COSTANZA

COSTANZA

RACHEL BLACKMORE

RENE
GADE

RENEGADE BOOKS

First published in Great Britain in 2024 by Renegade Books

1 3 5 7 9 10 8 6 4 2

Copyright © Rachel Blackmore 2024

The moral right of the author has been asserted.

*All characters and events in this publication, other than those
clearly in the public domain, are fictitious and any resemblance
to real persons, living or dead, is purely coincidental.*

A CIP catalogue record for this book
is available from the British Library.

Hardback ISBN 978-0-349-13109-2
Trade paperback ISBN 978-0-349-13110-8

Typeset in Jenson by M Rules
Printed and bound in Great Britain by
Clays Ltd, Elcograf S.p.A

Papers used by Renegade Books are from well-managed forests
and other responsible sources.

Renegade Books
An imprint of
Dialogue
Carmelite House
50 Victoria Embankment
London EC4Y 0DZ

www.dialoguebooks.co.uk

Dialogue, part of Little, Brown, Book Group Limited,
an Hachette UK company.

For Mum and my sister Kate
and in memory of Harriet

Prologue

'Bad Omens Gather'

Rome, August 1638

Despite the great heat the man is hurrying – half walking, half running – through the streets of Rome.

It is mid-morning, the sun is high and all those who are gainfully employed are hard at work. The roads throng with sellers and the air hums with the strident percussion of stonemasons and carpenters; a strange, clanging, sawing anthem played for the glorification of God.

Bad omens are gathering, so say the superstitious. This heat, they whisper, is lethal. The old and the sick – their bodies already dry from age and ague – are dying quicker than they can be buried.

Then there was that Barnabite priest, on his knees, praying in the San Carlo ai Catinari when he was struck by lightning. Tell me that is not a sign of divine displeasure?

Someone's neighbour heard from her sister's friend that the holy father was covered in lesions, great fronds of fire creeping across his body as he drew his last breath. Not to mention the Jewish quarter being set ablaze, flames tearing through the tinderbox houses.

It is all a sign.

Dust flies up from the man's feet, covering his breeches, gritting his eyes, causing him to spit out dry grime from his mouth. He feels intensely alive. More alive than he has ever felt before. His body quivers, delighting in the quickening of muscles which tense and stretch against his bones with each step.

This man is a servant to an artist – a famous sculptor who creates the likenesses of popes and kings from marble – so real people think the stone heads might start talking at any moment.

The manservant carries two flagons of wine. His palms are slick, wet with sweat, and he is glad for the twine which has been twisted around the top of each bottle, to prevent slippage. He grips harder, the harsh fibres of the rope pushing against his palms, rubbing small welts into the skin, but he does not register this mortification of flesh.

In the pocket of the servant's breeches is a razor, carefully folded in against itself. He feels the reassuring heft of it, banging in a constant rhythm – thud, thud, thud – against his leg as he scurries on. The blade is the type artists use. Finest money can buy. The edge of its gleaming metal has been shaved against the whetstone, sharpened for the particular purpose of harm.

The servant has his orders. Very specific instructions. Today he shall deliver justice. He hastens, heart pounding with the potential, the possibility, the anticipation of his deed.

Cast of Characters

Costanza, Her Family and Friends

Costanza Piccolomini
a twenty-two-year-old woman
living in Rome, Italy

Matteo Bonucelli
Costanza's husband, a sculptor

Leonardo
Costanza's father

Tiberia
Costanza's stepmother

Cecilia
Costanza's teenage stepsister

Michele
Costanza's younger stepbrother

Cleria
Costanza's younger stepsister

Giuliana
Costanza's best friend

Marco
Giuliana's husband

Tomaso
Giuliana's son

Luciana
Costanza's frenemy

Riva
Costanza's friend

Bluma
Riva's girlfriend

Mazzi
the midwife

Nino Marotta
the apothecary

Francesco Neve
the barber surgeon

Livia
Costanza's maid

Widow Vanna Falto
Costanza's neighbour

Sourpuss
Costanza's cat

Bess
Costanza's puppy

The Bernini Court

Lorenzo Bernini
the sculptor

Luigi
Lorenzo's younger
brother, also a sculptor

Pietro
Lorenzo's father, also a sculptor

Angelica
Lorenzo's mother

Dorotea
Lorenzo's older sister

Stefano
Lorenzo's manservant

Ranallo
the Bernini family lawyer

Paolo Panzetti
a sculptor and art dealer

Caterina Panzetti
Paolo's wife

Giametta
Caterina's maid

Finelli
a sculptor who formerly
worked with Lorenzo

Andrea
a sculptor at the
Fabbrica workshop

Vincenzo
a sculptor at the
Fabbrica workshop

Thibault Martinet
an artist friend of Lorenzo's

Makepeace
an envoy from the
English Court

Giovanni
Caterina's dance master

Franco Fortuna
a bear baiter

Elena Merletto
a sex worker

Ennio Balotelli
a cloth merchant

Cristoforo
a society tailor

Catherine Tezio
Lorenzo's betrothed

The Vatican & The Law

Pope Paul V
declared Lorenzo a
child prodigy

Pope Urban VIII
Lorenzo's patron

Cardinal Barberini
nephew of Urban VIII
and Lorenzo's boss

The Governatore

Marcello Sagese
a member of the sbirri,
the street police

The Fallen Women

Rosa	Silvia
Lisbetta	Lucia
Serafina	Frederica
Carlotta	Carmina

The Sisters of The Casa Pia

The Abbess

Sister Apollonia
serves the women

Sister Benedicta
the welcoming party

Sister Illuminata
supervises the washroom

Sister Chiara
the welcoming party

Sister Lidwina
a clerk to the Abbess

Sister Zita
runs the infirmary

Sister Perseveranza
serves the women

Part I

Chapter One

'Beginnings'

Rome, January 1636

It is January, named for the god Janus. A heathen. The god of endings and new beginnings, who looked both ways, backwards and forth. Some days the sun rises low, bathing the city of Rome in honeyed light, soft and warm like a baby's breath. On others, the cold runs through you like a sword.

This is such a day.

Two cups of ruby port are set upon the table at which I am sat, which has been so scrubbed with lemon and salt, so as to be almost bleached of colour. My toes feel tight in my best stockings, which have been carefully smoothed along my sturdy calves and tied prettily at the knee with scarlet ribbon. To aid fertility. I push my feet against the floor, which has been swept and mopped. All about there is an air of respectable tidiness, scented with citrus and anticipation.

Given our lodgings are but two rooms, and sparsely furnished, you could be forgiven for thinking such cleaning is quick work. It is not. I have spent the best part of the day, petticoats tucked about my waist, hair stuck to my face, making good this place. The bed curtains are shaken, mattress aired, the linen washed and folded, and my mother's precious silver candlesticks gleam. I sigh and pick at my nails where the skin is raw. I have an uncommon loathing for mopping, and dusting, and scrubbing.

Sprucing myself is a pastime I like better: rubbing at my face with secret preparations of broad beans soaked in honey and goats' milk. With my high forehead, I'm not as pretty as some, so it is not as much vanity as *sensible* to enhance my finer attributes.

The bell of Sant'Andrea delle Fratte chimes four times, sonorous and low.

My husband is late.

I reach for the cup. The first sip tastes of false pleasure, a rosy merriment slipping easily into my empty belly. I turn my face to the fire and close my eyes, like a cat seeking warmth. I have set a blaze going in each of our rooms; my stepmother, Tiberia, would be appalled.

'Two fires?' I imagine her rasping. 'I didn't bring you up to be so profligate. Such taste for extravagance must come from your mother. Whatever happened to putting on a shawl?'

I think on this for a moment. Despite my being hot-humoured, it is a wickedly cold night. Bending down, I pick up another log from the basket at my feet, weighing its pleasing heaviness in my hand.

Tiberia is not mistress of this house; I, Costanza Piccolomini am. And what's more, my husband, Matteo Bonucelli, is making his way in the world. He has a new commission from Lorenzo Bernini.

The Bernini.

'It is because of my prayers,' Tiberia had said with lips pursed while preparing the meal last Sunday. 'I asked for a sign that Matteo would be favoured,' she continued. 'That a door would open, and an abundance would be provided for my family. And so, it has come to pass.'

I had continued stirring the pot in silence. My stepmother is often more pleased with herself than she ought to be. It was not Tiberia's prayers but my husband's talents that caught the eye of Lorenzo Bernini.

For Bernini is a man who knows carving, who works miracles with Carrera marble, turning unyielding rock into the softest flesh which quivers and ripples. A man whose talent can recreate the intricacies of the finest lace from densest stone. What's more, Lorenzo Bernini is famous throughout the Christian world. An intimate of the Pope, feted by princes. Hailed by anyone who knows but a sliver about art as the greatest sculptor in all of Europe.

I casually aim the small log I am holding into the flames. Tiberia was right about one thing: my husband's new commission means a little more abundance in our modest household, so why should I not enjoy a modicum of luxury?

Finally, I hear Matteo's footsteps. There could be a hundred gentlemen climbing the stairs and I would pick out my husband's tread every time. Heavy, like an ox, with a stomp of such conviction and verisimilitude that no one could doubt, here comes an honest man.

The door swings open, and Matteo's broad body fills the frame. Being so tall, he must tip his head as he enters.

'Evening wife. How do?' he asks. Then he walks across my newly cleaned floor, big, dirty boots flaking ghostly footsteps of marble dust as he goes. Heat surges in my belly; I stand abruptly, all ragged, red with wrath.

'Mind my floor, you careless man!' I want to cry. 'With your great, hulking boots. Such scrubbing took me an age.'

But I am mindful my evening will not be bettered by a scold's tongue. Instead, I press down the thought, stretch out my hands and greet my husband with a gentle smile.

'I am well, husband.' My eyes flicker to the floor momentarily. 'How fared your day?'

'Cold. But mustn't complain.'

Matteo sits in his usual chair, as I kneel at his feet helping to shrug off the offending boots.

Not taking his eyes off me, he leans down to kiss me on the cheek. 'You are a good wife,' he says. Such words quell my heat, like river water poured on fire. I know I am lucky to have a good husband: one who is neither idle, nor insolent, nor always intoxicated. Despite his dirty feet, in our four years of marriage Matteo has never once thundered at me, unlike some of the other men of our district. Neighbours who belch such mean-spirited words at their wives – sometimes I fancy I can see their hate-scented breath rising like a fog in the night.

'Here.' I stand and hand him the drink ready and waiting on the table. He swallows it in two gulps, before giving me the empty cup to be refilled. 'We shall eat before we leave.'

I fetch more port, then slice dried sausage into thin discs, dropping them in steady regularity onto the pewter plate, which is near worn through in places. The rust-oil bleeds onto my fingers, staining them the colour of red earth and leaving my skin infused with the scent of sweet paprika and garlic.

Matteo eats with relish, and I watch in fond satisfaction. There is something very becoming about the way he opens his lips wide, revealing teeth so huge that Jupiter himself would be proud. We talk of his new commission, sculpting cherubs for St Peter's Basilica at the Fabbrica, God's workshop, where men sweat and toil, carving stone and casting bronze.

The soft boom of Matteo's voice fills the room, even though it is scratched by the dust he breathes, and his sandy whiskers dance delightfully on his chin as he talks. Through mouthfuls of sausage, he tells me of the designs he has been given. Plump putti with celestial curls, fat, impish fingers and a smile dancing on their full, little lips.

When Matteo talks of Lorenzo Bernini – the chief architect – 'Il Cavaliere' as he calls him – it is as if he is describing a deity. A prodigious talent, a human marvel, who has such dexterity with a chisel that the men of the Fabbrica workshop can only gawp at. Movement, motion, drama, theatre: Bernini's sculptures have it all. Such awe is most unusual coming from my husband, a man of such evenness he could rival the baker's scales.

After he has eaten, I bring fresh linen and Matteo strips in front of the fire, his strong body flexing in the low light. 'We should make haste,' he says, fastening his doublet. 'The men will be gathering, and we don't want to be late.'

I feel a flash of annoyance. I was waiting a long while. 'There was no need to collect me. I could have walked myself. I know these streets well enough.'

'What, and have people say that Matteo Bonucelli does not take care of his wife? The streets are not safe. To walk alone is to *invite* trouble, for the only women who walk abroad are the harlots from the brothels, now they are closed.'

I am fastening my cape, but my back straightens as I turn. 'You think I would be mistook for a harlot?'

'Nay,' Matteo responds carefully, while pulling on the affronting boots. 'I am saying men care not if you are – or aren't – a strumpet. They will have you regardless.'

'Men are a menace,' I say, throwing back the hood. 'Well … most.' I catch his eye in conciliation and he offers me a smile.

'Gloves and lantern?'

I place my husband's mittens on the table. They are well-knitted in rough brown wool, not by my hand, but by the neat, flying fingers of Tiberia. 'Shall I leave the fire?'

'Put the guard up, but leave it lit.'

A small smile creeps about my lips in eager anticipation of my husband's embrace, he wants the place warm and ready for us when we return.

Chapter Two

'The Weakness of Woman'

January 1636

The sunlight is fading as we step out of the house, the ground glittering with ice crystals that crunch underfoot. As I turn my face into the street a cruel wind whips through the air, wrapping us in a blanket of freezing haze so that our breath billows in clouds.

To reach the inn, we must walk towards the River Tiber, that wending stretch of water which has succoured Rome for centuries. In times gone by, such was the greatness of this old city that people lived right up to its walled boundaries. Now, most of the poor cling like rats to the riverbank, persuaded by neither land nor healthy air to move to the edges. There is no money to be made among grass and cows; coins only flow where popes and cardinals reside.

And make no mistake, coins are flowing, specifically into the hands of the architects and goldsmiths, the artists, urban planners, masons, bricklayers and plumbers. This city is once again a building site. The haphazard streets of Imperial Rome are disappearing to make way for huge, processional avenues linking breathtaking basilicas to star-pointed piazzas, in which stand wondrous Egyptian obelisks, shipped to Rome by slave hands. At every corner there are chapels in their infancy, the groundworks of neat, new townhouses, and great columned civic buildings, half-constructed. The foundations of a renewed Catholic majesty.

As we cross the Via del Corso I draw my cloak closer. Matteo's legs are long and stride at a pace unnatural to any but a giant. He is ahead of me, and I find myself tripping to match him, my feet running against my pattens despite them being old and well-worn.

'I beg you do not hurry so,' I shout to Matteo, my chest feeling the knife-cut of cold air as I breathe. It's a relief when he slows to accommodate my teetering tread on the treacherous road. As I catch up, Matteo loops his arm in mine, which both surprises and comforts me. He doesn't often show his affection in public, and I catch myself hoping that some of the district may see. Wanting to maintain the proximity, I begin to chat.

'I do not think I know any of the gentlemen who will be in attendance tonight. Perhaps you could tell me who will be there, so I might make good conversation?'

Matteo gives an affectionate laugh. 'I have never known you lost for words, wife. You find something of interest in everyone. And they in you.'

'That may be so, but to be forewarned is good . . . is it not?'

'True enough. Well. There will be Andrea, who works with me on the putti. And Vincenzo . . .'

'New to the city,' I interject. 'From a village beyond Pisa. Just finding his feet?' I am pleased to have remembered the name, and the opportunity to demonstrate my wifely interest.

'That's right.' There is a note of surprise in Matteo's voice. 'I know what it is to be a stranger in a big city . . . and he is . . .'

My husband pauses, and I wonder if he is thinking of his own arrival in Rome, just twenty-five, a fresh-faced boy from Lucca, seeking favour and finding it among the many Portuguese and Spanish nobles wanting to have their features captured in stone.

'Vincenzo is a decent man?' I offer helpfully.

'Yes. He is steadfast and works hard. Vincenzo is . . .' – he pauses again – 'a man of his word. Worth helping.'

'Not unlike you?' I squeeze Matteo's arm and feel a little jolt of joy when he presses in answer.

'Then there will be Paolo.' Even in the gloaming I know Matteo's lip has curled. 'He is something of a sobersides. Thinking much of his own talent and intellect . . .' Matteo leaves the thought dangling like a loose thread. 'And maybe Paolo's wife, Catherine, or Caterina or somesuch. They say she is talented in all sorts of ways.'

I raise an eyebrow, wondering what skills this Kate possesses and suddenly feel proprietorial about my husband.

I wait for a few moments to pass, then ask the question that has been clamouring at me, 'Will Lorenzo Bernini be there?'

All I know is Lorenzo Bernini exists in the same firmament as princes and emperors. So famous that all of Rome knows his name. A man to whom my husband is in thrall.

'Lorenzo does not frequent taverns. Doesn't drink. And Luigi favours more lawless places.' Matteo says the name 'Luigi' with a mild inflection, the merest catch to the throat, but I hear it.

'Luigi?' I ask lightly.

'Il Cavaliere's brother.' He thinks for a moment. 'Much younger.'

'I see.' My tone is placid, but my bottom lip protrudes. At thirty-two, Matteo may have a decade on me, but I am not so young. I worry I will seem like a girl to these men, in my plain dyed red wool skirt and my dark hair braided with ribbons. It is a well-practised style, and one I consider becoming, but it is not of courtly fashion.

The hood of my cloak rubs gently against my head and I feel my curls escaping their binding, undoing my earlier artistry and coming to rest in tendrils about my forehead like a child's. I silently curse. A quietness falls across us and we breathe in unison, sending wordless clouds into the cold night air.

* * *

The White Hart near the Ponte Sant'Angelo is an artisanal place, frequented by the congregation of men who grind stone, create wonders from marble, carve columns and weld bronze into fantastical shapes in the Fabbrica workshop. The great foundry where the dreams of popes are forged from earth and fire.

Trade is brisk. This Pope's yearning for heavenly glorification means he is spending a fortune. It follows that when artists find their coin purses bulging with papal scudi, they will find a tavern in which to fritter their earnings.

As we step over the threshold there is the low music of men's voices, a deeply timbered hum of masculinity accompanied by the acrid smell of hard work, leather and pipe smoke. Right at the back, beyond the crowds, sits a group from which a large, not quite corpulent, man waves and beckons. Matteo returns the greeting and I follow shyly behind him, holding on to his black doublet as we push through the crowds to the table. The excitement I felt earlier has unexpectedly alchemised into nerves, which flutter and flush through my veins. It is a bigger crowd than I had imagined, so I must force a smile to my lips to hide the hammering within my chest.

I find myself sat next to Andrea, the man carving cherubs with Matteo. His head is thin and his face long, like a medieval martyr, with deep-set eyes which dance when he smiles. The man seated opposite is the soberside Paolo; his wife, Caterina – as she is properly called – is seated next to him.

Caterina is the only other woman in the company. She is older than me, but by how much is difficult to tell, given the artistry of her toilette and the well-cut nature of her clothes: a dress of fine blue wool in the latest style. Her pale yellow hair is meticulously studded with tiny pearl pins; I cannot help but push and smooth back my own errant curls.

Caterina has a sharp sort of beauty, with high, angular cheeks, pale blue eyes and fair eyebrows, giving her a northern air. But what transfixes me more than anything are her lips. I wonder if their lascivious nature is due to their unnatural staining, the blood red of wickedly expensive cocciniglia, but I rather suspect their libidinous aspect is a natural attribute of Caterina herself.

They say women are gossips, but I have noticed when men start talking on any subject they know a gnat's wing about, they like their voices to be heard. There is much loud opining on every matter, and a great deal of talking over each other in the most certain terms. For the most part it is hearsay: 'I hear Giovanni Baresi is dallying with Fabriso's wife,' Paolo will say. Or, 'Did you see Armando De Marco has fallen foul of Il Cavaliere again? Drunk out of his five senses and late for work.'

When Andrea turns to me, I am a little embarrassed; 'And what about you, Signora Costanza Piccolomini? What do you make of all these comings and goings?'

A flush seeps from my chest to my ears, but the wine in my belly gives me courage. I stammer; 'These things of which you talk are not my world, so perhaps it is not my place to comment.'

Andrea begins to open his mouth, but my thoughts are gathering speed and I find myself adding; 'But it strikes me that this workshop ... this Fabbrica ... is no different from a farm.' I continue, the words now flowing out of my mouth like a stone rolling along the riverbed, washed along by the current. 'It's like this. There are farmers who know exactly the right moment to stick their hand in and pull the lamb from the ewe, and so rarely lose an animal. And then there are those who are ... lazy sods.' I finish with a smile and flourish, quite satisfied with my argument.

When Andrea roars with laugher I am mortified. I have said the wrong thing. My eyes desperately search for Matteo, but he has not heard our exchange, and is instead deep in conversation with another man, about my age, with oddly short-cropped hair, whose name I did not catch.

'Well-spoken, Signora Piccolomini.' Andrea chuckles. 'There are too many in our world who become puffed with grand notions of *artistry*. Lest we forget, we are all here to serve our master, just like any farmhand.'

I blush, blood heating my face.

'And your name, "Piccolomini",' he goes on. 'Like the popes?'

I am surprised. Not many make the connection – the last Piccolomini pope reigned over a century ago. But then these men rely on the patronage of the Church, so know their pontificates well enough.

'Yes, Pius the second – and third. I am of the same blood.' As the words leave my mouth, I worry they are too boastful. Equally, I am not bred to be the object of jest.

Andrea nods solemnly. 'Your nobility is well carried, signora.' Is Andrea playing me, I wonder? But when I look at his face, I see it is well meant.

'I may have the lineage, but sadly not the scudi,' I add smiling, rubbing my third finger and thumb together, and this time we both laugh.

Suddenly, where there had been the general hubbub of conversation and merriment, a hush falls over the place, like river reeds falling still when the breeze dies. I look up. At first, I cannot discern what has caused such quietness; perhaps it is a raid by the sbirri, the street police.

It takes a moment to register that it is just two men entering the tavern. As they progress, the crowd is rendered momentarily still, then mightily animated, nudging and pointing at their backs.

I am amused; it is a curious phenomenon. The man leading is slim, dark haired and chiselled cheeked. The second is taller, wider, with a more athletic build; he too has black hair and an angled face, but carries his strength in a more obvious swagger.

'Il Cavaliere ... Luigi!' Andrea shouts, waving at the first man who begins walking purposefully towards out table, his gaze unblinking. I should avert my eyes. It is the modest thing to do in the company of strangers. But I cannot.

Matteo had said neither Bernini brother would make an appearance, yet here they both are, making their way towards us. I take Lorenzo, the older, more famous brother to be the man in front. His features are striking, his body sinuous and compact, moving with feline gracefulness through the crowd.

The second man, Luigi, I believe, seems more at ease, stopping to share a joke with one man, slapping the back of another, certain of his place in the world.

There is an empty spot at the other end of the table. The taller man makes for the opening, grinning as he slides himself onto the bench, vigorously shaking hands with the Fabbrica men, playfully thumping the arms of others, shouting for 'wine and cheese, and don't forget bread, not the cheap black shit, but the good stuff. And olives too.'

Lorenzo Bernini waits a moment and examines the scene, as a priest might regard his flock. My breath quickens as I realise he is motioning for me to move up. The space is tight, but he can squeeze in beside me, and opposite Paolo and Caterina.

As everyone compresses themselves to find space, I feel his body manoeuvre round the seat, his thighs easing into the place next to mine. Even through my skirts and petticoats, I can tell they are not trunks like Matteo's, but are strong nonetheless, like a dancer, pushing wide as Signor Bernini spreads his legs to find comfort.

I steal a glance at him now. His face is not so much handsome as carved, with fine bones protruding from his cheeks, and startling beetle-brows from under which wide-set, crow-black eyes stare, penetrating and unflinching. But there is something more. Under the inscrutable face, there is an insatiable restlessness, a longing for something I cannot understand, for Lorenzo is famed and brilliant. What more could he want?

'Signora.' He offers his hand, 'Lorenzo Bernini.'

As if I did not know.

I offer him mine, undaunted, matching his stare straight on. 'Costanza Piccolomini. Wife of Matteo Bonucelli.' He does not smile but nods, continuing to look at me intently. To my annoyance I feel another flush rising, pinking my neck and cheeks.

The conversation changes with Bernini in attendance. No more gossip, but instead an eviscerating examination of Rome's patrons and other artists, detailed discussions of rich men's peculiarities and proclivities, each conversation rounded off with a thorough exposition of how the men around this table eclipse all rivals.

Later, after more drinking, talk turns to the nature of women. It's not long before Paolo shows his true colours, spouting words all foul and misshapen. 'That men are nobler is plain to see,' he says casually. 'It is obvious. The natural order of things. Women do not hold office. Nor can they be trusted with power of any kind. The weakness of women is evident . . . If Eve had not eaten the forbidden fruit like a whore . . . we would not now . . . all of us . . . live in a state of original sin.'

A drop of wine runs along Paolo's chin. I watch it slide inexorably downwards before he wipes it away as if swatting a fly. He goes on. 'Women are inconsistent. It is a truth declared by every poet who lived. In writing of women's feebleness and frailties, they are presenting a reflection of the world. Do the medics not teach that we men must be patient with the deformities of women: their smaller bodies and brains? To be hot, strong and dry, like a man, is far superior to women's cold, wet, and weak humours.'

There is a low murmur, but no outright concurrence. Perhaps it is the wine, or perhaps my womanly pride which makes me speak, but before I know it, I am making a vigorous riposte across the table.

I lean forward. 'Signore,' Paolo looks up, startled. 'I must strenuously disagree. Eve ... a woman ... was made by man's rib, was she not?'

Paolo nods, eyes narrowing.

'And Adam ... well, he was made from mud ... was he not?' I continue without waiting for an answer. 'Is being made from a rib not more dignified than being crafted from mud? As Eve was made from flesh, not clay, then she must surely be at least an equal to Adam?'

Paolo raises a hand and begins to open his mouth, but I have only just begun. 'What's more, we know from these self-same poets that as the world progresses, it becomes better. We are now more enlightened in the Catholic faith than our forefathers ever were, worshipping as they did many gods. Jupiter, Mars, Venus and such like. So does it not follow that a woman must at least be equal to God's first ...' and here I hesitate for a moment, '... and practice creation, Adam?'

There is a silence. Paolo's face reddens. He takes a gulp of wine before answering. 'It is a good ploy but flawed thought, signora. St Paul himself preached that a woman is not allowed to teach a man. Nor should woman usurp any kind of authority over a man. Instead, she must . . .' Here Paolo emphasises his words, enunciating slowly, as if talking to a child, 'Stay. Silent. Adam was made first. Eve second. So, it is she who must demure. Adam was not deceived. It was the woman, Eve, who was deceived and transgressed.' Paolo gives me a look of pure malevolence.

Growing up in my district, I quickly learned that words cannot bruise, and bullies do not like being challenged. My veins warm as I compose my sweet response. 'Ah, so now I see. It is the man who must always instruct the woman. So then . . .' I put my forefinger to my lips and cast my eyes skywards, as if thinking great thoughts. 'If this be the case, then if anyone's sin is greater, is it not Adam's? Since it was Eve who persuaded her husband to disobey, and he, being the Head – The Man – and wiser than Eve, should have guided her away from such an error, should he not?'

The table has fallen silent. No one will meet my gaze. My blazing bravado now deserts me. I seek out Matteo, but he can only respond with a silent question, eyes pleading, 'Why must you speak your tongue so?'

I drop my head as the heat of my humours turns wet in my eyes. A voice shouts out. It is Luigi, from the other end of the table.

'What say you, brother? Do you not have a view?'

All eyes now turn to the elder Bernini, gauging how he will respond. A moment of silence. The beat of a wing. Then a loud, slow clapping of hands.

'Bravo!' calls out Lorenzo Bernini. 'Bravo! Brilliante! Well put, Signora Piccolomini.'

Everyone applauds and shouts their agreement. All except Paolo, whose mouth forms the shape of a smile which does not reach his eyes.

When the chatter moves on, Signor Bernini lays his hand on

mine, his fingers long and light, and the leather of his black jacket so fine it rubs like silk against my skin. I feel his stare. 'You have a rare fire,' he murmurs, smiling. It is the first time I have seen him smile all evening.

I know men and their ways, and fancy I know what Lorenzo Bernini is doing. But then he pulls his hand away abruptly, as if he never intended to brush my flesh at all. I lay my hand over the spot so recently touched by him, and my skin feels warm, as if branded by an iron.

Chapter Three

'The Bedchamber'

January 1636

In the bedchamber, I have set a small bowl of civet and amber burning over the candle. An expense, but Nino Marotta, the apothecary, assured me a room perfumed in such a manner will benefit conception. A necessary investment. For how can I be a good wife if I cannot give my husband a child?

By the time we arrive home, Saturday has slipped into Sunday, and the embers are glowing their red farewells in the hearth. The old straw mattress sags as Matteo sits on the bed and pulls at the ties of his breeches. He stands to help me unlace my bodice, and I shimmy off the layers of my skirts, until I'm standing in my chemise and stockings, shivering slightly.

I wait, aching for him to take me into his arms, to touch me with a hunger born of longing, but instead he climbs between the clean, tautly pulled sheets.

'Are you not coming to bed, wife?'

Disappointment and shame wash over me as I climb in beside him. Matteo lies rigidly flat on his back, arms resolutely locked by his side like a boy playing at being a soldier. Instead of blowing out the candle, I reach for my husband's hand and lift it to the soft light, so I might see it better. His nailbeds are grey and impregnated with marble dust. It is the state of permanent artistic grace sculptors carry, a stain that can never be quite scrubbed away.

I turn his hand over, so I can see the callouses which have formed on his palm where his fingers meet the joints. I press down firmly, provocatively, on the saddle of his thumb, which is strong and meaty, and tenderly start tracing his lifeline, stretched like the River Tiber across his great hand. My fingers pause where the chisels and tools have made little scars which criss-cross his fingers, some faded white, others still violent beet. It is a matter of constant astonishment that hands such as these, as large as the bowls we sup from, can carve such intricacies. I want him to touch me the same way he inspects his marble carvings, to run his fingers along my body, the furrows and plains of my skin.

Matteo puts his other hand over mine, stilling my fingers from their loving movement. Its weight says more than any word, and I am felled. Then he adds, in case his meaning is not clear, 'Wife, I am tired.'

My hand lies mute under his, no longer able to issue its invitation. 'I thought you wanted the fire left, so we could . . .'

'I wanted the fire left for the icy night and in case we might need to warm some water on our return.'

'Please, Matteo.' My eyes wet with unpermitted tears. 'If we are to have a child, we must lie together. Our home is empty when you are gone all day. It is all anyone asks about . . .' I gather my last thought, unsure whether to let it escape my lips, so sad does it make me feel. 'We are four years married and I am yet to beget. I am lost on my own.'

He looks at me, his chestnut eyes foretelling the apology about to spring from his lips. He is sorry, this much I know.

'It is the Sabbath. Marital relations are forbidden on the . . .'

'Please,' I whisper, my voice cracking with humiliation.

Matteo grunts as he turns over and pulls me to him. The mattress dips under our weight, and the bed linen is so chilled that my legs are gooseflesh when he parts them with his hand, snorting as he climbs atop.

'Here,' I want to whisper. 'Here is where I want to be pressed. Here is where I want you to explore the hamlets of my body, to conquer my desire.'

Yet I never do.

I wait for his tongue to find my mouth and fill it with kisses, which are short and sharp, like the stabbing of him within.

When he cries out, I do not.

As Matteo sleeps, I lie stock-still, listening to the sounds of the night, the drunken husbands weaving their way home to gob execrative spittle on the cowering mistress of the house, and foxes screeching in painful copulation. Even though I am in desperate need of the chamber pot, I dare not move in case any of his seed seeps away.

Chapter Four

'Sewing Circle'

January 1636

San Lorenzo in Lucina is home to all manner of people: builders and carpenters, sellers of herbs and pastries, makers of hats, shoes and keys. There are also a good many artists, enticed by cheap rooms, low tax and a liking to be with their own. On warmer days cortigianas lean from the upper rooms of the tall townhouses, cheeks flushed with artifice and sin, parading their wares to tempt the next man up their well-trod stairs.

Papa and Tiberia still live on the Vicolo San Silvestro, near the Church of San Lorenzo in Lucina where I was married. For most of my life these bells have signalled the start and end of everything: waking, meals, when to put the cat and candle out. And Tiberia's Wednesday sewing circle.

They are chiming one o'clock and I am late.

As my feet move swiftly along the hard stone road my ears pick up snippets of the tongues spoken here, Polish, French and Spanish, and the dialects of Venice, Perugia and Florence.

Even though I was not born of this place, it is all I can remember. I was just a fat-fisted infant when Papa loaded me onto a cart and into the lap of my new stepmother for the slow journey to Rome. Papa always said he left Viterbo, his birthplace, because he wanted the chance at a better life. But I have long suspected that Papa's wanderlust was really driven by the heartache at losing his beloved wife and my sister to the birth-bed.

There are no paintings or drawings of my mother, no sketches or miniatures. I have never seen her likeness, except in the mirror, for Papa says I look just like her with my wide forehead and dark curls, yet I too feel her presence here in Rome, and wonder whether we ever really leave our ghosts behind?

When I reach the house, I adjust my linen cap. The door is tall, and the house narrow. I knock loudly and it is Tiberia, my step-mother, who answers. The same woman who held me awkwardly all those years ago. She blinks her eyes like a sparrow, as if the light outside is too bright, too harsh, and smooths fluttering hands down her workaday grey wool gown. I brace myself for imminent admonishment.

"Tis nice of you to bother joining us, daughter. Giuliana is already started. But better late than never,' she wheezes.

It is on the tip of my tongue to tell Tiberia everything that has befallen me. I lost a shoe, then could not find the box of pins, and then Sourpuss came rubbing at my legs, begging for a pet.

But the real reason I am late is I have been much preoccupied by thoughts of Lorenzo Bernini. His smile. That touch. The way my skin tingled after his fingers brushed my hand. The feeling that I have been seen. A sensation which sits oddly within me, like a snowflake falling in August.

'Aye,' I confess. 'Sorry, Mother.' I bend down to kiss Tiberia on the cheek and take in the familiar smell of goose fat and cloves, the former smeared upon her chest to ease the coughing, the latter sucked for the state of her teeth. Nothing reminds me more of my childhood than this scent. 'Still, I am here now,' I add cheerfully, as I step over the threshold.

The room is filled to the brim with small things; little bunches of dusty herbs hanging from the beamed ceiling, diminutive bottles of tinctures refracting rays of emerald and sapphire, bowls of pins and ends of twine, miniature replicas of saints' heads cast in tin, devotional crosses propped up along the fireplace, and delicate prayer beads strung over hooks where the candles are lit. It is as if Tiberia, a woman of bird-like stature herself, likes to be surrounded with things in direct proportion to her size.

As Tiberia tells anyone who will listen, it's nothing short of a miracle that she, with her narrow hips and tiny waist, birthed not one but three healthy babes, while the first Signora Piccolomini, a woman as broad-hipped as any who lived, perished in childbed.

'How do, Giuliana?' I say, ferociously hugging the young woman sitting at Tiberia's kitchen table. Giuliana Gavia is my oldest friend, and never fails to miss any Wednesday, this being the allotted time when we come together to make the endless list of household linens required to keep a body and soul together: shirts and chemises, cuffs and collars, caps, kerchiefs and rubbing cloths.

'Good of you to grace us with your presence.' Giuliana grins as she motions for me to sit by her. 'Mother Piccolomini has already started, as you can see.'

There is a large section of linen laid out on the long, wooden table, weighted at each corner. Given the size, there can be no doubt of the intended recipient. It is the beginnings of a shirt for Matteo.

Tiberia grunts, standing on her tiptoes to pull and smooth the cloth, while I eye the expanse of material warily.

'I cautioned that you might want to see the proposed design before we took scissors to it,' Giuliana says.

I bite my lip. I have not been here two minutes, and fear I am already on course to upset the equilibrium. 'It looks very . . .' I edge my tongue along my teeth as I search for the word '. . . big, does it not? Are you sure it will not be too large? Even for Matteo?'

Tiberia waves her arms to gesture the expanse of my husband's form, releasing a pungent avian scent as she does so. 'For a great, galumphing man like your husband?' she rasps. 'Nay, girl.'

My stepmother begins to motion like a duck flapping its wings. 'A man like him needs to move with ease. Besides,' – her breath sounds like the old fire bellows being squeezed to within an inch of their life – 'men like a bit of volume in their sleeve, do they not?'

My stomach sinks. I shoot Giuliana a pleading look. This is well-trod ground; Tiberia's knowledge of men's fashion is at least twenty years out of date. If I take such a voluminous shirt home, Matteo will ask for it to be unpicked and taken in. And the only thing worse than sewing a shirt once is sewing it twice.

Giuliana blinks her understanding of the predicament, a silent acknowledgement she has been impish to let Tiberia get this far.

'Mother Piccolomini,' Giuliana begins gently, smiling beatifically. 'I have no doubt it is the case that most men prefer volume.' She pauses to gauge Tiberia's reaction.

My stepmother is listening, head cocked to one side, but does not betray any emotion, so Giuliana proceeds at a cautionary rate. 'But given Matteo toils at carving marble all day, with a great many knives and chisels, which is a most vigorous work requiring much movement, would it not be better to . . . perhaps . . . slim the sleeve?'

Tiberia stops for a moment, assessing the cloth keenly, as if

Matteo himself were lying prone underneath its weave, while Giuliana and I wait in silent anticipation.

'You make a fair point, child,' says Tiberia, and I feel a little puff of air escape from my mouth. 'I shall adjust the sleeves,' she continues. 'It must be a practical garment, as well as handsome.' She looks up at Giuliana and winks. 'Not unlike the man who will wear it.'

Tiberia bends over again, chuckling at her own quip, and it occurs to me, not for the first time, how much easier it would have been if Giuliana had been Tiberia's daughter, for they are much better suited to domestic harmony. There has always been a rub between my stepmother and me. Like a piece of grit caught between toe and shoe.

Tiberia is neat and proper in everything, keenly observant of the right – and wrong – way of doing things. It's not that my childhood was lacking. More it was always noticeable how quickly Tiberia would rush to comfort my brother and sisters. How their fevers were fretted over just a little more anxiously, the salve applied to their sore knees with a lighter, gentler touch.

Her children were coddled, while I slouched, chewed noisily, walked with a boy's step, failed to stir the pot correctly, missed the corners when dusting, made a sloppy bed. Even when I left the house I would be rebuked; remember to avert your eyes from men, pull your cap lower, shirt higher, smooth your skirts and take smaller steps, learn modesty in all things, for a woman who parades herself always comes to no good.

The truth is, I knew I was different from the minute Tiberia gave birth. The moment I saw her clutching her own child tenderly to her breast. The way she gazed at my doll-like scrap of a new brother, Michele. A mother's love. An adoration I had seen before but could not remember. Golden. Fierce. Unyielding. Unending. It's not that I wasn't loved, it's just I wasn't loved *like that*.

'Thank you,' I mouth theatrically to Giuliana, while Tiberia pulls busily at the cloth, muttering as she goes, lightly retracing the new shape with charcoal.

As my stepmother picks up the scissors and steps closer to the table to cut the cloth, a child begins to wail. Tomaso! I had clean forgot about Giuliana's boy, sat under the table.

'Baby wants feeding,' Tiberia says, her lips hardly moving for the quantity of pins held between them, eyes fixed upon the exacting process of drawing the blade at a steady pace through the linen. I have no doubt that had Tiberia been born a man, she would have made a fine butcher. Or assassin.

Giuliana folds her needle into the tiny nightshirt she is fixing, and lifts Tomaso awkwardly from the floor, balancing him on her knee as she loosens her bodice. The child, being over a year now, finds his own way to her breast and nestles in, pawing at her hungrily as he suckles. My friend makes a quiet sigh, and gazes down fondly at his head, which is covered with thick brown curls.

Tiberia's eyes rest briefly on the child. I know what she is thinking. Giuliana's babe is small for his age, hardly thriving. Had it been anyone else we might have exchanged glances; this child, we would have said to each other in words unspoken, is sickly. This child, we may have blinked, might not be long for this world.

Giuliana is tall, like me, but straighter: her figure, hair, her long nose and almond eyes, the green of summer lichen. We have always done everything together, but it was only ever me who made a stand. When we were girls playing in the dirt of Vicolo San Silvestro, it was me who'd square up to the boys brandishing their sticks. Later, when we were sixteen and still virgins, walking in the dowry parade dressed as Our Lady in cornflower blue with flowers woven into our hair, it was me who insisted on betrothal to a man making his way in the world, while Giuliana accepted her first match. And now here we both are, married, making and mending for our men every Wednesday afternoon.

'Here.' Tiberia hands me the wretched bits of shirt. I bite my lip. 'He is *your* husband,' she continues. 'If you insist on marrying a big fellow, then it follows you must be prepared for more than a bit of stitching.'

Even with Tiberia's adjustments, the shirt still billows like a sail on a trader's ship. I take it and shake it out. 'It shall take me months!'

'Nonsense,' clucks Tiberia. 'If you make a start now, you will finish the sleeves by next week.'

I groan as I lean forward to search in the basket for a bigger needle to work with, while Tiberia begins her gasping chatter again, pricking her needle in and out of some well-worn stockings. 'Did you hear about Raffaella Laurito?'

'Raffaella? The niece from down the road?' asks Giuliana.

'The same. Well ...' Tiberia pauses to ensure she has our full attention. 'She has been arrested!' There is more than a cruel hint of triumph in my stepmother's voice.

'Arrested?' I cannot hold the surprise from my voice. Women are not *arrested*, even in a district such as San Lorenzo.

Tiberia leans forward and crosses herself, before looking up at the emaciated Christ on the wall. 'For fornication,' she breathes.

'God's blood!'

'Do not take the Lord's name in vain, Costanza,' Tiberia admonishes.

'How did it come to pass?' Giuliana presses on.

'Raffaella was wilful. Forced her mother's hand.' Tiberia rubs at her scrawny belly, as if with child. 'The husband was not blessed with longevity. Raffaella was left with two babes and not a scudo to her name. Well ...' Tiberia trails off into a coughing fit, the bones of her back protruding like the spines of a sea urchin. 'It seems the girl found one way to pay her rent.'

My heart thumps, 'Where did they take her?'

'The monastery at the Casa Pia,' Tiberia whispers. 'Imagine. Being locked up with a whole army of fallen women.'

Just then the door slams and there is the unmistakable sound of my fifteen-year-old stepsister's footsteps stomping heavily through the house.

'Shhh,' says Tiberia, 'You girls must cease your gossiping. For here comes Cecilia, and your low talk is not for her young ears.'

The door to the kitchen bangs open. 'You sent for me, Mother?' Cecilia is diminutive like Tiberia, but no less fierce for it, and speaks in an angry wasp buzz. Her face darkens at the picture of womanly domesticity laid before her, and she can barely manage a nod in the direction of Giuliana and I before flinging herself ungraciously onto a chair.

'Aye, I did,' says Tiberia, calmly ignoring the display of maidenly petulance. 'Time you started to learn the ministrations of a good wife, for you will be married soon enough.' Cecilia looks pained but does not respond, and almost snatches the sewing from her mother's hand.

The four of us sew until the light fades and dusk is upon us. There is no more talk of Raffaella, and later, before I leave, I see Tiberia quietly stealing Matteo's shirt from my basket. She will unpick the stitches and secretly make good my shoddy work. I do not say a word.

Chapter Five

'The Next Michelangelo'

January 1636

This is a busy time for Lorenzo Bernini – Il Cavaliere, Architetto di San Pietro, Impresario Supreme. His fortunes are riding high, yet he sits in his study in front of his papers, quill in hand, doing precisely . . . nothing.

It's days since he visited the workshop, and longer since he lifted a chisel. There are the robes on the carving of the Countess Matilda to finish. The folds of the cloth are not yet right, and every piece must be perfection.

When he is distracted, he allows his mind to wander. Costanza. The girl with fire in her belly and skin like marble. He liked the way she lacked the guile and sophistry of the courtly women in his circle. It is charming. Innocent. Indeed, the more he ponders upon it, the more he thinks Costanza is interesting for her very ability to exist in the moment, without thought for what others will make of her. He considers there are very few women left in Rome who dare to present themselves as they really are, without first calculating how to flatter or dissemble.

He looks again at the architectural drawings on his desk, sheaves of thick vellum, each scratched in fine detail, but he has no mind to concentrate on angles or figures.

Outside there are children screaming, playing some kind of chasing game.

Jesu!

He shits blood to be this successful, is nearly driven mad by the effort of pulling living figures from solid rock, and he must put up with this?

Of course, they all take it for granted. His patrons always want more. The men at the workshop who gripe and bellyache. Luigi, skulking in the shadows, muttering he too could have been a brilliant artist, had he not had the misfortune to be born the brother of a genius.

The sculptor still hears his father, Pietro's, voice as he works: 'Better, Lorenzo. You can do better than this.' What did his father know? Bernini surpassed Pietro's skill at sixteen and has never had a commission returned as unsatisfactory in his career.

Lorenzo Bernini was eight years old when his father put him in front of the Pope, his eyes cowed by the high ceilings and the abundance of light falling in trellised shafts on the floor.

'Show them what you are capable of, son,' Pietro had whispered as they walked into a room filled with silence. 'Make it wondrous,' he had hissed.

So, little Lorenzo sat on the floor, all velvet breeches and spindled legs, and asked God's representative on earth, 'Your Grace, shall I draw now?'

The great man had solemnly nodded. Taking his cue, Bernini's hand skimmed across the page making charcoal smudges, like the first flutter of fledging wings. The marks joined to form the face of an apostle, holding a martyr's sword and a book. The word of God. Saint Paul for Pope Paul V, of the famous Borghese family.

It took no more than twenty minutes, Lorenzo becoming so absorbed in his work he failed to notice his rapt audience. When he had finished, the boy had stood shakily and turned the portrait for the Pontiff to inspect.

The magnificent man stepped forward to view the vellum more closely.

Had Lorenzo Bernini done enough?

Pope Paul was quiet as he studied the boy's work, face inscrutable. Then he raised his arms, palms turned to heaven, and spun round to his cardinals: 'Gentlemen,' he declared. 'We are looking at the next Michelangelo.' The men in red murmured their concurrence and the child let go of the breath he didn't know he was holding. His father would be pleased.

'Uno, due, tre . . . dieci, undici, dodici.'

Pope Paul dropped the silver medals into Bernini's gowpen hands. Twelve, because that was as many as the boy's childish fingers could hold.

* * *

Now, there is more screaming from outside, excited shrieks and yells. Bernini grabs a measuring stick from his desk and charges to the door, seized by such a forceful momentum he forgets his jacket.

It isn't until he is outside that the sculptor realises it is raining. Drops falling down his collar, snaking down his back, making his linen shirt stick to his skin. He casts about for the children who have moved along the street and are huddled in a doorway over a game of jacks, dressed in scraps and drenched like wet puppies, impervious to the downpour.

Bernini runs towards them, stick aloft, when he sees three cloaked figures at the end of the street. But it is the person in the middle, a woman with dark curls, who makes him stop. Bernini, with his hawk eye, knows for certain it is her.

The boys at his heel giggle at his abrupt start. Making the most of their momentary reprieve they make to run, but Bernini is too quick. Like a dog with a rat, he catches one of the boys by the arm. The child squeals and squirms, his bare feet losing purchase in the claggy ground.

'Ow. Signore, that hurts.' An accent dredged from the river-ghettos. Aware she is approaching, Bernini realises his advantage.

'Mister, I beg thee. Let go, or I'll ... I'll fetch my Pa.'

'I'm surprised you've got a Pa, you little bastard.' Bernini's voice is faint in the clatter of the rain, but the menace is plain. 'Here. I'm going to give you some coins, and ...' Bernini grips the boy so tight he can feel an agitated heartbeat pulsing under the tips of his fingers. '... you are going to be so grateful that you are going to scrape and bow until your head touches that sodden floor. Then I never want to see you again. Do you understand?'

The boy nods. The sculptor releases him so suddenly the child falls, the side of his face hitting the mud, which runs thick and black down his face.

'Here,' says the sculptor, reaching into his pocket, pulling out a coin purse, and counting out twelve scudi. A ludicrous amount, he knows. Enough to feed a family for months, but he likes the pleasing echo of it: the great man counting out his money.

Bernini indicates the boy should hold his hands together like a supplicant's bowl, and begins to drop the coins, one by one, into the outstretched fingers. 'Uno, due ...'

'How now, Il Cavaliere!' Lorenzo Bernini looks up in feigned blitheness. It's the husband, Matteo. Three Putti Matteo. For this is how he remembers all his workers at the beginning, by the description in his ledger. He finishes counting. The boys, understanding they will never know the like of such riches again, are gratifyingly obsequious. One child even begins to cry, uttering his thanks through coursing sobs, his emaciated body heaving with the anticipation of a hot meal.

The sculptor raises his arm in a half-wave to the approaching group, as the boys run off, coins secured. The rain is falling heavily now, and it is only as they near that he realises who the third figure with Matteo and Costanza is. The trio are nearly upon him, and the sculptor's pride will not allow anything but temperance to reign.

'Matteo, Signora Piccolomini and ...' a pause. The sculptor slightly inclines his head. 'Finelli. Let me offer you some respite from this filthy weather. I live but a few short steps from here; we can take shelter from the downpour.'

If there is a hesitation within the group, he does not see it, striding at the front of them, leading the bedraggled ensemble quickly along the sludgy street. Once within his own home, Bernini is firmly in command, calling for cloth to mop his guests and the floor, and a new shirt to replace his own sodden linen.

'What brings you this far from home?' The question is directed to Finelli, but it is Matteo who answers.

'Ah, we have just come from mass at St Peter's Basilica. Finelli is an old friend of Costanza's father. We thought we would worship together. A chance to praise God *and* appraise the craftsmanship of the Fabbrica workshop in glorifying St Peter's.'

'An admirable act of efficiency. And how did you like the sight?' Lorenzo Bernini looks directly at his old rival Finelli this time, so there is no doubting who should provide an answer.

'Perhaps it is a little ... overwrought. But none can doubt the masterly conception of such unrestrained work.'

And there we have it. Finelli is a man so tight arsed he manages to make every sculpture almost pucker with tension. Yet he is one of the most gifted artists the sculptor ever worked with. Such talent makes it so much harder to share the limelight. Still, it was a loss when Finelli walked out of the workshop, and neither man forgives easily.

The sculptor cannot let the slight go, 'The light is not good today, Finelli. Perhaps you should visit again when the chapel is at its heavenly best. The combination of Michelangelo's dome and my bronze, is, so they say, a wonder.'

'I'm afraid I shall not be back too soon to genuflect at the feet of Bernini,' Finelli replies, holding the sculptor's gaze.

He sees Costanza wince at the comment. She is clearly discomfited. Being churlish to Finelli will not serve his purpose. After all, by leaving, did not Finelli make himself an irrelevance?

'Ah 'tis a pity; I had an invitation for you,' the sculptor turns his face away from Finelli and towards her. 'But I see I shall have to be content with the pleasure of Matteo and Signora Piccolomini's company. It would do me a great honour if you could attend a small soiree I am holding here at my house. For Carnival.'

Bernini studies Costanza's face intently as he speaks and is rewarded with the merest hint of a smile on her lips. It is enough to know the prospect of a party excites her. At the same moment, the door opens, and the hounds and servants clatter along the tiles, descending on his guests with linens and towels for the purpose of drying themselves.

Costanza takes a long line of linen and gives stuttering thanks to the maid as she shakes out the folds before beginning to delicately wipe at her face, around her chemise, across her firm décolletage. Bernini observes each act, and it is all he can do to stop himself from sinking his teeth into the fleshy white skin of her neck.

Chapter Six

'Advice'

January 1636

I am sitting in Bernini's carriage, lent to us as the weather is not for turning.

How many times have I trogged home from the market, pattens sinking treacherously into the mud, laden with wares, and *dreamed* of being swept to my door in a carriage? Of being steadied by a liveried groomsman as I step daintily down from the small metal grate, swiftly followed by a maid loaded with a myriad of parcels – not beet, nor bean, nor cabbage, but delicate silks, fine lace – and pretty shoes.

Now I find myself being transported in such a fashion I cannot savour it. Instead, I stare out of the window at the sodden, muted day, the heavy wet wool of my cloak wearing sore welts into the back of my neck, having feigned a headache to avoid making dull conversation with Matteo and Finelli.

At the tavern I had told myself that first touch – Signor Bernini's sudden impropriety – had been a mistake. Is he not an artist? And aren't such people known for their dramatic ways? A mistaken touch is nothing, a fancy to be dismissed. But at the house just now, as we stood in the great doorway mopping the drips from our skin, I understood Lorenzo's look most well. It was unnerving and unseemly, if not an outright affront; am I not married?

And yet.

To be gazed upon in such a manner, when your own husband is not so amorous, is, perhaps, a reassuring thing? For Signor Bernini is a man who, so I've heard, likes his women. And then there is the party. I have never set foot in a place as fine as his house, well, no further than the kitchens in the great houses where Father worked as a groomsman. I knew Matteo's commission could only bring good fortune, and so it is proving. To be a guest at a party held by Signor Bernini. I am determined to go. Although, it may be wise to keep a decorous distance from the man himself, so as not to invite more dark stares.

We arrive at Papa's house in Vicolo San Silvestro. Tiberia is already standing on the steps, drawn outside by the mighty clop of the fancy carriage. Despite her tiny stature, my stepmother is given to a great extravagance of movement and is currently waving her arms in such a gravely immoderate manner that I feel equal parts tenderness and mortification.

'Holy Mary, Mother of God. What is all this?' she exclaims, as I tentatively place my foot on the small iron tread to dismount gracefully from the carriage. It is a tricky thing, made no more dignified by Tiberia's rambunctious excitement.

'Good afternoon, Mother.' I lean in to kiss her cheek and take in the comforting scent of cloven goose. 'I shall let Matteo explain.' I am in no mood to give an account of our chance encounter, for I am both sodden and troubled.

Finelli and Matteo follow, almost leaping from the carriage onto the cobbled road. Tiberia does not cease her jabbering, but wheezily hurries us into the house. She is all a-fluster, with never-ending questions about the great Signor Bernini, the transport, his house, our health and what irresponsible coves we are for taking Finelli out in the rain. We do not disclose it was his idea.

Inside there is a great shedding of bedraggled garments. Cloaks, shoes and jackets, set to dry alongside various fires lit within the house, and it is not long before there is a rancid smell of wet sheep seeping about the place.

Tiberia, chirruping about our bad fortune turned good, the carriage (ye gods, the carriage!), and the propensity of colds to fall on the chest at this time of year, pulls me to the bedchamber she shares with Papa. Closing the door, she searches among her things for a clean chemise, dry body and skirt. I am not inclined to wear my stepmother's clothes, not least because they make me look like a behemoth, straining as they do to fit, but she is insistent.

'You cannot stay in damp attire, daughter. If you are with child, your humours will be too chilled for the poor little thing to survive.'

I do not respond. This is her way of asking the same question she has asked most Sundays for four years. Besides, my courses started but three days past and when I saw their staining, I wept.

''Tis a kindness, Mother. One I am grateful for.' She surreptitiously inspects my belly as I undo my skirt and brushes her hand over it as she pulls at my bodice.

'Well, I shan't pull too tight, just in case,' and although she is behind me, I know there's a puckish grin on her face. 'Some maids have no clue. I had a friend, Cosima Gelli, who—'

'Thought she had bellyache and called for the pot to relieve herself, only to find she was delivering a child, having gone nine months in ignorance of her state. I know.'

Irritated I have finished one of her favourite tales, Tiberia adds, 'Well it is not unknown for dozy maids to miss all the signs.'

I inspect myself in the small mirror on the wall, and it is a most ill-fitting image that is revealed. The worsted skirts show my ankle bones, and the stays are laced so loosely they gape around my bosoms, which are more ample than Tiberia's. I laugh at the sight and think if only Signor Bernini could see me now, he would cease his lip-licking in an instant.

'I hear Giuliana is expecting,' Tiberia continues. Poor Giuliana is indeed with child again, weeping in my arms as she told me her news, for she laboured so long and hard with Tomaso, and is barely recovered from it.

'Luciana, the one you used to play with? I saw her the other day at market. She is *huge* with child. Enormous.' Tiberia gasps on holding her arms out, as if circling a melon. 'It must be her time soon. And then it will be your turn. I pray to the Virgin every day that you may be blessed. Look at you! You and Matteo are both so handsome, you will make a fine baby.'

I pat her hand and nod. 'What is meant to be, will be. I, too, pray.' I ceased long ago discussing the issue of my barrenness with Tiberia. Although she means well, her words sting. 'But until then, downstairs we have men and children to attend to, have we not?'

'God's blood!' Tiberia raises her hands to her face in horror. 'What are you doing keeping me here chittering about women's matters, when the men are all on their own, with no one to look after them?'

Tiberia is out of the door before I can respond, leaving only the mildest scent of grease, and my loose tied stays, as evidence of her recent presence.

* * *

Tiberia serves veal in a sweet sauce with raisins, in portions which are hardly parsimonious. It is a far cry from my own childhood, but Papa is doing well, and I do not begrudge his delight in being able to provide such generous hospitality. He has always enjoyed doting on those he loves.

The only mar is Tiberia, who is constantly up and at it. The meat needs more salt, the table more oil, the pitcher must be filled with fresh sweet water from the well despite it being half-full.

Papa wears Tiberia's fussing with well-practised fortitude. I wonder how much love is left between them, if indeed there was any to start with. Tiberia was a practical choice for a widower with a young child. She was healthy and knew how to keep a house.

I am sat beside Papa at the table, which has been my place since girlhood. Every now and again, he lays his fingers over my knuckles and squeezes them. A small act, but enough to tell me he misses me still. Although men should conduct themselves without emotion, Papa has been known to weep on my behalf.

The day I left to become Matteo's bride, my poor father accompanied me to the church, eyes rimmed red, nose inflamed from the prodigious blowing which had started early that morning and continued throughout the ceremony. I look at Papa now and feel a fond smile upon my lips, which is rewarded with another warm squeeze of my hand.

I am so absorbed in the chatter of the table that I fail to hear Finelli addressing me.

'Do you not think it was a gaudy show, Costanza? All that ostentatious counting out of money. The false largesse?' Finelli eyes are trained on me, and it appears he will only brook one answer, which I am not inclined to give.

'I'm afraid I have no proper knowledge of this gentleman – Bernini – nor his manner. But I believe he must have been genuine in his sentiment, for had he not started the counting before our eyes alighted upon him?'

'Poppycock.' Finelli breaks some bread and dips it in the juice on his plate before taking a bite. 'It was a callous display designed to impress the innocent.' He stares at me. 'Which it clearly has.' Finelli continues to talk as he chews the bread, visibly churning it between his teeth. 'Matteo, I will speak without hair on my tongue: Lorenzo Bernini is untrustworthy.'

Finally, Finelli swallows the bread and takes a swig of wine before beginning again. 'Lorenzo and I worked *together* on the sculpture of Daphne and Apollo. It was my artistry that created a moment of transformation so miraculous, so wondrous it drew breath from the critics. Gasps! But who took the credit?'

We all know the answer, but we wait for Finelli to give it. 'Bernini,' he says, almost spitting.

Finelli pauses for another drink, but it is clear he is not done. 'Work for Lorenzo Bernini if you must. Take his scudi. Meet the patrons. Then move on. But do not get involved with him, or any of his little band of toothless acolytes. That goes for the brother, Luigi, too. Never easy being the second son, eclipsed and obscured, a simple quirk of birth relegating you to watch from the wings. It twists a man is all I'm saying. All that self-pity and frustration—'

'Signor Finelli, you know I have a great respect for you.'

I look up, surprised. Matteo usually takes the course of least resistance. It is not in his nature to contradict or confront.

'Your professional difference with Signor Bernini is well known,' my husband continues. 'It is true Il Cavaliere did not act with honour. But I must go on the evidence of my dealings with him, which have, thus far, been fair and equitable.'

Finelli, who is seated opposite at the narrow table on which we sup, leans forward in a manner of great urgency. 'Lorenzo

Bernini – and his brother Luigi – are arachnids, fanged creatures who spin their webs with fantastical delight, not caring who gets caught. They live for themselves, and themselves alone. It is not a world for good, decent people.'

Matteo shifts in his chair; these kinds of conversations draw a deep discomfort in him. 'I understand. But I am a poor man from Lucca trying to make his way in the world, and for that I need Master Bernini.'

Finelli falls back, defeated. 'As you must. But if you will not take my advice to steer clear of the Bernini brothers, then at least have a care. There is something beyond arrogance which drives them both. It is a rivalry more dangerous than that of Romulus and Remus, brothers who could have worked together to build our glorious city, but instead Romulus killed Remus, and ruled alone. Imagine,' he says morosely. 'Imagine killing your own brother.'

Matteo stares at his plate for a moment before speaking. 'I thank you for your words. But I hope you understand, it is necessary for us to accept Bernini's invitation.'

Finelli lifts his hand, weathered by work and dry as fallen leaves, and waves it in dismissal.

'Don't say I didn't warn you.'

Tiberia has been hovering at the edge of the table, the burgeoning disagreement causing her great pain, for she fears disharmony more than the Devil himself. 'More wine?' she offers.

* * *

By the end of the afternoon, I am pleased to be back in my own clothes and to take leave of my family. There is no carriage home for Matteo and me, only our God-given legs.

Just as we are to go, Papa pulls me gently back. I look to the floor, as I did when I was a girl and he would gently admonish me.

'Have a care, my little firecracker. Finelli speaks fine words which came at a high cost. He was badly used by Bernini. It worries me that Matteo refuses to see fault in such a man, a proven swine, so you must be watchful for your husband.'

'Have no fear, Matteo and I will take care of each other, Papa. We always do.'

Chapter Seven

'Aurora'

February 1636

Riva Carpanetti's shop can be found in a narrow alley near the Pantheon, a part of town as yet untouched by Rome's aggrandisement.

In truth it is two rooms. This first is dingy, crammed with baskets filled with old clothes: stinking shirts and frayed petticoats, broken bodices, breeches stained with grease.

This is all most people see. But I know there is a second, secret room, where Riva keeps clothes for the wealthy. Fine skirts and delicate collars, embroidered jackets and voluminous sleeves slashed with silk. A place I only know about because once, very late at night and after many glasses of port, Riva confided to me of its existence.

Riva, and her assistant, Bluma Bianchini, live above the little shop. There has long been talk of what exactly passes between these two women, tittle tattle. It is said they love each other as husband and wife. But they are both Jewesses, and heretics in the eyes of most, so damned anyway. It is also known that Riva's father is a money lender, notorious for holding the debts of Rome's rich, which is also to know this city's most sinful secrets and makes you no friends.

The bell rings loudly as I enter. There is a stench of people even though the shop is empty, ghostly odours rising from the garments themselves.

Riva appears in seconds, a spectre hovering at the back of the room. 'What's this? Costanza Piccolomini, as I live and breathe.' Her voice seeps through the air like liquid smoke, husky and warm.

I wait for Riva to step forward, but she remains still, standing in the shadows, so it is I who must advance. The sour-smelling shop is forgotten momentarily as she comes into view. Riva has always filled me with wonder, ever since we were very small. She stands like a man, upright and strong, her hands placed firmly on her well-built hips. From her broad shoulders rises a face which is chiselled and handsome, her bronze eyes are edged black with soot from a taper, and she has a wildness of dark curls piled precariously on her head.

What's more astonishing is her outfit. For Riva is wearing a man's waistcoat, the colour of ripe olives, decorated in tiny gold stitches spelling out traces of strawberries, rosehips, and carnations, so fine they can barely be picked out in the light. Clothing forbidden in all respectable places.

'It is good to see you,' I say, and I mean it. Until this moment I had forgotten what Riva stirs in me: a heady recklessness, as if the world is there to be taken rather than to be walked through feebly.

She does not smile back. 'I thought the Piccolominis didn't extend their coin to heathens?'

I pause. 'Those are my stepmother's words. Not mine. I have always thought you a friend. I have not had the coin for a new dress. But now I am in sore need.'

Riva extends her arm, palm facing up, and sweeps it across the room, as a street conjuror might declare his trick. My eyes remain fixed on her face.

'Nay. I am not here for your usual wares.'

She raises an eyebrow. 'I'd heard your husband is working for Lorenzo Bernini – a man who holds even the Pope in his thrall, so they say.'

I take another step forward and lower my voice, even though there is no one present. 'I need a magnificent gown. Better than I, or any of my friends can make. Please, if you have such a thing, will you help me?'

Riva does not move but looks at me intently, weighing her next words like gold. 'Oh, I have such a thing. The question is do you have the coin for such a thing? Nothing is given on tick.'

'Don't worry.' I shake my skirts. From deep within the folds comes a jangling sound. 'My husband suggested I should wear this,' I let out a little laugh as I ripple my red wool gown vigorously, revealing the places it has been artfully patched, knowing they will be visible to Riva's practised eye, even in this sepulchral light.

She frowns and I add quickly, 'But I have put him right on the matter. We are attending a gathering at Signor Bernini's this Friday. "Husband," I told him. "If I am to acquit myself well, then I must be properly attired."'

Riva's eyes narrow. 'And you thought of me? Not one of the Catholic tailors in the new quarter?'

'Well,' I feel sheepish, 'I don't have enough to *purchase* a sumptuous gown. Only enough to rent a little splendour for the evening.'

Riva looks me up and down. 'So, it seems you *are* in the right place. Wait . . . Friday? It is only a week away, if it needs altering . . . Ah, I see it now. Your husband took a little persuading, did he?'

Riva is a wily soul. It has taken the best part of three weeks to persuade Matteo I need a new dress. 'You will be admired whether you wear wool or silk,' Matteo had maintained, his voice dulled by the repetition of my requests. 'We cannot afford a new dress. To buy. Or rent. I am putting money away for the house, as you want. Here's the rub, wife. You cannot have more rooms *and* more dresses. 'Tis one or the other.'

'It took time,' I admit, 'but I persuaded him in the end.'

Riva considers the news carefully. 'I know of some who frequent the Bernini house, ladies, courtesans, they will be in silks and brocades ...'

'I know!' I let out, relieved to have some understanding at last. I have only discussed the matter with Matteo, having not raised it with Tiberia or Giuliana. 'I must have something ... lovely ... so I will not look out of place.'

I cast my gaze desperately about the room but can only see coarse frieze coats, skirts with torn hems, yellowing shirts, and ancient tunics made of canvas, coated in linseed and the brine of the sea.

Seeing my concern, Riva makes a gravelly laugh. 'Not here. This way to find your dress.' She motions to the small, gloomy passageway and pushes open a second door revealing a room with huge candelabras rising like forest saplings, fine chairs upholstered in damascene, and vast, ornate chests, each lined in traces of luminous mother of pearl. On the opposite wall hangs a huge looking glass, surrounded by gold, curling vine leaves and fat bunches of grapes.

'Take a look,' Riva says, stepping aside.

The first thing I countenance is my own reflection. At home I use a tiny hand mirror to check all is as it should be, whether my hair is well done, or my eyes are not swollen or red. It is disconcerting to see the whole: my skirts, worn of colour in places, raw hands, old leather shoes.

'I am taking a look.'

'Not at yourself, at the wares.'

There are furs hanging from pegs, shining pelts of mink and ermine. I reach out to take one and it yields to my fingers, downy and soft, no longer smelling of animal, but of perfumed oil, opulent notes of mandarin, pepper and plum, myrrh and musk, conjuring images of a queen in a far-off place, surrounded by palms and blue skies.

'I had no idea . . .'

'Why should you?' Riva says. 'You have had no need of such things until now. Besides,' she stops to stroke the nap of a crimson gown, 'most of my clients are women who rent, rather than buy their clothes. They work in a precarious profession where you must look the part, even if you come from the streets.'

'You mean they come from the back streets . . . only to work on their backs?' I laugh.

Riva looks up sharply. 'Those are my customers you are talking about. We show less judgement and more understanding here.'

I feel the pinking of shame rising in my cheeks. It is the kind of thing Tiberia would say. 'I'm sorry, I did not mean to judge so. I came to ask for your help too.'

'Aye, well. I will not have women starving. Besides, there would be no trade – mine nor theirs – if men were not willing to pay for it. This is the world in which you will be moving.'

I nod and feel bile bite at the back of my throat. How little I know. And Matteo, too. For sure, my husband can carve a decent putti, but when it comes to fine company he is as green as I.

'Show me your coins, then we know what we are working with.' I pull out the pocket and shake the money into my hand. 'Good,' Riva says approvingly. 'This is plenty for what you need.'

She unbuttons her own jacket, revealing a lawn shirt, so fine it is almost sheer, edged with small, scalloped, lace-like seashells.

'It gets hot,' Riva says by way of explanation, 'lacing and unlacing women into dresses. Jackets look fine, but ones such as this are made to be seen, not worked in.'

Riva swoops in and out of the chests like a graceful kingfisher, pulling out a series of dresses which catch the light like the iridescent scales of fish.

As she shakes out the clothes, the air is filled with the scent of the women who once wore them: a stale perfume, rose, musk and ambergris, heavy with a hint of luxury and debauchery. There are other smells too – pungent liquorice from the powdered anise and the soft, buttery orris to keep the pests at bay.

'This one?' Riva holds up a silk gown the colour of bluebells, with matching sleeves slashed with white, but I shake my head. It makes me think of Caterina in the tavern.

'Something to flatter my colour and complexion.' I hold out an arm, still carrying the faded kiss of the sun in its darkened tone. 'Red, or gold. I want to . . .' I hesitate, but I know I can trust Riva. 'I want to walk into Signor Bernini's house, hold my head up high. Show him – them – that a girl from San Lorenzo is as good as anyone.'

'I understand.' Riva says solemnly before casting her eyes rapidly about the room, mentally searching the many trunks. 'Yes!' It is the first time I have seen Riva smile. 'I have just the thing.' She kneels in front of an unopened box, slowly lifting the heavy lid. 'What about this?' Riva stands and turns towards me, holding out a set of velvet skirts the colour of old gold, and a matching bodice and sleeves. They look as if they have been stitched not by mortal hands at all, but are instead held together by air. 'Well?'

'They are beautiful.' I whisper. For truly I have never seen anything like it except for the garb of holy women hung upon church walls. 'Can I try them on?'

Riva clicks her tongue. 'Of course. That's why you're here. We will make you as grand as any noblewoman, you have my word.' The words seem to slip more naturally from Riva's lips now, as a friend rather than a dress seller, and I am glad for it.

She helps me to unlace and slip out of my dress, then slides the honeyed skirts over my head, pulling at the bodice to fit my shape, before attaching the sleeves with small ties. These are, I note, fashionably, wondrously voluminous, and I can't help but feel a little trill of pleasure as Riva cinches the sleeves with a ribbon just above my elbow.

When she has finished, I am turned back towards the long looking glass. I hold myself very still, trying to conceal what I truly feel. For in this mirror, in this flickering light, I see reflected an image so clear, so revelatory, it makes my heart rumble: there is something magnificent about me.

It is not just the dress, which flatters my skin and fits like a glove. I hear in the rustle of the skirts the whisper of possibilities. So great is the alteration it fills me at once with both satisfaction and guilt. I have many blessings in my life – I am loved, I have bread in my belly and a roof over my head – yet it has always lacked a certain splendour.

Here, now, in the back room of this small shop, it is as if I have just been magicked into being by Riva, birthed again by her haberdasher's alchemy.

This is what I am meant to be: a noblewoman of the Piccolomini house.

Riva sighs. She has seen it too. As much as I wish to hide what the mirror image shows me, I cannot. She stands behind me and I feel her breath on the back of my neck. 'Costanza. You look like Aurora, Goddess of the dawn, Earth's morning fire.'

I soak up the refracted rays of the candles, the opulent dress and

Riva's bronze gaze, and laugh. She laughs too, then Riva reaches to an open jewellery box, lined with plump purple silk, and pulls out a rope of pearls as big as hazelnuts which she loops about my neck.

'There,' she says, satisfied. 'My friend, you will be magnificent.'

There is a clattering on the stairs behind us, and I turn, suddenly embarrassed as the door opens. There is a gentleman standing in the doorway, tall and well-dressed, staring at me not in admiration, but in something approaching fear. Bluma, plump and red-faced, stands behind him.

'Signore.' Riva bows. 'Apologies, I had forgotten your appointment.'

She walks to the mirror so quickly I must take a hasty step back to let her pass. I am surprised to see a handle to a door hidden among the foliage. Riva opens it in one movement and there is a sudden blast of cold air, whipping at the candle flames.

'A good day to you, Signoria Carpanetti.' The man half bows, then hurries through the room and out of the shop, without even acknowledging my presence, while Bluma hovers in the doorway, grinning.

'This is Costanza,' Riva explains. 'An old friend, in need of a gown.'

'Indeed.' Bluma takes it all in: the dress, the pearls. 'Found one I see.' Then she looks directly at me with a defiance rarely seen in a woman. 'Hope he's worth it.'

I am about to respond, but Bluma has already turned on her heel to make her way back upstairs.

'I . . .'

Riva shakes her head at me. 'Don't mind her.'

'It's not that. What Bluma was doing. With that man. The authorities . . .' Riva raises her hand to bat away my words, but I catch her wrist and hold it. 'They are arresting women.

Tib— someone told me of another girl. She is our age and has been taken from her home for fornication. It is not safe.'

Riva's eyes narrow. 'You know nothing of being unsafe. To be a Jewish woman in a Catholic city is not safe. To be living on the streets because we cannot afford the lease is not safe. 'Tis why we rent gowns to women who want to appear more than they are.'

Her words bite at me. 'Is that what you think?'

'Nay. It is my turn to be sorry. I know of the arrests, but what can we do? Besides, it is only women who come here to be dressed – and men to be undressed. Father has some powerful protectors. Now, shall we get your dress and pearls wrapped? It will be dark soon enough.'

Chapter Eight

'An Education'

February 1636

It is Friday, and a milder night than the many which have passed recently.

Outside the Bernini house the huge iron braziers have been lit. The amber flames attract the moths of the sculptor's circle, those who work with Bernini at the Fabbrica workshop, rivals, priests and patrons endlessly arriving, some on foot, others in carriages, all attired in the latest fashions.

I have waited for this moment, yet now it is here my heart feels like a bird's wing beating against a cage. It's a strange phenomenon, that when the thing you have longed for finally arrives, there is a small part of you so afraid it will disappoint, you almost wish it done before it has started.

Matteo and I are met by a footman dressed in black wool, his uniform expensive and well cut. I hand him my cape and take a moment to smooth my skirts, arrange my body, so all looks as it should. Just before we enter the banqueting hall, I slide my fingers along the smooth pearls which have been warmed by the heat of my blood, loosening their bind on my throat.

'Quite magnificent, wife,' Matteo whispers as we walk in, but I'm unsure whether he means me or the spectacle before us. The hall is astonishing: not unlike a place of holy worship, with its high beamed ceilings, dark panelled walls and elaborate marble-tiled floor, alternating in patterns of black and white. Yet this place is no more dedicated to the worship of the eucharist than a brothel, it being entirely filled with entertainment for the body and the senses.

There is the musky smell of perspiration and rich perfume, roasted meats and woodsmoke. The guests are a symphony of colour and jewels glinting in the light of hundreds of lanterns. The air is warm and thick with voices loudened by drink, over which flows music from the nimble fingers of men on lyre and harpsichord.

Above all these notes of bacchanal, there is piercing, soaring soprano. I look at the stage at the far end of the room expecting to see a woman, but it is a man wearing a satin jacket of apricot brocade with heavily rouged cheeks.

Matteo leans into my ear. 'A castrato. Emasculated as a child. A favourite of cardinals, and not just for his singing, so very well connected.'

I pause for a moment, it is a strange thought, to know something so intimate about a person I have never met. 'Come,' Matteo pulls at my arm. 'It does not do to stare. Let's get some food, I'm hungry.'

The table is laden with delicacies: roasted fowl and suckling pig with truffle sauce, cured meats, fruit preserved in slick syrup, dainty honey cakes, sugared nuts and candied fruit. A compulsion bubbles up inside me, a sudden desire to plunge my hands into the dishes, tear the meat from its bone, to dip my fingers in shining glazes and suck on the succulent fruit. I content myself with taking a morsel of as much as I can. We are offered wine and I sup quickly, the salted meat, the crush, and the nerves, making me thirsty.

We hear him before we see him: a lone voice rising stridently above the noise of the room. 'Matteo! Signora Piccolomini!'

As he approaches, people part like waves: Lorenzo Bernini, walking with arms outstretched, welcoming Matteo and me. In this light there is a shimmer about him, a spark, like lightning about to strike, not borne of one single thing but a combination of everything: the sheen of his hair, the satin lustre of his doublet and polish of his boots, the strength of his body, vibrant, vibrating, hardly able to contain the sheer lifeforce emanating from his slim frame. Matteo puts a hand around my waist.

The eyes of the party immediately fall upon us, examining our hair, clothes, the warmth of the maestro's welcome. I hear a woman whisper, 'Who are they?'

Lorenzo Bernini ignores it all. 'I am glad you came.' He hesitates for a moment, as if the words have not been judged so well. He turns to Matteo, 'You are a Fabbrica man now. It is only right you should join us at our festivities.'

The men chat and I listen, trying to follow the gist, but they talk rapidly of business, how carvings are progressing, dates for completion and shipments, the merits of one design over the other, the impatience of patrons. The talk never strays from the topic of work and for a time I am quite glad to be forgotten, as it affords me the luxury of spying about the room unhindered. I was right to insist on a luxurious dress; even though it is hot and heavy, and the necklace pulls at my throat, I am more than equal to the people here.

The place is even busier now, and somewhere on the other side dancing has begun, a steady clap of hands marking the time of the music, women's bodies being lifted by unseen hands high into the air, like swifts swooping in the sky.

I skim the room for a face I recognise. There is no one, until I spot Caterina right at the edge of the crowd. She is dressed gloriously in silk the colour of a midnight sky and talking most animatedly with a gentleman who is not Paolo. I have never seen a woman talk in such a way to man who is not her husband. Caterina reminds me of a peacock flashing her feathers, fingers fluttering at her chest and strands of hair, flashing a shy half smile as she peeks from under her eyelashes, which is both coy and seductive.

I hope that Caterina might look up, might recognise me, and I will give a small wave in return. I imagine a flicker of surprise in her eyes as she takes in Costanza, the tavern girl in the plain wool dress transformed into a creature of the court. Except Caterina never takes her eyes off her companion.

'A dance, Signora Piccolomini?' My attention whips back to Matteo and Lorenzo Bernini, who are both staring at me. Matteo looks embarrassed, Bernini bemused.

'I said I think our conversation has left you more than a little bored. For which I can only apologise. To make amends, I shall invite you to dance. It will be my first of the evening.'

The thought of having the first dance with the maestro should fill me with dread, but it does not. I feel a little jolt of excitement, a ripple of anticipation, and find myself suddenly eager to take to the floor, longing to be seen.

As we make our way to the dancing, I surreptitiously examine his face. It is not quite as I remember. Bernini's cheeks are a little higher and the bones more wideset. He is flushed, the heightened colour only serving to set off his eyes, which are as pitch as night, giving him an impish look, so absolute is their darkness. His doublet is open, and underneath there is a fine linen shirt, so loosely tied I can peep at his chest, luminous white skin stretched over sinewy muscle, doused with fine black hair. I feel myself quenching a thirst I did not know I had.

We wait for the music to start. He does not take his eyes off mine and as the first notes sound, I feel the room watching me, silent, predatory. My chest tightens; either I allow myself to be swallowed by this moment or I can rise above it and soar to the rafters. For some reason I trust this man, feel safe in his company, so I throw my head back and laugh, letting the sound roar from my throat.

The melody begins in earnest, the castrato singing an old folk song set to a modern arrangement; the words are quick, bawdily describing how young lovers must succumb to springtime love. Bernini dances wildly, pulling me this way and that, so I have little choice but to yield to the demands of his hands upon my waist, twirling and clapping with the greatest of fervour. He lifts me high and I am made airborne, my skirts turning olive, then ochre then spun-gold as I whirl around, the crowd becoming raucous and loud.

We twirl and bound and leap until we are breathless, so when we finally stop, we must find rest by the wall.

'I have not danced with quite such abandon for a long while,' he says, still clutching his side.

'Well, in that case you have not been dancing properly, Signor Bernini. For to dance is to be free of all cares.'

'If that is the case, I have not been free of all cares for a very long time.' He takes a gulp from the cup a servant has brought. 'Call me Lorenzo. Please.'

'That I can believe, *Lorenzo*. All you do is talk of work, work, work. Is there nothing else which entertains you?'

He laughs loudly. 'Aye, there is plenty which entertains me, but nothing I can discuss with a married woman.'

I feel myself bristle, my words falter. 'I am not a prude ... if that's what you think.' I answer, scuffing my toe against the floor. 'But you are right. I am married and it is not seemly to begin tawdry talk.'

Lorenzo stands up straighter. 'My apologies. Art is both my entertainment and my work. The truth is, when I am not talking of art, or making it, I am utterly dispossessed. An empty vessel. So, you see, I have no choice. I am impatient for the modern world. I cannot sit and wait for it to come to me. Instead, it is I who must create it.'

'I see.' I push my toe harder into the tiled floor. 'I . . . despite being married to a fine sculptor, whose work is very good, and I am deeply enamoured of . . . I know very little of . . . well, about art.'

His eyebrows arch. 'You surprise me.' Another sip. 'You clearly come from a good family, Piccolomini. And are wearing a fine dress. Did your father, or Matteo, not take you to see the churches and collections of Rome?'

'My father is a footman. He waits on important men but is not one himself.' I hold out my skirts. 'The dress is rented. And Matteo works many hours to put food on the table . . .'

He nods, looking at me, but still does not reply. Suddenly I am infuriated. What does this man, standing here among such riches, know about my life? Lorenzo Bernini has no understanding of the ordinary world, and I am no poor creature to be pitied.

'Do not be so sorry for me! I am not without learning. My father instructed me in my letters and numbers. I know how to run a house and run it well. It is just I do not know about art. We are not all like you, who needs it to breathe. I think I must take my leave now, for I have taken up too much of your time. You have guests to entertain, and my husband will be looking for me.'

I make to go, but Lorenzo catches my arm. 'Will you allow me to show you some time? Art, I mean. And what it means to me?'

I hesitate. 'I don't know if it is proper ... Dancing in a roomful of people is one thing.'

'Just art. Naught more. You have nothing to fear from me, Signora Piccolomini.'

'*Costanza.*'

He smiles gently, not just his lips, but his eyes, face, his whole being radiating a sudden affection. I feel my heart beating in my throat.

'I have been warned you are dangerous company.'

'By Finelli, no doubt. You were with him, in the rain. What have you to say about dangerous company?'

'That is my problem. It seems all my life, even if I do not court danger, it courts me.'

'I am not dangerous, I am obsessive. About my work. And that seems dangerous to men who lack their own drive and talent. That is all.'

'I see.' I realise I am waiting for a sign like before. A subtle touch, a lingering hand about my waist as he makes to move us through the hall, but instead he bows.

'So, will you permit me to educate you in the making of the modern world? It would be good for your husband's career to have a wife well-versed in the latest thinking.'

A playful smile hovers about my lips. 'Ah. If it will be helpful to my husband, then I suppose I have every reason to accept, have I not?'

'It is settled then. I shall send an invitation. You are quick, Costanza. Curious. I think you will find the instruction of use to yourself, as well as your husband. But for now, let me escort you back to him. As you say, my guests are waiting.'

* * *

The party lasts until the early hours. He glimpses her from time to time. At Matteo's side. Dancing with Andrea, or one of the other sculptors known to her husband. But she does not say goodbye to him, and he does not see her leave.

In the velvety hours of the morning, as the fire's embers are dying in the grate, the sculptor sits in the high-backed chair in his studio, the rush of hosting still coursing through his veins. He thinks he will rest for just a few hours, before going to the Fabbrica.

The door to his studio is ajar. It usually gives a sign he does not mind being disturbed, but tonight it is open thanks to his absent-mindedness and nothing more, for he does not expect company. It is a surprise then, when the door is opened wider, and he sees a figure standing in the frame, face indistinguishable in the darkness of the outer reaches of the room. But the sculptor does not need to see the man's face to know who it is.

'Luigi. What can I do for you?' The figure lurches forward, and Lorenzo Bernini can smell the evening's entertainment on his brother's body: stale wine and a sour carnality. 'You are drunk.'

'Lighten up. God's blood, brother, it was a party!' Luigi stumbles into the second chair by the fire, and reveals the full effect of over-indulgence, hair askance, stains on his shirt, legs splayed, eyes struggling to focus.

'Seems you took your pleasures a-plenty.' Lorenzo can hardly contain his disgust. To lose control in such a way; to lack the self-discipline it takes to abstain. To throw your talents away on drink, and women, fights and gambling. To abuse all those who cross you, and those who don't. For even now, sitting on the large desk, in the pile of invoices and accounts, there are bills – or to use a more accurate term, pay-offs – to the victims of Luigi's fists, or his uncontrollable prick, both of which are used with impunity in the taverns of Rome. Payments to protect the name of Bernini.

'I repeat. It was a *party*. What else is a party meant to be, if not pleasurable?'

His brother is taller, broader, better-looking, in the eyes of some, possessed as he is of long thick hair, even boyish features, cheekbones which would look hard on a woman but devastating on a man, eyes which foretell of mischief. Around his neck hangs a gold chain, thick and ostentatious, and from one ear dangles a large pearl. He is a rake. Although unkempt and unsavoury to the nostrils, there is, Lorenzo can admit, a debauched charm about his brother.

'Parties are good for business. They create camaraderie, loyalty among the men who work for us. And their wives. They keep our friends, enemies and patrons close. We are introducing a new order, brother. The innovator has many enemies, especially those who have done well doing what has always been done. We must make men believe in our methods. Our art.'

'You are obsessed with being the first. And do not quote Machiavelli at me, you hypocrite. For business …' Luigi spits into the fire, the globule lands heavily, causing the coals to hiss. 'I saw you with that girl. Half your age. Are you really telling me that was not pleasurable? Your hands all over her body. It was an embarrassment.'

'I am tired. It is late. I have no stomach for your bullshit. It was none of those things.' It is true. He is tired. He thinks of his feather bed and its heavy hangings, of the work of the day ahead, for there can be no rest.

'So, you don't mean to have her then?' Luigi idly picks at some gristle lodged between his teeth. 'Then you won't mind if I do? I bet the little chit moans for Rome.'

The sculptor feels a rush in his ears, a tornado of rage circling in his lungs as his breath quickens. Before he has had a chance to collect his thoughts, Lorenzo finds he has leaped from his chair and his hands are wrapped around his little brother's throat, the beat of life throbbing under his fingers.

Luigi holds his hands up in surrender. 'Jesu, Lorenzo.' The words are squeezed out with venom and not a little spittle, which lands on the sculptor's face.

Why does Luigi do this? Want to sully all that is pure?

He takes his hands off his brother's throat and feels the pounding blood in his veins ease just a little. Lorenzo states his words with care: 'You will leave Costanza Piccolomini alone. That is an order, Luigi.' He wipes at the spit on his face with his sleeve. 'Lie with every woman in Rome if you must. But if I find out you have touched her ...'

Luigi pulls at his collar. 'You will what?'

'I will kill you.'

Chapter Nine

'Not a Pinch of Romance'

March 1636

Giuliana Gavia still lives on the Vicolo San Silvestro, and we are lying together upstairs on the big old bed once occupied by Mother Gavia. Until she died. I sometimes wonder how Giuliana feels sleeping here, or making love to her husband.

My friend looks toad green.

'I thought the midwife said that while you had milk, you could not conceive a child?'

'Aye, that's what she said.' Giuliana rubs her stomach. 'But the evidence is to the contrary.' She sighs. I want to tell her it is a blessing, but this is what old women say, without a mind for the mother, for I have never seen Giuliana looking worse.

'I cannot shake off the sickness. Lord knows how I'll cook my husband's meal. I haven't been to the market in a few days.'

I nod, having already noted the empty vegetable basket and the hardened haunch of bread on the board. 'Do not worry,' I say gently. 'I will leave it ready.'

Giuliana sniffs, then turns on her side to look at me. 'You hate cooking.'

'When I am filled with baby sickness you will tend to me,' I say, planting a tender kiss on her forehead.

'How *is* Matteo?' she asks, eyes closed and pulling her shawl about herself.

'Matteo' – I pause – 'is busy with his new commission.'

Giuliana notices the hesitation. 'My mother used to say that in a marriage, it is often the case that there is one who kisses and one who offers the cheek.'

'Do you remember when we were girls and used to talk about the men we'd wed, and the husbands they'd make?'

'Aye. I wanted to marry the baker's boy, and you were to marry the young duke who passed us in his carriage on the Piazza di San Lorenzo.' Giuliana grins. It's a long time since I have seen her smile. 'We only saw him once, but you swore he would hunt you down, and when he found you, he would ask for your hand with a diamond as large as a rose.'

'Aye, well. He was very handsome.' I turn over and softly squeeze her arm, which is thin. Propping myself on my hand, I look for the Giuliana of my childhood, but can only find a woman's face, pinched and drawn. 'How we longed for love and marriage.'

'Nay, you longed for love. I hoped for a decent man, who would put food on the table and not beat me. Love and marriage are not the same thing at all.'

'You have not a pinch of romance,' I admonish. 'But did you find him?' I tease.

'Marco does not beat me. But the leather trade is tough, foreigners bring their wares and undercut his prices. And he has a mannish appetite for marriage.' She touches her belly without thought. 'But don't they all?'

I do not tell Giuliana of Matteo's reluctance. In her state she does not want to know. I am pondering this when Giuliana surprises me by crying out in a voice so piteous it makes me wince; 'I fear another birth so soon after Tomaso.' She burrows into my arms, like she did when we were small, and I stroke her thinning hair.

The irony that Giuliana fears what I long for does not escape me. I nuzzle at her neck. She smells sweet, of sickness. 'Do not be afraid. I promise I will look after you.' I want to make things right, if only for a moment, so slip a piece of gossip into our conversation, like a welcome breeze on a hot day, to keep my friend occupied.

'This Friday, just past, I danced with Lorenzo Bernini.' The sound of his name upon my lips feels awkward, a secret language, so I must strain to keep my tone from straying into excitement.

The revelation does the job. Giuliana pulls back and looks at me aghast, her sickness momentarily forgotten.

'You wench! You've been here all this time and you did not think to tell me? I must know it all!' Her voice is loud and hurried, which causes a stirring from the curled figure at the end of the bed.

'Sshhh, Tomaso. If he wakes, we will have no time to talk.'

We both look at the boy, breath held until he settles.

'How did it come about?' My friend whispers now, but with no less urgency.

'Well, he had a party, and there was music.'

'I am no simpleton. I know how a dance happens, but not how you came to be at Maestro Bernini's party?'

His name again. BER-NI-NI. The hard sound of the 'B' followed by softly rolled 'N's.

'Tell me, how did you end up there?' Giuliana prompts again.

But I find I cannot say his name for fear of blushing.

'He ...' I stumble. 'He invited us ... well, Matteo. He invited Matteo. And me. As Matteo's wife.'

Giuliana does not notice my misstep. 'Sweet Mary. What did you wear?'

'The most beautiful dress of gold velvet.'

'But how?'

'Riva Carpanetti.'

My friend nods at the explanation. 'I wish I had seen you.'

'Oh, how I longed to show you, but it was a rush.' It is a small lie. 'And I have been ill. So, what's he like ... this Lorenzo Bernini?'

I think of Lorenzo's hands on my waist, lifting me high. Of the way he looked at me. Of that single moment, captured in flight. Of the rhythm of the music, the flex of his muscles, his body pulled tight against mine. Of the way he looked, playful and imposing all at once.

'Aye, he is fair enough,' I answer. 'But with an air of choleric about him, like a river running too fast.'

'Did he speak with you?'

'We danced ... And discussed art.'

Giuliana puts her hands over her face. 'Good God. You know naught about such things.'

'I know. He offered to educate me on the subject. Said I was curious. I piqued his interest.'

'Please tell me you did not accept? It would be most unseemly. You are married. He is a notorious lothario.'

A nervous laugh flutters from my throat. A decision. This way, or that?

'Nay, of course I did not accept. As you say, his circle is not decent.' I drop my voice. 'There was a castrato singing.'

Giuliana crosses herself. 'These are devil's things. Not natural. Men such as Bernini may be fine artists, but they live lawless lives.'

She is silent for a moment. 'Caravaggio too was feted, then he knifed a man and fled. You must take care.' She wipes her brow.

We lie side by side like an ancient couple entombed in a mausoleum, and stare at the ceiling. Giuliana continues: 'Good women do as their husbands, and the Church, bid.'

I examine a patch of bark-coloured mould creeping from the corner in curdled lumps, and consider the truth of her words for a moment. 'Aye. We are here to bear babies, keep the house and our personages nice, and cause as little wifely grief as possible. That is our pact. For this, men love us well. For what more is needed in life?'

Giuliana pats my hand. 'Indeed. 'Tis well spoken.'

For this is what I have believed, ever since I was a child. But as I say the words, I feel them obliterate my place the world. As if ribbons, and sweeping, and a ripe belly, which has always been my purpose, is but a step away from the grave, where I will be swallowed up in the dirt without having ever experienced life. Is this what all women come to understand? That our living is small, and we are only a hair's breadth from the muck that made us?

Chapter Ten

'Caravaggio'

May 1636

I t is some weeks since the party – and Lorenzo's offer.

At first Matteo was wary of accepting. No man, he argued, would offer such a thing as *art lessons*, unless the man in question wanted something else entirely.

This was, I retorted, a base way of thinking. Lacking a certain sense of Christian altruism. Is it not possible to see beyond a woman's body, and into her mind? Do not men of learning yearn to tutor? Would not having a wife well-schooled in all things art – instructed by a famous sculptor no less – help a husband's earning? Especially when that husband worked all the hours God gave – and had little time nor inclination to instruct his wife. Is it not an offer that we should be grateful for?

The discussion had been relentless, each passing parry a whetstone sharpening my resolve, honing my conviction. The ceaseless friction forcing an edge to my reasoning, my words gradually gaining precision, until I mastered the power to cut through my husband's counterpoints and rebuttals, so he had no choice but to concede.

It is cool inside the basilica of the Sant'Agostino, not far from the Piazza Navona.

Spring has slipped into early summer, and these are the quiet hours between Prime and Terce, before the sun has warmed the day. My skin prickles with cold and nerves as I wait for Lorenzo. What if he doesn't come? And what if he does? Either way, I have come. And in this act, I have declared my desire to be something, to be different.

The chiming bells woke me, as they do every morning. But instead of curling back asleep, I slipped from the bed and dressed by the light of one candle, Matteo having already left for work without a word. The candle flickering as I laced my patched red dress, fingers moving deftly, as I tried to suppress the nagging feeling that such presentation might somehow disappoint Lorenzo Bernini, the candescent creature in the golden gown having been carefully folded and packed away. He has, I reminded myself, seen me like this before, at the tavern, and still invited me to look at pictures. All will be well. All *will* be well. I repeat the words over and over as I pull and tug at the ties. All. Will. Be. Well.

The church is quite unassuming from the outside, with its stolid dove-grey stone portal sparingly adorned. Inside it is a different story. I drink in the high domed ceiling, the ornate patterns on the floor which remind me of sweet things, in their shades of cream, apricot and nutmeg. The tall columns which rise to the roof like the smooth trunks of pink marble trees, gold cornices shimmering against their rosy hues. It is so modern, so opulent, it dazzles me, as it has been designed to do, for every church should reflect the glory of God. I have chosen the last pew, at the very back so that I may better hear the heavy door opening and prepare myself properly for the imminent arrival of Lorenzo.

The door bangs and is followed by footsteps. I hold myself taut and I turn expectantly, preparing myself, telling myself to be calm; I am doing nothing wrong by being here.

It is not Lorenzo, but a woman, so heavy with child her steps are ponderous. Young, round-faced and pale, she makes no attempt to acknowledge me. Instead, she makes her way to the statue of the Madonna del Parto – the Madonna of safe delivery – where she awkwardly drops to her knees.

I study Our Lady for a moment. The statue has the face of an ancient goddess, with flowing robes tied under her breasts and a veil set upon her head. She holds a plump child-Christ, like an empress presenting an heir, a placid smile on her face.

'I pray to thee,' the woman murmurs. 'I pray to thee Blessed Mother of Childbirth, give me your protection. I commend the fruit of my womb to thy grace, for I have naught else.' The woman begins to rock and moan. '*Have mercy on me.*' She repeats the words over and over again, the low cry of pain turning gradually to sobs. 'I do not want to die. Spare me and my child, so we can be your devoted servants.'

I turn from her heaving shoulders, in part embarrassed; devotion is a private thing. It is a misconception that holy places are for serenity, when people more often than not come in shame or dread. Fear is such a lonely realm. But her distress turns my stomach too, such that I am compelled to close my eyes, bow my head and start muttering my own intercession: 'Holy Mother, bestow your mercy upon this poor woman. Take away her anguish, but not her life. Do not let her die for being a woman.'

It is because I am praying that I fail to hear Lorenzo arrive, until he slips into the pew beside me. Embarrassed he has heard my pleas, I stop and wait for him to greet me; it is not seemly for me to speak first, but he does not say a word. So we sit in perfect stillness for some minutes, listening to the crying woman.

'I am sorry I interrupted you,' he says eventually.

'Nay. Well, yes. I was just . . .' I nod at the statue and the woman. 'Our Lady of Childbirth . . .'

Lorenzo looks at his hands. 'A risky thing. Not that I am well acquainted.' Then he looks at me. 'Are you . . . ?'

'Jesu! No!' I say, a little too quickly. 'My mother; she died this way.' It feels too intimate a confession to a man I hardly know.

He pauses. 'With you?' I look at him and his eyes are alive with a sincerity, a reassurance, as if I could tell him all that has happened in my life and he would comprehend it.

'Nay, a sister.' I pull at some ragged skin which has caught at the edge of my nail. 'She perished too.'

'I am so sorry. Your poor father.' I can only nod and stroke out the folds of my dress in an attempt at a sereneness. This is not how I wished to start. Then it dawns on me: I must change the tempo, for he will not.

'It was a long time ago,' I say briskly. 'And not the purpose of our meeting. I say we leave the lady to her soul and get on with the matter in hand.' I imagine I see the briefest flicker of relief crossing his face, then it is gone. 'I must say you have picked a strange place – and time – for my education. This is the chapel of courtesans, is it not? Where fallen women attend mass brazenly and are laid to rest in consecrated grounds?'

'Whose bones are laid here is little concern of mine. I come for the art. And as for the time, I felt it best to meet early.' He looks about the empty church and murmurs in a hushed tone, edged with a hint of mischief. 'For if they see Lorenzo Bernini with a woman in chapel it will surely set tongues wagging and I shall be declared married before None Prayers.'

I let out a laugh, for it is true; Rome feeds on salacious gossip as a bird gorges on worms. 'Now that *would* ruin your reputation.'

'Quite.' He looks upon me warmly, and makes a small, apologetic smile. I decide I like it.

'Come,' he stands, 'I have something to show you.'

Lorenzo walks to one of the high archways in which hangs a large painting, leaving a waft of oranges, mingled with cinders and dust, in his wake. He takes a taper and begins to methodically light the candles in front of the painting.

While he does this, I desperately try to collect my thoughts. This is the moment I have been dreading. He will ask me about the painting: what I know, what I see, what I think.

And what I know is nothing. It feels as if serpents have begun coiling and uncoiling in my stomach, moving in giddy anticipation at the thought of my stupidity about to be revealed.

The more I look at the picture, the less I see. It is a painting of the Madonna, that much is clear. She holds a young Christ in her arms, and stands in an ordinary doorway, the like of which are common all over Rome. What confuses me is that there is no gold, no ethereal angels with trumpets, no blazing blue sky, no cherubs lying on pillowy-white clouds edged in silky apricots and rose pinks. The pilgrim kneeling at Our Lady's feet is almost vulgar, dressed in rags. I can find little to commend in such a painting.

'Have you heard of an artist called Caravaggio?' Lorenzo asks gently. The serpents slither, tightening their grip. A familiar story surfaces: thirty years ago, a man, Ranuccio, fighting with another, the same Michelangelo Caravaggio. There is a dispute over tennis – or money – or a woman. Rannucio attacks Caravaggio. Or perhaps it is the other way round? There are many accounts, and no one can agree on the facts.

What is recalled is that first there was a knife in Ranuccio's thigh. Then his back. A crimson tide spilling forth from the wound, the air thickening with a metallic scent of fresh blood. Caravaggio staggering back from the body. Years later people would recount in whispers how Ranuccio's blood seeped into the ground, congealing to a black mess in the cracks of the stone. And how, over time, the sun's rays and the soft summer rain extinguished all trace of Ranuccio's existence.

But this is not the answer Lorenzo is seeking.

I remind myself this is no frivolous endeavour, but an opportunity to become a person who knows about art, who can converse with ease on such topics as culture, sculpture and literature. A woman who voices opinions, without fear of ridicule. A wife Matteo can be proud of.

I shake my head, ignoring the serpents' fiery gaze. 'I cannot . . .'

'You can.' His voice is tender, coaxing.

The serpents hiss and spit.

'I do not know . . .'

'Tell me what you see. Look closely.' Lorenzo murmurs, the words barely perceptible.

I screw my eyes and open them again, but it all looks the same.

'Tell me what you see.'

I feel the acid rise of venomous panic at the back of my throat. All I can see are people . . . people like me.

'The door . . .' I falter.

Serpent eyes flash. *This cannot be right.*

'Yes,' his voice has some animation to it, urging me to say more.

'The door . . . It could be the door to Papa's house. Or any common place in Rome.'

'It looks humble?' He is leading me now, in this dance, I know.

'Aye ...' the word forms a long sigh as it leaves my mouth.

'Do not be so unsure, Costanza. You are right, it is an ordinary door. And what of the Madonna and the pilgrim? Trust me. Say what you see.'

He is taking you on a fool's errand, hiss the serpents. The question is too simple. The painting too confounding.

'Well, she ... Our Lady ... looks like ... she could be a woman from our street. Excepting she is so peaceful and serene.'

'Yes. Yes! Exactly! And what about the pilgrims? The man and woman kneeling?'

I begin to comprehend. It is all meant. The ignoble dirt, the seediness, the sheer ordinariness is all deliberate. The serpents fold their heads in unison, one fluid motion, settling together into a smooth loop.

'The people are filthy. The woman is haggard and the man's feet, are ...' I examine them closely now, and they are a true depiction of someone who has walked barefoot in dirt and horse shit, and all the nasty things found on roads. 'They are grimy, calloused ... hardened to the life exacted upon them.'

'Quite so!' Lorenzo is not far off shouting such is his excitement, and I cannot help but send him a look. The woman is still crying in front of the statue.

'Yes,' he says more quietly, standing so close now that I take in the musky citrus of his skin, the quiet strength of his form. 'Examine the painting closely. There is great theatre at play. Caravaggio paints commonplace people. He does not care for an idealised, spun-sugar version of the divine. Those pretty and perfect visions of heaven and humanity we can never hope to attain.'

Lorenzo breathes out and looks at the painting, examining it closely as if it is the first time he has ever seen it. 'Caravaggio depicts corporeal reality ... the flesh and blood of people like you and me ... and in doing so begins to show us how great the drama of the Bible is. Mary was a mother with a young child. She carried him, swaddled him, fed him pap on a spoon, held his hand as he fell asleep. But we know what will happen. We know that Mary will be forced to watch her son suffer the most grotesque pain. That she will feel the unbearable anguish of a mother who must bury their child. The saints who died defending Christ? They suffered great torments too. This is emotional truth. Unadorned.'

I look again. The darkness hidden in unlit corners, the lurking threat of night-time streets, the single beam of lamplight picking out the Madonna's features. It is as familiar to me as the Silvestro.

'I see it. It is us, and it is not. But it *is real*.'

'It is! This is what art does, Costanza. It holds up a looking glass to our own ecstasy and suffering. It provokes a reaction precisely because we recognise it to be true.'

I stand still for a long time, as the mysteries of this most ordinary of scenes begin to unravel and rearrange themselves into something I understand most keenly.

Chapter Eleven

'A New Friend'

July 1636

My education continues through June and into July.

As the heat builds in the city, I spend my days in cool churches and perfect propriety with Lorenzo. He escorts me to see more of Caravaggio's work: *The Crucifixion of Saint Peter*, *The Martyrdom of Saint Matthew* and *The Penitent Magdalene*, not naked and cunning as she is usually painted, but dressed in her street clothes and doused in remorse.

After we are done, I revisit these paintings alone, returning again and again between my chores to uncover their secrets for myself. I find it startling that in keeping this quietest of company, I – Costanza, a girl not known for her patience – am provided with the greatest of comforts. I sit and study the finely drawn figures, with only my blazing mind and the travails of deities for companionship.

At night, my dreams are filled by men possessed by a compulsion to paint, women who are unapologetically flawed, ordinary people elevated to mythical status, faces filled with rapture and the greatest terror, of towering churches and talking statues, regal lions, graceful peacocks and delicate songbirds hopping from branch to branch, of saints facing death with stoic resolve, of the divine, of the greatest suffering. Sometimes Lorenzo is there, always standing behind me, voiceless, his breath on my skin. I wait for his touch. But it never comes.

Instead, Lorenzo shows his friendship in gifts. There have been near a dozen now. Baskets of myrtle filling our rooms with the astringent smell of pepper, green and fresh; sharp-scented goats' cheese; batons of meat, cured and dried; rounds of marchpane; cold-stored apples; candied fruit; and a jar of pickled lemons.

While these are hardly the gifts of a paramour, I worry it lacks judgement to accept. I still have not found the words to tell Giuliana or Tiberia of my lessons. When I ask Matteo, all he does is shrug his shoulders.

'But do you think it seemly, to take lessons *and* baskets from Lorenzo?' I say, looking at yet another hamper, loaded with food, sitting on the scrubbed table.

Matteo takes a hunk of salami, biting it with his big white teeth, taking off a large chunk and chewing it noisily, Sourpuss miaowing at his feet.

'You are not taking this seriously,' I complain.

'The notes are addressed to "Matteo Bonucelli and Signora Piccolomini", are they not?' He takes another bite.

I think of the fastidiously neat script and strong black ink. 'Aye. To both of us.'

'Then what is the problem? Lorenzo is generous,' Matteo says dismissively. 'It is well known he takes peculiar fancies to favourites. What can I say? His humours are hot and unstable. It is what makes him so good at what he does, but also unpredictable.'

'But is it well meant?' I press on. Part of me misses the early objections my husband made to the lessons; now he just accepts the presents, the tutoring, the *time* I spend with Lorenzo.

'It depends what you mean by "well meant",' Matteo says. He is infuriating.

'I mean, is it proper for a wife – for *your* wife – to accept such things from a man who is not her husband? Or should we send them back?'

Matteo stops chewing for a moment and thinks. 'You cannot send it back,' he says gravely. 'Understand this, it is Lorenzo Bernini we are talking about. It would cause grave offence, and neither you nor I can afford that. You accepted those lessons willingly, and I did not stand in your way. But whatever you have got caught up in, you will have to see through. At least for now. Just tell yourself the baskets are for both of us. Besides, I would hardly call pickled lemons an amorous gift.'

'I suppose you are right.'

Matteo wipes his face with the back of his hand. 'You say he has never laid a finger on you?'

'Never.'

He contemplates the stub of meat in his hand like a boy staring at a lesson he does not understand. ''Tis strange, but perhaps he means to mould you, as if he is King Pygmalion.' Matteo lets out a great guffaw. 'Yes, that is it, wife! Perhaps Lorenzo is tired of the court women with their loose morals and ill-mannered ways, and instead of carving a statue like Galatea, more perfect than any living woman and falling in love with her, he chooses you. Flesh and bone, to be made perfect. For it would be bad form for the Pope's own sculptor to go begging a heathen goddess like Venus to make his statue real.'

I pout. 'Do not jest with me husband. You no more think I am perfect than he. All I wanted to know was whether we should be accepting so many gifts. But if you are content that all is well, then so am I.'

My husband stuffs the last of the meat in his mouth, speaking as he chews. 'We cannot send them back. And why would we? Il Cavaliere's taste is exceptional.'

He stands and wipes his hands on his breeches before taking me into his bear-like embrace, smelling of spice and garlic. 'It works for both of us. Lorenzo's tutoring means we can set up business together. I have been thinking, I should start dealing in antiquities. There are many to be recovered and most will need a little restoration. And you will help me sell them. Then we will make our own money, and shall not have to rely on Lorenzo or his gifts.'

I lean into his chest and nod. That he wants me as part of his business comforts me, but the thought of cutting ourselves free from Lorenzo does not. I tell myself I am taking lessons to better myself, and my husband's standing, but deep inside I know there is another part of me that never wants to be free of Lorenzo Bernini.

* * *

Alongside Bernini's baskets, another invitation arrives. For a woman who never receives correspondence, I have picked up a remarkable habit for letters.

I hold the message to the light of the window and examine the unfamiliar hand. It does not have the hallmarks of Lorenzo's tight and scrupulous script; these letters are extravagant and curled, confident. I turn the letter over and inspect the seal, a thick, waxy drip, deeply imprinted with a carving of honeysuckle and bees.

It is an unfamiliar badge; I cannot think who has sent it, so I rip open the wax and run my eyes down the page. At the bottom of the short note there is the most surprising name written with a great, looped flourish. Caterina.

My dearest Signora Piccolomini,
    I should be charmed if you would do me the honour of visiting
next Thursday afternoon.
    Caterina Panzetti

After the success of the gold dress, I have been impressing upon
Matteo the very dire need for one good outfit. Not for a party, but
for everyday wear. I smile. This will tip the balance, for even Matteo
would not want me visiting Caterina in my patched red wool.

It is with a lightness of step that I set out the following Thursday
in my new dress, the colour of rusted autumn leaves. As soon as I
leave the house, the heat envelops me in its suffocating embrace, the
warmth of the day clinging to my skin. The sun burns my cheeks,
and my movement is necessarily slow to accommodate the hot air
stealing breath from my lungs. In my pocket, tied to my dress, are
three little linen bags of lavender, onto which Giuliana has sewn
tiny sprigs of forget-me-nots in the neatest stitches you have ever
seen. I chose the thread carefully, picking out the same colour blue
as Caterina had been wearing the night of our meeting.

Without the scorching temperature it is a good half-hour walk to
the west, with the sun beating down it is more like an hour. The city
is busy, the streets filled with carts selling leather goods, and bread
hardening in the sun, tall jugs of wine brought fresh from the cellar
and baskets of birds calling and clucking from under their covers.
Dogs roam in packs, and donkeys pull drays filled with barrels,
there are jugglers and gamblers and pickpockets in the squares,
clerics and lawyers hurrying in black, carrying the business of the
day on their shoulders.

By the time I stand at the door of the address, my undershirt
clings to my body, my dress is damp, and my face is dusty to the
touch. This house is situated on the other side of the river, near

the Vatican, where the properties are large and stand in their own grounds.

Caterina's door is surrounded by heavy travertine blocks in geometric shapes, square and solid; and impeccably manicured gardens stretch all the way around the house's perimeter. It occurs to me that I might be in the wrong place, and I want to get the letter out of my pocket and check it again, but I have already read the address a hundred times, and know I am right.

I ring the bell and the door swings open to reveal a maid, young and skinny, peering anxiously at me. 'Good day, mistress.' Her voice is timid, her accent strong and from the country somewhere west.

'Is Signora Panzetti in? She is expecting me.' The girl looks at me but does not move, then squints mutely up the stairs. There is a shout from inside. 'Is that Signora Piccolomini? For goodness' sake, girl, let her in.' Only once this instruction is issued does the maid nervously nod her head, while beckoning me through the door.

Inside, the floors are tiled in expensive marble and the staircase wrought in bronze. There are paintings hung on every wall, some modern, in the style of Velázquez, while others depict bowls of perfect lemons or ripe figs in the Dutch style. I am proud of myself for recognising the schools. There are statues, their faces worn by time, missing noses or limbs, and new ones, with sharp features, cherubs and fawns, which I take to be the work of Paolo. I note, with not a little satisfaction, that Matteo's are better.

The girl's feet make a light patter as she runs ahead of me, up the stairs to a room on the first floor. 'The mistress's private salon.' She steps aside, so I might enter first, then follows me in.

'Ah, Signora Piccolomini!' Caterina moves in one long, elegant motion towards me, a picture of refinement. I notice now I am standing near that she is smaller than me, and dressed in yet another silk dress, a brilliant saffron, the colour of spring crocuses.

Her hair is pinned into a bun at the back of her head, and curls – made by hot irons rather than nature – fall artfully around her face and shoulders. Unlike the last two times I have seen her, Caterina's lips are natural, and when she smiles, reveal a regular and complete set of perfect teeth.

'Please sit.'

I hesitate. There are a number of places I can sit: a long settle, painted gold and upholstered in crimson velvet, set in front of large windows, hung with green-fringed brocade; and several chairs, each more extravagant than the last, with exuberantly carved backs and twisted arms in darkest ebony.

'Here,' Caterina motions to the settle. 'Sit with me. For we are friends, are we not? We must not stand on ceremony.'

I sit, not realising I fell into the category of 'friend', the discovery of which makes a most pleasant surprise. Caterina turns to the maid, who waits fretfully, shifting her weight from foot to foot. 'How many times do I have to tell you not to jig, Giametta? Bring two glasses of port and some hot spiced cordial, set upon the silver tray. Be quick, but do not spill it.' The girl is nearly out of the room when Caterina shouts, 'And bring some of those sugared almonds which arrived from Il Cavaliere this morning.'

There is something about that last instruction, the way Caterina bares her teeth just before she smiles, the way her eyes slowly come to rest on me, that makes me think it was not an afterthought at all, but something far more deliberate. I feel the serpents inside shift. I am not the only one, not the only woman who receives gifts from Lorenzo Bernini. A pang. A hiss. Foolish girl, did you think you were special?

There is a movement from the corner of the room. I break Caterina's gaze, turning to see an orange-plumed songbird in a huge gilt cage. It stares at me with unblinking, obsidian eyes, then jumps onto another perch. It is, I decide, the most stylish thing I have ever seen.

'My apologies. My usual maid is sick. Giametta is the kitchen girl. Not used to waiting upstairs. Needs instruction.' Caterina sighs. 'You know how it is training servants.'

I do not, but nod anyway. 'She is very sweet. I am sorry you have been inconvenienced ... Oh.' I stand abruptly. 'I brought you these.' I thrust my hand into the small pocket and pull out the lavender bags, which I am disappointed to see are looking creased and crushed, and not at all the elegant little gift they had seemed in my kitchen.

Caterina offers her palm, and I tip the homespun parcels into it. She examines them as if a child has made them, before declaring, 'How charming, the needlework most dainty.'

"Tis all my own hand,' I lie.

'Exquisite. You are clever, I can't sew a thing.' I wrinkle my nose; I think she is humouring me.

Giametta reappears with the tray on which is balanced the port in small etched glasses and the cordial served in ornate silver cups, filling the room with a highly fragranced steam. Accompanying the drinks is a small plate of sugared almonds, the colours of a spring sky, pink, and white, and pale blue, and dusted in sugar. Everything makes me feel large and awkward and gauche. I wait for Caterina to pick up her cup, watching the way she pinches her fingers daintily, and try to copy her manners.

In the strong light of day she is older than I had first thought, but I still cannot place her years. Although her skin is milky white, almost translucent, there are a myriad of fine lines upon her chest and around her eyes, accentuated by the light dusting of white powder she wears.

She sits close to me and takes a shallow sip of the hot drink before placing it on a little table. Then, in a manner more intimate than I would have imagined, she places her hand over mine. I stare at her fingers. Each one sports a heavy ring, hazy amethyst set against fiery opal, copper-green malachite and burnished amber, each competing with its neighbour for dominance.

'Signora Piccolomini, I must confess, I asked you here for a reason.'

'And what, pray, is that?'

'I understand you are taking *lessons* from Il Cavaliere.'

I hesitate for a moment. 'That is true. How did you hear?'

A knowing smile creeps across her lips. 'I am an old friend of Lorenzo's. We have known each other many years.'

'I see.' I cannot fathom her meaning, nor where this is going, and it makes me feel uneasy.

'There are few wives in the Fabbrica inner circle, it being populated with so many bachelors. It is a relief to have you and Matteo join us. Il Cavaliere does not extend his friendship to many, and those he chooses he treats well.'

It begins to make sense. 'Lorenzo – Il Cavaliere – he sends you baskets?'

'Of course. Have you been receiving gifts too?'

I hold my hand still under hers, and nod.

'And have you felt – how shall I put it – a sense of unease about these gifts?'

I hesitate, but Caterina's fragrance is cloying, enveloping me in a fustiness of feminine confidences.

'You can trust me.'

I am overcome by a compulsion to talk, to explain how I have been feeling. Caterina understands me in a way a man never could. I tell her of my longing for knowledge and advancement, how I wish to wipe away all notions of what my life has been destined for and live it anew. I tell her that Lorenzo is nothing but a tutor, but that I still worry about impropriety.

'You have no idea what a relief it is to talk to you!' I say as the words fall out of my mouth in a jumble; that Matteo has accepted things as they are, but it will be badly understood by those I love, for where I grew up things are different, and married women do not consort with unmarried men.

Caterina holds my hand throughout, and her words, when they come, are like a cooling balm on my inflamed humours.

'There is good reason confusion reigns within you,' she says eventually, 'for you are moving into a different world.'

Caterina touches her throat, which is adorned with a delicate silver and garnet necklace, as she looks out of the window. I can see a thread of veins running like blue tides under her skin. Outside, the sky is cloudless, the ardent heat blunts all noise, so only the muffled sound of a carriage or stifled bark reaches us, making me feel entirely divorced from the life beyond this room.

Caterina continues, 'Il Cavaliere's world is … sophisticated, elegant. The rules by which ordinary people live do not apply to a genius like him. He is an artist. Driven by different appetites. Even Pope Urban knows this.' She turns to look at me. 'You know what His Eminence said?'

I shake my head.

She adopts the deeper voice of a man. 'It is a great fortune for you, Il Cavaliere … that your greatest patron has been chosen by God to become pope. But my fortune is even greater: that Lorenzo Bernini lives during my pontificate. Together we will leave a legacy which will live for a thousand years.'

Caterina turns to face the window, and I hear the dull sound of hooves upon dirt. Her voice softens. 'He knows no bounds, Il Cavaliere. Even the Church bends to his will.' She takes another sip of the spiced drink. 'It is a fickle world, and there are many who will use you to access Lorenzo Bernini. His temper is wild. Things can turn on a pinhead. I can be your companion, Signora Piccolomini, if you wish. We can spend time together. I can help instruct you in the ways of this life, for I see a great deal of my younger self in you.'

In this moment there is nothing I want more, to have a woman such as this as *my* friend. 'I should like that very much.'

She raises her small glass to me in a toast, 'To friendship, alla nostra salute!'

I smile. 'Alla nostra salute.'

Chapter Twelve

'Feast of the Assumption'

August 1636

It's a month since my first meeting with Caterina.

I continue my instruction with Lorenzo, studying the masterpieces of the past. Our conversations meander, and he listens to me intently, his attention so focused that it sometimes feels like there is a shift in the air between us, like a door being opened.

Instruction with Caterina is of an altogether different kind. I spend my days learning card games and how to consult with merchants of silks (which I cannot afford), and attending recitals and readings from writers I have never heard of. I discover I have opinions on many things, including literature, outfits and art.

But perhaps, most of all, I find an ally. In a world where everyone is either pregnant or mothering, it is simply a relief to be in the company of a woman who not is not only childless but seems perfectly happy with her state. Caterina tells me in a low whisper that she has never yearned to be pregnant and is not at all sorry she is unable to conceive.

This is how I find my worlds splitting in two. For today, I am back in San Silvestro. It is the procession of the Feast of Assumption when all of Rome stops to celebrate the arrival of the Madonna in heaven.

The sun is high in the sky and casts an unforgiving heat on the scorched city below. Matteo and I have joined Papa and Tiberia, and the rest of our district, to follow the statue of Our Lady through the streets. With my free hand I pull at my hat, lowering the brim to cover my eyes, briefly glancing backwards to check on Cecilia, who is trailing two steps behind, mortified.

Usually, I love this feast, held in the in the deepest dog days of summer, when everyone stops their shoemaking or carving, mopping or baking, and joins in celebration. Yet as I walk in the throng of the crowd I am ill at ease. Even the pomander I wear on my wrist cannot cancel the miasmas, the sourness of men left out too long in the sun and the stench of dead street dogs decaying in the deadly heat of Rome.

It is as if I am being swallowed whole. We make slow progress behind the statue of Our Lady, shakily hoisted aloft on two poles. My ears balk at the sounds of the trumpets, shrill and sharp, and the noise of muscular singing by well-lubricated men, their faces glistening from heat and wine; and my heels rub as my hot feet swell from marching on ground which is baked hard.

After the ceremony, the congregation spills out of the dim church into the square with a great din, like the squawking of birds released from a coop, and even though the sun immediately bites at my skin, it is a relief to be outside.

The formalities done, Matteo is restless. He wants to go and find the Portuguese traders, having talked of little else these past few days. There is a scheme to buy antiquities, which will be sold on for a profit to the rich merchants of Venice and Ferrara, and the nobles of England and France.

'Go. I know you are itching to,' I say, batting away a fly trying to land on my face.

A look of relief. 'I shall not be long, wife. It could be a profitable venture for us. These men have good contacts, but it is I who know about sculpture and can restore the worst pieces. We must seize upon this appetite for the ancients, the fashion for rich men to lend an air of learning to their surroundings.'

I think of Caterina's elegant home and can only nod. 'If you are looking for something old, perhaps you could slip Tiberia into your shipment?' I laugh, but he does not. I stick out my bottom lip. 'What? You openly express your desire to escape my family, but I cannot do the same?'

He grins and plants a pretty peck on my cheek. 'I would not willingly give up a moment of time with your stepmother, you know that. It is just my business is most pressing.'

I punch him in the arm. 'Pig. I am sure your business is *most pressing*. For that you can buy me a cup of wine, my mouth is as a dry riverbed in August.'

'Done.' He shakes my hand in jest. 'Giuliana is over there. I shall get her a cup too, for I am sure she would welcome your company. You have not seen her in some time, I think?'

It is a gentle chide. Matteo and I have not discussed in detail my lessons with Lorenzo, nor the amount of time I spend with Caterina.

This is because my husband is, for the most part, one of those men who believe if no words have passed on a matter, then it can be ignored. I find this the easiest path to follow too, for whenever I touch upon the chaste nature of my education, all Matteo does is grunt, making it clear my chatter is beyond his realm of comfort.

I screw my eyes up and raise my hand to my brow; the sun is bouncing off the white stone houses. It is a moment before I see Giuliana sitting in the shade. With a pang, I realise she is bigger than I remember, the child within stretching wide from her belly.

I push my way through the crowd, being careful not to spill my wine. Giuliana is sat with Luciana Cuore – and in this small act, the difference between us is laid bare. For Luciana and I have spent our lives in enmity, while Giuliana is willing to see the best in everyone. Even people who are wasps.

Indeed, were it not for Tiberia's friendly ties with Luciana's mother, I would avoid the hornet entirely, for Luciana and her mean mouth are trouble.

They both look up at the same time as I approach, like grazing deer disturbed.

'Costanza!' Giuliana cries, 'I had hoped you would attend. Come and sit.' Tomaso is playing with a little wooden windmill at her feet and gives a small cry of objection as he is shuffled along.

'You are looking well,' I say as I sit down heavily, spilling a little of the wine on my skirts.

'I look exceedingly round,' Giuliana says, patting her stomach. ''Tis not the same thing at all.'

Luciana wears a smug countenance upon her face, which is bovine, wide and plump, she too holds a sleeping newborn babe in her arms.

'Costanza!' Luciana utters in mock surprise. Then she whispers conspiratorially, 'We had thought you dead! Or at least that you had given Rome up for good, hadn't we, Giuliana? It's a long while since you have been spotted in these parts.'

'I have been about. Perhaps your sight is not as sharp as it was.'

'What is it now, a month? Time passes so quickly when you are important.' Luciana looks at the cup in my hand. 'No wine for me?'

I feel my lips purse like they did when I was eight. Forbearance, I tell myself.

'Oh dear,' I offer the cups into the air. 'My husband only bought two, for I am not sure he remembers who you are.' It is her turn to press her lips, and the gesture affords me a little satisfaction.

I hand the cup to Giuliana, who says. 'No matter, Luciana. You can share mine.' Always the peacemaker.

Mischief dances slyly about Luciana's lips, which are covered in sores. 'We have been discussing what to call the baby.'

I will the surprise not to sound in my voice, Giuliana had confided such things to me when she was carrying Tomaso. Instead, I determine to let Luciana play at her theatrics.

'Isn't that so?' Luciana rubs at Giuliana's belly in such a proprietorial way, it is all I can do not to snatch her hand away. Instead, Giuliana pats the top of Luciana's hand. I notice the gesture and all the intimacies of friendship it suggests, and it makes me wince.

'Pray tell me then, for I would love to know.'

'Well,' Giuliana begins, 'I was thinking if it is a boy, then Leonardo. Named for your father. For he has always been so good to me.'

'It is a kind thought, is it not?' Luciana watches me carefully.

'It is a truly wonderful notion.' And I mean it, for I cannot think of a better name for a child than in honour of my father. It would make him so happy. 'And if it is a girl?' I wait with some half-formed thought that the next word I shall hear is 'Costanza'. For if Giuliana is thinking of Leonardo for a boy, then surely she will choose my name for a daughter, as I am her oldest friend.

'And for a girl,' Giuliana clasps my hand and squeezes it excitedly, 'I am thinking of naming her for Tiberia. What do you think?'

I see Luciana on the other side of Giuliana, face flushed in triumph.

'Tiberia . . .' My words falter. 'Tiberia,' I repeat more firmly.

'Is it not the most perfect choice? For since Mama died, Tiberia has been as a mother to me, and I have nothing to give in thanks, except my daughter's name.'

Tiberia. It is a rotten notion, is what I *want* to say. Who thinks to saddle a child with a name such as Tiberia? It is too . . . too cruel. Instead, I catch Luciana's anticipatory grin and know I cannot give her the satisfaction. So, I squeeze Giuliana's hand in return and say, 'It is also a superior choice. For who would not want to be blessed with such a name, and after such a woman too?'

'Oh, Luciana said you would be pleased!' and Giuliana reaches to pull me into an embrace. 'You know how much I am dreading what is to come, but at least I can think of Leonardo and Tiberia's happiness, and it is something.'

I look into my friend's face. 'It is a very thoughtful gesture. One they will treasure. And you will be fine, for the world needs you. I need you.' I kiss her on the forehead, and refuse to even glance at Luciana, for she may parry with Giuliana's good nature, but I will not allow any satisfaction to come of it.

Luciana sits back and observes the square, which has settled into the kind of frenzied inebriation that a holy festival brings. 'So, what has been keeping you busy, Costanza?' She scratches at her cheek, and I consider her square jaw and ample bosom, and her straining bodice, and think of Caravaggio's ordinariness. It occurs to me to turn braggart for a moment, to render Luciana speechless with the sophistication of Caterina's salon, and tales of sumptuous gold dresses locked in Moorish chests.

'My husband has a new position at the Fabbrica workshop and is establishing his own business. It requires a wife to run a lot of errands. Notes to lawyers, making the acquaintance of the ladies of his new circle, picking up packages . . .'

Luciana yawns loudly and picks at her nails. 'Sounds like he has you running rings; I always thought you the kind of wife who would hold such scurrying at bay.'

'Oh, nay,' Giuliana interjects. 'Costanza is the most happily married person I know. Aren't you?'

'I am.' I smile. Luciana's baby starts to cry. She hoists a hefty bosom from its lacing and the child sucks hungrily. I do not watch, but close my eyes, and pull my hat down over my face, not wanting my skin to darken in its rays.

'God's blood, it's hot today.' I feel a trickle of sweat run down my belly, a schism. And I contemplate just how much I keep my old life from my new.

Chapter Thirteen

'A Change of Plan'

August 1636

Guilt has been silting my gut since seeing Giuliana at the feast, for I realise how little I have seen her these past weeks. It has become usual that, on Thursdays, I attend Caterina's salon, but with the baby so near, I send my apologies and decide to visit Giuliana instead.

Matteo rises early for work; I kiss him goodbye and go about doing my chores, as I do every morning. Then, instead of setting off for the river for my walk west to Caterina, I make my way to the market, where I buy a plump chicken, pink and plucked, and some carrots and onions to make a good broth. As I climb the stairs back up to our rooms, I plan how I shall scent the soup with the rosemary that hangs in comforting bundles near my fire, and ladle it carefully into the pots I have borrowed from Tiberia, so it may last Giuliana a few meals.

My thoughts being so occupied, it is not until I turn the last corner to our landing that I see something is amiss. Sourpuss is sat outside crying and the door to our apartment is slightly ajar. Not much. But I am sure I had let down the latch and locked it before I left. Such is my uncertainty, I feel for the iron key in my pocket to make sure it is still there. Aye. It seems either someone has gained unlawful entry to our rooms, or Matteo has come home early.

My stomach turns with the awful possibilities an early return would mean. Perhaps Matteo has been hurt in a Fabbrica accident, carried home by his workmates, and is, even now, lying abed mortally injured, a man watching by his side, as another runs with urgent strides for the barber surgeon, and medicines to tend his wounds?

This is the eternal fear of Fabbrica wives. That their menfolk will be returned unexpectedly. Hurt in some awful manner; unrecognisable from burns inflicted by molten metal in the foundry, or else missing a hand, crushed by a falling block of stone, or blinded by flying marble from a chisel.

If it is not Matteo injured, then it must be a thief, intent on taking what few possessions we have. It occurs to me that I should run downstairs and fetch Widow Scutari, who lives below. But it is not a good plan. Two women would be no match for one determined man, and besides, Widow Scutari is so old that if she were to receive a fright, or worse, be knocked to the ground, it might kill her.

A cold shiver creeps along my back and raises the hairs on my arms. A fear demanding of answers. Almost without thinking, I find myself setting my basket silently down on the stairs, then creeping to the wooden door and gingerly pushing at it a little more.

Immediately I breathe a little easier, for there, right by the door, are Matteo's grubby boots. It is a relief to know he must be well enough to at least have taken off his boots, which is a newfound consideration.

I step inside with less trepidation now, expecting to see my husband splayed out on the big kitchen chair he favours, perhaps with his eyes closed, taking advantage of a quiet house. But Matteo is not in the kitchen in his usual seat, as I had expected.

Beyond, by the door to the antechamber, I notice a strange thing. A second pair of boots, abandoned. By them, a jacket pooled on the floor, the shape of the wearer still held within. It is black, and made of coarse leather, the grains so impressed with marble dust they give the appearance of stone. I feel a moment of confusion. Why would anyone leave their boots and coat like this, discarded in our good room?

It is only now I register that there are noises coming from the chamber beyond: low groans and high tides of sighs. Matteo is making sport with another woman. I listen, feeling a rising tide of disgust. That he has brought his mistress to our home, the apartment I clean, to lie with her in the sheets that I wash, it is ... fury-inducing. I feel a choler shooting through my veins, and am about to storm into the room when something stops me. The sounds coming from the bedchamber; they are familiar yet they resonate differently in another pitch.

I progress warily, tiptoeing around the edges of the floorboards known to creak. The door is not quite closed, so I can stand in the half-light without being seen. I peer beyond, into the next room and see Matteo and another man.

They are lying on the bed, their bodies shamelessly tangled above the sheets, both as naked as the day they were birthed. Their sighs keep time with the rhythmic thrusting of their bodies, their flesh peeling and slapping together. It takes me a moment to place him. Then I realise where I have seen the gentleman before. That night in the tavern. He is Vincenzo, the one with strangely short hair.

My blood pumps harder, and my breath becomes as hoarse as theirs. I had not, could not have, imagined.

He does not want me, but this . . .

I want to run into the room, shrieking. To hurt them both. To drag my nails across their flesh and gouge their bodies with my teeth until blood pours.

But I know I must not be seen, for *I could not bear* for these two men to witness my mortification, for pity to form in their eyes, even as they panic at their discovery. Instead, I take a step back, then quietly retrace my steps, taking every care to remain invisible.

* * *

Outside, I stop a moment to take in the air around me, which smells unaccountably fetid, of rendered fat and peaty manure. The rest of the world carries on: mothers urging their children to hurry up, boys running errands, men in fine linen coats striding with purpose.

I want to stop everyone who passes and demand of them, 'Did you know? Did you know my husband has betrayed me? Did you know he is upstairs right now, lying with another man?'

Heart pounding, I pick up my skirts and start walking, my shoes sliding in the holes and muck. So furious is my pace it is inevitable I should catch my foot and fall. I cry out as I land heavily on my knees, tears rolling down my face. Without looking, I know there will be wounds, and a trickle of blood creeping down my shinbone, staining my stockings.

A man rushes to my aid. He is young and has pale watery eyes. 'Signora.' He pulls me up in one great swoop, then bends back down to deposit the chicken, now covered in brown dust, and the rest of the vegetables back in the basket.

'You are most kind.' I look down and see to my dismay the tumble has cost me a hole in my new rust skirts.

'Can I escort you somewhere?' The man waits for me give an address, somewhere I can be taken and comforted. But there is no such place. I cannot go home; Matteo is there. Papa and Tiberia would fuss, and Caterina? She cannot know.

Not for the first time, I ache for my mother. Not Tiberia, but the woman who birthed me. I could turn to *her*, bury my head in her skirts and weep and she would give me sweet words and wise counsel.

'Signora,' the man repeats, 'are you well enough to walk? Or should I fetch someone?'

'I am fine,' I say, the shake in my voice suggesting I am anything but.

'You seem . . .' His voice trails off.

Eager to be free of this good Samaritan, I take a step to show him how well I can manage. ''Tis only a few scratches, I have endured worse,' I assure him.

'Where shall you go?'

'My husband, he is expecting me.'

The lie scrapes at my heart, but there is nothing better than the mention of an attentive husband to banish unwanted attention. The stranger nods farewell, and I stand and watch him take off down the street, back to his business, or whatever he was doing before I fell. I turn towards San Silvestro.

* * *

Giuliana opens the door just a fraction, asking nervously, 'Who's there?'

'It is Costanza,' I say, wondering who she is so wary of on this street where we know everyone.

Giuliana opens the door a little further, taking a moment to assess my state, before crying out, 'What's all this?'

'I had thought to surprise you.' I look down at my bloodied hand and torn skirt.

'Look at the state of you.' Giuliana rushes, almost stumbling in her hurry to put her arms around me.

'Do not fret,' I lift my head to see if the neighbours, or worse, Tiberia, are watching. The last thing I need is more questions.

'Here, let me help you.' Giuliana begins lifting the basket.

But I brush her hand away, 'Leave it. 'Tis naught. Just a few scratches. Anyhow, it is I who should be helping you.'

'Nonsense. I am not an invalid, just with child. And you are hurt,' she says firmly, taking the basket from my grip. 'Here, lift up your skirts, so you don't catch them again on the stairs.'

Once inside, Giuliana begins fussing, pressing a glass of grappa into my hands and dabbing at my grazes with a cloth. I sip the drink, savouring the heat as it slips down my throat.

Only when she has wiped the worst of the dirt away and smeared a thin layer of oily balm that smells of bark on my cuts, does Giuliana step back, assessing me with the certitude that twenty-two years of friendship brings.

'So . . .' she says expectantly.

'I had meant to make you soup, but I fell. And the chicken got dirty.'

'We can clean the chicken. Yet you are still sitting here with grazed knees and red-rimmed eyes? There is more than soup to this business.'

I stare at Giuliana but in my mind's eye I see Matteo and Vincenzo, dishevelled and woven as one.

'Did you have an argument?'

I look dumbly at my friend, before my eyes slip to the Christ on the cross hanging behind her head on the wall.

'An argument?'

'With Tiberia? I know she can be hard on you, but she loves you and means well . . .'

'Nay. Not Tiberia.'

'Matteo then? Have you had a falling out with your husband?'

I stare at the cross. Christ's face etched in pain, the crown of thorns pushed into his mortified flesh. A pressing realisation is forming: the peril Matteo has put himself in if he is caught. The danger he has put us both in. A sickness rises in me as I think of convicted men floating in the Tiber, churchmen uttering prayers over their bodies, and their penniless widows, pitied and shamed, crying on the banks, facing a life of poverty. A sob begins to rise.

Giuliana sits clumsily on the bench next to me, manoeuvring her cumbersome frame into position.

'It is natural for a wife to feel cross every now and again.'

I waver for a moment, so desperate am I to share the burden of my heartbreak. I look into her eyes, and remember her devotion to the Church, the fervency of her prayers.

'Aye, we had a fight.'

Giuliana and I have shared everything: boys and betrothals, menses and the loss of our maidenhoods, our hopes and fears, everything we have wanted from life and everything we have not. Yet I am unwilling to share this most momentous of storms.

Giuliana wraps her arms around me, but when I return her embrace it feels insubstantial.

'What did you argue about?'

I try to think of something Giuliana will not question, and glance down at her belly.

'Begetting a child.'

It is a truth of sorts. A carapace.

Giuliana self-consciously smooths her skirts, 'Oh my love, I am so sorry. The Lord sends many things to test us. It is a hard cross for a woman to bear, I shall make an offering for you, to the Madonna at Sant'Agostino.'

I do not respond. I had thought Matteo was different, that he would not be a husband who humiliates his wife by lying with other men's wives. Or whores. But then Vincenzo is not either of those.

'I have no need of such cheap offerings to a God who does not listen,' I snap.

Giuliana sighs deeply. It is not her fault Matteo has chosen Vincenzo. That she is fecund, when I am barren. I know well enough that being fruitful brings its own sorrows.

'I had meant to put herbs in it. Rosemary.'

Giuliana looks at me astonished. 'Rosemary?'

I nod. 'In the soup. I have them hanging by the fire at home. But then, Matteo ... There was a change of plan, and I forgot to bring any.'

She glances over at her own fire, which is unlit. I cannot put my finger on it, but the place feels sparser, and I wonder if Giuliana has perhaps rearranged the furniture in anticipation of the new child, to create more space now Tomaso is crawling.

'I have no herbs.' Giuliana's voice sounds strained. Seeming to realise this, she adds with a false gaiety, 'But no matter! We can make the soup without. All we need is some water to wash the chicken and make a stock.'

'You could go and ask Tiberia? She is only over the road, and always has some to hand.'

'Nay!' Giuliana says, a little too quickly. I feel my eyebrow rise. 'Nay,' she says again, in a more measured tone. 'Let's not disturb Tiberia on my behalf. She has been very generous to me of late.'

'So be it. Then we should make a start before the chicken spoils.'

Giuliana hesitates before standing. It is as if she is giving me one more moment, one more chance to tell her the truth. I imagine telling my friend what I have seen, spitting out the tale of Matteo and Vincenzo. How I am discarded, as one throws away an unneeded thing. I feel the words in my mouth, but they taste bitter, like yarrow.

'Aye, we should make a start.' As I rise, a thought crosses my mind.

'Who were you afraid of? When I knocked? You were . . .'

At that moment there is a childish wail, as Tomaso wakes from his nap. Giuliana pushes herself wearily to standing as she calls out, 'Hush, bambino, Mama's coming.'

She looks back at me, eyes wary, hair hanging lankly across her shoulders.

'Nothing. It was nothing.'

Then Giuliana turns to retrieve her screaming son. As I watch her leave the room, shoulders slumped, I understand it is my friend's turn not to tell the truth.

Part II

Chapter Fourteen

'The Moste Dangerouse Beast in Rome'

August 1636

The carriage creaks so loudly I can hardly hear Lorenzo's voice over the hammer of iron horseshoes hitting the cobbled road. He is speaking rapidly to Stefano, his manservant, who accompanies us.

A small chill rises up my spine as we approach the Colosseum. The grass at the side of the road has been bleached to the colour of sand by the harsh sun. When we come to a halt I step boldly from the carriage, determined not to show my nerves. As my skirts move, I catch sight of the small, darned patch where I fell on the ground after finding Matteo. A stark reminder that my husband is the guilty party – not I.

I shake my petticoats so the mended fabric falls into a fold. If Matteo cannot bring me the love I desire, then I shall make the most of what he *can* bring me: a place in Lorenzo's court and all that means.

We leave the carriage and Stefano ties the horses to a tree. He is a thick, squatly built man and handles the beasts roughly, pushing their necks and shouting at them.

Lorenzo and I set off and I am surprised when Stefano begins to follow.

'Is he to accompany us too?' I whisper low enough that Stefano cannot not hear.

Lorenzo glances behind and smiles. 'Aye, Stefano must walk with us, for we are headed into a notorious place where bandits and the destitute reside.'

'But we shall not be ...' – I pause, as it is unseemly for me to be here at all, let alone unchaperoned – 'by ourselves.'

Lorenzo laughs. 'Stefano will be discreet. He knows my business well. Has been part of our household since we were boys. Lost his parents young. My own mother took him in. We grew up together.'

I think of Stefano as a small boy, alone, frightened, facing destitution. 'Your mother is a good woman,' I venture.

Lorenzo looks at me. It is the first time we have discussed his family, and I wonder whether it's a line he wants to cross.

'Yes,' he replies slowly. 'My mother is a woman of uncommon kindness. I think she wanted me to have a male playmate. To fight and practise my rapier skills with. She had seven girls. Five before I arrived.' Lorenzo grins. 'Can you imagine my father's relief when he held me?'

I think of the pride men feel in having a boy to carry their name forward. Instead, Lorenzo's father was burdened by daughter after daughter.

'He must have been pleased.'

'Very. Fearing he wouldn't have any more boys, my father took no chances on names, I have two you see – Giovanni after my great-grandfather – and the name I use – Lorenzo – after my grandfather.'

'Your mother made up for it. The lack of boys I mean. By having you . . . and of course Luigi.'

He raises his eyebrows slightly and I realise I know very little about Lorenzo's family. 'Do you have more brothers?'

'Five.'

'Five?'

'Five. Francesco, Vincenzo, Luigi, Ignazio and Domenico. Vincenzo went into the Church. My father also taught Luigi and Francesco to sculpt. Francesco was more talented than Luigi, better suited to the exacting nature of the work . . . but he died nine years ago.' Lorenzo pauses. 'He was just twenty-three.'

We walk on in silence, his grief so dense it swallows our words. I want to ask about his sisters – all those women – but know it is too late. I accidently stumbled upon a wound, blundered into a place he shrinks from. And now I do not know what to say.

It is a relief when the shadow of the great building falls upon us. There are vines growing in thick, luxuriant ropes, stones covered in verdant moss and yellow lichen, while caper and fig trees spring from the crevices between the walls.

'Here, this way.' Lorenzo takes my arm, and directs me to a dank passageway, which stinks of rotting vegetation and effluence. I grip him, for there is a great part of me which is reluctant to go deeper into the shadows.

He feels my fear and breathes into my ear, the proximity of his body and unease at the place we find ourselves making me unsteady. 'Do not be afraid,' he whispers, 'I am here. Stefano too. This is a wonder, trust me.'

As we walk through the darkness, my feet pass over decomposing slime and I say a hurried prayer to the Madonna. There is the scurry of small animals, then suddenly we are drowned in the brightest daylight, surrounded on all sides by vast tiers of stone.

Lorenzo shields his eyes with his hands. 'Is it not magnificent?' he asks, his voice hoarse with excitement.

'It is a wonder,' I answer, for it is true. It is thrilling, to feel one-self in such vastness. I imagine the grind of men to create such a spectacle, and my pulse quickens with the boldness of it.

Lorenzo picks his way through the dung and fallen masonry, the remnants of a wool-making workshop long abandoned, and holds out his arms like a ringmaster at the circus. 'Right here is where the ancients would fight leopards and lions, pit gladiator against warrior to keep the ordinary man entertained.'

They are creatures I have only seen in paintings, snarling and roaring.

'Imagine,' Lorenzo continues, 'the mortal blows on skin and fur. The baying crowd, hungry for blood. Come.'

We climb over the boulders, and Lorenzo extends his hand, so I may steady myself on the slippery stones underfoot. It is an over-familiar gesture, and I know Stefano is watching. My instinct is to pull back. I hesitate for a moment, then grip my hand in Lorenzo's, unexpectedly grateful for the stability he provides.

Here and there, there are blackened patches of land where fires have been lit, rags caught in thorns, broken pots among the weeds. For all the splendours of the past, today it is a place for the home-less and the abandoned, those who have lost hope. I look nervously behind for Stefano, who nods in my direction, his hand perched on his dagger.

Lorenzo kicks at a rectangular patch of bare earth, raw and freshly exposed, as if a fallen gravestone has recently been taken. 'Thieves,' he spits and looks up, as if half expecting to catch the criminals in action. 'They are plundering the relics, looting. Sometimes selling them as antiquities, sometimes just for the stone. Desecrating their own city's history. Philistines.'

I think of Matteo. I have never asked where the statues he plans to trade will come from. Men need coin. It occurs to me that the preservation of antiquity is the pastime of the privileged, but I do not say so. Lorenzo kicks again, running his boot back and forth in the madder-red earth. I look about at the arches above our heads, congested with weeds, the ruined columns, the overgrown plot under our feet, and I am struck by both its permeance and fragility. It is all brokenness and decay, yet there is magic contained within it.

Lorenzo sits on a boulder, and I join him.

'Rome is the centre of civilisation.' He looks up at the stone structure. 'Here, the Emperors sought to enlighten a barbarous world. It is a legacy we must continue, to fight against the self-satisfied Puritans who would rid the world of its beauty.'

I nod, for I know about the men in black who throw rocks through glass windows, smash statues and burn books.

'This' – he thrusts his arms into the stadium – 'is our heritage. My father came to Rome for a better life. The temples and triumphant arches, the monuments, murals and mosaics of this city. They shaped me. I spent my hours drawing the rarest things, examining every detail of Michelangelo and Raphael, searching for the epitome of beauty. This is what I wish to create, but with a chisel. Art so lifelike, that people must touch what they see, for they believe there must be a heart beating within.'

He places his hand on my heart. It is most unexpected and intimate. I should push him away, tell him it is an affront. But I do not. I want his hand to rest there, against my shallow, breathless chest, my blood flowing under his fingertips like a burning river.

'I wish to show all that is human – joy, pain, grief, elation – in a fleeting moment.'

I cannot move. The sky above us seems endless, and my heart is thundering as loud as the roaring Tiber.

'When we are dust, my work will live on. For generations people will feel the same awe we do here, in this place. It will be my legacy, just as this building is Emperor Vespasian's.'

He plans to conquer death with permanence. It is like the need for a child, who will still be warm-blooded when you are cold in your grave.

* * *

Over the next hours, Lorenzo lures me into a world of gods and emperors, slaves and sacrifice. We tramp around the ruins until the light begins to fade and the blue sky blots with pink.

Lorenzo stares at it for a brief moment. 'Dusk will be upon us soon enough,' he says, 'and this is not a place to be at night. Even with Stefano and his dagger.' He shouts the last line into the distance behind us, and Stefano roars in good-natured answer.

'You go on,' Lorenzo calls to Stefano. 'Make ready the horses so we can leave quickly.'

His manservant nods and sets off at a clip towards the place where we left the carriage.

Lorenzo and I proceed at a more leisurely pace, my arm in his, and postulate on the construction of the stadium, and the thousands of years which separate us from those ancient footsteps which trod on the very same path our feet walk now.

We are halfway to the carriage when a man unexpectedly steps out.

Lorenzo and I stop abruptly. The stranger is tall and dressed in an old leather jacket and breeches. He has the manner of a confidence trickster – or something worse – about him.

The stranger takes a step towards us. 'Good day, signore.' He tips his hat at me. 'Signora.' The words roll from a tongue stained claret red.

It is then that I notice a large brown bear in the shadows behind him, wretched, in manacles and tied to a staff. Bigger than the man, she looks as old as the scenery, her fur matted into tufts and peaks. Here and there lie patches of grey skin, livid with red lesions where lice have raided the creature's flesh. Beside her there is a sign propped up by a cart: 'Beware! Blind Bess. The Moste Dangerouse Beast in Rome.'

I feel Lorenzo's back straighten beside me. 'Good day, Signor . . .?'

The bear lumbers onto all fours, turning towards the sound of Lorenzo's voice as best as her shackled limbs will allow. She sniffs at the air for scent, her eyes open but clouded. I look to the distance to see if Stefano is still in sight, but he is gone.

'Fortuna. Signor Franco Fortuna.' The man makes a dramatic bow. As he straightens, his eyes take a practised pass over us: assessing the wealth of our clothes, our presumed naivety, our vulnerability.

Lorenzo tips his head and pulls at my arm 'Come, signora, we must make haste.'

Set far enough from the bear to be safe is a large basket. Squirming within are a litter of puppies, climbing over each other. They move in a tumult of fear, little pink mouths barking and yelping in terror. The bear growls.

Signor Fortuna turns to the basket and, as he does, a knife glints in his belt. I take another step so I am stood almost fully behind Lorenzo, I want to tug at his arm and urge him to leave, when the man swings round holding a tiny dog.

'What about a pup? For the lady?'

'Ha!' Lorenzo bellows. 'Signor Fortuna, you truly are a man of surprises.' I groan inwardly; in the time I have known Lorenzo I have come to understand he has a fierce love of theatrics. 'What an idea. What do you think, Signora Piccolomini?'

I look at Lorenzo, horrified. The last thing I want – or need – is a puppy. I have enough trouble looking after myself and I have Sourpuss, the best mouser I've ever owned.

'Do not look so affronted. It would be a gift. A token of my esteem.' Lorenzo considers the dog for a moment. 'A keepsake of our afternoon.'

Before I can speak, Signor Fortuna, having expected a rebuff and clearly delighted at this unexpected turn of events, seeks to press home his advantage.

'Here,' he says, thrusting the small red and white dog into Lorenzo's arms. 'Take a proper look. Got this from an English sailor. Seems maidens have been seized by a madness for them. Small enough to sit in a lap. Good looking enough to warrant a portrait. Long muzzle. Silky ears. Nice to pet.'

'It is a very fine creature indeed,' agrees Lorenzo, inspecting the dog at arm's length. I sigh, suspecting that while Lorenzo knows a great deal about composition, he knows very little about canines.

'I am not sure—' My words are stopped by Signor Fortuna's interjection.

'Come now. It does not do to be ungrateful, signora. This gentleman wants to make you a gift; you are lucky. For what lady would not care for such a sweet love token?'

I wait for Lorenzo to explain that there has been a misunderstanding. That we are not lovers, but friends. But he says to Fortuna, 'My companion is of a delicate disposition.'

I feel my stomach curl. I am not any such thing, but neither can I question Lorenzo Bernini. Lorenzo turns to me laughing as the dog squirms in his hands.

'What do you think? Is it not perfection? A present. My treat. In appreciation of our friendship?'

The men wait expectantly.

Giddy, I hold my arms out to take the puppy, which immediately nestles itself into the nook of my elbow.

Lorenzo unties his coin bag from his waist to pay, and I half expect Fortuna to pull his knife and take the lot, but he does not.

'What say you, Franco Fortuna, to a good price for this pup? I think the lady has taken a fancy to it, and having offered such a gift, I must now secure the deal.'

Lorenzo tips some coins into his hands with his usual largesse; it is more than any puppy, even one from England, is worth. The money glitters in the gloaming and Signor Fortuna's eyes light like a magpie's.

With a flourish, he snatches the coins from Lorenzo's fingers and tips his hat once more, before hitching the bear to his cart to leave.

* * *

When I arrive home, Matteo is awake and sitting in the kitchen, weariness etched on his features.

He stands, pulling at his dishevelled shirt.

'I waited. I was ...' he runs his hand through his hair, 'I was worried.'

Matteo's concern creeps under my skin. I am holding the puppy, which I set down on the floor, and she begins to sniff around the kitchen as I undo my cape.

'I was with Lorenzo.'

Matteo looks at the animal, bewildered. 'Costanza ...'

'Do not say it, Matteo. Do not talk to me of Lorenzo. It is not I who have erred.'

He looks at me, a sudden wariness in his eyes. 'I have not ...'

Anger and fear oscillate within me. 'Have a care, husband, in what you say next. I know the truth. I saw you. I saw you with Vincenzo, Thursday hence.'

Matteo crumples as he sits back down and puts his heads in his hands. He makes a low groan, almost animalistic, which rises from the depths of his body.

There is a churning in my stomach, a whirling, claws ripping and tearing the same way they had that afternoon. I want him to stand, to face me – to face what he has done. But he does not.

For better or worse, Matteo is my husband, and as such we are yoked to each other in perpetuity, like oxen ploughing the field until one falls and dies.

Matteo lifts his head from his hands. 'I am sorr—'

'Do not say it. Do not justify it. Or apologise. Do not do any of those things. Our marriage is a lie.'

'I tried . . .' Matteo looks at me, but his features no longer look familiar. He shakes his head. 'It was not like that.'

'You did not try. We have not even been married five years. All that time you allowed me to think it was my fault that you did not desire me.'

His shoulders heave, and he begins to weep. His sobs fill the room and as I stand and watch my husband cry, something breaks in me. I feel the energy and heat seeping from me, as if doused by his tears. For, despite it all, I love him.

I close my eyes and feel his pain. It is my pain too.

Chapter Fifteen

'A Messenger'

Late August 1636

'Signora Piccolomini!' It is a child's voice at the door. 'Please, signora. Open up!'

It's late and my level of irritation at being pulled from my bed is high. Even if it is the Devil himself demanding an audience, I shall not be leaving this house. Matteo is out – Lord knows where – and I have not slept since I returned from the Colosseum. Thoughts of Lorenzo and Matteo are loosening my mind, and at times I feel as if I am ready for the asylum.

'Signora!' There is now a fearful banging.

'Hold your horses. I am not fit.' I throw a shawl about my shoulders and open the door to see a boy standing in front of me. He is about ten, barefoot and dressed in tatters. 'State your business, child. And be warned, I am in no mood to be involved in a petty argument or a neighbourly dispute.'

'It is Signora Gavia, mistress. She is sick. Mortally, so they say. She calls for you. You must come.'

Giuliana.

I look at the boy's face; his eyes are wide, fearful. I grab at his arm and pull him inside. 'Who sent you?'

'The midwife, Signora Mazzi. Says you are to come quick.'

My heart thuds. It is what I have feared. What Giuliana predicted. What I told myself could not happen, and yet it has. The moment is here. The beating inside my chest is large, loud, overwhelming, so I cannot hear myself think. Yet I am speaking, instructing the boy. 'Tell me everything that has happened. I need to dress. You see that room there?' I point to my bed chamber. 'I shall be in there, so you must shout it at me.'

I am in my trunk, frantically pulling out my clothes – cursing as nothing is where it should be – when I realise the boy is not saying anything. Why does he not speak?

'What happened?' I shout. 'Have Mistress Gavia's pains started?' I search at a desperate pace through my things, to find something, anything I might wear. Here, an old grey skirt and bodice. This will do. No need for ceremony.

'Nay, mistress.'

'Then what has happened?'

'She has given birth already.' He pauses, then clarifies. 'To a babe.'

My fingers still on the laces of my bodice for a moment, as my mind catches up to the information he has given. Giuliana is already laboured. Ye gods, is this boy mute?

'And what is it?' I prompt.

'What is what?' he asks, mystified.

'The babe.' My heart is galloping now. Giuliana, my poor, dear friend. 'What is it? A boy or a girl?'

'A boy or a girl?'

Sweet Jesu. 'The babe. A boy? Or a girl?'

'Boy!' he shouts in triumph.

'Aha.' I give one last pull at the body and fumble tying the lace. The next question is one I dread. 'Alive or dead?'

Please let him know the answer to this question.

'Alive!' comes another little triumph. I whisper a simple prayer to Mary. Thank you. Thank you for giving the child breath.

'Why did she not send for me earlier?'

'I came. Not five hours past. But there was no sign, and your neighbour said you would be out for the day.' Another pause. 'Gadding,' he adds.

I had promised Giuliana that when her time came, I would be with her. I pin my hair quickly in place. Mixed with the fear comes shame, creeping over me like a shadow, black ink seeping through my veins. I half tie my skirts. My mind is working now. I rush back into the kitchen and grab a basket, a hunk of honey cake, bread, ham, herbs, a flagon of wine.

I leave a short note for Matteo, put the dog to bed and make to leave. The boy does not move. I realise he is waiting for his coin. I let out a sound like a soft mewl. My friend may be dying and he waits for his coin? I go to our chest and take out the purse, pocketing the whole thing. Births can make for expensive nights. 'You will be paid when I see Signora Gavia.' My tone is harsher than I intend.

The boy carries the lamp, and the two of us make our way back to my childhood street and Giuliana's house. When we arrive the apartment is silent, save for the scrabbling of mice in the walls, and the groan of the stairs as I tread. There is no sound, not from Tomaso, nor the babe. The boy waits at the door for his payment, and I give him some money to be on his way.

I find the midwife boiling a pan of water on the fire. At her feet are a great pile of sheets, soaked through with blood, already starting to stiffen. I am seized by a premonition: Giuliana, white as marble, emptied of blood, still.

'Signora Mazzi,' I say. The midwife nods in response. I hardly dare ask. 'How does Giuliana?' Mazzi has been delivering babies in our district since she was a child herself, standing at her own midwife mother's side.

'I won't lie. She is perilous.' The midwife washes her hands vigorously in a bowl of water, scrubbing her fingernails, the muscles in her forearms flexing as she turns the soap in her hands. 'Giuliana was weak before the birth and had not the strength to push the child. The boy came feet first.' I wince at the thought.

'She suffered greatly,' Signora Mazzi continues. 'There was a tear, but she was so gone by the time I sewed it she could not scream.' I take a breath at this news and the image it conjures, hurling it from my mind. What cruelty God inflicts on us, just to bring his image into this world.

'And the child?'

Mazzi splashes her hands in the water, then shakes them before drying them on a strip of linen. 'Sickly.'

'I need to see her. Giuliana, I need to see her now.'

'Aye.' She stops to look at me. 'You have not much experience of birth, have you?'

'I saw Tiberia.'

Mazzi nods: she delivered all of my stepsiblings. 'This is different. Tiberia, for all her complaining, is a strong woman. Giuliana is not. It is ...' She searches for the word. 'It is worth preparing yourself for.'

I nod, as if understanding, but have no idea how to prepare myself. Giuliana is like a sister, my twin; our lives have been as entwined as any who lay in the womb together. Taking a candle, the midwife leads me through the blackness of Giuliana's apartment.

Even though I have been warned, when we enter Giuliana's bed-chamber I am shocked. The room is warm, and smells of metal and dung. My friend – my vibrant, beautiful friend – lies like a wraith, tinged with such a deathly pallor that even her lips are blue. Next to her is the child. He is small and yellowed, and hardly any more animated. Giuliana opens her eyes to look at me. It is an effort, but she tries to smile, and it breaks my heart. Her eyes look as if the flame has already been extinguished, leaving her mortal body to follow. When I take her hand, it feels lifeless in mine.

My voice cracks as I speak. 'You have a boy! Leonardo.'

A tear rolls down Giuliana's cheek, but she does not move. We sit like this for a few moments, then I return to Signora Mazzi, who is standing at the end of the bed. 'What can be done? There must be something that can be done to ease her suffering?'

The midwife turns her back on Giuliana, so that my friend is sheltered from her words, and whispers to me. 'It is the manner of the delivery. Feet first can cause inner wounds. Turn the womb even. Giuliana is still bleeding and will die unless we can stem the flow with a physick.'

'Then why do you not give it to her?' I demand.

'She has not paid me for the delivery. Giuliana's mother was my friend. I brought Giuliana into this world with these hands.' Mazzi holds out her muscular arms, and I wonder how many lives have started in their embrace. 'I cannot procure more medicine; I do not have the means. This work is not well paid.'

'Then Marco?' It suddenly occurs to me Giulana's husband is not here. 'Where is he? Surely Marco should be here?' Someone else is missing. 'And where is Tomaso?'

'Luciana has taken Tomaso. She was here. She helped with the birth. Marco is out. He no longer works for himself but is tied to a new workshop on the other side of town.' Signora Mazzi's eyes narrow and her brown eyes dance like a bird on a wire. 'Just how long is it since you last talked with Giuliana?'

I squirm. 'I have been busy with my own husband's work.'

'So I heard.' *Luciana.* Signora Mazzi clicks her tongue. 'Friendship is forged from constancy, not turning up to save the day.'

'My concern is Giuliana. What herbs does she need? I shall go and rouse the apothecary.'

'You can try.' I have the feeling Mazzi is keeping something from me but know it will not help to tarry with her. 'And if you fetch the herbs, then I shall have my fee for the birthing too.'

'Don't fear. You will be paid.'

I turn back to Giuliana and kneel by her bed. She smells of iron, and something sweet, as if death is beginning to blossom inside. 'I will not be long, I promise. While I am gone you must stay. Stay for me, please. Do you understand?'

She looks at me with terrified eyes. Her lips are dry and cracked, and move without sound. 'Aye.'

I turn to Signora Mazzi. 'And you will stay with her?'

She folds her arms. 'I won't leave Giuliana. But for her dead mother's sake, not yours.'

* * *

I take a lamp. The moon is low and the air is warm. Outside it is so dark it is like a chasm has opened up and stolen all the light. There are glimmers of stars here and there, but even they seem diminished by the grim knowledge of Giuliana's pitiful state.

The apothecary shop is down the tightest of alleys, hidden. A bad location for passing trade, but an excellent one for men and women who do not want the world to know their business. It is a place I am very familiar with.

I bang on the door in panic and shout up to the window where I know Nino Marotta sleeps. It does not take long for his neat head to appear.

'Signora Piccolomini! What do you mean by such noise? I beg you cease immediately, for I have neighbours who will not take kindly—'

'I am on urgent business. I beg you, come down.'

Nino emerges wearing a dressing gown of silk, a most sumptuous item and incongruous with the neatly bearded, unassuming man who mixes my potions. 'It has been some weeks. I had hoped . . .'

'I have been discovering life, not begetting it,' I say impatiently. 'But I am here for Giuliana Gavia. She has given birth and is gravely ill. You must give me something to stem the blood and relieve her of the pain.'

The smile disappears from Nino's face. 'Signora Gavia owes me a lot of money. I cannot give you any more medicine before she settles her account.'

I draw myself up to my full height. 'Signor Marotta. I cannot believe you would be so mercenary. Giuliana is gravely ill, in mortal danger, her child too – she must be helped.'

'Signora Piccolomini, we are all dying. Some quicker than others. If I gave free medicine to every sick person who walked through this door, the bailiffs would come knocking.'

'Put it on my account then. But hurry.'

He does not move. 'It will not help. I have been giving Giuliana medicines for months precisely because she is your friend.' He tugs gravely at his beard and pauses, weighing his words like the precious tinctures he keeps in the bottles behind. 'I am not one to listen to rumours but . . .' He stops, and I can feel my exasperation bubbling. I do not have time for this.

'But?' I prompt.

'They are behind on the rent and about to be evicted. Giuliana has been taking alms from all and sundry to feed her boy. People's patience has worn thin.'

I am struck for a moment, left quite without words. How could this be? How could I not see what was there in plain sight all along? Poor Giuliana. An indignance swells, blooming, filling my belly. Her husband had a duty to care for her.

'How has this happened?' I buzz with outrage. Nino shifts. He is a man who keeps secrets and the spilling of them does not come easily. 'Signor Marotta. What has occurred that should leave my friend in such a low state?'

'I...'

'Yes?'

'Marco. He likes to gamble, *so I hear*, and is beholden to money men.'

I feel the weight of the situation dragging me to the floor. I could possibly cover the cost of the medicines from Nino from our savings, even a month or two of rent. But Matteo would never allow me to give money to a man who gambles. Good money after bad.

'I see.'

Nino shuffles his feet. 'They are desperate. I cannot fund any more...'

I am decided. 'I will settle Giuliana's bill.'

'You have not even asked how much it is.'

I bite my lip. Then I think of Giuliana lying in her bed, nearly lost. It matters not, for I will find the money. Whatever the cost, the apothecary must believe I will pay.

'No matter,' I say dismissively. 'We have means. My husband is a sculptor for Il Cavaliere, Lorenzo Bernini.'

'So I heard.'

Nino is already writing down an amount on a piece of paper and pushing it towards me. It is enough to keep a family fed for months, but I nod. 'I will bring your money. Here is a down payment.' I tip my coins onto the table, less Signora Mazzi's fees. 'You know everything, Nino. How much does Marco owe everyone else? And the rent? How much is the total amount?'

This is the thing about apothecaries: they, like the barber surgeons, know the men everyone else fears. It is the apothecary and the surgeon who stitch and mend the stab wounds and tend to the injured.

He shakes his head. 'I do not know for certain.'

'A rough figure?'

'This is the amount I have heard.' Nino writes down another number and pushes it back to me. I read it and try not to wince. It is far more than I had feared.

I nod slowly and smile, as if it were a trifle. I must give the impression all will be settled, or else Nino will report back that the Gavias are lost, and if birthing doesn't kill Giuliana then destitution will.

'Payment will be arranged.' If Nino is surprised, he does not show it. Two can play at bluffing, it seems.

'Very well. You are a better friend than many, and far more than Marco deserves.'

'It isn't Marco I want to save.'

* * *

Nino's tiny glass bottles glimmer like jewels in the candlelight. It is either very late or very early in the morning, but I have lost track of the ringing bells which mark our hours. Giuliana is finally sleeping peacefully, the slumber of the exhausted, and I leave Mazzi snoring in the battered chair in the corner while I try to think.

Marco has proved himself no protector, but Giuliana is tied to him. As I pace the floor, my resentment bristles; it is always the women who must sweep up. Each time a board creaks I falter and check it has not woken anyone, but Giuliana is securely locked in her poppy-induced fugue, and Signora Mazzi is almost dead to the world.

The cat shuffles her hind legs and makes to pounce, emitting a growling cry as she sinks her teeth into a small mouse whose body twitches under her paw, and I realise I have not eaten for hours. I stop to look upon Giuliana's scant face and try to imagine what it would be not to hear her voice again; to live when she does not. But the thought causes such a rendering within my heart, I must push it away the instant it forms.

There is a disturbance which ebbs and flows, a question which tarries back and forth, but I cannot find the answer. I know someone who has the money, who has the means to protect Giuliana from death, but what would it cost? If I want to save Giuliana, I must prostrate myself at the feet of Lorenzo. And if I throw myself on Lorenzo's mercy, I become beholden to him. If I am beholden to him, it will cause an irrevocable change in the manner of our friendship. Then the whole edifice of my questions tumbles, causing me the greatest anguish. Not because I fear being beholden, but because I suspect I desire it.

The sun is rising, washing the sky with muted threads of lemon and grey. At first light, I gently shake Signora Mazzi, and she opens her eyes immediately, looking over to the bed in alarm.

'Nay, they are fine. Still sleeping. I am sorry to wake you, but I must go.'

'Where?' her voice is still thick with the night.

'I cannot say.' She pulls a face of disgust.

'It is to help Giuliana,' I interject quickly. 'I learned many things from Nino Marotta last night.'

Mazzi grunts. 'So you know about the debts?' She looks over at the baby, eyeing the sunrise. 'He will need feeding soon. Giuliana is not strong enough to keep them both alive.'

I feel a new alarm creeping in my breast. I cannot save Giuliana, only to lose the child. 'What needs to be done?'

'He needs a wet nurse. A healthy young woman, with bright cheeks and children who prosper.' She sniffs. 'Such girls do not come cheap.'

'But you know of such a person?'

Mazzi sniffs again. 'I know where to find the best wet nurses in Rome.'

'Send a boy then. Make sure Leonardo gets a nurse. I do not care for the cost, it will all be paid for.'

'Where will you get such a sum?'

I hesitate. It is far from assured. 'Worry not, I will get the money.'

She stands, letting out a great groan as her body creaks, and it takes a moment for Mazzi to reassemble herself upright.

'Has Marco returned?'

'Nay, he has not.'

'What a louse.'

We look at each other. It is something we can finally agree on.

Chapter Sixteen

'A Request and an Order'

Late August 1636

'This is an unexpected pleasure.'

We stand in the hallway as housemaids scurry past carrying buckets of water and firewood, plates of food and linens. If they are curious as to why a dishevelled woman has called for their master before the Prime bells have been rung, they do not show it, but instead remain at their tasks, eyes cast downward, feet moving forward.

When I arrived, it caused such a commotion that Stefano had been called. Could he, the maid asked, verify whether this woman – this *unexpected visitor* – was a good enough excuse to disturb the master? Il Cavaliere had given *express instruction* not to be disturbed.

As soon as he saw me Stefano had barked, 'Fetch Il Cavaliere at once, you stupid chit. The master will want to see her immediately.' The girl had scurried away as quickly as she could.

When Lorenzo appears, my courage deserts me. For what have we between us but some instruction on art, and my husband's employ? This is not the stuff of favours or loans. 'Thank you, for seeing me,' I stutter. 'I am sorry for the imposition. I need to ask . . . I need to ask for your help.'

'You had better come in then.'

He looks me up and down. I am a sight, in crumpled old clothes flung on many hours before, and my hair loosely pinned, rather than elaborately styled. If he is curious, he does not show it, nor does Lorenzo see me into one of the many reception rooms downstairs. Instead, he makes to walk up the stairs. 'We shall talk in my studio,' he offers by way of explanation.

I pick up my skirts to follow him. As I do, Luigi is coming down the stairs. I have encountered this brother only a handful of times – in the tavern, at the dance, here in this house – but I know well enough who he is. Matteo and the men of the Fabbrica all talk of Luigi, of his unpredictability and vice, that there is little in life he will not take if he wants it. As Luigi passes, his gaze meets mine with a smirk.

'Good morning, Signora Piccolomini. It is early for business?'

Lorenzo stops. 'Enough.'

They remind me of two street dogs, teeth bared, hackles raised, growling their intent.

Luigi does not look at his brother but continues to stare at me. 'Well, whatever it is, I hope you can settle it quickly. My brother likes solving problems.' I feel a cold shadow, like a bird of prey passing overhead, then it is gone.

'This way.' Lorenzo begins climbing once again and I follow, not looking back at Luigi.

Lorenzo's studio has windows flanking one side, floor to ceiling, an expense which could only be afforded by the Pope's favourite.

Against every wall are stacked paintings, and one on an easel: a portrait of a man from three aspects, wearing a fine lace collar and blue riband. There is a large table on which sit paints, pestles and mortars, and glass containers of pigments which will be ground to release their colour. On the desk there are inkwells and papers, and stacked on the floor are abandoned sketches, more than I can count.

Morning light floods the room, making the air swirl and dance with dust, and the place smells strongly of turpentine. On the table there is a half-eaten meal. It is meagre for a grown man: some ricotta and honey, with a single slice of bread.

'I am disturbing you . . .'

I trail off, and still Lorenzo does not speak but stands with his back to the light, watching me. There is some quiet melody at play between us, but it has no words, only a rhythm of its own. I am suddenly struck by the inevitability of my standing here: the touch in the tavern; the light on the face of Mary Magdalene; the sight of Matteo, of Giuliana's blood, her child. As if all the moments in a life create a momentum which, once started, cannot be undone.

'Tell me, how exactly do you need my help?' He does not move.

I falter. However I respond will determine Giuliana's future.

'Something terrible . . . has come about.'

'Matteo?' I see a slight flicker in his eyes but shake my head.

'If not Matteo, then who?'

'It is my oldest friend, Giuliana. We were raised as sisters, and she is as dear to me as anyone on this earth. She birthed a boy yesterday and finds herself in the gravest danger.' I wait, but he says nothing. 'This is women's business, I know.'

'Go on.'

'She – Giuliana – is very sick. She needs medicine from the

apothecary. Expensive medicine. The care of a midwife. And the baby needs a wet nurse.'

'What about the husband, why does he not provide for his family?'

'Marco? He is a leather worker. But trade is tough. He lost his job at the bottega, and has not been able to sell his wares. They are behind on their rent.' There is no point in pretending, the amount I need to ask for is too large. 'He owes money.'

Lorenzo waits. He knows what is coming and is not going to give what I need easily. He wants to hear me say it.

'And they ...'

What next? It only occurs to me now that there is a very real possibility that Lorenzo will not lend me the money. That my certainty in coming here has been misplaced. It had seemed easier when Giuliana was lying in a rusting pool of her own blood.

I take a step towards him, deciding there can be no artifice in this conversation. 'Matteo and I are ... well, it is strange between us. Something has occurred. And Giuliana is in the most desperate danger.'

He takes a moment, then says, 'So you came to me? It is not a small thing, Costanza, to ask for money. I have been approached many times, by many different people, and cannot save everyone. It is just not possible to give alms to everyone who needs it.'

The air is thick with the clean, sharp stench of paint. If he says no, it will kill Giuliana. He takes one step nearer to me. 'I can see how much your friend means to you.' Lorenzo's tone is so level I cannot read it. My fingers stretch and curl against my dress. I want to shout, 'Aye or no?' To tarry with me is a dreadful thing. I am just about to open my mouth when he speaks: 'I shall give you what you need.'

It is as if the world has contracted then opened up, and I am standing on a great plain, open land, an expanse of meadows smelling the sweetest air. Relief floods through me, flushing out the anxiety which had hemmed me so. I take a step towards him, and hear the rasp of my voice as I speak: 'Thank—'

He puts an unexpected finger on my lips. 'Nay. I do not need your thanks.'

He has not even asked the amount, but he is willing to save Giuliana, and it consumes me. That great expanse shifts, a mark on the horizon. I feel a sudden drop, a lurch in my stomach, a pang of sudden and unexpected longing.

That this man, who has for all these months offered his friendship and protection, should mean it. My husband has professed to be all these things but has not been any. The thought of Matteo stings. He would hate me being here, begging like this. I see his face, hollowed by my betrayal. Then another image flickers: my husband, in bed, another body, not mine. Nay, my husband could no more save Giuliana than he could save me.

Lorenzo stands and waits; it is clear he will not meet me halfway. I need to touch him. Taking his face in my hands, I feel the hard lines of his jaw carve into my fingers. I am surprised by how my body leads my mind.

'Thank you.' The words are a half-formed murmur as I move my face towards his. Only now does he move; there is a thrilling moment as our lips meet. Sensitive, searching, delicate. It feels wildly exhilarating, like a chase coming to its end. He is in no hurry; our mouths meet and part, creating an involuntary force of such magnitude that all I want is his hands on my skin, his body pressed against mine.

It is as if Lorenzo instinctively understands. He puts his lips to my throat and lets out a low groan. My body is expanding, and I am falling. He pulls at my bodice, his hands fondling, releasing, stroking, strong fingers pressing into my flesh. I am astonished at the sensations, the sounds. We are on the pallet in the corner of the room, I lift my skirts. He eases his body into mine, a murmur of contradictions, slender but sturdy, flesh of moonlight streaked with hair as black as coal. I can see his muscles slipping and moving under his skin. We find a rhythm without words, a wildness, a feeling of such fierceness I am swept away.

* * *

It is mid-afternoon and the workshop is at full pelt. Beyond the huge awnings the air is damp and hazy, and the sky is filled with rheumy clouds which periodically weep gauzy tears onto the ground.

Lorenzo Bernini would normally take his time walking through the Fabbrica, checking on progress with a carving or a casting, appraising his workshop with the eye of a master, dripping a word of praise here, a critical review there. But today this is not his business. He is looking for Matteo; there is a conversation to be had. Some of the workers try to catch his eye, beckoning him towards a piece they have pride in. Others – the lazy and those who lack sufficient talent – turn their faces away.

'Where can I find Matteo Bonucelli?' he enquires of a puckish man, his face red with exertion, who waves his hand to the far corner of the workshop. Matteo has chosen a spot on the margins for his space, unshowy and unobtrusive. It tells the sculptor something of the man he is looking for.

Bernini could have called the husband to his house, had this conversation in the private confines of his studio, but here there is less opportunity, less propensity for an emotional outburst. If things get heated, there are plenty of men to restrain Matteo, who is as large as any brute who fights for a living.

At last, the sculptor reaches the far confines of the workshop.

As promised, there is Matteo, his sandy head bent diligently over the putti. Even at a distance, Bernini sees Matteo is competent. A safe man who will turn out what is expected of him, and not go beyond his remit. A trait which could be helpful in the current predicament.

Bernini is determined to have Costanza. But he knows she is a fawn, easily startled. One word of reproach from her husband at this stage could undo everything. The sculptor understands it is his job to ease Costanza's path to him, to dismantle the blockade, to assuage the guilt that would prevent her from pursuing the noblest of causes, human desire. He is, in fact, helping Costanza to realise her full potential as a woman.

'Matteo Bonucelli!' he calls. Matteo stops, and slowly turns, in the manner of a child about to be accused of some wrongdoing he did not commit. Andrea is working at the next station, watching, curiosity flickering in his eyes. With the merest nod of the head, the sculptor gives command for Andrea to leave; he is not needed for this conversation.

'A word?' Bernini asks the question out of politeness, knowing there is only one answer, but he has learned that men like the courtesy.

Matteo wipes his dusty hands on his leather overalls and nods. Bernini steps into the confines of the canopied workspace, close enough to intimidate. The husband stands solid, almost motionless, save for a small lick of his lower lip which betrays his uneasiness. Good, thinks Bernini. I like it when they are nervous.

'I shall speak plainly. I have come to talk to you of your wife.' There is a flare in Matteo's nostrils, slight like the single beat of a butterfly's wings. A man less observant than he would have missed it. But Bernini is a sculptor, used to noticing the tiniest of details.

'What of my wife?'

Bernini leans in and speaks quietly. 'Come now, do not play the innocent. There is something which has passed between Costanza and me.'

'I see.' Matteo shifts his feet uncomfortably.

Bernini understands why the man is upset: he is cuckolded; it is a blow to his pride. But then to be cuckolded by Bernini is different.

'You know how things work in our world. That while we sculpt for the Church, we are no more confined by its teachings than those cardinals who favour boys.' He pauses for a moment, wondering whether to use the information he has to hand. 'And being partial to boys is something you know a little of, isn't it, Bonucelli?'

The man's head pulls up and his eyes focus jerkily on the sculptor. 'I cannot fathom . . .'

But the rising colour in his face suggests otherwise.

'I know everything that happens in my workshop.' Matteo's face flashes with fear. 'So, let's agree that your marriage vows are not as sacred as you like to pretend, and I shall see your wife as I like?'

'She is young, Il Cavaliere. She does not understand the world.'

'Given my reputation, you may not believe this, but you have my assurance that I will treat her kindly.'

'And . . .'

'What is it?'

'She desires a child. Costanza. She has never fallen pregnant, despite . . .'

Bernini is intrigued. Perhaps this sodomite's seed is weak, or Costanza is unable to bear children, which would be a blessing.

'I shall have a care. I have no desire to become a father, but it is a natural consequence of . . .' He stops. No need to say it in front of the husband. 'But rest assured, if Costanza does bear my bastard, I shall pay her handsomely. With this, are we agreed?'

Bernini looks into her husband's eyes and sees contempt. He

cares not. For a moment he lets his impatience show. 'Are we agreed?' he repeats, and immediately regrets asking twice, for Bernini doesn't even have to ask the Pope twice.

'We are agreed,' says Matteo.

Chapter Seventeen

'Physick'

Late August 1636

'I cannot go home.'

I find myself in Caterina's salon, her silk skirts sighing as she moves about, pouring wine, ordering broth and fresh linens to be brought. I am sat on the long bench, overcome by shame and confusion which has settled like an acrid smoke upon me, clinging to my skin, cloying and heavy, reason dulled by the abandonment of my propriety and the reality of my betrayal.

On the one hand I am indignant; did not my husband break his vows first? Filled with a sense of righteousness, my mind reasons that Lorenzo Bernini has cared for me, tutored me, protected me, helped me when I most needed it, given me succour; he desires me, shows me great affection in all things, and is more than any of the best husbands boasted of by their wives. And yet: he is not my husband. I have behaved foolishly, rashly, grievously, as if a devil has taken up residence within and suppressed all the things I know to be right. I have acted against God and against my husband.

* * *

After I had left Lorenzo I made haste to Giuliana's house, my heart triumphant and my purse heavy with coin, the scent of him still on my skin. It had been the greatest relief to find my friend was sleeping peacefully, the child too.

'They have done well, to have got through the last few hours,' Mazzi had said approvingly. 'But we're not out of the woods.' She had taken the money I handed her with less equanimity, eyes narrowing. 'Lord knows where or how you came across this coin, although I can guess. You are fit for no purpose in this state. Go home, rest, and return when you have slept.' It was then the dark smoke of dishonour and humiliation began to curl around me. As I stood on the street in my old district, dishevelled and distracted, I knew I could not face Matteo.

Not yet.

* * *

Caterina sets the glass upon a polished brass table, and pats her hand reassuringly on my arm. 'You will, at some point. But not now. You must stay here until you are feeling better.' She rubs at her chin. 'Tell me of your friend, Giuliana, how is she now?'

'She has rallied a little,' I make a sign of the cross and look skywards. 'Thanks to the mercy of Our Mother Mary, the apothecary's potions and Mazzi, the midwife.'

Caterina smiles. 'A woman's holy trinity. It is a relief to hear your friend is recovering. She is lucky to have you.'

I feel a crumbling inside, a cliff falling into the sea, the edifice of my goodliness failing. 'I am not a good friend. I have paid her scant attention these past few months.'

'You have just saved her life.'

'It was not I. She ... Giuliana ... her husband has debts. So, I went to Lorenzo.'

Quick as a polecat, Caterina does not miss a beat. 'You went to see Il Cavaliere? To ask for money?'

I nod. 'You must understand. It was of the utmost urgency. Giuliana was going to die.'

'He gave it. Just gave the money to you?' Caterina does not look shocked, more questioning. Then she adds, 'He is a most kind and generous man.'

I remember our previous confidences and feel if I can tell anyone of my undoing, it is Caterina. I close my eyes as I finally admit what has been troubling me. 'I have done something very wrong.'

When I open them I find Caterina at my side, eyes brimming with concern. 'My dear, whatever has happened?'

I remember the peculiarity of Lorenzo's touch, his lean form, how different it felt against mine, the novelty of running my fingers through his thick curls, so unlike Matteo's straight, fine hair. The newness of it all. 'I have betrayed my husband ... betrayed Matteo and in doing so have committed a mortal sin.' I begin to cry, and feel Caterina's arms circle me, holding me as the tears fall. 'I am full of guilt,' I sob.

Caterina stands to find a handkerchief. 'My dear Signora Piccolomini, you cannot get so vexed.'

'But I have broken my marriage vows,' I whimper. 'And the most awful thing is, I wanted it so.'

She kneels and hands me a small square of fine linen. 'It does happen. You are not the only woman in the world to whom this course of events has transpired ... How was Lorenzo when you left him?'

The sound of his name jolts me. 'He was ...' I think back now to the murmurings, the wrench I felt leaving his arms, how he tried to coax me to stay, and how I insisted I must leave; Giuliana was waiting. 'Lorenzo was full of tender words. Said he must see me again, that his dreams are alive with thoughts of me, that he cannot live without me, that he will find a way.' I throw my arms from my lap. 'But it is impossible! I am married.'

Caterina grips at my hands to steady them. 'Signora Piccolomini...' she begins.

The songbird begins to trill and flap his wings, and deep sobs begin to well from my belly.

'Costanza!' she says more sharply.

I look up, momentarily quietened by my name, and the tone of her voice.

'Listen to me.' She is soft again now, like a mother speaking fondly to her child. 'Do you have feelings for Lorenzo?'

I give a tentative nod.

She tips her head to one side and studies me. 'And he has feelings for you?'

My voice cracks with exhaustion and misery. 'I believe he does. Yes.'

Caterina rubs her hands soothingly over mine. 'What of Matteo?'

'He does not love me as a husband should.' I cannot say any more, for even with Caterina, it is delicate and too dangerous.

'So, you wish to be with Lorenzo?'

I nod slowly, and more tears squeeze from my eyes. 'It is a most hopeless situation.'

Caterina lets out a loud rush of air from her teeth.

I look at her. I cannot work out what the noise represents. Annoyance, condemnation, frustration? A panic rises in me, a fear that she too disapproves; I have ruined myself and my reputation. But instead, Caterina pulls herself to a regal height and places her hands on her hips, more like a fish seller in the market than a satin-clad hostess in her salon.

'My sweetness. All is not lost. Indeed, it is a most fortunate turn of events. You are not ruined. You have not been loved and discarded. Lorenzo wants you as his mistress, yes?'

'It is impossible.'

Caterina's voice dips to a hush. 'We are friends, are we not?'

I nod slowly.

'Then I shall tell you a story. I was sixteen when I married. Young. Beautiful. A great match for an ambitious man, had my father been more imaginative. But he wasn't. Paolo was the safe choice. The dullest pairing. You've met him. A bore who opines on everything, whether he knows a jot about the subject or not. Can you imagine?'

It is, I admit, an awful predicament for a young woman to find herself in. I hold Caterina's stare, embarrassment preventing me from moving my eyes anywhere else.

'So, I had to conjure a better life for myself,' she continues. 'Using my own assets. I began to understand that I could have all that I wanted: to be surrounded by beauteous things, pretty jewels, sumptuous clothes.' She drops her voice. 'My desire sated.'

My heart thuds at her bluntness. 'I have been brought up to be—'

'Everything you have been brought up to be – all that is taught to women is imparted by men: your father, your husband, your priest. Now you have a woman teaching you. Our sex has few advantages in this life. You are attractive.' She pushes an errant strand of hair back from my face. 'Be very sure, there is something about you that men want. That Il Cavaliere wants. And *he* is a man even the Pope wants. It is done now. You will quickly forget the shame of lying with a man and think only of the power that comes with it. Your husband cannot object to his master's choice. Il Cavaliere is his superior.' Caterina tucks the curl behind my ear. 'Marriage is a bond which can be loosened without being entirely severed.'

She can't mean ...

'They will come to some sort of agreement. Men do.' The light in the room has fallen, as clouds gather, and I hear the first drops of rain falling against the glass. 'Make the most of what you have, Costanza. It doesn't last long.'

My mind is a tumult. All air is pressed from my lungs. Is it really of no consequence whether a wife keeps her vows? Then the image of Matteo and Vincenzo runs through my mind.

Caterina adds, 'There are ways of preventing a child.'

'I had thought ...'

She turns quickly, concerned. I hear the first drops of rain hitting the glass. 'Sweet girl. It is best not to be foolish in this matter. Matteo will not want to raise another man's infant, and Lorenzo does not want a bastard. Think of his position – he is the chief architect of St Peter's. And you certainly do not want to grow fat and cumbersome, nor deal with the wreckage of birth. Do you think Il Cavaliere will still want you then?

I am like a child taking instruction on how to sound their first letters. How could none of this have occurred to me? I begin to feel faintly foolish, for what Caterina says makes perfect sense, and in this moment I am intensely grateful for her friendship.

'If I were ... I mean, how do you manage to prevent it?'

She smiles. 'There are means. A discreet apothecary. A physick of laurel, madder, sage.'

I breathe out properly for the first time since I arrived at Caterina's house. It had not occurred to me that I could be with Lorenzo and still live with Matteo. That I will not be forced to confront this truth, but the men will speak. A momentary flash of relief passes through me, followed by a dampening sadness, that

Matteo would so readily agree to such an arrangement. 'Do you really think it is that simple?'

Caterina's lips widen. 'Where Lorenzo Bernini is concerned, anything is possible.'

There is something else I am longing to know. 'May I ask one more question?'

'Of course.'

The rain is falling heavily now, and the room is cast in the shadow of the thunderous clouds outside. Men will be scurrying home in the falling light, before the storm truly breaks.

'How does it work? With Paolo?

Caterina sniffs, 'I consider Paolo's comings and goings none of my business. And he has adopted the same position. It is what has kept us happily married for so long.'

It does not sound happy to me. 'So, your husband does not care for the appetites of his wife? Nor who you consort with? That is not the understanding I have with Matteo.'

Caterina looks at me steadily. 'Are you so sure?'

I meet her gaze and am startled to realise she knows. If she knows Matteo's secret, then so does Lorenzo.

From this moment on, my path is set.

Chapter Eighteen

'Makepeace'

October 1636

'Where are we going?'
I have been Lorenzo's lover for two months, enough time that we have found a familiar pattern to our days. We are walking swiftly towards the river; the afternoon is winding down, causing the narrow streets to be so busy with traders on their way home from market that I must dodge the heavy, creaking wheels of their carts.

Lorenzo flashes me a wicked look. 'We are to the country.'

His answer puzzles me greatly. 'The country? On foot?'

He laughs. 'Or what passes for the country in Rome. A villa, in Trastevere on the other side of the river. Come.'

He grabs my hand so that I must skip to catch up with him. Even his touch, the strength of his fingers wrapped around mine, feels so delightful I cannot stop my stomach from dancing. So great is my anticipation for the adventure ahead, I meet his stride as we walk, and think contentedly how evenly we are matched in our humours.

We turn the corner and meet the river. The sun is beginning to lower in the sky, and the fast flow of the water shines aqua-green against the muted pinks and bright white of the buildings and bridges. The tall green-black Cyprus trees are crisply silhouetted by shadowed light. It is a sight that never fails to delight, the Tiber in late autumn sun.

We walk quickly, the pace of our conversation complementing the speed of our steps, talking about all the things that have happened since we last saw each other, though it has only been days. Lorenzo points to the place he is taking me to, and I scrunch up my eyes so I may see better against the sun's glowering rays.

'There, between the trees. Do you see a loggia, facing the river?'

So great are the thickets and vegetation it is not a clear view, but I do not want to say I cannot see it. 'Aye . . .' I declare, somewhat unsure, 'I think so.'

'That is for the players. Behind the gardens there is the most wonderful villa, built by Agostino Chigi. A banker from Siena.'

'I see.' Everyone knows bankers are even richer than clerics.

Lorenzo squeezes my hand like an excited child. 'I have arranged for us to view the rooms. But we must be quick, to see them before the light fades.'

'Did the bankers not take their art with them?'

He laughs, 'Nay. We are to see frescoes, which cannot be moved.' Lorenzo pulls at my arm. 'We must go to them.'

On we hurry, going with the flow of the traffic. We have just reached the bridge to cross the river when there is a shout.

'Signor Bernini, if I am not mistaken?'

Lorenzo mutters under his breath then shouts. 'Signor

Makepeace! What a fine chance to see you here.' He steps forward and slaps the stranger on the back. 'How in the devil are you?'

I hang back – this is clearly business – and take a good look at the gentleman. He wears a cap favoured by the English, which I take him to be due to his accent. His clothes are sober: plain grey wool with no embellishment. From under his headwear hangs hair not curled, not straight, but some kind of frizz of a light colour, and his face is pale, despite our climate, with no strength to his features.

The gentleman does not even acknowledge me, but instead directs his conversation only to Lorenzo. 'I am well, Signor Bernini, I trust you are too?'

While I acknowledge the discretion Lorenzo must observe, this pretence that I do not exist still smarts.

'His Holiness keeps me busy.'

'Not too busy to complete my liege, King Charles's commission, I hope? For you are revered by His Majesty.' Makepeace throws his arms in the air in false exaggeration. 'Exalted!' he continues. 'Above all men who have the talent and exercise your profession.'

Lorenzo makes a loud laugh which has no soul to it. 'Si! Do not worry so, Signor Makepeace. It is nearly done; it matches the painting you sent. I think His Highness will be very satisfied.'

A wash of relief washes across the man's face. 'Nearly finished? This is welcome news indeed. The dispatches of London ask frequently for updates on Signor Bernini's carving and Mr van Dyck's painting. For both are dear to the King's heart, and what is dear to the King's heart is dear to all Englishmen's hearts.'

I dislike this Makepeace. He is so snivelling.

'Have patience, my friend. It is all in hand and will be finished on time.'

Lorenzo looks to the sun which is beginning its descent,

burnishing the water of the river with her golden rays. 'If you will forgive me, I must make haste. I have an appointment with an old friend.'

Makepeace makes a bow, deep and toadying. When he rises, he looks straight at Lorenzo. 'Of course. We shall speak again soon, Signor Bernini. In the meantime, enjoy your evening.' At this his eyes make the merest glance in my direction. I expect a smirk, but there is none, only a weaselly frown of disapproval.

As soon as Makepeace is out of earshot, I cannot help myself. 'I did not like the way that man looked at me,' I say petulantly.

His eyes narrow. 'Mr Makepeace is a Puritan and I am walking as the sun is setting, with a handsome woman with a wedding ring on her finger. Well . . .'

I make to say that the gentleman would not have noticed such a detail, but Lorenzo puts his finger on my mouth to quieten it.

'Perhaps if you had pretended I was one of your sisters, or a wife of a friend, he would not have looked at me so?'

'Nay.' He says softly. 'I know this man. You are too beautiful. He understood immediately what you are to me. I could not acknowledge you, as he would report such gossip as fact back to the King, who is a notorious censor. This commission would not be in doubt, but the next one?' Lorenzo shrugs. 'Maybe. A man like me is only as good as his next commission.' He taps his head. 'The English take a very dim view of Catholics. I do not need to confirm their worst fears.'

'Your words make sense,' I answer grouchily. 'But I do not like being ignored. It is enough to have the gossips of the Fabbrica pick over the bones of my reputation.'

Lorenzo looks at me, and for a moment I do not know which way he will turn: to fury or forgiveness. Then he puts his hand on my arm and smiles. 'It is getting late and I think you must be hungry. I could no more pretend you do not exist than deny the stars in the sky.'

Then he kisses me full on the lips in the middle of the street. It is beyond propriety. I want to refuse him, but he holds my arms so I cannot.

When Lorenzo lets go, he leans over me, whispering in my ear. 'There is no denying you now.'

* * *

As we walk, order is restored and Lorenzo tells me of the man who built the villa.

Despite receiving little formal education, Lorenzo knows the history of this city well enough. Or perhaps it is fairer to say, Lorenzo has made it his business to learn the lineage of Rome's benefactors – and their money.

'The man who built this house was called Chigi. It stands on the ancient site where Cleopatra entertained Mark Antony or so they say. Our man Chigi lent money to foreign kings and popes, the Borgias, the Medicis, the Piccolominis.' At the mention of my name, he makes a small, playful bow. 'Anyway, when Chigi's wife died he promptly fell in love with a shopkeeper's daughter named Francesca.'

A rich man and a tradesman's daughter. It cannot end well. 'What happened to Francesca?'

'They lived as common-law husband and wife for many years, and she begat him numerous children, while he remained the Pope's banker.'

'It is surprising, is it not, what can be tolerated when you have the scudi?'

'I guess Chigi's fine living caught up with him in the end. He proposed to Francesca and dictated his will at the same time.'

'So, good old Chigi made an honest woman of Francesca?'

'Aye. With the blessing of the Pope, too. The wedding was a fancy affair, attended by poets and princes, nobles and cardinals.'

A whistle emanates from my lips. 'It is not often you hear of a fallen woman like Francesca finding her feet again.'

'Indeed. It is the reason I have bought you here. We are to gaze upon one of the hidden wonders of Rome. The fresco Chigi commissioned Maestro Raphael to paint in honour of Francesca at her wedding banquet. Hurry,' Lorenzo pulls at my hand. 'The light is against us, and we have already been too long delayed by that fool, Makepeace.'

We walk swiftly, our feet moving across the cobbles in a steady beat, alongside the exodus of carts of goods and tired men making their way from the city to the farms beyond. As we do, I cannot help but wonder if there is hidden meaning in Lorenzo's words. The man who hid his mistress in plain sight, and eventually found a way to make her his wife.

Chapter Nineteen

'Venus'

October 1636

The villa stands on the west bank of the Tiber, a large estate shrouded in overgrown shrubbery, set in dappled quietude.

Lorenzo leads me to the formal gardens, their once-neat order and geometric paths near vanished, overtaken once more by nature. Cedars, laurel bushes, bergamot trees and evergreens. In some places the vegetation has grown so thick it has all but swallowed up the flower beds, vast shrubs choke the borders, and lilacs and rose bushes grow high into the sky.

As we push our way through this maze, I see glimpses of the villa itself. An elegant counterpoint to the wildness all around, undimmed by time, the house is of classical structure built from light stone, with tall, symmetrical windows. It is a place of harmony. I think of Francesca and the first time she saw it and wonder if she too was awed.

Lorenzo and I pick our way along the path. When we reach the door, he carefully places down the bag he is carrying and I hear the faint clink of glass; he has come with provisions and I am glad, for the walk has made me thirsty.

He pulls a heavy key from his pocket. The rusted metal lock is stiff, and Lorenzo curses as he struggles to turn it. For a moment I am worried we will not be able to enter, souring Lorenzo's mood – and our whole afternoon – and am relieved to hear the click of the lock as it moves.

The day is beginning to shake its shackles, but the sun refuses to admit her waning power, obstinately washing the villa in a pink-gold halo. Even this celestial effort cannot prevent a slight chill creeping across my back as Lorenzo pushes at the heavy door, and we pass into the dark.

He immediately sets about pulling at the great wooden shutters, causing motes of dust to dance in the soft light. There is a smell of damp plaster and I try not to think about the river rushing not far from where we stand; so tightly is Rome bonded to the flowing Tiber, our ancestors believed floods to be divine punishment for depravity.

As if in defiance of these gods, I impulsively kiss Lorenzo on the side of his neck. He turns, grinning, surprised at this unexpected act of longing, and returns the kiss, full on my lips. Blood rushes through my veins and a soft ripple runs up my thighs as I embrace him.

'You are quite exquisite,' he murmurs. 'Now, I have something to show you. It cannot quite match your beauty, but it tries.' I stare, not grasping his meaning. 'Look up,' he whispers. 'Look up ... and feast your eyes.'

I tilt my head and gasp. Above is the most wondrous scene, densely decorated with the naked bodies of gods and nymphs.

'It is so unexpected.' I knew he had a fresco in store for me, but I had thought it would be one wall, not a whole ceiling. 'It is a spectacle. My eyes do not know where to rest.'

'I knew it!' There is a note of triumph in Lorenzo's voice, his enthusiasm palpable and infectious. 'I knew you would love it. Isn't it magnificent? Bravo, Chigi, you outdid yourself with this one!'

'It is astonishing,' I agree.

Above us, the ceiling is painted as if we are standing under a pergola. There are rampant garlands festooned in all manner of exotic fruit and flowers, the vegetation so lush it feels as real as the shrubs we have just walked through.

Then Lorenzo makes his favourite ask of me. 'Tell me what you see.'

I begin hesitantly, for there is so much to take in. 'There are gods. It is a feasting scene of some kind. And the colours . . . the colours are a riot. A clear blue summer sky, red earth, delicate pinks, the perfect contours of flesh and fruit.'

'The garlands are painted by Giovanni da Udine, from Raphael's studio, made with ground stones from across the world. You see the blue? It is lapis from the East. And here, this green? From Verona. The red is cinnabarite from Spain. The bright blue is smalt from Bohemia. Even the paints tell us of Rome's greatness and how far our traders travelled. Pomegranate from Persia; bitter orange from China; watermelon from Africa; pumpkin from the New World; aubergine from Asia. It is all of earth painted in the skies.'

My footsteps echo as I wander back and forth along the loggia, I am unable to settle for long before I start searching for more treasure, like a magpie. Cupid. The Three Graces.

'Have you worked it out yet? What the story is?' asks Lorenzo with rising delight.

'It's a feast. A story of the ancient gods. But I cannot work out who.'

'A good start. Here let me help you.' Lorenzo stands behind me and circles his arms around my waist, I feel his breath warm on my neck as he points ahead, whispers, 'Look! Here is Cupid.' Then he shifts his hand, and points at another scene, 'And there is Venus.'

A half-formed memory stirs: of sitting on Papa's knee, hearing ancient stories. Psyche, the youngest of three mortal daughters born to a king, so beautiful she incurs the wrath of Venus. The goddess instructing her son, Cupid, to make the girl fall in love with a monster. But Cupid falls for Psyche. A vague recollection of Psyche being taken to a palace and a falling out between the lovers, but the bit I remember vividly is Venus setting tasks for Psyche. Each one increasingly difficult. The devastation of Psyche failing her final mission, followed swiftly by elation when the gods agreed to make her immortal anyway, so she can live the rest of her days with her true love, Cupid.

I remember the relish with which Papa told the tale, and Tiberia admonishing us. 'Leonardo Piccolomini,' she would snap. 'You should be instructing our daughter in Christian stories, not the ungodly antics of pagans.' How Papa would laugh good-heartedly. 'You provide our girl with good schooling in how to be a modest maiden. It is the fashion to know of old myths and legends. Our daughter will make a good match and shall have a need for such learning.' Then he would smile conspiratorially and pinch my cheek.

'It is Venus whispering to Cupid,' I say to Lorenzo, looking around the room and seeing more of the story painted into the arches. 'And here,' I say, pointing, 'here is Psyche carrying a vessel to Venus, on one of her trials. Oh, and in the centre, that must be the Council of Gods deciding whether to admit Psyche. There's Zeus in the middle. And then here, the wedding celebration. A fitting end.'

'Perfecto, exactly!' Lorenzo is as delighted as any tutor could be with his pupil.

'You have solved the riddle. Psyche achieves immortality through her commitment to love.'

He kisses the back of my neck, lips brushing my skin as he murmurs his words again. 'A commitment.' Another kiss. 'To love.'

Leaning against Lorenzo I gaze at the ceiling, dappled by the fading light and the trees outside. In the distance I hear the shouts of the ferrymen on the river, the birds making their sundowner plans; and I have never felt more complete in my life.

Abruptly, the moment is broken, as Lorenzo pulls his hands from my waist and walks to the bag. 'Here.' He pulls the drawstrings open. 'Have something to eat.'

There is a blanket for us to sit on, some stubby candles which he sets down in tin holders, dark rye bread, cured ham wrapped in waxed cloth, a flagon of water, two goblets, and a small knife with which to cut.

I half watch as Lorenzo meticulously cuts the food into bite-sized morsels with practised ease, the unthinking way he progresses with his tasks, setting out the cups, pouring wine, and suddenly have the unshakable feeling this is all staged: a practised seduction. The revelation blazes and I find the words have escaped before I have had a chance to rehearse them.

'Have you been here before?'

Lorenzo looks up, like a man sleepwalking and awakened from his dream. 'Yes,' he says after a pause. 'Of course. To see the Raphael and Giovanni da Udine . . . he painted the plant festoons. Any artist would want to see such a—'

'That is not my meaning. Have you been here before? With a woman?'

A cloud crosses Lorenzo's face, and I cannot be sure if it is shame at the cheapness of his action, or anger at having been discovered. For a moment, no words pass between us. I feel an inferno raging as

I imagine him here with another woman. Same words, same meal, same motive. The thought of it wounds me. I want to be special. Different. I am not naive; I know Lorenzo has had many lovers. Matteo has never spoken of what passed between him and Lorenzo but had only said men like Bernini are incapable of constancy, that sooner or later they need a new fixation. I had near shouted at my husband, telling him he knows nothing at all.

Lorenzo scrambles to stand. Such is the quickness of his action that I almost cower. Instead, I stand firm, eyeing him with fury. He moves slowly towards me, hands not outstretched in placation but by his side, hot, black eyes fixed upon me. When Lorenzo reaches me he does not speak, but instead traces his forefinger over my cheek, and wraps around it a ringlet which has worn loose at my temple.

He smiles, a hound baring his teeth. 'You are as cruel and jealous as Venus.' The finger at my temple runs over my ears and along my jawline. His face so close his breath replaces the mildewed air. 'That is what I shall call you: Venus; my goddess. A jealous goddess, green-eyed and hot humoured.'

I make to push him back, for Lorenzo has not answered my question, but he catches my hands, forcing them downwards, and kisses me again. It never ceases to surprise me how swiftly desire can rise, in the pushing of his body against mine. Furiously I relent, meeting passion equally, biting and nipping at him, while I revel in the pleasure of his touch, his hands gripping my back, mine slipping under his shirt and feeling the flesh along his slender ribs.

We lower ourselves to the floor, almost falling in the struggle of our bodies trying to find their way to each other. His hand is under my skirt, his lips a madness upon mine, his fingers feeling for me. My breath quickens as the tightness rises – a pulling, a gathering tautness – as he touches me at my centre, again and again.

When it comes, it is a pleasure which is not confined, but spreads through my whole being. I reach for him and kiss him with such fervency I am entirely spent of breath. He holds me as I learn to breathe once more, then pulls me atop, and we rock in the long shadows of the dying day until he too is spent.

Afterwards, while Lorenzo sleeps, I lie among ghosts on the thin blanket, the cold tiles pressing against my back, and stare at the ceiling. I think about Francesca and feel the vastness and the richness of her world; of colour, and light, of decadence and gorging, of naked flesh, of love and passion, of ecstasy, of touch, of the sweetest, ripest fruit and blowsiest blooms.

My eyes rest on Venus and I hear Lorenzo's words, realising he never gave me an answer. I study her closely, saffron robes flying, Cupid in her arms, cheeks flushed with high colour, the divinity of her body, rounded and soft, with firm flanks and high breasts as she points below. Venus is powerful and utterly beguiling. She is perfection.

Here, lying in Lorenzo's arms in this place of love, of Cleopatra and Antony, of Francesca and Chigi, a new confidence unfolds in me. I imagine our future. A premonition of sorts. A room full of people, gathered to celebrate a marriage feast. A fine ceiling, painted in a riot of colours and entwined bodies, a paean to the power of enduring love.

Chapter Twenty

'Dancing Lessons'

October 1636

'I said step to the left, Signora Piccolomini.' Caterina's dance master, Signor Giovanni, is exasperated.

Her salon has been transformed for the occasion, the furniture having been pushed back against the wall and the rug pulled up.

'Left! SINISTRA!' Signor Giovanni yells again. I do not take kindly to the screaming but these lessons are being paid for by Caterina's purse. Or rather, Paolo's pocket.

The invitation had subtly been slipped into a conversation a couple of weeks before, as we watched a rather tedious salon concert.

'I am to take some lessons,' Caterina had whispered, wafting a fan in front of her face.

The declaration had taken me aback. 'Lessons?'

'Yes. Lessons.'

I had turned to face Caterina. 'Lessons in what?'

'Dancing.'

I was mystified. 'In dancing?'

The fanning continued. 'You sound a little . . . underwhelmed.'

'Nay . . .' I had murmured. 'It's just that . . . well, dancing lessons. It's . . . a most startling proposition.'

'How so?'

'You already move with such grace, I'd have thought you in little need of further instruction.'

Caterina had laughed quietly. ''Tis true. I am blessed with an elegant gait, but it becomes a woman to know the latest fashions. The French, Venetians, the Spanish – they are busy inventing new dances all the time. A good wife must be able to show off her husband's investment in her.'

'And Paolo has agreed . . . to pay for these lessons?'

'Of course. He is keen I am kept amused. I can be quite lonely when he is away on business.'

Rarely have I seen Caterina happier than when Paolo is away, but I commiserate nonetheless.

'Your husband's absences cause great despondency.'

'It would do you good too.'

I had laughed. 'Lorenzo doesn't have time to learn new dances.'

Caterina fluttered her fan, then pressed it into my arm, tapping in time with her words to emphasis their meaning. 'Ah, but if he sees you dancing it with another (tap) man (tap), his jealousy (tap) might be aroused (tap) and he will pay you . . . more attention (tap, tap).'

I was sceptical. Tempting Lorenzo's jealousy didn't sound sensible. Nevertheless, I held my tongue and agreed to the lessons, not wanting to disappoint Caterina. After all, I could do with learning a little more finesse.

Which is how I come to be at Caterina's villa, going right when I should be going left, attired in one of my more practical gowns – while she is beautifully dressed in hyacinth blue, with a full toilette, hair artfully arranged and cheeks richly rouged.

The reason for Caterina's rich ensemble is clear: Signor Giovanni. A heavenly creature. Taller than most, blessed with an athletic frame, broad shoulders and a nipped-in waist, not to mention strong legs. Even his face is exceptional: skin unblemished, eyes dark and penetrating with a slight flirtation about his lips at all times.

'Arm higher, Signora Panzetti. That's it. Very good.'

I shoot Caterina a poisonous look and she arches her eyebrow at me.

'Nay, Signora Piccolomini! I said step to the left and head to the right – not step to the right, head to the left.'

Mother of God. Is 'nay' this man's favourite phrase?

'You must be a gazelle on the dance floor,' he continues, 'quick and light. Pick up your feet. Quick! Quick! Turn!'

Signor Giovanni bangs his stick on the floor in time to the music and when Caterina makes a small misstep, the dance master rushes to correct her, arm resting lightly on her waist, finger slowly running along her arm. 'Better, Signora Panzetti. Better.'

Then he whispers into her ear, knowing that I can hear but not caring. 'The way you move is like sunlight rippling on the water.'

Caterina blushes and I feel both sorry and ashamed for her.

Then the dance master claps his hands. 'We shall take a break. The ladies need refreshment before we start again.'

Giametta, no longer a kitchen girl, but promoted to upstairs maid, serves a light wine, sweetened with honey, and some small almond biscuits. I fall upon them ravenously as Caterina sits on the ornate sofa, her eyes wild with excitement. 'Didn't I tell you Signor Giovanni was a masterful instructor?' she gushes. 'We shall acquit ourselves very well at the next masque.'

There is no way of dressing up the question I am burning to

ask. I speak, still chewing on the biscuit. 'So, is Signor Giovanni your lover?'

Caterina looks nonplussed for a moment, clearly assessing the propriety of the question – of which there is none.

She takes a sip of wine. 'He is.'

I nod. The biscuits are difficult to swallow. 'Does Paolo know?'

'He suspects.'

'And he doesn't mind?'

Caterina takes another sip. 'It is our agreement. Gio makes me happy, and Paolo is content when I am happy. It is ... convenient. But Gio would be devoted to me, lessons or no.'

I watch the dance instructor talking to the harpsichord player on the other side of the room. The late morning light falls upon his face, he is young, handsome. While I do not know him, I know his sort; there are many in my district. Pretty men, born poor with no way to rise unless they keep rich company. It is the same sport as the cortigianas on the top floor make, except Giovanni's wares are flaunted in the private rooms of Rome's finest salons. I am mystified that Caterina cannot see it.

I tread tentatively. 'He must be in demand.'

'Of course. He teaches many ladies, but' – and here she whispers – 'Gio says that he will wait for me to become a widow, however long it takes, and claim me for his wife. I will have no need of another rich husband; I have no children and all of this will be mine.' Caterina sweeps her arm around the room, and Paolo's extensive art collection. She pauses and I wonder if she regrets sharing this last confidence, then asks, 'Talking of great loves, how is Lorenzo?'

I feel the need to repay the trust Caterina has just shown. 'He took me to see the Raphael at the Chigi Villa.'

'He did?' She turns a ring on her finger. 'And how did you find it?'

'Arresting. A supreme tribute to love.'

She nods and smiles but does not reply.

'On the way we met a man from the English court. A Signor Makepeace. He looked at me with, well, with contempt. Thought I was Lorenzo's mistress.'

'But my dear, you are.'

'I know. But it made me feel like a foul secret.'

'From the English court you say? They frown on all pleasure as sin. You must take no notice of such things.'

We sit and watch Signor Giovanni in full flow, his arms expressing the words we cannot hear.

'Lorenzo and I ... it is always snatched time; we can never be in a place which belongs only to us. We can never just be ... together.'

Caterina looks at me kindly, but quizzically. 'What do you mean?'

'It is just ... I hate hiding. The subterfuge. Everyone watches in Rome. Even the statues.'

She waits for a moment, listening, absorbing my words. 'Go on ...'

'I wish Lorenzo and I could spend time together, 'tis all. Away from prying eyes and gossips. He is so ... capricious. I wish we could go somewhere we could be just like carefree newlyweds. It is easy for you. You have a beautiful house and no doubt a comfortable bed, and a husband who doesn't care.'

I had not meant for those last words to fall from my lips, and immediately regret them.

'I am sorry. I didn't mean ...'

'Shhh. No harm done. It is true ...' She studies me for a moment, her gaze intense, as if weighing my words like a goldsmith at his scales. A generous shaft of light falls across her face, and I hear the bass murmur of Gio and the musician deep in their own conversation.

Then Caterina speaks slowly, 'Yes . . . I can see . . . It is vexing . . . It would be good for Lorenzo. A few days away to . . . indulge in a little . . .' Caterina smiles, 'a little pleasure. It might be just the thing.'

I hang my head and speak quickly, quietly. 'I have no means, no money. I am married. It is impossible.'

'Not so fast cucciolina. It might be. There could be a way.'

She taps thoughtfully at her chin with her fan.

'I have an old friend. Rich merchant, new money. Likes to flaunt it. He's just built a villa outside the city: far enough to escape the claustrophobia, near enough not to be an arduous journey.'

'Do you think?' Then I remember Lorenzo, his work, the Fabbrica. 'Nay. Lorenzo would not tolerate being away for too long.'

'That is true . . . And yes, this merchant is a discreet man. Ambitious.'

I wonder how Caterina knows this merchant, rich enough to afford a new villa but discreet enough to want to lend it to her, but do not care for the answer. The idea of spending a few days alone with Lorenzo is so wondrous, I have no need for the details of how it will happen.

'And you think he . . . the merchant . . . would lend it to us?

'Oh, I am sure I could persuade him. He likes to help well-connected friends.'

But this is only one side of the problem. 'Do you think Lorenzo would agree?'

Caterina laughs. Not the giddy laugh she saves for the dance master, but verging on bawdy. 'Oh, come now little one. Persuading Lorenzo is your job. I am sure it will not be difficult. He is completely enamoured with you.'

I laugh too, but feel nervous. It is true. Lorenzo lusts after me, sends me presents and flowers, letters and tokens of his esteem, but tearing him away from his work is quite another feat.

'Do you think we could go? Soon? Before the weather turns for winter?'

Despite myself, I begin to imagine it. No servants. Just Lorenzo and me. A simple life. Man and wife in all but name, and a little ray of hope bursts forth and jolts me. Is not hope the most dreaded of all emotions? It can be so easily crushed.

Chapter Twenty-One

'Supper'

October 1636

He is sat in his father, Pietro's, chair at the head of the table. The arms are worn conker-smooth where the elder Bernini's palms have rubbed at the grain, the hallmark of years of frustration.

It is Lorenzo Bernini's talented fingers that grip the curved edge now. The sculptor's mother, Angelica, is sat beside him, doused in voluminous black. Seated along either side of the table are his older, unmarried sisters, arranged like saints watching a catafalque. They too are demurely dressed. He prefers a less ostentatious kind of Catholicism in his own house, dresses of brown and grey, under-shirts fastened at the neck, hair tightly braided and caught under the cover of pristine white coifs: hardly the fashion anymore, but becoming of women of good standing. Understated, humble, chaste.

The sculptor dips his spoon into the liquid on his plate. The menu is light to his liking. White meat, broth, nothing to inflame his already hot humours.

'More bread.' A voice from the other end of the table. 'And some cheese ... and olives.'

Lorenzo looks up sharply. 'The meal is not to your liking, brother?'

'The food is most adequate, but it is not plentiful, and I am hungry.' Luigi stares at him, something, not quite a smile, upon his lips.

A rustle of women's clothing, bodies moving, a collective intake of breath so quiet it is almost inaudible. A sudden drop in temperature. The sky darkening before a storm.

The sculptor's pulse quickens. He looks up and down the table. The women have all found something of great interest upon their plates.

'I must apologise, brother. Sincerely. That this establishment, this *victualling house* I appear to run is not to your taste. Perhaps you might find something better to your liking if you were to leave and live off your own efforts?'

The women listen to the air like hawks. His mother's eyes blink shut, as unseeing as they were before his father dropped down dead seven years before. The servant hovers at the door, unsure whether to stay or proceed to the kitchen.

'Jesu, Lorenzo, it is just some bread and olives.'

But it is not just some bread and olives. It is the challenge, the questioning, the always wanting more, the fact that Luigi, his brother – his *younger* brother by twelve years – has somehow concluded that he knows better than Lorenzo Bernini. There are many things this brother does not know.

The sculptor waves his hand at the servant. 'Fetch the bread.' The boy scuttles out. In the kitchen he will tell the cook that trouble is brewing. The cook will raise an eyebrow and whisper to the lad that, in the natural world, male cubs leave. It is the females who band together in companionship, gather to hunt, watch their young with a protective eye. It is not natural for a man to be kept by his brother as Luigi Bernini is kept by Lorenzo.

Upstairs, the conversation continues. 'And how, pray tell me, brother, could I leave and set up my own household when you refuse to give me a commission of my own?'

A gust of wind fanning the flames. Costanza and Caterina have cooked up a plan. A villa. He likes the idea of being away from here. Away from this. Of having her with him, knowing she will not have to return to her husband, if only for a few days. He is surprised at how much he craves her, how his imagination fires when he is with her, like sparks flying from an anvil. He thinks of the complaints sitting on his desk, the piles of notes demanding money for his brother's unruly behaviour.

'I pay your keep in many more ways than putting food in your belly and a roof over your head, as well you know.'

There is a clatter as Luigi lets his spoon fall against the metal plate. 'I am sorry to be such a burden. I could relieve you of the necessity of settling my debts if you would give me the opportunity to earn coin of my own.'

The gowns rustle. The breeze picks up pace. Such whining from the man-boy: he cannot stand the ingratitude. He wants to be away, with her soft gaze and yielding flesh.

'This has been much discussed.' The sculptor's tone is full of suppressed fury. 'You cannot be trusted to run a commission. You cannot even look after yourself or curb any of your excesses. You bring shame to the Bernini name.'

'Ha. You think it is I who brings shame upon our father's name?' The younger brother's voice is raised now.

The women cease all movement, hands are held motionless in laps, heads bowed, lips still. The mother has taught them well. To observe, anticipate, brace themselves for the tempest.

'It is not I who has bedded a married woman,' Luigi continues. 'It is not I who walk all over this city . . . brazenly . . . with her. Who genuflects at the feet of His Holiness, only to rush back to a harlot. Who knows, you're probably not even her only lover.'

Each word acts as kindling. By the end of Luigi's speech there is an inferno blazing, a ferocity of heat searing through the sculptor; his hands grip at the chair, white-boned knuckles pushing against the skin. He feels the eruption flowing fast now, like lava from his core.

'Enough!' he bellows. 'You ungrateful, whining turd. You will not speak of her, or anyone else in this manner. You will not have a commission until you have proved yourself worthy. And I know you will not leave this house, not because you love our mother, or our sisters, but because you could not survive out there in the real city, where men must toil, put in a real day's work to put bread on the table, while you lounge here like some overfed lizard.'

Luigi stands abruptly, pushing the chair so it scrapes against the wooden floor. For a moment, Lorenzo wonders if his brother means to fight him. Such arrogance. He readies himself nonetheless. But the younger brother merely throws his napkin on the table, muttering, 'I've had my fill of this.' He walks out without taking another look at the sculptor.

It is an end, but an unsatisfactory one. Lorenzo Bernini turns to one of the servants and screams loud enough for his brother to hear, 'Tell Cook to forget the olives, they are surplus to requirements.'

* * *

The younger brother grabs at a long wool cloak hung by the door. As he departs, he exhales deeply, nostrils flaring like a thundering, wild stallion.

It is dusk; the noise and bustle of the day has receded. The streets have an altogether quieter air, as if the city is holding its breath in anticipation of night's arrival.

As Luigi Bernini makes his way from the house towards St Peter's Basilica, he is propelled forward by a familiar compulsion. The need for risk. A craving to shock. Untamed desire, untrammelled domination. His heart pounds, hooves drumming.

The fading sun casts a final few rays across the half-finished buildings, before dipping below the horizon, leaving the ancient city draped in a tapestry of shadows.

The darkness is his friend. Onwards to the precincts of the great church. There is a place, a quiet doorway where a brazier glows. One side illuminated, the other obscured. He will stand and wait in the gloom.

He knows who he is waiting for. Not the exact person. But knows it will be someone young, unsuspecting. Weak. Someone he can startle, upset, humiliate.

The younger brother pricks his ears; his hearing is impeccable. He has learned to decipher footsteps. The heavy tread of clerics, the patter of serving women, the light scuffling step of the many children that populate the precinct, choristers and kitchen maids, the lads who wait on cardinals and clean out the horses.

He bides his time, slowly unlacing his breeches. He must pace himself. Not win the race too soon. He laughs. His brother thinks he has no self-control, yet in this act, this place, he has perfect restraint, iron self-discipline.

There they come now. The person he has been waiting for.

Luigi Bernini steps like a fox from the shadows, his much larger frame pinning the young girl in the doorway.

She looks down and recoils. But the man sees only fearful admiration. The power, the pleasure he feels from the shock of his victim is palpable; he has controlled this this girl without even touching her. Provoked a reaction. His gratification peaks. Hand jerks.

In this moment, Luigi Bernini feels invincible.

Chapter Twenty-Two

'To the Country'

November 1636

Miraculously, Lorenzo has agreed to two days. I fabricate a story for Giuliana and Tiberia, telling them I am to be away on business with Matteo, and to my surprise they ask not one question. Instead, my husband takes himself off with Vincenzo – I know not where.

The merchant's villa is as beautiful as Caterina promised. Set high on the hills outside the city, just over half a day's travel from Rome, it is built from white stone, which reflects the sun in a blinding glare. Around the veranda, lemon trees are planted like sentries with olive groves beyond. At the end of the garden there is a pond, dark and cool, in which fat carp idle, while the shadows of kites pass overhead.

Being with Lorenzo is a rarefied place in which only he and I exist. Living for the moment we reach for each other's bodies, touch dominating sight as we explore, learning to traverse the ordinance of each other's bodies; the dip of a back, the softness of an inner thigh, the hollow under an ear, and the sharpness of a collar bone.

We take shelter in this place. Within hours we are living like the cicadas, according to the rhythm of our bodies, the rise and fall of our desire, making love then sleeping until hunger and thirst drive us from bed, paying no heed to the needs of anyone or anything but ourselves.

We lay small foundations. Sharing our past. Creating our own castle, memory by memory. I tell Lorenzo of Papa and a childhood filled with music and stories. How the lightness of Giuliana's voice fills my heart, and the sweet way my small sisters would nuzzle into me, their baby hair softly grazing my cheeks. Lorenzo shares stories of duty: the sting of his father's hand on the back of his legs, the exhortations to be better, deliver more, to surpass everyone, and the guilty relief he had felt when Pietro died. He makes me promise not to breathe a word.

Lorenzo runs his hand through his hair and shares how his brother Luigi is becoming increasingly erratic, difficult to manage. He has spoiled the boy by indulging him. But then does he not have the Bernini name to protect? Not long ago a man – a father – had come banging on the door, half demented, demanding to know what Luigi Bernini's intentions towards his daughter were. It had been a costly mess, Lorenzo says with a sigh. More expensive than usual, because this time the girl had been a virgin, and was willing to swear in court the child was a Bernini. In this way secrets pass between us, shoring up the walls in which we are bound.

* * *

Below the villa, about fifteen minutes' walk into the valley, is a village. A humble place with rough-hewn stone cottages, populated with people who live off the land. No one here has heard of Il Cavaliere, the great Bernini, and for this alone, it is perfect.

The women talk, know I am from the villa on the hill, and have mistaken our desire for privacy and the ring on my finger for something more. When I pass through the market they tempt me with nuggets of ricotta, rich and creamy, soaked in honey or steeped with the scent of rosemary. Slim-hipped girls call to me like sirens, 'Take a sip, signora! Your husband needs his fire!' They laugh as they offer small clay tumblers of clear spirit which burns with the taste of citrus blossom. I buy it all, and return laden with good, simple food.

Lorenzo is stood shirtless at the table, pestle and mortar in hand, grinding herbs. There is a pan over the fire, in which he is frying small orange-red tomatoes, and onions which have turned golden and slippery on the heat. Stood on the table is an earthenware jar of sardines preserved in oil, which he must have brought with him.

I walk up behind Lorenzo and place my hands around his waist, gently resting my head against the place where his shoulder blades meet.

'What is all this?'

'My mother used to cook this dish when I was a child. I remembered it and wanted to taste it again. Wanted you to taste it. Here,' he holds up the jar for me to smell. I sniff and take in pungent fish, sharp green oil and briny salt.

'It's how I imagine the sea to smell,' I tell him.

'You have never been?'

'Never left Rome. I came when I was a small child, and have only ever known my district, the city. This is the furthest I have ever been.'

He frowns. 'One day I shall take you to the coast, and you will stand and let the small waves wash your feet and you shall smell of the ocean.'

The thought fills me with unbridled longing.

When he has finished cooking, Lorenzo serves the tomatoes and sardines with bread I brought from the village. We sit at the broad table in the kitchen used by the cook for preparing feasts, ignoring the echoing dining hall upstairs. 'If we are to live simply, then we shall dine as such,' he declares.

We eat like famished animals.

'It is very good.' I say in between mouthfuls. 'Is there anything you cannot do?'

He laughs and shrugs. 'It is the food my mother cooked. Dishes she brought from Naples, recipes she learned at her own grandmother's knee and taught me. Food is like language. It anchors us. Teaches us who we are and where we have come from. Binds us to our own. This is a Bernini recipe. So, you see, Venus, you are mine. You are a Bernini.'

If only familial connection was so easily transferred.

After we finish our meal, we sit outside in the autumn-nipped air and watch the sun fall slowly from the sky. In the distance, brown tilled fields become dark woods, which morph into verdant hills and shadowed valleys, stretching until the earth meets the sky at the blazing edge of the horizon. It makes me feel infinitesimally large and unfeasibly small all at once. Lorenzo and I do not speak, but rest in silence, arms draped languidly over each other. Kindred spirits.

Spending unaccustomed hours with Lorenzo has helped me to understand how he operates when I am not with him. His art runs through him, bubbling ferociously, spitting out ideas which he must commit to paper the moment they seize him. The villa is littered with charcoal drawings. They lie everywhere, across every surface and the floor, bits of parchment scratched with lines of half-formed things, the beginnings of an idea as yet indecipherable, abandoned too soon for another thought. I see how his mind races, with new contemplations, occurring in such frequency he can hardly contain them.

I am astonished when he sighs and says, 'This is the greatest peace I have felt in years.' The stark black lines, the scattered paper, none of it speaks of peace. 'It's you, Venus,' he breathes. 'Knowing you're mine.' Lorenzo shifts, arm still round mine, but it's gripping harder now. 'You are mine, aren't you?'

The question takes me aback. I start to answer, but he does not wait for my reply.

'Tell me you never lie with him now?' Lorenzo almost growls. 'Promise me . . . promise me he does not lay a finger on you.'

'It . . . I . . . no! I could not. He is my husband, but we do not . . .'

'Do you swear it? I could not bear to find out you had been together.' I feel Lorenzo's fingers digging deeper into my flesh, and I am thrilled and horrified all at once by this sudden depth of feeling. 'If you and your husband . . .' he continues. 'I would know. And I could not bear it. Could not live.'

I raise my free hand to his face, not knowing where these thoughts, this jealousy has come from. Alarmed by the intensity, my only thought is to reassure him. 'I am yours. Never think anything else. I promise. I am yours.'

He sighs. 'Do I sound like a lunatic?'

'Nay. Not at all. Your life is a rush. Here we have found time.' I think of Luigi, of the Fabbrica, of Matteo and what I had thought we would be. 'A small peace.'

He pulls himself straighter, not looking at me, but watching the dusk-swept horizon in stillness. 'Who would I be if I did not rush? Do I not complete commissions faster than any other artist? Do I not have the boldest concepts, the bravest of convictions to fashion impossible structures from the elements of earth and stone?'

A fleeting thought brushes past at the very edge of my sight. A nameless waxen face. My mother. His brother.

'You would still be Lorenzo Bernini,' I say. 'These things are not the sum of you. Am I not here? I am not here for Bernini the great artist. But Lorenzo, who is a good man.'

He grips my hand. 'This is why I need you ... when you talk like this. You are a balm and a poison all at once. A physical pain. I am a wretched sinner who steals men's wives. But it is because you are rare. Your intellect. The fire which flickers within. There is something about you which cannot be contained.'

It is strange to be talked of in this way. To be desired so. It makes my chest swell and my heart flutter with a wild recklessness.

I squeeze his hand. 'I understand,' I say. But I am not sure I do.

The sun has dropped below the horizon, and the light, so fantastical just a few minutes before, is beginning to be swallowed by the inky night.

'Come,' Lorenzo says, standing and offering his hand to pull me up. ''Tis time for bed.'

We light candles and lock the door, then climb the stairs to the great canopied bed which lies unmade. Unlike most of our previous encounters, which have been frenzied, lustful and quick, here we have the privilege of time to make slow sport.

Lorenzo walks to me in deliberate steps and with unhurried movements begins to work my bodice free. I deny my desire to pull him to me, burying my impulse to have him immediately. Instead, I allow his fingers to move delicately across my skin, tracing faint muscles in my arms, lingering across my breasts, across my jawbone and behind my neck. As night descends, darkening the room to blackened firewood, Lorenzo pulls me down onto the bed. A brush of his head at the top of my thigh, a soundless tongue. I feel a circling desire building like a furnace at my centre.

A metamorphosis. I am molten. Mythical. Malleable.

Forged to woman.

Later, in the stagnant dead of night, I sleep. The kind of earthly sleep that comes when you are sated and the air is cooler.

Lorenzo begins to shake me. 'Venus!' He more shouts than whispers.

'Venus!' He says it again and again, a tone of urgency lacing his voice.

I am slow to shake off the heavy slumbers but open my eyes when my mind finally hears his insistent tone.

'My love,' I ask anxiously, 'are you hurt?'

'Nay! I am not hurt.' Lorenzo jiggles my shoulders, his grip hard and unforgiving. 'Oh, Venus, wake up, I have something to show you!' He holds a candle to my face, my eyes flutter, not yet adjusted, having so recently been shrouded in dark.

'Wake up, Venus!'

'What time is it?' I ask thickly.

'Night. Deep night. But that does not matter. Look, I have been working!' The notes of his voice are brittle, as if about to break.

My eyes, finally used to the meagre light, look into his, which are shining as if possessed. This morning I had gently wiped Lorenzo's body with a lavender-scented linen cloth, lifting his arms, running the cloth over the dark thatch of hair that nestles in his armpits, along the line which traces from his chest to his groin. Afterwards, I had rubbed scented oil into his smooth skin, and he smelled sweet. Now, his brow is studded with small beads of sweat, and the sweetness has been overtaken by a sour, stale odour which rises from his naked body.

Such is the chaos about him, his eyes, lit by the slice of candle-light across his face, are so wild, I wonder for a moment whether Lorenzo has taken a potion, laudanum or poppy.

'Are you sure you are not ailing? With an ague or fever?'

'I am quite well! It is you whose wits are slow! I said come!'

He tugs impatiently at my arm and begins pulling me from the bed. I am naked as a babe, and the night air feels cruel against my warm skin. I try to fall back against the sheets, but he tugs again. I hiss and kick at him, like an old cat being moved from its favourite spot in the sun. 'Leave me be. I am resting, I will look later.'

I make to fix my head upon the pillow, but he pulls again. 'Venus, you little hellcat. I said come!'

It is no use; I shall not be allowed to rest. 'You win,' I say with one last kick. 'I shall come, but let me rouse myself.'

The air is cold and my skin rises to little bumps. I see Lorenzo's shirt on the floor. As I slip it over my head taking in a lungful of his scent, as familiar as my own.

In the corner of the room there are huge sheets of paper covered in drawings. It is a frenzy. An outpouring from his mind. I am shaken by the intensity of the effort it must have taken to produce so many finished etchings in the time I have been asleep.

I stare at them, not knowing what to say.

'I am sometimes afraid,' Lorenzo says eventually.

'Afraid? What have you got to be afraid of? You are Bernini. You can do anything.'

'That God will punish me. Take away my ideas. Injure me so I can no longer practice my craft. Cause some great calamity, so people will say, "Lorenzo Bernini has lost his touch. Has reached for the sun, and has flown too close, and now is plummeting to earth, the fire of heaven having melted is wings."'

I want to ask why Lorenzo believes God would punish him, but I know. I hold his body close to mine and feel sinews and muscles flexing under moon-hued skin. I stroke his hair but do not offer any words, for it is not the comfort he seeks. Another secret bound into the wall of our fortress.

He shows me the drawings. Great fountains, elaborate structures gushing water at such a rate, it seems the gods have sent a flood to Earth. An elephant – I recognise the beast as Don Diego, who came to Rome about six years ago. Papa and I joined the crowd to watch him walk, the large ears and mournful eyes, and the marvellous tricks he performed with a trunk that moved like a hand, but this rendition is something altogether more detailed. Astonishing even. The swiftly drawn lines capturing the bulk, the shape, but something more: the maudlin, noble spirit of the animal, as if it is about to lumber off the page. Lorenzo has captured everything perfectly. From memory.

'You see, Venus!' Lorenzo cries. 'You see what you do for me? What you make me do? This is my penance. For my perfidy and sin. To redefine. To create the world anew and place beautiful objects among mortals.'

'I see it,' I reassure him. 'I see it all.'

Then Lorenzo picks up a length of charcoal and starts to scribble again, and I know I have lost him to the other side of this wide, moonlit night.

Chapter Twenty-Three

'A Good Subject'

April 1637

It is seven months since I became Lorenzo's lover, and I am becoming many Costanzas: mistress, wife, friend and daughter.

Every Sunday Matteo and I still dutifully eat with Papa and Tiberia, mutton or pike, sometimes with guests, sometimes without. We call each other husband and wife, and smile indulgently at each other's jokes, we talk of plans to move, of the success of our new business buying and selling art and old statues, which keeps me busy and is gaining customers and a good reputation. To my surprise, I find I am more and more content to be childless, but I know it is with quiet disappointment that my parents stop asking about the state of my womb.

At home, Matteo and I live like brother and sister, not man and wife. I am learning how to manage his accounts and negotiations on shipments abroad, and he is grateful for my help. We talk of trade and patrons, but not Lorenzo. My husband never asks me where

I am going nor when I shall return; he knows I am to Lorenzo's bed, and that I shall always come home. We are married and must remain so; we live united by day, but when the moon rises we go our separate ways.

Lorenzo sends for me almost nightly, and we are lovers of such fervency that society beyond the Fabbrica knows, but I have no care. The idea that anyone could stop me ... stop us ... is laughable. Lorenzo Bernini is not a person who tolerates being told what to do. He cares not for who people ought to be, only who they are.

* * *

This evening, I am to Lorenzo's great house by the Basilica. The maids are no longer confused when I arrive, and it is always Stefano who greets me, leading me by the light of a candle up the wooden staircase to the first-floor studio. It is a place I have come to love, like the man who resides within. At night you can see the stars flame from the huge windows, and through the rising smoke, the great dome of Michelangelo, imposing itself on the skyline to remind all of Rome of the glory of the Church and the genius of its artists.

As I step into the studio, I have the vaguest sense a chaos is forming. Lorenzo is working harder than ever, the paperwork for multiple commissions lies about the floor. A strong smell of oranges pervades; Lorenzo has taken to eating them night and day to keep his wild humours at bay. There is discarded peel on his desk and on the floor, spent and coiled at the edges.

'Venus,' he steps to me, his immaculate black eyes shining. 'I have a gift.'

Laid neatly on a chair are women's clothes, new and freshly pressed.

'For you.'

I know what is expected, this is not the first time Lorenzo has bought me clothes. Indeed, the first lovers' gift he ever made me was a new gown. It is a thing I am most grateful for, that Lorenzo likes me to dress in a manner befitting his status, in colours he believes are flattering to my countenance. Matteo never cared much for my wardrobe.

I peel off my petticoats and loosen my sleeves. There is even a new chemise for me, edged in lace. The skirt and bodice are made from a burgundy silk, shot with grey and black, which shimmers like a butterfly's wings. The deep red-purple colour reminds me of ripe plums, or a blossoming bruise, depending on the way the light falls,

I carefully place the skirt over my head, and pull the laces on the body tight, so that I am transformed into his desire. Lorenzo looks at me approvingly, and motions to the full-length looking glass at the end of the studio. Each time I regard myself, I am amazed by how little is left of Costanza, the girl who grew up in San Lucina and had to beg a dowry from the Church. Now I am Costanza, a woman worthy of adoration.

'You like what you see?' he asks, gently.

'Very much,' I respond. 'I always do.'

'I am glad, for I take great care in choosing exactly what would suit you best. Now come, sit here, and let's arrange the dress in such a way that the shadows play across it.'

I sit and he moves about me, pulling the fabric this way and that, relaxing my shoulders with his hands, and turning my face. A strand of hair falls loose across my brow, and Lorenzo tenderly pushes it back. I flush, and he smiles. 'You must learn to be a good sitter, Venus, and not care about the artist's gaze.'

Lorenzo has taken to sketching me incessantly, whenever we are together. He stands some distance away, his eyes darting between the page and me, so fast it is a wonder his rapid movements do not make his head sore. I cannot see it, but I hear his hand skimming the page. A look, a mark. A look, a mark. It goes on at a relentless pace, the sound of his charcoal grazing the paper.

He explains sometimes, 'Every sitter is unique. The measurements of their face, the slope of their shoulders. If a candle is placed behind someone it is possible to recognise them just from their shadow; no two people have their heads placed on their shoulders in the same way.'

The truth is I do not find it comfortable, sitting still for so long under his intense scrutiny. My own eyes flicker around the room, at the statues, headless torsos and bodyless limbs, plaster casts of faces, canvases of kings and saints, women dressed as the playthings of gods. I long to see what he has drawn. How he has configured me, how those marks have rendered my spirit in charcoal upon the page. But he makes no such offer, and I do not ask.

At last, he declares, 'I am done for now.'

He takes my hand and leads me to the pallet in the corner of his studio, where he begins to peel off the layers of clothes I have so recently put on. I feel a pulse of desire with each garment that drops to the floor. New lovers experience a certain blindness so that they cannot see each other as mortals. Instead, they believe the force of their love to be such that nothing on this earth can stop it. That is how Lorenzo and I are. My body constantly craving his touch, feeling ecstasy when his embrace finally comes.

* * *

Concealed in the shadows of the landing upstairs, Luigi watches as Costanza, his brother's latest whore, leaves. This one has lasted longer than most, with her high forehead and noble nose. And those lips. He'd have her in an instant.

Lorenzo is returning. His brother does not go back to his studio, but instead makes for the bedroom, so Luigi slips into the work-room, a place he should only enter if invited.

He wants to see where his brother makes love to her, the site of Lorenzo's deepening desire. Luigi knows his brother well; Lorenzo is infatuated.

On the easel are a series of studies. Freshly made, well executed. Costanza in the costume his brother has provided. Luigi knows all the tricks: the way Lorenzo likes to dress his women, presenting the clothes as gifts. Well-dressed women in sumptuous costumes, befitting of the title 'Bernini's lover'. The little puttanas always too avaricious to ask any questions, just pathetically grateful to have a new gown.

Luigi looks at the sketches with a practised eye, for he too has great talent. Lorenzo will not be satisfied with this effort. Although the likeness is fair, the light falling on the hollows of her skin and the dimensions of her face (one would expect nothing less), Lorenzo has failed to capture the complexity of the girl. The sensuousness of her look and movement, coupled with the youthful unsophistication of her gaze.

Then he sees a pile of clothes in the corner. Her clothes. What a gift. Luigi kneels among them. He discards the outer skirts, it's not what he is looking for. He wants her chemise, the material she has worn next to her skin. He finds it tucked beneath the rest and pulls it out. The cloth is rougher than his own shirt, and he likes the thought, that she is not as good as he, her accent and manners unpolished.

He lifts the shirt to his nose and inhales her scent; it is musky and sharp, but sweet, with notes of camphor, eucalyptus and lavender. There are marks where the material has pressed against her skin, and he feels aroused at the thought of it. At touching her, feeling his hands on her body, pulling her to him. Hand in breeches,

Luigi lets out a low moan in the gloaming of the studio. His breath is hot and fast now, his body spiralling in a need which spreads from his loin to every limb, then he spasms unsteadily onto her clothes. This is *his* mark. He sinks to his knees and feels a darkness released from within – and something more, a change of ownership. That somehow Lorenzo no longer owns the right to this girl, because he has had her too.

Luigi picks up the chemise and roughly wipes his hand, using the cloth to clean in between his fingers and across his palm, before tossing it onto the floor.

Chapter Twenty-Four

'Birthday Party'

April 1637

From the gardens of the grand villas comes the scent of blossom, delicate and sweet, a portent of good things to come.

Usually, a birthday only involves a gathering of the family, but Tiberia has decreed Cecilia's sixteenth birthday celebrations must involve new associates, as well as old friends. In this city it is one thing to feed your own family, but quite another to feed someone else's.

Neighbours from the nearby streets begin to assemble. People who dandled me on their lap as a child and gave me candied fruit on saints' days, and their children too, now grown, arrive with mewling babes of their own.

Judging by the number of dull, bookish young men in attendance, I have an inkling Tiberia fancies a more sober profession than sculptor for Cecilia. While she is enamoured of the change in Matteo's circumstances, she is less keen on the new dresses and parties.

The day brings much noise and laughter, and as the sky begins to leech its light, the men pick up wooden stools and make their way down the courtyard. This is my favourite moment of any party: when Papa and his friends take up their instruments and play the tunes I've known for ever – songs about changing seasons, heart-break and love.

Papa sets down his special stool, the one where the edges have been smoothed to perfectly fit the shape of his legs. He lifts a small wooden pipe to his mouth and begins to play, the trill of the notes pricking the early evening air with their sharpness.

He is joined by the old boys, who take up residence on seats beside him. Signor Faggio, with his knotted hands and warm-timbred lute; Signor Cacciatore, bent nearly double over his viol. And Father Collina, as lively as a cricket thanks to the afternoon's hospitality, blessing the small troupe of music makers before taking up a drum. They look to Papa, who counts the beats, and the melody begins.

I am my father's daughter. No sooner has the music started than I grab Giuliana's hand and pull her into the middle of the yard. When we were girls, our bodies still babyish and soft, we would dance for hours. Now, when I grip Giuliana's waist, I can feel her hip bones poking sharply from under her skirts.

As the pace picks up, Giuliana and I are forced into wilder, ever more inelegant forms of dance, skipping and clapping, twisting and twirling, our faces flush from the pace of the music and the exuberance of life running through us. There is no place for Signor Giovanni's mannered and measured steps here.

We whirl around faster, our skirts flying and the air filling with our laughter. Others join us, and soon we are surrounded by neighbours who whoop and stamp their feet as they dance. I spot Cecilia, standing at the edge of the courtyard, trying but failing to show displeasure at our antics.

'Come!' I shout. Cecilia shakes her head. 'Come, birthday girl. Dance with us!' She shakes her head again, but I brook no reluctance.

Instead, Giuliana and I pull Cecilia into the middle of the crowd as she feigns unwillingness. Before long the three of us are holding hands, hopping madly in a circle, Cecilia's small body, usually so taut, loosening with every step as she bounces along to the music. Finally, Cleria and my little brother Michele push through the throng, desperate to join the merriment of their older sisters.

Lorenzo, I think idly, would enjoy such a spectacle. The warmth of this thought turns hot. What if someone in the crowd could read my mind? These are good people, who work hard and still have little. They would see me in an instant for what I am. An unfaithful wife. I kick away all notions of Lorenzo, grip my sisters' hands harder, and urge them to go faster.

The musicians take a break and as we leave the makeshift dancefloor I see Marco, Giuliana's husband, waiting for her.

'Can't he leave you be, even allow you a little pleasure?' I whisper to my friend.

'He is my husband,' she explains, hurrying.

Marco pulls Giuliana to him, 'I have been lingering a while, did you not see?'

It is I who answer, in my sweetest voice. 'We were dancing Marco, did you not see?'

There is a flare of hostility in his eyes. 'My wife is needed elsewhere.'

Giuliana pulls at Marco's arm, 'Come, let us find the boys.'

My siblings have already left to find their friends, so I join the women sat on stools lined up against the wall.

I rest for a moment, eyes closed, listening to the sounds of my neighbourhood: mothers swapping stories, children shrieking, the loud grumble of well-wined men complaining about the world. A shadow falls over me, a guttural breath, the sound of skirts being patted down, like goose wings flapping against the fabric.

'How do, Mother?' I greet Tiberia without opening my eyes. 'It is a good gathering, full of happy company. I hope you are well pleased?'

Tiberia sits next to me with a loud wheeze. 'I saw you making great revelry with your sisters.'

My heart sinks, and my hackles rise like a street dog. I sit up and open my eyes to look at my stepmother. Her face is in shadow. She looks older than I remember, the creases deeper, the rattle of her chest crueller.

'It was not a show, just little fun, 'tis all. To dance on a spring evening while Cecilia is still a maid.' I pause. 'And for Giuliana and me to feel our youth again.'

Tiberia clasps her hands and lays them on her lap without looking at me. 'You mistake me. I do not seek to admonish. It's a long while since I have seen Cecilia smile, 'tis all. My daughter is so angry with the world.' Tiberia pauses to take in the scene. 'So vexed with me.'

Tiberia turns, and she looks sad. 'You may not believe it, but all I have ever wanted is for my children to be happy.' She sucks air through her teeth.

I do not respond.

'I may have been hard on you, but it was for the best. So you would have the security of a good marriage and a man who provides.'

Given Tiberia's reflective mood I seize my moment. 'Why didn't you tell me about what happens between a husband and wife? On their marriage night. I didn't know what to do.'

She sighs. 'You found out quick enough, didn't you?'

'Do you not think Cecilia should be told?'

'Nay!' Tiberia's tone is shrill.

I think of the cold nights, the reluctance of my husband, then of the warmth of Lorenzo's breath on my body. 'Is being prepared not better?'

She sucks at the air again. 'I wanted to protect you.'

'Protect me? From what? Being a loving wife? All you did was keep me in darkness. A marriage bed shrouded in mystery does not make the best start, I can tell you.'

'Shhh,' Tiberia hisses. 'Do you want the whole district to know your business?'

'You care too much what the neighbours think.'

'And you, too little,' Tiberia counters. 'My silence protected you from scandal.'

I think of Tiberia, with her starched caps, constant prayers, dark eyes which judge every action, and a little snort escapes from my mouth. 'What would you know about scandal?'

'More than you would imagine.'

At this moment Cleria rushes up to me and flings her arms around my neck, giving me a wet, childish kiss, before depositing her poppet in my lap. 'Will you keep Juliet safe for me?' she asks, eye reflecting the seriousness of the request.

'Of course; I will protect her with a lion's heart.' I reply solemnly, picking up the doll and kissing it on the forehead as a demonstration of my oath.

It is enough to satisfy Cleria, who runs to re-join her friends. When she is out of earshot, Tiberia begins speaking again, but there is a change in her voice: it is thick and choked.

'You love my children well.' We watch Cleria playing cat's cradle, her little hands deftly pinching and turning the scrap of string. 'I was a little sister once.'

The revelation is like a bee sting, sharp and shocking. 'I've never heard you speak of your family.'

Tiberia watches Papa and his friends. They are laughing and joking; he catches us looking at him and nods, his face folding into a smile.

'Her name was Teresa. She was a year older than me.'

'Why didn't you tell me?'

'For the same reason I didn't tell you about the marriage bed: to keep you from harm.'

'What harm could knowing about your sister possibly do me?'

'Plenty!' spits Tiberia. 'I adored Teresa. When she was about Cecilia's age, Teresa was told the truth of men and women in such a way that she craved love. It happened soon enough. With the son of a merchant. Teresa fell with child. Unwed. The boy denied all knowledge. My parents cast her out, and the whole town watched as my sister got fatter and fatter, living off alms.' Tiberia pauses; my own breath is shallow. 'Teresa and her child died. No one would wed me after that. Shamed. Sullied by scandal, unwanted by men, discarded by the town.'

I look at my father. 'But Leonardo?'

'Knew me as a girl; we were neighbours. He was older. When your mother died, he was a widower with a child in need of a competent wife. He took me away. I have done my best to give you what I very nearly did not have: a future.'

I am too stunned to speak. My father married Tiberia and in doing so saved her – and probably me.

'That is why your love for your sister is appreciated.' The glint reappears in Tiberia's eye. 'And why I would stop at naught to protect you, and them, from having their reputations besmirched. Because it can cost everything.'

Chapter Twenty-Five

'An Offer of Help'

May 1637

As the days grow warmer, a deeper current flows.

While the mortal danger Giuliana faced has long since passed, some deeper malady persists. My friend no longer laughs as she once did, the colour of her skin has become a permanent grey, and she suffers from pains which leave her bent double in the middle of the street.

Tiberia prescribes fresh air, before the heat of the city brings the sickness. 'You girls go for a walk by the river,' she all but demands. 'Spend some time in your own company, there is precious little opportunity for it. I shall watch the children.'

We pass through the cross hatch of alleyways, past gardens alive with scratching hens, barking dogs and goats chewing, eying us philosophically as we pass. It is a cloudless day, the air warm, and there is a sense of newness, fresh scents, a slight breeze. Everything is shifting: insects crawling in the grass, the flutter of butterfly wings, quivering stems, and the constant shake of leaf-dappled shadows.

While we stroll, we talk of the small things, reacquainting our-selves with each other's lives. The young dog Lorenzo gave me, who I named Bess after the bear, meanders at my feet, for our pace is slow.

'How is Marco?'

'He is better. He drinks ... less.'

I note her hesitancy and hear my husband's voice. Good money after bad.

'How is the gaming?'

It is dangerous territory, but I worry Giuliana may slip from my view once more, and this time I will not be able to pull her from the rapids overtaking her life and she will drown in Marco's debts. And after all, did I not rescue her? I have a stake in her future, for we are bound.

'He is ...' She is choosing her words well. 'Marco tells me he is being more cautious. He knows that you and Matteo did a won-drous thing for us and is determined never to allow us to reach such a sorry state again. He has a new job, nearer home. He seems to be doing well.'

'The only way to stay safe from debtors is not to bet any stakes.' It sounds glib, and I immediately regret the simplicity of the statement.

Giuliana holds onto my arm as she picks her way over some stones, her weight hardly registering. 'I cannot ask the impossible. My husband is a man with appetites. I pray incessantly he finds a way to curb his excesses.' She looks skyward. 'At the moment, it seems the Lord is listening.'

I have a question which burns and know I must ask it, as Giuliana will not survive another birth. 'Has he appetite for his marriage rights?'

We have reached the river where the sun dances on the water in little waves, and as we walk the grass feels fresh beneath our feet. Giuliana does not answer me, nor does she look in my direction, but instead holds her head resolutely out to the river. 'He is owed his rights as a husband, as any husband is, and he takes them.'

I wince. 'If he loved you . . .'

'Love!' Giuliana says, her voice cracking. 'Love? Oh Costanza. Do not give me such talk. You are not a girl but a woman – and married.' She takes a breath. 'Men must have their due. It is what I promised at the altar in front of God. It must be borne, like all things.'

Now is the moment I have been waiting for. 'What if I had a physick? A potion which could stop you from begetting a child?'

Giuliana continues to walk.

I press on with my words. 'So even if you must lie with Marco, your body has time to repair itself from the damage done birthing Leonardo.' I catch her arm. 'Giuliana, you will surely die if you have another child so soon. You must know that!' She continues to walk, and I am sure she is thinking over my words, so I continue. 'I had never heard of such a thing until a few months ago, but many use it. It is a secret passed from woman to woman, so we may not face the ordeal of the childbed when our bodies are worn. An offer of help.'

'Pray, who told you of such help, for you to tell it to me?'

'Someone from the sculptor's circle who understands the mysteries of women. It is common practice among those who know.'

'What you suggest is against all morality.' Her words are completely unexpected and come in a breathless fury. 'You are so mixed up in this godforsaken world, you have forgotten ... forgotten where you came from, and how good people live.'

My defences spring, ready and spiked, for how dare she stand in such judgement upon me.

'You know not of what you speak. This is what women must do, not to be beholden to men and their own body. For we cannot say no. And for you to stand in adjudication, like the priest in the pulpit. This world in which I move knows more about humanity than any of yours and I am glad for it.'

'What horseshit!' I have never heard Giuliana swear in her life. Her face is reddening. 'It is not humanity but heresy, Costanza. You talk of preventing life from forming with such ease, but it is a mortal sin. You stand there in your fancy clothes as if all is the same, but your reputation is being passed from lip to lip by the gossips of the district, ruminated upon, then spat out like soured milk. You think you are so much better than all of us, but you are not. What are you becoming?'

I examine Giuliana. My friend whose life is filled with babies, and puke, a husband who can hardly provide for her and pays her no kindness at all, and I feel a great pity.

'I know it is a shock, but you should think on . . .'

'Stop!' Giuliana ceases walking and holds up her hand as if to repel me, her lichen eyes set deep in their sockets, a ruination of black shadows.

'Do not. I live a hard but good life. I *will not lie* to my husband. I will not damn my soul to an eternity of torment. Because if you take this physick, Costanza, a fiery hell is where you are destined.'

Her words reverberate through me. 'You think I will be sent to hell?'

Giuliana looks at me and something changes in her face, the tumult slowing. Then she says quietly. 'What has happened to us, and we have only been twenty-three summers on this earth? I worry so much for you.'

'And I you. You were dying, Giuliana. I love you too much to allow that, you must take the physi—'

'God's blood, Costanza!' she erupts. 'Can you not see? You did not save me. The Lord in his infinite wisdom did, and I shall not betray his mercy by perverting the natural order.'

She turns away and begins to walk once more, a slight figure making her way along the crowded riverbank. Our conversation is done.

I run after her. I want to shake her and beg her to take the physick, but I do not. Instead, I walk in silence with Giuliana, my friend who I have loved since a child, the woman who knows me better than all on earth. Our quietude cuts at me like a knife, and I tell myself acceptance is the cost of true love.

Chapter Twenty-Six

'An Intimate Portrait'

June 1637

In the sour hours between midnight and daybreak, Lorenzo is awake.

She is asleep beside him, her face upturned, as she has been for nearly a year now, ever since that morning she came so unexpectedly to him. He feels an irresistible urge to touch her, to run his fingers over her flesh, to indent the mounds of her cheeks, to push his fingers into her mouth, which is slightly open, showing her small teeth, almost like a child's. He watches as her inhale and exhale with each breath, deep and slow, an arm flung across her breast, which lies uncovered in her slumbered immodesty.

Was it always like this, with the others? The burning skin, slick-bodied dance rising and falling, an innate understanding. He wants to wake her; such is his necessity to hold her. Touch her. Enter her.

But he stops.

The sculptor thinks of the words his brother, Luigi, uses about

Costanza when he thinks no one is listening. Slut. Whore. The way these words make him feel like a rapidly unspooling thread, as if he is experiencing a great unravelling. In this moment the sculptor realises something astonishing. A piece of information so rare in its clarity, it both moves and disturbs him in equal measures.

Looking at Costanza's soft face in the flickering light, Lorenzo Bernini understands that he loves her. What's more, that he loves her in a way that cannot be contained, because she has become as necessary to him as breathing or eating. Another thought rises in him, restless like a wild beast. He has never depended on anyone. Not even his mother.

For a moment he hates Costanza. He hates her for making him so vulnerable. For speaking her mind. For coming to him in such distress he felt compelled to comfort her. But, most of all, Lorenzo hates Costanza for taking what is not hers. His steadiness. His certitude. His heart.

He hates himself too. For having ceded this control of his heart to her, in all its red, raw, beating glory. Now that it thrums in a state of such childish need, she could kill him if she wanted to, by not loving him back.

There is something else. He understands he must take control.

He watches her. Examines her, the curve of her eyelashes, the bones of her brow, the soft curls at the nape of her neck, the folds of her flesh as it falls over the muscles of her arms, the way her ribs fall fallow as she exhales.

An idea forms.

An idea of such audacity, he laughs into the spring night air, and the world falls silent for a moment in response.

He will make her immortal.

He will create a portrait of Costanza for himself. Not on commission, not for sale, but for his own collection.

It will not be like any other marble woman; it will not be an imagined goddess, or an immobile rendition of a staid princess, her royalty wrapped up in a dull-eyed stillness. No, this portrait will look as a woman does. He will capture a moment in time, as if Costanza were to speak, or had just risen from their lovemaking. A speaking portrait.

Love is by its nature tactile. It is his language.

Lorenzo begins to imagine the stone. What people seldom realise is each piece of marble is unique. It contains flaws, just like people. Sometimes the flaws are deeply hidden and revealed too late.

Like the crack which appeared across the forehead of his master-piece, the bust of Cardinal Scipione Borghese. Standing in front of his patron, the sculptor had taken his chisel and lightly tapped the statue's forehead, grinning at the Cardinal's unfolding horror as the split appeared – only to produce a new marble portrait, as good as the first. Such a fine joke.

That is the beauty and terror of marble. It has lain so long, pushed by the pressure of the earth, the matter is temperamental; each blow just one step from disaster. The breathless surge, the heightened anxiety, is when he feels most alive.

This portrait of Costanza will be his, and he will work on it alone. The ultimate expression of desire and love. Dante and Shakespeare courted perfection; he, Bernini, would give Costanza all the vitality of a living, breathing, carnal woman.

He gets up, his naked form reflected in the mirrors about his studio, his body thin and lunar white, his long-veined feet cold on the floor. He cares not. He needs to find his paper and make a start.

Where is the damned charcoal? In the low light of the fire Lorenzo rummages among the debris on the table, which is covered in fine marble dust, dulled velvet, paper coated in the light, dry particles. Here it is. He pulls at a pile and chooses a large piece of paper, and a board on which to rest it.

He has left Costanza on the linens and furs. She sleeps on, unaware he is watching her, his crow eyes darting from her face to the page, measuring her aspect, the orbital bone shining above her brow, the depth of her lips, the cleft of her chin and the tilt of her nose. He will examine her from all sides, at all angles, so when the viewer walks around the portrait, they will see her from every perspective just as she is. His hand flies across the page, marking and outlining, flashes of black denoting density and shadow. Collar bones, the slide of her chest, the folds of her neck.

Eventually he can stand it no more and slides back onto the bed, where he presses against her, his desire evident, placing precise, demanding little kisses down the back of her neck and across her shoulders. 'Venus,' he whispers. She stirs and turns instinctively towards him, tasting of stale wine and honey, and he wants to cry he needs her so much.

Chapter Twenty-Seven

'Susanna'

July 1637

I am a better wife, now I am Lorenzo's lover.

Matteo remains a constant of brotherly love. As he slices his bread in the mornings, he tells me he worries for me. He says the risks are grave for him, but the only thing a woman has is her reputation. And as he passes the oil, I tell him I remain steadfast in my choice and repeat that while we are both happy, who but us should give a care? As I pull my husband's jacket onto his wide shoulders, he reminds me that we have the protection of Il Cavaliere, which is why no one cares, and nothing lasts for ever. As I stand on my toes to kiss his cheek, I tell him I am undaunted by worries because love is infinite.

After Matteo has left, I open my chest to inspect my wardrobe, the contents of which have been exclusively paid for by the Bernini scudi. Each outfit selected and commissioned by my lover, the cut, the colour, the material – each chosen with an artist's eye.

Lorenzo will collect me at ten. Where once I would have dallied and become distracted, now I get ready quickly, and listen for the bells tolling a quarter to the hour, so I may gather my things in good time. Lorenzo does not tolerate tardiness, and I always make sure to be ready and waiting on the doorstep.

He steps from the carriage on the hour. 'Morning, Venus.'

Stefano is driving today and tips his hat towards me. I have taken care to wear Lorenzo's favourite dress and hope he will notice. He does not, but instead helps me to the steps of the carriage.

It is a hot morning. Lorenzo likes the small window of the carriage down, and I feel welcome breeze rushing against my face, making my cheeks blot with colour. My lover is not talkative today, and I have learned that when he is so vexed it is best to treat him with quietness and kindness, and to strive to be as amenable as any woman could be. He has a pope's ambition resting on his shoulders, so it is I who must be understanding.

We travel up the Via del Corso, and veer towards the river to a part of the city known for its vice, eventually stopping outside a large building which not so long ago would have been grand, but now has a decrepit quality to it. The steps are dirty, the windows broken and there are weeds growing from the foundations.

I am puzzled, but do not say it. Usually we stop at churches, or private houses which contain dazzling art galleries. As if Lorenzo has read my thoughts, he lets out a great, 'Ha! This is an important day, for you are going to buy your first piece of art.'

My eyes widen, 'I cannot afford . . .'

Lorenzo laughs, baring his teeth as he smiles. 'I shall fund the purchase, but you shall choose it. Call it a test, if you like, of all you have learned. 'Tis a good notion, do you not agree?'

My stomach feels as if a millstone is falling within. I am not ready to make such judgements, but he stares at me expectantly and I dare not show the hesitation I am feeling.

'Oh! I am …' I stutter. 'It is …' I begin again, with a bravado I do not feel. 'I think it is a most excellent idea. And here is where we shall enjoy such a venture?' I look up at the grimy windows, some of which are boarded.

'Have I not taught you well enough? Do not judge only by appearances. We are here to see Thibault Martinet, a Frenchman and an artist I greatly admire.'

He cannot be doing that well, I conclude, for this house is poorer than many in my district.

'You declare your hand too early, signore. For you may admire his work, but it is I who have the choice today. Must I not admire it also?'

Lorenzo dips his head in mock deference, enjoying this game in which I am a spirited pupil. 'That is indeed so. But you will be kind to this man I admire, for he has been ill. And, by way of his suffering, has fallen on hard times.'

'Well, I am pleased he is still breathing, for all other aspects of my education have concerned dead artists: Caravaggio, Michelangelo, Leonardo. This is the first *living* artist I shall study!'

'Indeed.' Lorenzo's tone changes. 'But I must tell you, Martinet has been,' he pauses for the right word, 'he has been beset by sickness.'

A dull alarm rings, though my tone stays light. 'It is not catching, is it?' I think of the plagues and quarantines, of people dying in the street, and feel a compulsion to raise my pomander to my mouth.

'Nay! Well, not unless you are planning to lie with him.'

I hate it when Lorenzo speaks with a vulgar tongue, as he does in the company of his brother or the men from the workshop.

'Martinet has the French pox. Nearly died of it. Now all his commissions have dried up. Poor man. That's why it pays well to choose a girl who only has eyes for you.' He tucks his fingers under my chin and tilts my head up so he can kiss me.

'You have taught me that the beauty – and brutality – of an artist's work has nothing to do with the morality of its creator.'

'I have.' He places another soft kiss on my lips. 'Besides, we are hardly in a position to lecture anyone on morals, are we, Venus?'

Inside the building the limestone walls are peeling and peppered with something growing in black, swampy clouds across the walls. There are canvases propped up against every surface, alongside the furniture, in the hallway and up the stairs.

Monsieur Martinet matches his surroundings, in that he is a pitiable specimen, a skeleton dressed in skin, his mouth encrusted with sores and features sunken, so it is hard not to feel sorry for him. His clothes fare little better: a shirt which is old and patched, over which he has draped about him a woollen scarf the moths have enjoyed. There is a small cot in the corner, with a meagre mattress and a blanket which is more holes than thread. This is a charitable act Lorenzo is performing, and I cannot help but feel my heart swell. He is a man who would give all he has to those in need.

'My good friend.' Lorenzo pats Martinet on the back so hard I think the poor man might fall over. 'We come as patrons. This is Signora Piccolomini.'

Martinet bows, but I do not offer my hand for him to kiss.

'She is an ingenue when it comes to many things, art being one. We have embarked on a period of, how shall I put it? Collective study.'

'Aye. Is that what they call it now?'

Martinet smiles as he ushers me into the room. I should feel cross at the slight, but he is such a sorry man, he inspires more sympathy than judgement. 'Can I offer you some refreshment? I have some wine – it is scant but good.'

'Nay, keep your wine. We are here for your talent, not your hospitality.'

In the studio stands a stool and easel at one end, under which is a cloth thick with paint.

I wait for Lorenzo to start looking through the canvases. But he makes for the cot, there being no chair to sit upon.

'What are you waiting for?' He motions about the room. 'I am buying, but you must make the choice, signora.'

'I . . . ?' The words do not form, but my head is shouting. How can I choose? Everything I have learned about art, form and composition, leaks from my head. What if I get it wrong? What if I choose something Lorenzo does not like, or thinks is insipid or second rate somehow?

I turn to Martinet and try to converse, but he hangs back, making it clear he is desperate enough for coin that he will admit us into his studio, but reluctant to engage in whatever game Lorenzo is playing.

My throat needs clearing; the air is suddenly dense with fumes and dust. I cough and watch the motes flying dreamily in the sunlight as I calculate how best to please Lorenzo.

The conclusion comes to me in a blaze of clarity.

The only way to do this is to please myself. If I choose something I am taken with, I will be able to argue with conviction and justify my purchase.

'So, Monsieur Martinet, the game is afoot!' I take a spirited step towards a large pile of canvases, which are rolled like ancient scrolls against the wall. 'It seems I am to have the final say, so I shall need to see everything you have.'

I do not look at Lorenzo, but know he is watching intently, his dark eyes fixed on us.

'It would be my greatest pleasure.'

Liar. He wants the sale, not to babysit Bernini's mistress.

Despite his diminished state, Martinet is stronger than he

appears, and shifts his work to and fro for me to inspect. There are
some fine landscapes executed by a hand practised in perspective,
and some men playing at cards, their avarice and deceitful nature
made plain to the viewer. Then a paradise bird in a cage takes my
fancy, something about its vivid plume of pitch and emerald coupled
with its melancholy aspect, for birds are not destined by God to be
bound by wire, but should live weaving in and out of the sky.

I pause over the canvas.

'You like this one?' Martinet asks.

But something tells me to keep looking. 'Aye, but I have not seen
everything you have for sale.'

Lorenzo shifts. I still do not address him, but something tells me
he approves of my thoroughness.

'Here.' Martinet brings another armful of rolled canvases to me.
As he passes near I expect him to smell of sickness, but he doesn't,
and as he opens his arms wide to roll out the canvases on the desk
I detect the scent of something spiced, maybe cinnamon, or cloves,
and sweet, like plums in grappa.

There are more surprises on the table and these depictions are
more to my taste. Myths of the ancients and Bible stories made
real by Martinet's hand. The tone of the bodies pushing against
each other, muscles resisting or straining to catch their prey. He
unfolds a large-scale painting of Susanna from the Old Testament,
her naked white flesh almost burning with shame and indignation,
and something else . . . fear . . . as she realises she is being spied upon
by lecherous old men hiding behind the trees, their eyes shining like
wolves. Martinet puts the canvas to one side and makes to unfurl
another over the top of it.

'Wait,' I say, 'I want to study this one.'

There is something in the way Susanna looks, the panic in her
eyes, the way he has captured perfectly the risk she has taken and

her resignation at the inevitability of the intrusion. That a man should understand. But then Martinet has experienced rejection, and what it is to be cast out by polite society.

I look at Susanna again. Her vulnerability is exposed, her loveliness stolen by the eyes of men who believe it their right to possess a woman's beauty.

The scene is set in the deep, mossy green of a forest. The pond is cool and blue, and small flowers are just making their opening. The boughs dip their heads like fingers outstretched, wanting to touch her. But it is Susanna's feet that seal the decision: trailed about her toes are lilies, their long, slender trumpet stems delicately painted with highlights of gold trailing in veins across the blooms. Every time I look there is more to see. The doe peeping from behind the tree; the small birds, singing of Susanna's innocence; and the lilies, each one a tiny masterpiece.

Martinet shifts beside me. 'Have you found something you like?'

'It is such a fine composition. Mesmerising. Susanna's beauty, and the men, like forest predators, I find it very ...'

I search for the word. Certainly, I find it arresting, for who could not – the mastery of the figures, like flesh upon canvas; the colours, so rich and alluring – but there is something else.

'I find it very familiar.' For that is the truth.

Martinet dips his head in acknowledgement.

Lorenzo, who has been listening, stands. 'Familiar,' he repeats, in a tone I find uncertain, and I laugh.

'Familiar to women.'

Lorenzo walks towards me, his face as rigid as the stone he cuts. 'Pretty women must be careful, or else the beast will find them and want to eat them.' Then he grabs my waist and pulls me near, so he can pretend to bite at my neck. I do not like it, but do not push him away, for it would offend my lover in front of his friend.

Lorenzo turns to Martinet. 'Signora Piccolomini has chosen. We shall take this one. Write me an invoice and I shall settle immediately.'

Have I passed the test? I cannot help myself wondering, and ask, 'What do you think of *my* painting?'

Lorenzo examines the canvas, and I have the distinct feeling he has seen it before.

'Anything by Martinet's hand is extraordinary. Better than I could ever achieve with a paintbrush. Artistry, the composition of the bodies. But there is something more . . . which you saw. He has captured a moment, life as it happens, the distress of Susanna, the lust of the men. And commercially, this painting will be worth a great deal. For what husband or father does not want a permanent warning to his daughter or wife of the perils other men pose?'

He looks at me, a hawk once more. Challenging me to answer.

''Tis most true. Dangers lurk in alleyways and doorways, but also in plain sight.'

Chapter Twenty-Eight

'Statue'

August 1637

L orenzo works at the statue.

He feels along the lines of the stone, as if purblind, noting the delineation, understanding the possibilities of the material in his hands. Even though it is cold, inanimate, cut from the earth, it lives, speaking to him of unrealised possibilities. He knows she is within this block, at least, his vision of her, untamed and as yet unearthed.

He lifts the chisel, honed to an exacting sharpness, and it weighs well in his hand. It is one of his favourites and sits as if it belongs there, in a satisfying balance in the pivot between thumb and fingers. Lorenzo hammers into the marble, the auditory refractions a musical anthology of sounds, responding to every blow, telling him where to move next.

There is a resonance between the chisel and the hammer. He becomes attuned to the noise and starts to create a rhythm of tapping. It is the beginning of a hypnotic dialogue. As he creates her form, he loses his own, the marble becoming an extension of him, the stone impervious to his desire.

He works quickly, removing the dead matter: destroying in order to create. As he does so, there is a blooming, like well-water rising from under him, pushing, expanding into his mind, his hands, spilling over into the stone itself, aching to connect.

It takes hours of working into the silence, of hearing the quiet voice of the stone, picking out small drills and rasps, tapping with wide then fine chisels, to reveal her chin and broad forehead, her leonine hair; playing with the surface of the marble, smooth here, textured there, the curls at the nape of her neck, boring two holes into the centre of her eyes, which he will rub with black ash, to make her face as if living.

He becomes consumed not just by Costanza, but by this representation of her. Working ceaselessly, stopping only to eat and piss. He does not see his lover, and his commissions go untouched.

Luigi becomes frustrated, shouting that the business will suffer. 'Your obsession with this woman, Costanza, is affecting us all!' he yells. 'It would be better if you could leave her be.'

Yet when Lorenzo's brother looks upon the statue, he is astounded. It is as if she has just risen or is, perhaps, about to give one of her quick-witted opinions.

The days pass, and the brothers both become infatuated.

Chapter Twenty-Nine

'The Spectre'

September 1637

We have found new lodgings, a three-storey house, near the Pontiff's summer palace.

It is much grander than our former rooms, and still only a walk away from Papa, Tiberia and Giuliana. Being truthful, three storeys is too much for our art collection, but it is an investment. Matteo's reputation is growing, and we have money enough for good food and some small paintings. Downstairs there is a courtyard with a fig tree, and space for Matteo to set up his studio and a small foundry. Upstairs there is a reception room and a salon, where I can receive my visitors in comfort. It is simply decorated, but I have plans.

We can also afford a maid, so I have found a girl in need of a household, Livia. I liked her immediately; she has a steadfastness like a reed blowing in the breeze, anchored to the riverbed of the Tiber. I try to be a good mistress, but it is impossible not to feel relieved that I no longer have to keep house.

I sit in the salon, with my embroidery on my lap, Bess slumbers at my feet while Sourpuss stretches in a shaft of sunlight on the other side of the room, a good distance from the hated dog. Livia is at the market, fetching food. It should be a time of relaxation but, try as I might, I cannot rest. My heart is rent in agony.

Lorenzo has not sent word – nor called for me – in nearly a month. The question 'why' pulses inside me, day and night. I spend my hours trying to understand how I can have given such great offence, or caused him to cut me off. At other times, it is *I* who feels mightily offended, that *he* should profess deep love for *me* and then leave in such a cruel manner. I write phantom letters in which I beg forgiveness for whatever transgression I have committed. Then I compose notes containing the strongest of admonishments, for how dare he cut ties so brutally? It is as if I am a ghost.

It is all made worse by the simple fact that Matteo sees Lorenzo from time to time at the Fabbrica. My husband bears, with good fortitude, the constant questioning about my lover, when all he can do is assure me that Lorenzo is not only alive but working.

'What of Lorenzo's health?' I ask over the last meal of the day, picking at my plate. 'Does he look sick or ailing? Is an ague claiming him?'

Matteo does not look up as he eats, but doggedly chews through his boiled chicken. 'Lorenzo looks no worse than usual, but is working as hard as three men. What ails him is an ungodly obsession to work, naught more. He is carving a private commission and it consumes him.'

I am not satisfied.

'Is he with another woman?' I ask as we prepare for bed. 'You would tell me if there was such tattle?'

'Nay,' sighs my husband. 'Il Cavaliere works. As I said. He would be hard pressed to bring another affair into his business.'

'Then how *is* his business?' I ask at sunrise, as Matteo prepares for the day. 'Does the Pontiff still send for Lorenzo? Perhaps there are enemies marshalling against his favour, or there has been a complaint about a commission?'

'No complaints. Il Cavaliere is busy. The brother, Luigi, is running things for a while . . . and making us all fonder of our old master than we thought possible.'

I am at Matteo like a fly, buzzing with the questions that consume me. When each answer elicits a no, I move to the next, and the next, wanting to find any other reason for Lorenzo's absence from my life, other than that he has tired of me.

Eventually Matteo throws down the cloth he has been using to wipe his mouth, his blond moustache twitching with irritation. 'I am a patient husband. We have an understanding. But this incessant questioning of Lorenzo is not healthy. The man is a law unto himself. There is no indication his affection for you has waned, it is more that you are, and I mean this kindly, a distraction for a man who has business to attend to. He will call soon enough.'

Matteo leans back in the chair, and I know not to push further, even though there are several more questions burning at my throat.

Bess is sitting on my lap, and I stroke her ears as I look at Matteo. 'It is hard. To be left this uncertain.'

His voice softens. 'I know, but you must be patient. A man like Lorenzo does not like to be ruled. He is the one who rules. You have his heart, and more than likely it unnerves him.'

It is one of the dangers of love. It is like a hunger. All you care about is the touch of your beloved, and unless this need can be sated all other needs are made redundant. I have no appetite, and the white meat of the chicken is left untouched on my plate. The little dog whines piteously for it, and I give in, breaking off small slivers and feeding it to her straight from my fingers, feeling her muscular pink tongue licking at the tips.

'You treat that dog like an infant. She should be on the floor or, better still, outside in the courtyard.'

I scoop Bess up to my neck and allow her to nuzzle against my skin.

'Perhaps. But she is a comfort.' I kiss the dog's head for good measure. 'I have made up my mind, if he won't see me, I am going to see Lorenzo at the Fabbrica.'

Matteo sits up and leans forward across our small table, nearly knocking a glass onto the floor. 'That is a bad idea, Costanza. He will not thank you for it. There are hundreds of men in his care. His mistress marching through the place will not . . .' He stops.

'Go down well? But what else can I do? Perhaps you could . . .'

'Nay,' says Matteo firmly, shaking his head. 'Nay. Nay. Nay. Do not ask it. I will not turn messenger. This situation of ours is already complex enough.'

'Then I am resolved: I shall see him.'

Matteo leans back slightly and lets out an aggrieved sigh.

We sit for a moment, the dog turning in my lap trying to find a comfortable place to lay, and my unhappiness writhing between us.

It is Matteo who speaks first. 'Perhaps I am not the best person to give counsel on this matter. Have you spoken to Caterina? She is well-practised in affairs of the heart and knows Il Cavaliere well. She would be far better placed to advise.'

My eyes narrow for a moment, and my lip protrudes of its own accord. But then I begin to think he is right. Caterina is the one person who will understand, and I am sure she will agree that something must be done to break this interminable impasse.

* * *

'I fancy I shall walk down to the Fabbrica,' I slip in casually.

I am sat on one of the ebony chairs playing cards in Caterina's salon, which smells of perfume, hot house lilies and songbird guano. She is puffing on a pipe, which only adds to the fug and is staring over the top of her cards, daintily held by her bejewelled fingers. I can only see her eyes but know Caterina's lips are pressed into a frown.

'For what purpose?'

I lay down my hand. I have no appetite for pastimes, they bore me, as does everything now. 'For the purpose of seeing Lorenzo. For the purpose,' I emphasise, 'of asking him whether he still loves me. Or if I am to be discarded, like a fractured piece of marble.'

Caterina does not respond. The orange bird flutters in its cage, and quite unexpectedly, my mouth feels dry. I reach and take a cup of the honeyed wine, which has been spiced with too many cloves, reminding me of Tiberia, making my stomach turn.

Caterina studies me. Not as a painter, with eyes darting, measuring and memorising, but assessing me like a priest, peering into the health of my soul. Perhaps I am the poor victim of a bewitchment of some sort. Sometimes I feel I have wronged God so greatly, I deserve every unhappiness life will throw at me.

'You love him, don't you?'

I am surprised at her question. 'Of course.'

Caterina shakes her head and I feel a flush rising.

'He is everything to me.'

'Oh dear. You must never fall in love with them. Men like Lorenzo are incapable of loving anyone but themselves. You must take the trinkets and the lifestyle, so when it is over, you have had fun and are in a better position than when you started. It all comes at a price, and a woman's reputation can be bought for a ducat in an alleyway.'

'You have it all wrong. I love Lorenzo, and he loves me.'

'Is that so?'

'Yes.' I take a breath. 'He told me so.'

Caterina lays down her cards, fanning them on the table, with a careful deliberateness. 'Did he now?'

I immediately regret my outburst, for that was a private moment. Although Caterina is a friend, she seems to hold on to the revelation like a thief.

Caterina considers the rings on her hand. 'You must not be hasty, for if Lorenzo really does love you . . .' I open my mouth, but Caterina intercedes, '. . . which I doubt not . . . then he will return to your bed sooner or later. When he does, you must do everything you can to nurture his passion. In the end, lust binds a man to a woman more than ever a gold band on a finger ever did.'

I close my mouth. Her words make sense and a new hope bubbles within me, like a brook, fresh and pure. All might not be lost. It is a sudden and very great comfort to me.

'Do you really think he does? Love me? Then what shall I do?'

'Come come. There is no need for hysterics. In moments such as these you must not panic, but plan. If you go to the Fabbrica you will be challenging Lorenzo publicly. He will be humiliated. There is nothing more dangerous than a man who has been humiliated. Men have started wars for less. Did not Menelaus besiege Troy and slaughter a city because Helen, his wife, chose Paris? Nay, it is best not to poke at men's egos, for they are fragile and wont to crack.'

This is not what I want to hear, and I feel the annoyance glowing like a stone warmed in the sun. 'So what then? I should do nothing, and wait?'

'Nay, I did not say that.' There is a smile creeping across Caterina's red lips. 'I have a much better idea. We shall go shopping. And when you next see Lorenzo, you shall look like a goddess, so beautiful he will not be able to keep his hands off you.'

I think of Riva whispering, *You look like Aurora*. But there is a problem. 'It is not so easy.'

'Why?'

'Matteo will not give me the coin for such an outing, and I cannot accept your payment.'

'You misunderstand, my dear. I shall take you to Il Cavaliere's cloth merchants. The one where he purchased the plum silk you are so fond of. There we will find material for a new gown; you know how Lorenzo likes a well-dressed woman.'

I run my hand through my hair, smoothing my curls against my scalp. 'But won't he mind? If we charge his account?'

Caterina leans forward and pats my hand with her ornamented fingers. 'It is a small price for Il Cavaliere to pay to keep you happy, when he has wronged you so. It is all part of the game, my sweet. Come. Fetch your dog, we shall go today.'

* * *

It is like a rainbow within Ennio Balotelli's store house, a place where the shelves are filled with bales of shot silk the colour of crocuses, luscious greens, regal purples, the blues of all the skies in nature, and rich reds.

He bows as we enter. 'Welcome. Take a look. My wares come from all over the world.'

The cloth merchant is one of the most charming men I have ever met, having spent a lifetime persuading ladies to part with their scudi for the benefit of their beauty. He is tall, with evenly spaced features, and his eyes are a deep kind of blue, as if the seas he has travelled have seeped into them. His face is covered in a crossing of lines, but I can still see the shadows of the young man he once was, in his brows and at the cut of his jawline.

'There is cloth from the East Indies, Africa, Spain and the New World, expertly woven and dyed here in Rome,' he continues.

I try to imagine these far-off places but find it impossible. I know they cannot look like Rome, so I conjure lush forests and gleaming lakes, plains of sand and palm trees, like those I have seen in paintings.

Tiberia only ever used the merchant near our district, who sells a plainer cloth, worsted wool and coarse linens, and I am dazed by the jarring colours. Caterina, however, picks through the bales of material with the eye of a connoisseur. Bound within this weft and warp are the fortunes of the men and women who will wear them. In Rome's high society, what someone wears tells you everything: who is rising through the ranks, who is courting the favour of the rich, the young girls being readied for marriage and those, dressed in their plain attire, who are destined for the convent; and who is hoping to catch the eye of a lover. The whole of the city's yearnings are caught in the threads of this place.

'Here, this one.' Caterina indicates for Balotelli to pull down a bale of velvet, as supple as a baby's skin and the colour of blackberries. I tentatively touch its sumptuous lustre.

'It is quite beautiful.' I do not carry on, although I feel a 'but' caught at the back of my throat. It is too old for me, and more like something Caterina would wear.

'Hold it to your neck,' she instructs.

I do as Caterina says, holding the cloth against my collar bone, which is white, thanks to the effort I have made to conceal my skin from the sun. She stands back to look at me.

While it looks good against me, it would sing against Caterina's blonde hair. There being something of the winter about her pale blue eyes and pink cheeks and her cold, dry, womanish humours, which I envy.

'You should try it.' The words are out before I can stop them. Some habits die hard.

'Yes, maybe you're right.'

Caterina walks over to inspect the cloth more closely, but eventually she finds it lacking and she waves her hand. The bale is returned to the shelf by a young lad who looks hardly big enough to lift it, but he hoists it onto his shoulders with great dexterity.

We go through the same exercise again and again, Caterina choosing a bale for me, shot silk the colour of a spring sky, green damask the colour of emeralds, heavy velvet the hue of honey plucked from clover. There is such an excess of choice I lose track of what I like, as I hold cloth after cloth against my cheek.

Signor Balotelli bears it all with the patience of a man who knows there is a long game to be played, and the wait will be handsomely rewarded. Sometimes he is on my side; 'nay,' he mutters. 'Nay, nay, nay, this is not the one.' Other times he agrees with Caterina, 'Such a becoming colour, and very fashionable,' forcing me to stutter my objection.

We are all getting weary when I see what I have been looking for, right at the back. A bale of silk, which switches colour in the late afternoon sun, one minute flame orange, the next minute copper, aquamarine, the rust of paprika, as if the cloth itself is on fire. I remember Lorenzo's first words to me: 'You have a rare fire.'

'There,' I point at the roll of cloth, that one.

Caterina turns and wrinkles her nose, like a cat at curdled milk. 'It is too gaudy, Signora Piccolomini, pick something more moderate; a little restraint would be better.'

'Nay. This is the one. It is what Lorenzo first saw in me, and I have forgotten how to be that woman. Now, I shall remember.'

My little dog barks excitedly as the boy scoots up the ladder like a rat, scrabbling at the corner of the roll to tease and then pull it out. When he returns and unravels the glimmering cloth, I feel as if something lights inside me. I touch at it, and it is stiffer than it appears, a chimera of molten colours like flames flickering, and when I hold it to my throat my cheeks heat and my eyes burn brighter.

Caterina sees it too. 'Perhaps you are right after all. Yes, we shall take this . . . And fourteen lengths of the blackberry velvet.'

As Signor Balotelli tots up our spending, Caterina adds more to the list. Some delicate Italian lace which looks as if it has been spun by faeries rather than a woman, a bolt of fine lawn for a nightgown, and half a dozen French silk stockings to be held up by a ribbon of baby blue. She is leaving nothing to chance.

'To be charged to Signor Bernini's account?' Ennio Balotelli has a look of deep satisfaction on his face; the patient man has been rewarded.

'Of course.' She lowers her head. 'And to be delivered to my tailor, Cristoforo, on the Via Castello, who will come and fit us both for new gowns.'

As we leave, Caterina loops her arm into mine. 'Now for the second part of the plan. I shall send a letter to Lorenzo, reminding him of his Venus. No admonishments, just a confession that we have been free with his scudi buying lace and silks, and other feminine things. A little enticement.'

We have spent in one afternoon what it would take Papa four months to earn. The uncommon manner in which Caterina takes charge is a lesson to be learned. Men command, but women can still call, like sirens. It is a quieter power, but no less potent.

Chapter Thirty

'Reconciliation'

October 1637

I sit down at my desk to write a short letter, full of appreciation for my friend, for who else but Caterina could have engineered such a swift reconciliation?

> *My dearest Caterina,*
>   *I am indebted to you and fear I can never repay you for your kindness. Not three days since you wrote to Lorenzo, he has summoned me to his side.*
>   *Thank you again, my true, dear friend.*
>   *Costanza*

I hand the note to Livia. 'You must deliver this straight into Signora Panzetti's hands. No one else, do you understand?'

She nods, not questioning the instruction, no doubt guessing at its content, for she has been unpacking parcels all morning. A nightgown cuffed in lace so intricate it is like a spider's web drawn with ribbons of blush apricot; and stockings that are but a milky sheen about my calf. The flame gown is not ready, but that matters not. I am not planning on wearing my skirts for long.

It is dusk, and I am nervous as Stefano opens the door to a wild clattering of dogs and barking. At least the Bernini hounds are delighted to see me. 'Signora Piccolomini,' he bows, as if there has been no absence of time since we last saw each other. 'I shall let Signor Bernini know you have arrived.' I watch him climbing the stairs as he takes his leave, jumping the stairs two by two; it is oddly childish for a such a dense, muscular man.

I do not take a seat in the hallway but stand and inspect the paintings on the wall: Venus; a Madonna and child; and a portrait of Lorenzo rendered in swift brush marks in the style he prefers, which looks like it might be a self-portrait.

As I ponder this, I become aware of someone watching, of a pair of eyes upon me, as a bird of prey searches for a mouse in the field. I know it is Luigi even though I am facing the wall. I feel him moving behind me. All about him is the stench of the tavern, pipe smoke and a shirt worn too long. It is the odour of the end of an evening, not the beginning.

'You would have done better to stay away.' His voice is low, almost a growl.

I turn to face Lorenzo's younger brother, and see he is the worse for wear, dark circles staining his eyes, hair rough and greasy. His stare is disquieting, but I am emboldened by the knowledge that he cannot touch me; I am his brother's mistress.

'Good evening, Luigi. You look well.'

Luigi takes a step towards me, almost nonchalant, but too close. His words are slightly slurred. 'Lorenzo tried to carry on without you, but he knows he can't. It is a dangerous place to find yourself. My brother would rather destroy you than let you go.'

The candles on the wall flicker, and I can hear the wood in the great room cracking as it splits with the fury of the heat of the fire.

'Lorenzo is insatiable,' Luigi continues, close enough that the hairs of his black moustache tickle my face. 'He consumes all those who cross his path like a wildfire, like Satan himself. He cannot abide anyone to have a seat at the table. Finelli saw it and escaped. I have the misfortune to be family. But Lorenzo will devour it all, the power, the love, the adoration, the beauty – he feeds on it until there is only a husk left.'

The proximity of his body unnerves me, and I feel a flare of panic pass from my stomach through my limbs to my fingers, even though I know these are the words of a green-eyed sibling, a jealous little brother who is a drunkard and a libertine. Any word from his foul mouth should be dismissed the moment it is uttered.

I step to one side. 'It is a cruel thing to be born a brother to a man such as Lorenzo, who is made of such talent and charisma. He is like the sun, eclipsing everything. Threats will not help you, Luigi, and Lorenzo would be displeased to hear you talking so.'

Luigi begins a retort, but at that moment there is a heavy tread on the stair. It is Stefano returning to collect me.

Luigi retreats far enough that Stefano would never know we had passed anything but pleasantries, yet I have seen something burning in his eyes. He cannot forgive me for loving his brother as he does not.

As I walk up the stairs, my heart races a little faster. I have always been wary of Luigi; he disturbs my peace entirely. Revolts me. I have not been to this house in weeks, yet here he is, waiting for my arrival. It is as if he spies upon my comings and goings, always watching from the shadows. And when we speak it is too intimate. The truth is, Luigi Bernini chills my spine.

I debate whether to tell Lorenzo, not now, but perhaps later? But I don't want anything to jeopardise our reunion. Stefano shows me into the studio and closes the door. I make no effort to move towards Lorenzo. Despite my nerves, and my longing, I have already decided it is he who should come to me.

'Venus,' Lorenzo stands and looks at me for a moment. The candles drip their wax onto the floor, and even in the soft light there is something raw and jagged about him. Every line – his ribs, cheeks, collarbone – is sharp. The lines of the muscles in his neck are pulled tight and there is a restless energy about him, like leaves quivering before a storm.

We face each other and the space between us fills with such stillness, it is if the world has ceased moving.

He breaks the spell by taking a step towards me. Then another. I control my breath, willing my body to cease the shake which threatens to erupt.

'Venus,' he says again. He is now in front of me, and raises his hand, tenderly, to my face. It is finely clammy; even a man well drilled in the art of dissemblance cannot hide his emotion from manifesting in such a way. My head turns slightly into this small embrace, and my mouth softens to a kiss, propelled by my body, which needs to fuel its addiction.

I look up at him again in silence. Then say softly, a quiet fury contained within. 'You will never make me a spectre again.'

His head moves almost imperceptibly, but it is a nod, an acknowledgement. Lorenzo puts his hand about my waist and pulls me towards him, and all at once I smell his perfume, oranges and paint and lust. Then I take him by surprise by kissing him with such fervency that he sinks into my mouth, his fingers pressing into flesh and bone.

There is no end and no beginning of us. His body on mine on his, a great breath of release and I cry out. Afterwards he pulls me up, and I let him curl my hair in his fingers as we lie as lovers once more on the long chair, kissing and talking as if nothing had ever been amiss.

My eye catches something on the floor. At first it looks like a nest of vipers, long coloured ribbons entwined, and I fancy I see serpents moving. As I study them more, I see they are not living, at least not in the conventional sense, but had once been part of a canvas, which has been slashed.

My eye is drawn to one of the curves, and then another; even in the low light of the night, I can see what has been etched upon them. There can be no mistake. They are lilies, their luxurious bells cut at cruel angles, the gold filigree tarnished by the dust and dirt of the floor. I look closer and see flesh, a woman's thigh or arm, pink and nubile and tattered so that the limb looks dismembered. A disfigurement of the cruellest sort.

I swallow my wine, which feels more acid than berry, feeling a sickening wildness come across me.

I sit up and look more closely. There is no doubt.

'What happened to my painting?' I ask, without looking Lorenzo in the eye.

He laughs. 'What do you mean?'

'What happened to my painting of Susanna, by Martinet? It is in a pile of ribbons over there.'

He looks. A heartbeat passes between us. He kisses me on one shoulder, then the other, takes my wine and pulls me back into his body.

'You are mistaken.' He kisses me again, the simmer of a lie upon his lips. 'It is common when paintings do not come together for my humours, for my choleric to rise so fast I cannot bear the failure. It was a tribute to you.' He kisses me and it starts again.

Later, when we are dozing in the firelight, I watch the shadows dance on the lilies and limbs, remembering the detail which called to me, and I feel a shifting. It *is* my painting, and Lorenzo destroyed it; I know not why, only that the ribbons are a testament to the violence and fury of his knife. I feel the smallest hairs on my arm rise and note the sensation, and nothing seems clear anymore.

* * *

Outside the room Luigi listens to her cries of ecstasy and his brother's animal grunts. He swells as he imagines their bodies, a great chimera, bucking in the soiled painter's rags of the studio. He closes his eyes and slowly the image changes, and it is he, Luigi, who is within Costanza, panting and pushing, harder and harder, the veins on his face filling with blood. Then he has his hands on her neck and begins to squeeze. He groans softly in the corridor and knows there is only one release.

Down the stairs. A cloak to hide his face as he unlocks the door, slipping out into the night. The moon shines her silvery light on the city's imperfections, the cankerous sins of the drunk and debauched. He has no need of a lantern, knowing as he does the cobbled pathways through the backstreets. He passes walled villas with their scents of pine and bougainvillea, avoiding the doorway sconces still lit to show hospitality and wealth. There is always danger, even in a holy city like Rome, and as he walks he hears the shadows grunting and vomiting.

Onwards to Ortaccio, a place even popes turn a blind eye to, because a ghetto where whores congregate means there will be fewer beaten wives and deflowered girls, less disease and not so many unwanted babes left on convent doorsteps. Here men find their release with women who will take a florin for the pleasure. Better that than some innocent maid being sullied.

The place stinks and underfoot he feels the slime of animal entrails, rudimentary sheaths of pigs' bladders and cows' intestines filled with the seed of men. Luigi would rather take his chances. He casts about the gloom, looking for a particular woman. She is older than he usually likes, with streaks of grey at her temples and a stomach which bags from having whelped so many children.

She is also desperate, and for a few extra coins will let him do things the other girls won't. To extract a level of violence upon her which causes her to cry out in pain, but it is so damn near the same sound of ecstasy, he does not care.

He finds her.

'Elena Merletto, there you are.' Luigi puts his arm around her in a parody of a loving embrace, and whispers, 'I need something special tonight. And I am willing to pay.'

Her bodice is low, exposing her skin to the cool night air which makes her shiver.

'I will charge you, Luigi Bernini, for every bruise, and every rib you break.'

He nods, and even as he moves to kiss her, in his mind she morphs into Costanza. There is an inn nearby which lets rooms for the whores of the gardens, when their gentlemen friends are either too shy – or too wicked – to do their business in public.

The landlord nods as she passes. For a small cut, he will send a boy to keep an ear out for their room, to make sure she survives the trick she is turning. He knows the gentleman she is with, and will pay special attention tonight, not wanting to have the bother of a corpse and the thugs of the sbirri on his arse.

The room reeks of all the bodily fluids that have seeped and shot out of the human body. Luigi cares not. His vast, fantastical imagination, used for the construction of the city's golden churches and glorious fountains during the day, has turned to a wilder hinterland,

and a passion for pain and destruction. He pushes her down onto the mattress covered in muck, and she pushes him back, causing a spark of wrath to light in his eyes.

'Money now. I won't be in a position to demand it later.'

Slowly, with his fine long fingers, he unknots his purse and counts the coins out into her hands.

'Enough?' he asks.

'For now. We'll see how I am at the end of it.'

He pushes the woman back down again, and this time pins her by the throat so she can neither complain, nor move, knowing there will be finger-shaped bruises when he finally releases her. Then he grabs her hair, pulling her head back in such a ferocious manner she cries out, as he turns her so she is lying on her front.

Still restraining her with one hand, Luigi lifts Elena's skirts with the other. He slaps her across the buttocks and back, again and again until great red welts appear on her flesh. Mortification. He hits her again, and wishes it was Costanza. How dare she speak to him as a servant, when all he wants to do is protect her. He is rigid, an apoplexy of rage and destruction as he mounts the woman on the bed. With every jerk of his body he imagines Costanza. Making her sorry. Making her wish she had paid more heed.

Making her wish she had chosen him.

Chapter Thirty-One

'An Unveiling'

December 1637

I do not see it coming, although I should have.

The year is almost at an end. I have not long arrived at Lorenzo's house and am about to take off my cloak when he appears, standing at the top of the stairs, leaning over the banister in the manner of an excited child.

'Do not disrobe, I have something to show you in the courtyard.'

I breathe in, then slowly out, and feel something resembling relief, like the first trickle of water after a drought. Lorenzo is in good humour, there shall be no second guessing his mood today. 'As you wish,' I say lightly, and begin retying the thick wool tapes.

He bounds down the stairs, jumping the last two steps and pulls at my arm. 'Come, Venus. Outside. It is a surprise.'

We walk through the hallway, to the back of the villa and into a square surrounded by a high stone wall on all sides. Winter has taken the firmest of holds, the bare trees in carved planters are encased in frost, the hard ground crunches beneath our feet and as we exhale we leave a silver stream in our wake.

Lorenzo is leading me to the other end of the yard, where a section is shielded by an oilcloth rigged tightly across the corner, keeping the statues standing below safe from the elements. It is a jumble of stone. There are busts on wooden plinths and figures half hewn. Some of the effigies are finished and so lifelike only the absence of white billowed breath betrays that they are not living.

I do not see her at first. Then my eyes alight upon a marble head. A glance. Then a double take. I stop, hardly able to fathom what I see.

For it is me.

And it is not.

It is my likeness in marble. The face I see reflected back from my little looking glass, from the windows at night, in the water of the pond at the villa, the mirrors that adorn Lorenzo's studio. It is my proud forehead, rough curled hair, high cheeks, smallish teeth, my chin, with the little cleft just like my father.

Yet it is not me at all. It is someone else entirely. Me seen through Lorenzo's eyes. I look at this Costanza, standing in the chill air and frozen in time, and understand it is the greatest betrayal. It is everything we ever shared laid bare. Lorenzo has revealed something intimate, private, something that was not his to expose.

The likeness is not a woman of propriety, the saints you find in churches or classical figures you see in salons. It is something altogether more sensuous. Shocking. Scandalous. My lips are parted, my chemise falls open, revealing a hint of my breasts, a swollen promise peeking from under the shirt.

Unlike this stone Costanza, I feel my blood coursing in my veins, the tight ribbons tied at the top of my stocking, the muzzled warmth of my fingers pressed against my squirrel-fur-lined gloves, the ache of a single pin against the back of my scalp, where I have secured my hair too tightly. I feel in one heartbeat the violation for what it is. I know what people – men – will see when they gaze upon this likeness. They will feel the prick of their own lust reflected back at them.

I have not given my consent, have not agreed to this version of me. I do not want men to gaze upon me in this way, as if I invite them all in. As if I am theirs. As if I am nothing but a petrified fragment of passion.

Lorenzo stands at my side. 'It is you,' he breathes. 'It is my tribute to our love.'

He is wrong. It is not me – but a stolen version of my image. I am no more this woman than any of the other figures standing in this place.

Lorenzo walks over to the statue, and runs a finger along her face, over her breasts. 'It is my best work. Capturing you ... like this.'

I hear myself saying, 'Yes,' my voice sounding thick, as if coated in tar.

'Do you not see how I have fashioned you in every way? From all sides?'

I give him a downward nod, not wanting to interrupt and wishing he would stop. How dare he speak of the way he has fashioned me, when I did not agree to his picking up a chisel and doing this? Making my image.

'It is a love letter, but writ in stone ...' Lorenzo looks at me unblinkingly. 'To endure. How many mistresses are feted like this? Are you not the most fortunate of women? First I gave you money, now immortality.'

He waits for my answer. My mind throws out lines like a fisherman, casting about for words he will want to hear. It is true. What woman would not want to be the subject of such love, to be commemorated in such a way by the greatest artist alive? And yet a part of me wants to push this statue to the floor, to take a hammer and smash at it, watch chips fly into the air, matter turns to dust. To grind the fragments, the remnants of this mightiest of duplicities, underfoot.

He holds my gaze with a frank expression, and I know only one answer will suffice.

'It is indeed glorious,' I say carefully. 'And I am the luckiest of women.'

* * *

Although it is a private piece, Lorenzo cannot help but show my portrait off to his guests, to hear them crow in wonder. The critics say it is a triumph, that the great artist has frozen time and achieved the incredible feat of there being two Costanzas in the same place. One the living woman, the other rendered in marble, as if alive.

The sculpture sits in pride of place in the courtyard.

'Magnifico!' they cry. I muster my bravado and smile.

'An ordinary woman celebrated in stone? Who would have thought it?' they declare, and all I do is nod.

Some men smirk when they see my likeness, imagining they know me in my flimsy chemise. These men I stare at brazenly, adopting the defiance they attribute to me, and try not to think of Tiberia, or Papa, gazing upon it, even though I instinctively feel their hurt and shame.

Lorenzo is beside himself, never questioning my duty to give up my body for him, to provide the raw material from which he can create. 'Look, Venus!' he says. 'Look at what *we* have achieved. An entirely new art form. Is this not what we are put on earth to do? To push the inventions of man forward? Galileo has his instruments of cosmic observation, and I have you. No one has ever plucked a woman from the streets and made her flesh in marble; you are the first.'

Of course, it is not about me, but Lorenzo. I was not plucked from the streets but am the wife of an artist. But then he smiles like this so rarely. The story Lorenzo has invented – the statue he has created – has brought me closer to him. Now when he draws me, I know what he is about. As he studies me, I study him. The skittish steps back and forth, his darting looks, the manoeuvring, adjusting. This is how I become even more intimately acquainted with his glossary of looks, the half-smiles and wrinkled brow, the pensive licking of his lips in the depths of concentration. It has enabled me to be even more alert to his needs, to anticipate what he wants before he even knows it himself.

And so I become a better muse.'

Chapter Thirty-Two

'La Puttana'

January 1638

There is a knocking at the door.

I wait for Livia to answer it and remember she is at the market. How quickly I have got used to this life. I walk down the stairs in a state of high dudgeon; it is not the job of the mistress to be up and down the stairs. I pull at the latch and swing open the door, only to take a sharp breath.

'Lorenzo!'

The pale winter sun is at his back and seeing his silhouette in front of me makes me so happy, I fall upon him and kiss him, full and long, for such is my joy I care not for propriety. He laughs at my enthusiasm, a low sound which vibrates against my heart, and runs his hand through his hair which has, over these last few months, grown much longer about his face.

'I had heard there would be a kindly welcome at this place,' he says, kissing me once more on the lips. Bess yelps and barks at his feet, making an uncommonly loud noise in delight at seeing her saviour.

'You had better come inside; I have a reputation to keep.'

'It is not your reputation I watch for.' He smiles and kisses me again in an act of friendly provocation.

When Livia returns from the market we are already to bed. It has occurred to me that Livia may not care to work in such an ungodly household, for I am sure Matteo has entertained Vincenzo here too. But she has never said anything, and I get the impression that our unusual arrangements matter not to her. If anything, it makes her life easier, for my husband and I live in a harmony, not always common among those who are married, and we are content to leave Livia to her work rather than use her to score points in a war.

It is after lunch by the time we tire, and my belly growls as we lie.

'You are hungry.' He kisses the soft mound of my stomach.

'You are hungry work.'

I stand, pulling about me a long shawl, embroidered with roses and insects, in needlework finer than mine, so good that the little creatures look alive and ready to crawl onto my skin.

'Shall I call for food?'

'Nay, I must return. There are many preparations for Carnival. We are rehearsing my play this afternoon.'

I nod. The play is all he has talked about. The premise, the script, which members of the great and good shall be pilloried, who will star, who will not. An annual event in the Bernini calendar, when work stops for nearly a month.

I bid farewell to Lorenzo at the door, still delighted by his un-announced visit. Only the keenest of observers would notice my hair has been roughly pinned, and my feet lack stockings. 'Tis a pity then that I live next to one of the keenest observers in all of Rome, Widow Vanna Falto.

As Lorenzo walks around the corner, the old woman appears on her own front step, her features scrunched into the middle of her face, which is cracked and worn like an old walnut shell.

'I see you.' She cackles, raising her crow arm, and pointing her bent finger at me. 'I see you both. You and your husband. There is no God under your roof, and this is a respectable area.' She sniffs the air as if she smells carrion. 'And on the doorstep of the papal palace.'

The familiar wrath rises. The sensible voice within me says just ignore her, she has no evidence, and what does she care? She is old and half-blind, and I have the protection of Lorenzo. She quivers about the Pope, yet Lorenzo is an intimate of the Pontiff. But the girl from San Silvestro emerges. Her anger swells, for who does this old bat think she is? Goading has always challenged me.

I do not choose the wise path. Instead, I stride off, in long steps along the street to Vanna's house. The road is rough and cold, and my feet immediately register the discomfort of it, but so warm is my blood, I cannot stop.

When I reach the widow, I stand at least three heads taller, my shadow falling upon her, swallowing her up.

'Say that again, you old crone.'

She opens her mouth into a contorted grin; most of her teeth are missing, and those that are left are decaying brown lumps, leaving her mouth a black hole, putting me in mind of a cadaver.

'I am not afraid of you,' she rasps.

Then she takes a step back, towards her own threshold. I sense the victory is mine. I have no need to truck further with an old woman, so turn to walk away. As I do, I hear a sharp intake of breath, making me turn back, fearing the widow is about to fall. My face comes square once more with hers, and something most unexpected happens. I feel a wet globule hit my face. When

I put my hand to wipe it, my fingers are laced with a yellowy, clingy spit.

'Puttana!' She expectorates the word with such venom I am momentarily taken aback. When my language returns, Widow Falto has already disappeared back into her home, and the next sound I hear is that of the bolts being locked inside.

I stand, my face covered in spit, and look upon the road Lorenzo has just walked along. I wish, not for the first time, we had met before I married.

Chapter Thirty-Three

'Firebird'

February 1638

I take Livia with me to see the society tailor, Cristoforo. A man of such fame he needs no second name.

We have much to organise ahead of the Carnival theatrics. I need new shoes, and more lilypowder for my face, and have ordered cochineal from Nino Marotta. But most of all, I need a gown which will dazzle.

Cristoforo greets us with a gracious bow as we enter his shop, which is spacious as befits a man who makes the outfits for the finest folk in Rome. The rooms are hung with brocade curtains and have elegant chairs with elaborate gilt work, and a private room for dressing, while above there is the workshop where nimble fingers sew garments of such intricate beauty it is almost impossible to believe it is the work of mortals. I think of Riva's shop, which I had once thought so magical, and see it differently, with its chipped paint and moth-eaten tapestries.

Livia takes a seat in the corner. It's a week since she helped me wash my face of Widow Falto's spittle and took the stained night-dress to soak. Her features are set, like a hawk observing. Livia never gossips with me, and I wonder whether she trades news with the other serving girls on the street.

Cristoforo emerges with the dress in the material I bought with Caterina. It blazes like a flame, rust red and sunset orange shot through with turquoise blue, and I can already see it is a triumph. I am helped into it by two serving girls, both dressed prettily in florals and smelling of roses. It fits me perfectly. Better than anything Tiberia or the old tailor ever made. Better, even, than the dresses Lorenzo has bought me.

The body is sleek and flatters well, while the skirts are pleated and fall long to the floor, with sleeves which are voluminous, and edged in lace which spills softly from the hem. The orange of the fabric has black repeating lines, which trace down the front, making a sharp left and right at the bottom, to create a pleasing geometry. Over the top he lays a net, which has been mightily embroidered and studded with feathers and scraps of material cut like flames, as if to transform me into a shimmering firebird. Atop my head, I wear a great fancy plumage of feathers, as if a mythical creature has dipped its wings in a birdbath of gold.

I cast a look at Livia, whose liquid eyes remain extraordinarily impassive.

Bess, in contrast, whimpers at my feet. 'Are you afraid of Mama?' I question, bending down to pick her up, but she squirms in my arms.

'I think she needs the toilet,' Livia says simply. 'I shall take her outside.'

She scoops the dog from my arms and leaves without turning back. I worry my maid's plain speaking is uncouth in such a place, but it is difficult to judge, for some of the people who speak the foulest language are the richest in Rome.

My attention returns to the mirror. 'I think the headdress . . .'

'Nay, signora.'

Cristoforo dives in front of me waving his lace-doused arms with ferocity. He is muscular, with a wide chest, broad thighs and mannerisms more suited to a Frenchman than an Italian – Cristoforo spent some time at King Louis's court – which is what makes him irresistible to fashionable Roman ladies.

'The head piece is the crowning glory. Without it, you have a pretty dress. With it, it is a masterpiece.'

He claps with joy and while I appreciate his fervour, I feel his judgement might miss the mark. Not being born to fripperies, I still have a little of the street beating in my soul and can see it looks wildly extravagant.

I move my head from side to side, making the feathers shake like a cockerel. This does nothing to increase my confidence that there is not some sort of farce being played out upon my skull.

It is at this moment Livia returns, Bess pattering at her feet. She takes a look at me. Not even a flicker. My admiration for her shoots like a star; this woman's card face is divine.

I cannot help myself but ask her, 'What think you, Livia?'

Without missing a beat, she says, 'I think it is perfect for its purpose.'

Clever. Had she been born a man she could have been serving the Roman state, not washing dishes on the Vicolo Scanderbeg.

'I shall take it all. Please package the dress up. And this.' I pick up a collar from one of the cabinets. It has a small lace detail, but not ostentatious. I will not make the mistake of buying something too lavish to wear, for although I was never a serving girl, I did live life where fashion is not a luxury to be afforded.

We return laden, and Livia immediately gets to work fixing Matteo some food, as he has been working in his foundry. He finds me in the bedchamber, unwrapping my day's work.

He stands for a moment, his sandy whiskers twitching.

'This is a pretty sight.'

'It is for Carnival.'

I look up. He has not moved.

'Matteo, do not begrudge me. For many years I watched the rich at their festivities, but we had not the money, and Papa and Tiberia are too devout. Now I can dress beautifully and act as I wish among people who value living, while we still walk on this good earth, rather than waiting for something beyond.'

He takes a step towards me, face sombre. 'It is not that I begrudge you, Costanza, but the way we live. What we do. It is forbidden by law.'

The hairs on the back of my neck rise. This is a hypocrite at work.

'I am well aware of that,' I say stiffly. 'As you were, when you first took Vincenzo to bed.'

'Aye,' he looks at me, and the old Matteo is there, in a perpetual motion of contrition. 'But Lorenzo ... I have seen the portrait; his obsession is obvious.'

I go to the bed and continue unwrapping the packages, untying ribbons, opening paper, laying out the sleeves and the skirts.

'Costanza.' Matteo takes a step closer and puts his hand on my arm to still it. He bids me to sit on the bed, and I feel the feathers of our new mattress give way softly.

'The portrait leaves no doubt as to the nature of your relationship with Lorenzo. Some will think it beautiful. Others will think it brazen. It breaks all the rules of portraiture; there has never been anything like it before.'

'It has been lauded.'

'If your parents were to see it . . . or any from our distr—'

'You are jealous. That's it. It is quite clear . . .'

'People talk . . . you cannot assume your family will not find out. It will cause great anguish. They might well cut you—'

'Do not come at me with that. Great anguish. You know full well no one from our street would be any place a Bernini portrait is on show. It is not worry for my parents which paves this path of mock concern. It is a smokescreen to hide your bitterness. You are envious of the attention the statue draws to me, while your own work is hardly rewarded.'

'You are mistaken. That is not it at all. This relationship with Lorenzo, it is like a craving . . .' Matteo speaks softly, sadly and hangs his head. I feel a spike of pleasure in his discomfort, which I know to be a cruel thing, but I do not like his tone, his knowing: his audacity when telling me of Lorenzo's feelings.

Matteo's eyes fall on the dress and headpiece laid out on the bed. In the gold and velvet of Cristoforo's shop it had looked radiant, a magnificent costume designed to set my lover's eyes alight. Yet here, set against our muted chamber, it looks gaudy.

'The world still turns, Costanza. There can be one rule in private, but in public we must show decorum. It is how Rome works. I hear you had a run in with the widow up the road.'

I wonder how, and immediately think of Livia. My stomach turns at the idea of my maid and my husband colluding.

'The Widow Falto is a nosy harridan,' I retort.

Matteo gives me a look as if to remind me to watch my language, but the time has long since passed for either of us to pretend our virtue.

'Maybe she is. But one of her sons works for a cardinal and the other is a successful merchant, and high in the guild. It does not do to make enemies when you have something to hide.' He looks again at the skirts. 'To make it so obvious, Costanza. To draw attention to yourself in such a way, dressed like this.'

In that moment I hate him. 'What? Should I skulk about like you? At least my love is natural. It may be fornication, but it is not sodomy. You promised to love me. You told Papa you would take care of me, stay by my side. But you couldn't find it within yourself to do that. So what was I left with? I blamed myself ... for four years. And now I am loved, you ask me to deny it?'

'I was wrong.' His mouth is slack, and his great body slumps. 'But I needed a wife, and you a husband. And whatever you think, Costanza, I love you. Perhaps not as you need me to, but I do. Which is why I am telling you, this must be contained. We live in a rare world where much is tolerated, but even now they lock up men such as Galileo for his thinking. We are *both* sinners in the eyes of the Church.'

The worm in my belly turns dark, and I am consumed for one awful moment with a thought of his death. Not violent, but that Matteo could be taken by disease or some such, leaving me widowed and free to the thing I want more than anything in the world: to be Lorenzo's wife.

Knowing myself well, I push away this canker. Even for me it is wickedly black.

'I should like you to leave now,' I say quietly, my fingers plucking at my skirts.

At first, I think he will refuse, that he will stay and insist on continuing these words until I spit out the truth. But he does not. Matteo never had any stomach for the fight. Before he goes, he takes one last look at the dress.

'Never was danger dressed in brighter colours.'

Part III

Chapter Thirty-Four

'Carnival'

March 1638

Lorenzo walks to greet me, arms outstretched. His face is high in colour, there is a jumpiness about him, and when he speaks it is in a voice a fraction too loud for the occasion. 'Venus! What a costume!' Then he whispers in my ear, 'You look magnificent.'

Livia and I have been rubbing creams, scrubbing, and dressing my hair for hours, but I will not let him know this.

'A firebird.' I lift my arms slightly, as if they were wings, setting off the flame colours in my dress with the motion.

He pulls me close. 'Nay, not a bird. You are my muse, my muse of fire.'

I close my eyes, and savour him and his nectar of citrus, his golden words, the heat of his breath on my skin.

But I only have him for a moment before he pulls away, the mask of the maestro straightened upon his face. He has company to keep and a production to run. All about, there is a throng of people pressing to say hello. They are dressed in their most lavish clothes, in silver and gold cloth, embroidered skirts, forests of jagged French lace growing from the cuffs and sleeves of men and women alike. Anyone who fancies themselves of consequence clamours for a place at Lorenzo Bernini's Carnival production, or they risk not having anything to say at the next gathering of polite company.

He takes my hand in his and leads me to the front, where I am to sit between his mother, Angelica Bernini, and Caterina. Matteo is already backstage, and I am glad not to see him. Things are still strained with my husband; our words have been few this last week.

Although no player, Matteo must take to the stage, and has thankfully been given a modest part to match his reluctance. All of Lorenzo's men are to take part, it being a necessary test of their loyalty. To refuse or to leave is a betrayal, as Finelli found out.

I curtsey in front of Mother Bernini, who offers a tremoring hand for me to take.

'Rise,' she says, and I kiss her knuckles, which shake as I lift the bone to my lips. I straighten my back, and feel it grow more than a few inches with satisfaction at this anointing. Even Caterina, who often treats me as a teacher does her pupil, nods her head in acquiescence to my daughter status.

'You make a fantastical firebird, Costanza,' Caterina whispers as I am seated. 'You made a good choice on that material, setting off, as it does, your hair and eyes, like flame and coals. And the headpiece is a triumph. You have such a talent for carrying off a cut and colours which other women would run from.'

'You, too, look beautiful,' I say, and I mean it. Caterina has never looked more noble, her face flawlessly painted, hair perfectly curled, and her dress setting off the lightness of her skin and sharpness of her pale blue eyes.

'But I have not the glow of Bernini's love.' She smooths the silk of her skirt, which is a striking turquoise and decked out with gilded butterfly wings. 'It is the most extreme fortune to have love requited. You are lucky to be adored by Il Cavaliere, for his love alters not and he is a rare man.'

I feel a chill, and think of my statue and Lorenzo's words: *Are you not the most fortunate of women?*

I do not reply instantly, and Caterina's eyes narrow.

'It is true. I am most blessed.' I rush my words, trying to catch up. I want to change the subject and am just about to ask about Signor Giovanni when Caterina sits up very straight, opens her fan, and begins talking to the woman sitting on the other side.

I turn to Mother Bernini. The profile of Lorenzo's mother's face is astonishing in its resemblance to her son's: contoured, her chin tapering to a point, eyes the same molasses black. She turns to look behind us, at the many acquaintances taking their seats in the vast auditorium, which has been constructed in the grounds of the Fabbrica.

'It is truly a sight. We came to this city as strangers.' She sucks the air through her lips. 'From Naples. From nothing. And now look at all these people.'

'They are here for your son.'

She nods unsteadily. 'Do you have children?'

I pause, and noticing the lapse, she continues.

'I see. You can always take the holy waters, my dear. Our Lady can take her time to bless a woman.' She considers this, then adds, 'I was pregnant when I married.'

I smile. 'It happens.'

'I was twelve and Pietro was twenty-five.' She rocks slightly, back and forth. 'I bore my husband thirteen children. Five daughters, then finally a boy. And what a son to have; he was worth the wait, and the pain.'

The music sounds for the play to start, and Lorenzo walks out upon the stage, commanding all with his presence. As he introduces the players, he looks for just one second at Angelica. It is a fleeting moment, but I see the flash of connection, atavistic and primeval, a lifetime of memories exchanged in a glance, his giver of life. I feel the deepest ache wash over me in the revelation, which always seems to hit me anew. I wish I had known my own mother.

The evening passes well enough; the audiences are charmed by the quips and japes. The satire is biting, with much fun being poked at the rich and the notorious, the cruellest lines getting the biggest laughs. Poor Matteo, with his large frame lumbering across the stage, manages to acquit himself honourably. He even raises a chuckle, and such is the relief I feel, I understand I must signal a truce.

After the play, the chairs are pulled back and wooden panels are laid on the ground for dancing. A thousand lanterns hang around, the breeze moving the lights like shimmering fireflies, so bright it is hard to see the stars.

When the music starts, Lorenzo leads me onto the floor. We are Lord and Lady of the Carnival dance. Slowly we begin to weave our bodies to the music, hands clapping, backs swerving, then he puts his hands on my waist and lifts me to the sky. The men cheer and soon many couples have joined us, their jewels catching the light of the lanterns as they move around the floor.

We dance until our breath is lost and our faces flushed, but as we make our way to the wine, I lose Lorenzo to his business. There are many patrons here, and each seeks their moment with the genius of the age. In Rome, proximity is power.

I have seen Matteo once or twice with Vincenzo, which I can hardly begrudge given my very public display. Some men join me in conversation, but their wives do not, unwilling to talk to Bernini's mistress in public. It makes me bridle, for they are happy enough to gossip with me behind closed doors, in Caterina's salon. I note with resentment who the women are and think not for the first time how this city is full of hypocrites.

It is in a fallow moment of conversation that I am caught. I feel Luigi's oily shadow upon me before I hear his voice.

'I saw you kissing our mother's hand.'

The hairs rise on my arm.

'Being so well acquainted with the family, it would be uncivil not to greet the lady of the household.'

'Aye, but you are not a lady to be feted as such. You are my brother's harlot.'

I do not dignify his goading with an answer.

'Why did you ignore my warnings?' Luigi's voice is hoarse, as if holding something back, which I dimly perceive as a threat. His face has lost its softer edges in the flickering lamplight, and looks instead harsh, his eyes glittering.

'What your brother and I have cannot be dammed like a river. It is not containable.'

Luigi grips my arm and puts his face into mine. I smell the grappa on his tongue, as bright and sharp as if he had just taken a sip.

'You should have been mine.'

His words are full of fury and my heart beats quicker, making my muscles taut, ready to flee.

'It is my greatest misfortune to be born the brother of Lorenzo Bernini. An accident of birth, that is all. That he comes first, and I second. All he does is steal my art, my ideas, and pass them off as his own.'

There is a fluttering in the darkness as people pass by.

'You are drunk, and this is unseemly. This is a conversation for your brother, not me.'

'Yet you know I will never have it, any more than you will ever tell him. For we are both afraid. Lorenzo is bound by nothing and demands absolute loyalty.'

'I am not afraid of him. And he should expect loyalty. Look at all he does for us. For *you*.' Luigi snorts. 'It is time you grew up and acknowledged everything Lorenzo has given you. Commissions, employment, the way he sweeps up after your ... cruelties.'

Luigi looks up, his face contorted with the revelation. 'Lorenzo told you?'

I do not say anything, there is no need, but it is obvious I know about the discreet bribes and payment of fines Lorenzo makes when Luigi is in trouble. Covered over, like dirt thrown on vomit. To keep the Bernini name free from scandal.

'Why shouldn't he pay?'

There are voices nearby and someone pushes into Luigi. Momentarily distracted, he loosens his grip, and I pull my arm from his, the skin feeling tender where he held it.

'It is all an edifice, Costanza,' Luigi nearly shouts.

But I am already walking away. I head to the heart of the party where I take a drink from a serving boy. The night is warm and my costume heavy, and I welcome the slaking of my thirst.

I search for Lorenzo, pushing my way through the guests, burning to tell him of Luigi's imposition, but cannot find him. I take another cup of wine, then another.

'Costanza!'

I swing round and nearly fall into Matteo, holding on to his arm to steady myself.

'I was looking for Lorenzo.'

'I have not seen him for some time.' Matteo takes a moment to look at me, taking in the slight sway of my body. 'Just as well you have not found him. Il Cavaliere would not be pleased at your sorry state.'

'I am just enjoying the party.'

'Here,' Matteo pulls roughly at my arm and drags me to a corner, finding a free bench, which he pushes me onto. I bridle at such unkind action and make to speak, but he does so first, raising his forefinger in the air to silence me. 'Wait,' Matteo commands, and I sigh as he turns, resting my chin in my hands as I watch his broad back moving through the throng. When Matteo returns he is carrying a large cup, which he hands wordlessly to me. It is wine, but so watered down it is almost undrinkable.

'Ergh.'

'Take it. You cannot be seen to be so loose, Costanza.'

'I need to tell Lorenzo something.'

'Nothing is so pressing as to warrant his wrath at your state. He will think you have done this to embarrass him.'

My eyes try to alight upon Matteo's face, but I must squint to make his features sit straight.

He crouches in front of me and whispers, 'What is so urgent you need to tell Il Cavaliere immediately?'

I gaze at him, mute for a moment, trying to form the words. Then I lean forward so as to speak secrets into my husband's ear. 'It is Luigi Bernini.'

There is a pause, while I think some more.

'Go on.' Matteo exhales a note of exasperation.

'Luigi is jealous of Lorenzo.'

'This is not your business, Costanza.'

I speak slowly and quietly so Matteo will understand. 'Luigi thinks I should be his.'

Matteo pats my arm gently. 'Even Luigi would not be so foolish as to try something on with his brother's mistress.'

A hiccup. 'You did not hear him. He means me' – another hiccup – 'harm.' I steady myself on Matteo's arm and fix my husband with a stare so he understands the gravity of the situation. 'I am sure of it.'

Matteo ceases to pat, and instead takes my hands. 'Listen carefully, Costanza. This is the drink talking; pay no heed to these thoughts. Whatever Luigi said, and Lord knows he can be unpleasant, you have interpreted it to be more than it is. Il Cavaliere is not a man to be trifled with, not least when it comes to his women or his business ...'

'I know what I—' But Matteo continues talking over me.

'There is no way Luigi would interfere. There is a resentment between these two brothers, of that there is no doubt. It is like tinder waiting to be struck, and I will not allow you to be the spark. We have had a fine night, and you have dazzled all with your presence, but it is time to go.'

Perhaps my husband is right. There is a torment between Lorenzo and Luigi, and now I try to remember Luigi's words they are hazy, lost to the night, leaving me only a dim feeling something is amiss.

Matteo looks at me expectantly. 'No more talk of Luigi, do you promise?'

'I promise.'

Chapter Thirty-Five

'A Tear in Time'

July 1638

Livia is out, and I am readying myself for an afternoon with Caterina when there is a knock at the door. At first I think it must be a tradesman, for now we have coin I am in the habit of spending, on fine food and wine, threads and pins, so all manner of parcels and packages arrive for me. It still surprises me how much upkeep there is in fashionable living.

The day is already singeing at the edges, and in a bid to keep cool, I have not dressed but am still in my light nightshirt. I put on a silk house-robe, wrapping it around my waist as I descend the stairs, navigating the paintings stacked on the landing, recent purchases ready to be hung. As my hands alight on the metal of the door I feel its warmth, where the sun has shone on the other side. I turn the handle and the door is gently pushed open from the outside.

'Luigi.' I am surprised to see him. 'Lorenzo is not here.'

'Good morrow, Costanza. I was expecting a kinder welcome. It is you I came to speak with.'

'Luigi, I—'

'Just a word.'

He pushes harder at the door, so it opens wide, and mindful of Widow Falto I step aside.

'What can I do for you?' I am wary, but do not want to appear impolite, for we must maintain the vestiges of civility.

'I've walked all the way here and I am thirsty. Fetch me a drink, will you?'

I wish Livia were here. To serve upon Luigi is an annoyance, but I resolve to do anything which will get rid of him quickly.

'Wait in the salon, upstairs. I shall fetch some wine.' I watch him climb the stairs two at a time, and then pause to flick through the stacked paintings, as if he owned them, not I.

When I return to the salon, Luigi is sat on the long settle. I set down the wine, which is well watered, and carefully pour us each a glass. Our new house is set on a quieter street than our old rooms, and there is precious little sound from outside. I miss hearing people about their business above and below me, as if the tenor of their industry afforded me protection, for someone would always hear you if you called out. Now it is as if a sleep has fallen over the city and Luigi and I are the only ones awake.

I make to sit opposite him, but Luigi motions for me to sit next to him. I do and suddenly feel frail and flimsy – in great danger – like a gossamer-winged moth about to be consumed by a summer wildfire.

It is swift when it happens. He leans over, pushing me down with his hand on my neck. My glass falls to the floor and my head bangs against the scrolling of the settle. I instinctively reach up to feel the back of my head, my fingers finding their way to where it hurts.

'No, I don't want to . . .' I gasp, but his fingers are pressing so hard I cannot make my words clear.

I want to squirm, to pull away, but every second he is about me he could hurt me more. I am also terrified that he will leave marks upon my body – welts, blows or finger-shaped bruises – rousing mistrust in Lorenzo, who would notice, ask questions, become suspicious of my fidelity, and how could I tell him they were made by Luigi's hand?

I turn my cheek to the wall and look at a small crack in the plaster, so fine it could have been spun by a spider. I look at the dimensions of its lines, long and thin, travelling not quite horizontal to the ceiling, and imagine another world beyond, a tear in time. I want to raise my hand, trace my finger along its path, but cannot move.

Assured I will not run, his hand leaves my neck and pulls up my nightshirt.

It will be over soon, I tell myself. It will be over soon, and if you do not struggle he will not hurt you any more than he must.

The crack on the wall glows the yellow of snakes' eyes and breaks open, shapes dance in front of my eyes, which leak tears without consent, but I push the sob in my chest down deep.

Afterwards he leans to kiss me and asks, 'Did you enjoy that?'

I cannot speak.

'When I come again we shall to bed, and I shall show you what real pleasure is. More than my brother has ever shown you.'

'I do not want . . .'

His eyes narrow. He is still atop me and holds my head, so he can speak plainly.

'The time has passed for that. I shall come and we shall go to bed. If you do not agree then I will tell Lorenzo everything. How *you* came to *me* and made your proposal. How you betrayed him with me. How your body felt in my hands. And it will end everything, for both of us.'

I cannot move, but my silence says it all.

* * *

He comes again, and again.

Always the knock at the door mid-morning. At first, I made arrangements to be away, but he cornered me like a dog and made his threats; that he would tell Lorenzo, nay, the whole world that he has bedded me. I beg him to cease, that I never wanted this, but he tells me I lie. He tells me I did not say no when he came, that I encouraged him and lay with him willingly.

He wants more.

I think of Lorenzo and my courage fails me. I am beyond shame. I am reduced, so small in my own estimation I can hardly bear to see my image reflected in a window or a looking glass.

It is always the same. The heat of the day rising, the air stilling to nothing; an absence of noise in the house, Livia being at market and Matteo at the Fabbrica.

When he is upon me, I feel myself lifting from my body. Hovering above, I want to stop watching but cannot; I see the drops of sweat fall from his face onto mine, trickling down into my eyes, their salt tang stinging, and eventually tracing their way to my mouth. Sometimes my body is submerged, and it is not the weight of him but the sodden earth that pushes down upon me. Thud, thud. Sods of mud falling from above on the box in which I lie.

My mind begins to close in on me.

Looping memories of these afternoons with Luigi, like a thread getting caught when a needle is pulled too quickly, snagging, tugging, too tight to unknot. I want to pull so hard the strand snaps and is freed, so there will be no stitches at all, no evidence of the last few months. I want to go back to the beginning when it was just me and Lorenzo, nothing more. But Luigi infects everything. My sleep. My appetite. My body.

Caterina complains about my company, that I have turned silent, pale. She holds my hand and asks what's wrong. 'Tell me,' she implores, 'tell me what ails you?' I speak a little of what has happened. Not all. Not the worst. I confide how much I detest Luigi: how he watches me, waits for me, menaces me. Of the way Lorenzo's younger brother lusts for me, his slippery hands, a finger running along my face, a touch of my waist, when he thinks no one else is watching. Of how Luigi sours the very air I breathe, and how my belly houses a deep-seated dread that this situation, this bloody awfulness, could descend into chaos at any moment should Lorenzo find out.

She looks aghast, and I see in her eyes she has guessed the rest, understands it all. 'You must tell Lorenzo,' she urges. 'Make Luigi stop.' I shake my head. I cannot. It is impossible. He will never accept what I say. Caterina pleads no more, but grips my hand, squeezing it hard in a silent acknowledgment that when it comes to powerful men, there is nothing that *can* be done.

Chapter Thirty-Six

'Revelation'

August 1638

The city is roiling, waiting for the storm clouds to burst. As for the city's inhabitants, they sweat in the infernal heat: men who are usually as strong as two oxen, weaken; food spoils as soon as it is bought; children, stripped to their lightest linens, scream in vexation; and all appetites are lost.

The Bernini house has its windows thrown wide open to encourage the breeze, but there is no wind, so the gesture is futile. Inside, the sculptor's close circle is gathered, but Lorenzo has not the inclination to be clever or witty and instead demands to be entertained.

He sits on his large chair, watching. There is Paolo: the weather torments the man, there are rashes about his face and arms, making his mood insufferable. Andrea, in good humour as always. Matteo and Vincenzo, together. They have given up pretending, he thinks.

Costanza's statue stands proudly in the corner, marble made flesh. Costanza doubled, one on a plinth, the other in his circle, as if she has been born with a stone twin.

She is with Andrea; their conversation flows back and forth like the tide, and she smiles a great deal. Her face lights from within, like some celestial animation. He casts his eye about again, but it always returns to her. He could, he thinks, watch her for eternity. She is his great undoing.

Despite the hanging of herbs and lighting of scented oils, bergamot and sandalwood, the room smells fetid, of sweat and women's blood, sewers and dust. With marble there is always dust. Maybe it is time to go to the country. He could take Costanza with him. The city is sickening, as if God is withholding rain as some sort of punishment for the hypocrisy within its walls.

The hounds at his feet slide their heads down upon their great paws and let out defeated sighs. There is nothing to do but lie and hope the humid day passes.

Here is Caterina. She sidles up to the sculptor, and he greets her with a wave of his hand, not wanting to expend more energy than is strictly needed. She has been unwittingly useful, he thinks, training Costanza and persuading her of the pleasures that would surely come from being his mistress.

Caterina hovers, like a dragonfly in shimmering silks, her perfume sweet and sickly. Now she has his attention, she leans in and whispers into the sculptor's ear, 'Do you think something ails Costanza?'

'Not that I have noticed.'

'Or perhaps Luigi?'

Costanza stands out, even in the middle of the throng, the head higher than most and her sturdy shoulders thrown back, chin high. But when he looks at her again, he fancies he can see something different about her, a tightness in her jaw, even though the light flickers prettily about her face.

And talk of the Devil: here is Luigi snaking his way through the crowd. Lorenzo sits forward and rests his chin on his knuckles, as if watching players upon a stage.

His brother makes straight for Costanza. She is facing Lorenzo and cannot see Luigi approach, although she seems to stiffen as if sensing his presence. She does not turn, or acknowledge his existence, even when Luigi stands right behind her.

The sculptor's hackles have been raised by Caterina's comments. His body becomes tense, like an animal as the sun sets, newly alert to the sounds of the night. Is it not odd? That Costanza would not acknowledge Luigi, in company such as this?

Then his brother does something which is most startling. Luigi slips his fingers subtly about Costanza's waist, so unobtrusive and slight a gesture that if you were not watching intently, you would not even notice the touch.

More startling is Costanza's reaction.

It is as if she has been stung. She brushes his hand away and moves abruptly, as if to shake Luigi from her shadow. Costanza makes no attempt to look behind her, but nods her head this way, then that. Lorenzo sees her jawline is implacably set, as she makes her apologies and gets set to leave the modest circle of friends. Luigi is left looking bemused.

What means this? Lorenzo hears many words clattering about his brain.

There can be only one explanation: that Caterina's foul hints are based on the ruminations of truth.

His own brother and Costanza.

Why else would Luigi presume to lay a finger on Costanza's body in such a way? And was her response not one of a woman wishing to conceal the tender touch of a lover? To cover up the secret of a familiar caress?

Bile rises at the back of his throat, and his heart pounds stronger as the truth, just born, begins to wail and screech in his ears. Wait, he tells the keening inside, wait. A man such as Lorenzo is built by years of self-determination and control. This is supposition. There is no evidence to support this vile subterfuge, this hideous betrayal.

His mind spins a cloth of virtuous lies which he will lay at the feet of the wanton lovers. He wills there to be no truth in this gesture, he wants to believe it is *he* who conjures falsehoods from its meaning. Costanza is his. She has lain in his arms and expressed her love and desire for him in the most ardent terms.

A drop of sweat runs down his back. He must know. One way or the other, he must determine the truth.

* * *

Lorenzo rises from his chair. His movement breaks the sleeping spell which has been cast over the listless room, and all eyes turn to follow the sculptor's progress as he makes his way to the small dais. The platform sits neatly at one end of the room and is usually reserved for the musicians who play at parties.

My belly tightens, as it always does when Lorenzo moves unexpectedly, as if he has a force which pulls me to him. I wait for his eyes to search me out as he passes, a knowing glance, or wink.

Lorenzo passes but does not look for me. Despite the sweltering heat, it feels as if I have slipped into the shade. He steps purposefully onto the stage. His determination puzzles me. Earlier he had been lamenting the weather, crying to the heavens, asking how long we must endure this fetid, feverish air which infects all men so they are utterly devoid of passion or purpose. Asking why God is punishing Rome, although we all know her crimes.

As Lorenzo stands raised on the small dias, the late afternoon sun shifts, and a beam falls upon him, as if Caravaggio has had a hand in the composition. The light dances on his face, illuminating his fine chin and strong cheekbones, and casting spectral shadows around the hollows of his eyes, which shine as if they are made of polished jet. He glances around at the upturned faces of the room but does not look directly at anyone, as if he is searching for something more ethereal than our solid bodies, something living in the warm silhouettes that fall from them.

Slowly, Lorenzo raises his hand, signalling that he will speak. A hush falls about the place. 'I have received some news about a commission out of town which needs investigation and will be leaving immediately.'

A low murmur breaks out, as the men of his employ speculate what could have caused this abrupt change of plans, and what it will mean. It is odd; Lorenzo has mentioned nothing of a trip. I feel as if I am playing a game in which the rules have suddenly been changed, and I no longer understand the order in which the cards should be laid. I look up hoping he will give some signal that I am to accompany him on his journey.

He continues. 'I will be absent for a few nights only. My brother, Luigi, shall take on responsibility for the business while I am gone.'

The murmuring grows louder. It is not unusual for Lorenzo to travel, but at this time of year, in this heat? It is unconscionable. Whatever the business at hand, it must be of the utmost importance. I turn as everyone does, to look at Luigi, and find he is looking directly back at me.

When I glance back at Lorenzo, he too is staring at Luigi, and I realise with fear that he must have witnessed the glance between us. A taste of dread rises within, acid revulsion kicking at the back of my throat and filling my mouth. With Lorenzo away, and Matteo with Vincenzo, I will be left on my own.

Lorenzo says nothing more but steps off the stage, reserving neither a glance nor a word for me. He strides from the room, the dogs at his heel, and signals for Stefano to follow.

I push people out of the way to follow Lorenzo into the relative peace of the hallway, meaning to ask him what has happened to cause such precipitous action, but when I get there, he is gone.

It begins with a demented rushing in my ears, like hooves, a hundred beasts thundering, panicked and rearing, the whites of their eyes showing. I pull at my bodice to loosen it, such is my fight for breath. It is a bad omen, this trip. I cannot think why Lorenzo would leave town so suddenly – and leave me. Leave me to . . .

Caterina's hand on my shoulder disturbs the thought. Her grasp is firm, and I steady my breath before turning, wanting to hide the fretfulness which bites at me.

'I saw you leave.' She looks at me and blinks; in the Bernini household, walls have ears.

''Tis the heat, and the crush of bodies inside.' I motion to the hall. Her hand remains on my shoulder, providing sisterly comfort.

'Oh, you poor child.' She speaks softly, with something of a whimper.

'I wish he were not going,' I say quietly.

'It will be a few days at most, and then he will return. It may even help your cause. Luigi does not run a tight ship; Lorenzo may decide to use his brother less if mistakes are made. And I shall keep determined company with you.'

I nod. 'You are right, of course. A few days. It's just . . .' I feel a small leak of the dam and the words rush from me. 'It's just I do not like it when he is away.'

Her hand grips harder. 'Lorenzo would not leave you unless it was absolutely necessary.' She twirls a lock of my hair around her finger, as a mother would with a child. I cannot meet her eyes, but stare uneasily at the floor.

'I have an idea.' She brightens and smooths my hair back over my ear. 'We shall plan a party for his return. That will be a wonderful distraction, and you can welcome Lorenzo home in style.'

Chapter Thirty-Seven

'Master of all the World'

August 1638

The sculptor tells his groomsman to pull the carriage up on the square, beyond her front door.

It is not really a square, but a small scratch of land in the winding backstreets of the Pope's summer palace. He knows the place intimately. He will be well hidden here, but still afforded a good view of Costanza's front door. The air presses upon Lorenzo Bernini's lungs and sweat trickles down his back as he waits.

He knows Luigi is already inside the building, having dispatched Stefano to keep watch. The heat invades the sculptor's skin, his blood is roiling, his fiery humours blaze so fierce they discharge devilish sparks in his mind. Terrible, tortuous thoughts of Luigi touching, his fingers delving everywhere that belongs to him. And Costanza, letting him.

He becomes so lost in the ugliness of his dreams – part despair, part incandescent rage – that his lips begin to move. The words he speaks are of the harm he wishes to inflict on them both. Stefano shifts: this whore has turned his beloved master into a muttering madman.

Time ticks on. The cicadas drum their many grievances into the darkness and the moths flutter with death-wish wings towards the groomsman's lantern.

Dante had conjured his muse, Beatrice, imagining her draped in a crimson cloth, then watched as she ate his burning heart, before dispatching her to heaven. Beatrice inspired Dante from afar, she was emblazoned on his soul, but never polluted his flesh.

Lorenzo can see the mistake he has made. Instead of putting Costanza on a pedestal, he has allowed this woman to climb inside the cavity of his body and take possession of his soul. The alchemy of their love drove his hands to cold stone and inspired him to render a vivid likeness, the softness of her flesh, the intensity of her gaze, the moment she parts her lips, it is as if she is with him.

His weakness was a mistake. So driven was he by carnal desire, to meet flesh upon flesh, he allowed himself to be taken by her.

She was *his* muse.

She *was* his muse.

The sculptor begins to drown in a storm of unrelenting violence. Thoughts burst from his mind and bridge into his body, the sinews in his neck drawing like a purse string, tensing his arms, hands, knuckles, his fingertips flex and pulse.

It's early morning now, moments before the moon gives way to the sun. The sculptor looks to the inky sky and comes to a decision which, although it pains him, is just.

Dawn breaks, light clouds streak the chiffon sky, painted in delicate hues of apricot, rose and gold. The heat has not broken; today will be as stultifying as yesterday.

There is a movement at the door as it opens. Lorenzo springs to a crouch, heart crushed as he watches his brother leave Costanza's house. Luigi's doublet is undone and he hitches at his breeches, pulling them about his waist as he speaks to her. When Luigi leans in to kiss Costanza, she offers her cheek like a chaste maiden.

The sculptor lets the moment run through him like a cat o'nine tails lashing, then releases a bitter laugh; it is too late for modesty now.

Unknowingly, Luigi walks towards his brother's carriage. Lorenzo holds his breath, ready to jump, but Luigi pays no attention to it. His brother never did observe as an artist should.

As he passes, Luigi scratches at his balls. This small, uncouth act causes Lorenzo such pain that he bursts from the carriage in blazing wrath.

Luigi, some strides on, turns and looks upon his brother, confused, then comprehending. The younger brother starts to run, boots sliding and catching in the dirt, kicking up a small sandstorm, as he attempts to secure better purchase. A dog barks in one of the courtyards, high-pitched and insistent, and is answered by another who growls, clamouring to be let loose.

The sculptor begins to give chase, his body impossibly alive, his chest heaving with exertion and rage.

The brothers pass south through the streets of Rome. Both are fine specimens, fit and able. They pass tradesmen starting about their early morning business, some of whom recognise the Bernini brothers giving chase. Later, in households and taverns, there will be boasts made, stories embellished. Luigi wild, running for his life half dressed. Lorenzo following, knife in hand, intent on plunging it into his brother's heart.

Luigi makes for the doors of the church of Santa Maria Maggiore; he will seek sanctuary from his maniacal brother in a house of God.

Lorenzo's lungs contract and expand against his ribs, which quiver in sharp, painful jolts. He cares not where his brother is headed, it makes no difference, he will have revenge.

The younger brother is at the doors, pushing to open them. Inside it is a building site, scaffolding all around, half-finished commemorations to the long dead. But it is the living that concerns Luigi, specifically the necessity to preserve his own life. His legs, unused to sprinting, give way beneath him, he rests his hands in the dust of the church floor and allows the relief of sanctuary to flood over him.

The holy men are startled. It is early for a man to be panting on his knees, even in Rome. And this man, Luigi Bernini, is notorious. The priests may have taken religious orders, but they are worldly enough to know trouble when they see it.

They exchange nervous glances and mutter. Some say they must get him gone, others argue that anyone can seek sanctuary, but all agree the appearance of this man will bring grief.

Then a number of things happen all at once. The silence is broken by a hammering of fists and feet on the wooden door. A quick-witted brother rushes to bolt it, while another helps Luigi from the ground, sitting him on a pile of wooden planks.

The pounding at the door continues. Outside, a man is yelling. He shows no respect for the sacred nature of the place but screams in disdain. 'I am Lorenzo Bernini, appointed architect of the Basilica. A personal friend of His Holiness. Allow me entry to this church or you will all be reported. To earn the ire of the Pontiff is a most grievous thing.' More banging. 'I'm warning you. Open this door or else I will have you arrested for denying the chief architect entry. Can you fucking hear me?'

The holy men huddle again, but it does not take a mystic to work out what will happen next. Someone, with one eye on advancement, opens the door, and Lorenzo enters like a flying banshee, words leaving his mouth in such a torrent of spittle and swearing that they are hardly distinguishable. He shouts of betrayal, of the fact Luigi has made him a fool – vulgar, nasty, unholy words about fornication and treachery.

Luigi, having recovered his breath, gets up quickly from the pile of planks, and walks slowly towards his brother, arms open in contrition, like a child trying to make peace with the playground bully.

The Bernini brothers face each other, while the holy men recede into the shadows.

'My brother. I am sorry. This is God's place ... let us talk.'

The sculptor laughs. The time for words has passed. Nothing but obliterating Luigi's vile countenance from this earth will be enough.

All at once the sculptor lunges at his brother, landing a punch on Luigi's face. There is a satisfying crack and blood spurts from Luigi's nose as he staggers back. The sight of the harm he has caused surges inside Lorenzo, expanding in his nerves and muscles. He needs more.

Lorenzo lunges again but Luigi is ready this time and hammers blows in return. The sculptor feels fists landing on his face, his neck, his skull, then experiences a moment of white silence before a screeching pain pulses under his skin. He is propelled backwards by the shock of his brother's blows and the force with which they land. The men in the darkness shift. Luigi looks stronger. This could be over sooner than they feared.

Lorenzo rights himself. He cannot believe his little brother has had the temerity to fight back; how fucking dare he? The sculptor's thoughts are filled with the eyes of the monks watching, how they will have seen his momentary weakness. Humiliated now, he will hold nothing back. He imagines Luigi lying on the floor, skull caved in. His brother cannot be allowed to win.

There is a momentary lull. Luigi, thinking his brother has come to his senses, relaxes his stance. But Lorenzo has seen something out of the corner of his eye. On the ground is a metal bar, abandoned. Luigi follows his brother's gaze but realises too late what is about to happen.

Lorenzo lunges for the bar; the weight of it feels reassuring in his hands. A calm descends over the sculptor. He is now in charge, in control; he will determine how this ends. Without giving his body instruction, Lorenzo Bernini finds himself running at his brother, a power surge, one word repeating, screaming, inside his head: justice.

Luigi has no time to arm himself. All he has left is words. He covers his head in anticipation of the blow, and shouts, 'Lorenzo, please, I beseech you, we must tal—'

But the younger Bernini does not get the chance to finish his sentence.

The sculptor lifts the bar high and the heavy iron hits Luigi across the chest. His brother screams as the metal makes contact. Another blow. Skin splitting, blood vessels bursting, bones breaking. Such is the onslaught that Luigi falls to the floor. The sculptor is a decent man. He will not pulverise his brother with metal while he lies on the ground. Lorenzo drops the pole and bends his knee. A boot in his ribs. Then another. The church echoes to the dull thuds of kicking and stamping.

'Please.' Luigi stammers now. He is beaten. The holy men are not moving. If no one stops his lunatic brother, Luigi Bernini will die on the floor of the Santa Maria Maggiore.

Blood foams and bubbles from Luigi's mouth.

The sculptor screams. 'You are no brother of mine.' And delivers another kick.

The priests are alarmed, shifting in the dark recesses as a slow understanding dawns on them; Lorenzo Bernini will not – cannot – cease. One rushes forward, his hands waving as if stopping carts in the street, trying to break whatever spell the sculptor is under.

'Il Cavaliere!' he shouts.

Lorenzo swings around, fists raised, ready to punch whoever even thinks about restraint, for no one will be spared his rage.

The priest stops; there is an edge of fear laced with pleading to his voice. 'Il Cavaliere, I beseech you. This is the most sacred house of God. He is your brother. It is against all justice, God and man.'

Lorenzo turns back to Luigi in disdain and delivers another kick. Luigi does not move now, but merely groans.

'Holy Mary, Mother of God,' shouts the man. 'Do you mean to kill him? Do you really mean to kill your own kin, Lorenzo Bernini? To kill your brother? Think of your mother.'

Lorenzo turns again towards the priest, spitting out his words. 'Luigi Bernini deserves to die. He is a thief and a man who has lost all honour.'

The holy man replies, 'It is not your right to take vengeance. God will do that. But if you kill him, you damn yourself.'

The sculptor looks at his brother lying on the floor: his face a bloody mess, shirt torn, the ground speckled with ruby drops.

'I stole nothing,' Luigi whispers hoarsely.

Lorenzo kicks him again.

Luigi whimpers. 'I stole nothing!' What little animation he has left is channelled into a final act of self-preservation. 'I stole nothing,' he repeats again. 'Costanza gave of herself willingly.'

As he hears those words the sculptor lets out a long breath and feels the energy draining from his muscles, seep from his pores. It was all Lorenzo had left: that his brother had taken Costanza under duress, that she acted unwillingly. For this truth he would have gladly killed his brother. But Luigi has made his declaration in a house of God.

It is finished. Irreversible. She has done what he always feared she would.

She has abandoned him.

Lorenzo walks out of the church without a backwards glance, his face splashed with the crimson of his brother's blood, a new plan fermenting in the bleeding edges of his heart.

Chapter Thirty-Eight

'An Ill Unlike All Others'

August 1638

Where does love go, when it is lost?

Lorenzo strides out of the church to find Stefano, his violence not yet sated. Still covered in his brother's blood, the sculptor wears a look of such savagery that his manservant steps forward in alarm.

'Sire ...'

Lorenzo holds his hand up. His body is shaking from the exertion of the chase, the exhilaration of the violence he has meted, but the matter is not settled.

She gave herself willingly. The words echo in his mind, as if he were back in the empty church.

'I have a task for you.' Lorenzo lays his hand on the Stefano's shoulder. This man is more than a servant, he is a brother-in-arms in this war. The only person left that the sculptor can rely on.

'Costanza has been ...'

It is the first time he has said her name out loud since the discovery, and he is surprised by how strange the word feels, like a foreign object in his mouth. It is humiliating to tell a servant of the betrayal.

He would not do so unless he knew Stefano's view. The groomsman is no admirer of women, having been betrayed by a maid he thought was a virgin who turned out to be anything but. He knows the words Stefano uses to describe the housemaids and the women he passes on the street. Scold. Bitch. Witch. Jade. Slut.

Lorenzo lays his soul bare. 'She bedded my brother. Betrayed me.'

The air between the two men vibrates with an ancient understanding. Eve was only the first of her kind.

Stefano lays his hand over the sculptor's in an act of solidarity.

'She must pay. You are Bernini. A man of God-given talent, put upon this earth to glorify the heavens. And she is a . . . a whore.'

Lorenzo dips his head at the heart-breaking truth Stefano speaks, then looks his servant in the eye. 'I cannot be seen to . . .'

A darkness surges and Stefano's eyes glitter with reciprocal exhilaration. 'I will do it.'

Lorenzo nods, and from his jacket draws out a cloth he has been carrying. Wrapped inside is a tool from his workshop: a razor. The sun is rising fast and the blade dances in the light, its edge freshly sharpened on a leather strap.

'Her face.'

It hurts him to think of the caressing detail of her lips, her tender cheeks. But it must be done. The world is laughing at him.

Stefano takes the weapon, turning it carefully in his stocky hands.

'It is a fine blade. She will be marked, bearing the scar of dishonour.'

'You will be banished if you are caught.'

'Aye,' Stefano's eyes gleam with anticipation. 'But I do not intend to get caught.'

'I will protect you if necessary.'

'I trust you with my life, sire.' Stefano begins to wrap the blade.

'Call home. Pick up two flagons of wine as gifts, it will rouse less suspicion.'

A cat, mottled and matted, slinks past and settles in the shafts of sunlight creeping over the top of the buildings, watching the two men with her sly eyes.

Chapter Thirty-Nine

'Dealt With in Fury'

August 1638

E ven though it is early, I gesture Stefano over the threshold with a smile.

He holds out two flagons of wine, offering them as he always does, but he will not catch my gaze. Instead, he looks at his boots, which are covered in a sandy grime.

I take both jugs, one in each hand. Their liquid weight pulls on my arm as I carry the flagons to the small wooden table ready for Livia to take to the kitchen. I glance at the ancient statue of Helen of Troy standing nearby. She is my latest purchase, and I am unequally pleased with her. Although beautiful, Helen's smile is faint and her eyes questioning; it must have been wearisome, all that being fought over, causing wars.

When I turn back there is a flash of metal. For a moment I am confused, then I feel an impression upon my face, a sensation before it is a pain. Then again. A surge of candescent heat springs where he has sliced.

He staggers back and I see, in his hand, a blade covered in blood.

A noise swells from my breast to my throat. It is not a sound my mind has conjured, but one my body has willed into being. A scream raw, and hoarse, and filled with such terror it is loud enough to rouse Livia.

So loud he drops the razor, turns, and flees.

I know I must stop the blood. I fall back against the stairs, frightened to feel my face for fear of what I will find. When I touch there, my fingers are immediately slick, and I can feel something else, a hardness between the carved tissue of my skin.

My white nightdress, soaked crimson, clings to my body as a pool of blood edges its way to the Turkish rug, darkening the knots and motifs with a terrible stain.

Livia is running towards me.

'Signora Costanza!'

Her face pales, aghast at the sight. I see her bewilderment as she looks around for the attacker. I shake my head trying to tell her he is gone.

'Linens.' My voice is muffled, my mouth filled with a metallic wetness, which splutters and leaves a trail of tiny red specks across her face as I speak. 'To stem the blood.'

She nods and leaves me.

My mind spits and stammers with a vision from my childhood. An old woman in rags, missing a nose. The gaping hole of her face making her appear as a skeleton before her flesh has even fallen from her skull. A roaring river of repulsion and fascination washing over me. ''Tis the mark of sin, daughter. Punishment for being a puttana. A whore,' Tiberia had whispered.

The minutes it takes Livia to return feel like hours. When she is back with a bundle of clean linens in her lap, I gingerly lift my fingers from my face. The wound feels naked.

Livia tries to hide her look of revulsion, but she is not quick enough.

'Is it bad?'

She nods.

'Do I still have a nose?'

She nods again. A small consolation.

Livia hands me a folded cloth which I press to my cheek, causing a pain to spiral through my body. The room is receding, my mind closing, overwhelmed by the calamity that has befallen me. 'Fetch the barber surgeon. Bring Francesco Neve,' I murmur. A doctor who learned his craft at university is no good. I need Francesco, a man who treats the foul fallout of street-fights and stabbings. 'But first, get me to bed.'

Livia nods, and pulls me up, both of us staining our feet in my blood, rust settling between our toes.

As she hauls me unsteadily up the stairs, I know only one thing – if I live, I will forever be a woman marked by calumny and shame.

Chapter Forty

'Fire is a Cruel Master'

August 1638

The sculptor stands at the window of his studio, dogs strewn at his feet. It's late afternoon and there is a tempest raging in his household. The Bernini women are gathered, steadying the ship, battling the rare forces that have washed over their family. They have weathered storms before, but never like this.

Behind him, Costanza's statue is positioned in the corner, her fixed form staring straight at his back. He had ordered the likeness to be moved after her betrayal.

The door is open. Left deliberately so, to better hear his mother and sisters talking downstairs. There is an uneven pulse of urgent, hurried female voices, of arrangements being made, of footsteps coming and going. He wants no part of whatever is happening below, yet he does not want decisions made without his consent. Without his express approval.

Evidently their family lawyer has been called – a capable but wily man by the name of Ranallo. He has just arrived and is standing in the hallway. This lawyer is someone who takes charge, smooths things over, makes his money from placation. The sculptor sees it in his mind's eye – Ranallo drawn to his full height (which is considerable), nodding gently as he takes in the facts, square face set implacably against the torrent of information.

The lawyer asks, 'Where is Lorenzo now?'

'Upstairs,' his sister Dorotea says.

'Alone?'

'Yes.'

'What is his mood?'

There is a pause. 'He is quiet,' Dorotea adds, almost inaudibly. 'Not always a good thing.'

'At least he is here and not at some tavern. We have to move quickly. Limit the damage, the fight between your brothers is already common knowledge.'

'A containment?'

'Of sorts. We may need to ask for some assistance . . .'

The lawyer drops his voice so the words are lost, and Dorotea speaks.

'It is the only way . . . and tell me, how is Luigi?'

'He is . . . comfortable. We have given him a fine room, large and light, and he is being well nursed by my wife and daughters. They are good women, well-practised in aiding recovery from these types of injuries.'

'And what of Luigi's wounds?' she asks. 'Are they . . . permanent?'

'The surgeon was there when I left. Your brother was lucky. It was a vicious beating, but he'll live. Broken ribs. A lot of bruising.'

'I should like to see him.'

'Not yet. Soon. I need to put the arrangements in place.'

The sculptor is amused. It had not occurred to him what would happen to his brother after he left the church. Where Luigi would go. So, the women have arranged for his little brother to be taken to the lawyer's house. It makes sense, the family fixer. Banishment, even temporary, will hurt Luigi as much as his injuries. And does his brother not deserve it?

'Are you making all the preparations? Mother is most anxious . . .' The words are indistinct. Lorenzo Bernini is fighting the desire to walk down the stairs and take charge.

'Some distance must be put between my brothers . . .' Dorotea trails off. Another voice, a servant, interrupts.

The lawyer says, 'Bologna. I have contacts and the city has an excellent university. I am arranging lodgings. Your brother can study with some of the best minds in engineering, it will help . . . *should* help when the time comes . . . to make his return easier. He will have new skills . . . be useful.'

'Is it far enough? From the scandal. From Lorenzo?'

For Christ's sake, thinks the sculptor. Everyone knows he is flawed; has a quick temper. So, famously, did Michelangelo. Fire is a cruel master. But was there not *severe* provocation? Did both of them . . . Luigi and Costanza . . . not deserve what happened? And here are his mother and sister creeping round to make the whole thing go away.

His own brother and his lover. It is a disgrace. Making a fool of him. Showing him up to all of Rome. No doubt laughing about him when his back is turned. The pair are lucky to be alive.

He turns and faces Costanza's statue, her gaze is direct, demanding, frank, unyielding. 'What?' He says to his inanimate beloved. Although he cannot name the sensation, it hurts him to look at her. To know that she is lost to him.

For one moment he thinks she might speak.

How is it possible that she was in his arms only a few nights ago, and now is wholly absent from his life? The stone face seems distorted; it is both her, and not her, not Costanza as she is now, flesh sliced. He is hollowed out by this thought. Her beauty ruined. 'Look what you made me do,' he spits. 'You ruined everything.'

The Bernini women do not yet know about Costanza. When they do, the sculptor knows they will judge him. Even though Costanza was a married woman who lay with two brothers – a hussy who has rained trouble on the Bernini house – despite all of these acts, his sisters, Dorotea in particular, will treat him most wrongly.

It is egregious he should be blamed in this way, when it is *he* who has been treated wretchedly. His family have shown no loyalty. No wonder is has ended badly. Costanza and Luigi were fools to try. He is stronger than both of them. Stronger than the binds of society, stronger than anyone who wants to restrain him. He could go downstairs right now and put a stop to whatever plan his sisters are hatching – but there is a long game to play.

His reputation.

He understands how this will damage him, his business; that he could lose everything.

The family, his friends, the men at the Fabbrica, they will all be told he went mad – *lost his mind* – to the wild, immoderate nature of his love. It is the only explanation. The whole of Rome will, for evermore, tell the story of Lorenzo Bernini's beloved and his crime of passion.

I shall not interfere, thinks the sculptor, but choose to play nicely.

Chapter Forty-One

'Venom'

August 1638

A man peers closely at my face.

I can almost feel the scratch of his beard, and his breath, which smells of meat, feels warm on my skin. It makes my belly turn so quickly I may need to retch.

His troublesome proximity means I cannot see his features, only the texture of his skin, which is sallow and marked by small, cratered scars.

I want to push him away, but my arms will not do as they are told.

Here he is again. Closer this time, and with that terrible breath. I make to turn my head but he holds me at my jaw, so firm I feel his strong fingers gripping at my skin. The act reminds me of some-one – another man I cannot place – but I want to bite his fingers clean off.

'You must be still, signora.' This is the voice of the man about my face. 'Hold still, or I cannot inspect your wound.'

I try to wriggle free. 'Livia!' the man calls. 'Livia, come here and hold your mistress tight, she is not fully of her senses and we must be quick. The lips of the wound must be sewn immediately if they are not to be altered by the air about us, for in this heat evil miasmas are strong.'

The air is hot on my skin, and my body is wet and clammy as if the Devil himself is lying upon me, making my limbs quiver and shake. I do not remember buying a crimson nightdress; maybe it was a present from Lorenzo. He has such peculiar ways.

'Will woo men, Neve?' I cock my head to listen more intently. It is as if I am in water, there is a great sloshing and whooshing in my ears, making the words indistinct.

I know him, this man with his long bony frame and lank hair. He is the barber surgeon. But what does he want with me? I must try to fight and push them away, for they are conducting evil business in this house and mean to do me harm. Why else would a barber surgeon be here? I must find Lorenzo; he will protect me.

'Aye, the wound should mend well. But there will be a cicatrix. It is inevitable with cuts to the face such as this. The neater I sew, the better it will heal.'

They are to take a needle to me. I push again at the arms which have hold of me. I am strong and I feel these foreign hands yield a bit.

'Signor Neve. I cannot keep hold of her like this. My mistress is ...'

I push again, and Livia bears down on my arms with all her might. Where is my vigour? Why can I not throw this chit off? I must be poisoned. Aye. *That* is it. My heart. It pounds. I cannot catch my breath.

There is something on my lips. More poison, serpent's venom. A strong syrup, thick, and sweet. The liquid falls into my mouth and numbs my tongue in an instant. Most noxious.

'She will settle soon, then I will be able to sew. But be warned: it is a strong potion ... and she will see magic. Maybe faeries and fantasies.' The words fade.

The man and girl are about me now. I watch the candle so I may not be mesmerised by their malevolent eyes. The flame flickers and the smoke slinks into the air like a black cat. Maleficence.

They are pricking at the skin of my face. This is how they check for witches. By inspecting the body for marks. Pricking the moles and dimples to see if they bleed. But my face? I have always had such fine skin. What can they find upon my cheek to warrant such needlework?

God help me. The flame flickers and it is Lorenzo's face. My love. My sin.

The man takes a step back to examine me from a wider angle. I try to look at him harder, but he is too indistinct. Perhaps it is Lorenzo painting me? It is impossible to fathom, but I move my head anyway, bending it back, so Lorenzo can artfully capture my best aspect.

'For Christ's sake. Keep her still.'

'Aye, sir.'

They mean to manacle me to stop me from flying away. My hand clamps at the sheets. There is a pain far away. Like an echo, calling again and again. I feel a pulling and tugging about my face and squirm like a child. I worry I will empty my bladder onto the bed and Tiberia will come and beat me. A dirty girl who makes a foul, pissy stench in the night.

There are small, rapid nicks at my face. Again and again, like insects biting. I am infested. I must wash. I cannot see Lorenzo in such a state, he is afeared of infestations.

The man stands back again. Is he here to judge me? Shall I be found guilty of witchcraft? A smile creeps across his hollow face, and his lips peel back, revealing yellowed teeth. I am done for. I shall be burned. The air about is suffocating, I need a breath.

They both leer at my face. The Devil and his nurse, in dual impish grins, their eyes burning black as night. I see now. All about they are covered in blood.

'I am most pleased,' says the Devil.

The Devil's nurse lets go of my arms, and the absence of her fingers feels odd. She too steps back and gazes upon me. 'It is very fine and neat.'

The candle flickers in fat flames, a livid licking, dragging my eyes away from the foul daemon pair. I see Lorenzo's shape shifting in the light, the shadow of his features just beyond the edge of my sight. I want to lift my arms, reach out my fingertips to trace the lines of his face, but my limbs are cursed and will not move.

There is whispering. The Devil's nurse strokes my hair, and her hands turn my curly strands into snakes, which squirm and slither about my scalp.

'Rest,' she says.

How can anyone rest with serpents all about? But they have stolen my voice.

'Rest,' she says again, and I close my eyes and give myself to the blackness, afeared I will never crawl out of this cavernous hole.

Chapter Forty-Two

'Banishment'

August 1638

Whene I wake, Matteo is by my side. He is asleep.

I blink and look at him. He looks like my husband, but is rough around all his edges; his whiskers are long, his hair unkempt, and his face lacks colour and vitality. My body feels as heavy as a millstone when I try to move. As I push myself up, a streak of pain passes through my head like lightning, and I fall back.

Matteo is up immediately and sitting next to me on the bed. He takes my hand warily, as if I am a wounded animal to be approached with caution.

'Do you remember?'

I have recollections: Stefano; a man with devil's horns about his head; Lorenzo's face. But these images reveal themselves as gauzy things, fluttering at the edge of my mind. I shake my head one way, but it hurts too much behind my eyes to move it back again.

'I will call for Livia. You need a drink, and sustenance. Then, when you have eaten and rested, I will explain.'

He starts by apologising for being a poor husband, for pursuing his own carnal pleasures before our vows. Tears roll slowly down his cheeks as he tells of how he arrived at the Fabbrica after spending the night with Vincenzo, to find the place in uproar – a riot of rumour that Lorenzo had half-killed Luigi.

'When I heard of Luigi's injuries, sustained in sanctuary, I knew you would not have been spared.'

Matteo's chest heaves as he remembers. 'I ran all the way from the Fabbrica. When I arrived, the hallway was awash with blood. I panicked.' He runs his hands through his hair. 'And then I found you alive – it was Livia who saved you.'

Matteo is quiet for a moment and grips my hand tighter. 'Luigi ... Did he?' My husband was never one for being direct.

'It was never my wish ... I should have fought.' Another tight squeeze. 'But I was afraid.'

Matteo's chin drops to his chest. 'Luigi told Lorenzo you lay with him willingly. You tried to tell me, but I did not hear.'

I feel a tear drop from my eye and down my cheek, its salty path burning my face. I lift my fingers to confirm what I already know I will find. A swelling, a dressed wound – the skin around it slick with ointment.

'Lorenzo did this?'

Matteo looks at me, his copper eyes boring into me like we have been parted for years and he is trying to find me again.

'He ordered Stefano to do it.'

The thoughts flow from me like branches on a tree, casting off from my core into new ideas, new possibilities.

'I must speak with him.'

Matteo looks at me aghast. 'With Lorenzo?'

'It is a mistake. Can't you see? I am glad for you, husband. I am glad you are here, but you and I both know that the love Lorenzo and I have . . .'

Matteo slaps his hand on his thigh and springs to his feet. 'How can you still say that, Costanza? We may not have loved each other the way you loved Lorenzo. But you are as a sister to me, family. When I thought you hurt or dead at his hands – when I thought I would never see you again, my grief was great.'

He turns his back on me to look out upon the street where the day has darkened, and tremoring clouds gather, granite in the sky.

'I did not see your youth and inexperience until it was too late. Lorenzo and Luigi preyed on you. Each in their own way. And it was me who introduced you to them, hid what I knew about them. Allowed you to become involved. I am as much to blame.' He turns to me again, his frame blocking the light meaning I am unable to see the features of his face. 'You cannot think of going back to Lorenzo. He has inflicted such violence on you. Your face, Costanza . . . he has maimed you for ever.'

I reach and touch again, and begin to understand.

'He is mistaken.'

'He is the talk of Rome. As are you. You must leave well alone.'

'In that case I shall write to Caterina.'

Matteo is out of the shadows and walking towards me. I can see something written upon his face but cannot fathom its meaning.

'You must rest.'

'I have done plenty of resting. I shall write to Caterina. She is my friend and knows the Berninis. She will plead my case with Lorenzo, as she has done before.'

'As you will. But first I will call Livia to bring some beef-bone soup and put some more of the tincture upon your face.'

I rest my head against the pillow, thoughts stumbling, disentangling the chaos. It is known.

All is undone.

* * *

A huge storm breaks, to the relief of the city, and rain falls for days so that the dusty stain of the summer is washed into the Tiber, and the streets become slick and miry, like a stewpond.

My face does not heal but becomes putrid, with tracks of vivid violet across my nose and cheek where the edges of the skin should knit. Nino Marotta sends a new poultice every day, and Livia dresses my face with egg white, oil of roses and omphacine.

I send word to Lorenzo and Caterina; I am filled with hope that remorse and plain sense will prevail, and they will see I am a woman greatly wronged. But as the days slip by with no word, I realise I am mistaken. My former life is dead. I find myself a ghost in search of a world she can exist in and, like all spectres, I am disappeared completely from view.

Matteo does not encourage me to leave the confines of my room. The tattletales are still full of stories of the Bernini brothers, the scandal of a shared woman, near-fratricide, face-slashing, and Angelica Bernini herself begging the Pope to call her reckless son to heel.

Matteo hears news that Luigi has left Rome, and Stefano too. He has no need to tell me that my reputation is as shredded as my face. Instead, he brings me threads to embroider and books to read – anything to stop me from stepping foot on the street where he fears I shall be spat upon, or worse still, set upon.

After the frenzy of my life with Lorenzo comes silence. A grief that runs so deep I am repeatedly brought up short by it: when I open a drawer and find a trinket he gave me; or smell linseed, such as lingered on his skin, or the scent of oranges, which he wore on his breath. All the stuff of life which can be happened upon in a day. At the bottom of a trunk lies the firebird dress, its iridescent beauty buried, and when I think of it, I am washed with shame at my pride.

In the stillness, I sit with Bess and try to remember the contours of Lorenzo's face, the ridges of his body. I do not dress in anything more than my nightgown, petticoats and house coat. I hardly eat. I do not venture out because I cannot bear to see anyone.

Giuliana calls. I suspect Matteo's hand. She sits on the settle in the salon, her hands neatly folded in her lap, and tries not to cry when she looks at my face. There is a gulf between us now, a great distance we must try and reach each other over.

'I am sorry . . . for what has happened . . .' Giuliana breathes heavily and speaks hesitantly. I can tell she is shocked by my appearance. Whatever she had imagined, the wound, the depth of the cut, the neatness or not of the stitches, the reality of how I present is worse.

'It is done. I cannot change it.'

She examines my face. 'Nay, that you cannot. It will heal though, in time it will . . .'

'It is part of me now. My face is altered, as am I.' Even though I am mighty glad to see my old friend and touched she should risk the opprobrium of such a house call, I am wary and have no urge to share more than is strictly necessary. 'How are the boys?'

'They are . . . well. Tomaso has finally shaken off his cold and Leonardo . . . well, he is taking his time, he is still small . . . but each day he gets stronger.' There is a false note of brightness to her voice. I nod and imagine the ferocity with which Giuliana tends her sickly boys, how she pushes back the world, encasing them in her fierce mother-love, feeding them pap, and wrapping their chests with rags soaked in oil when a cough lingers. The nights she has watched over them, praying for a just a day more.

She changes the subject. 'And Matteo? He looks well.'

Giuliana does not say it was a surprise to her, to everyone, that my husband did not throw me out.

'He is a good man.'

'I never doubted . . .'

'And my father, have you seen him?' I rush at the question, burning to know the answer and afraid if I do not ask now my courage will fail me.

The wariness returns. 'Aye, I mean at church . . . around.'

Giuliana is not telling me the whole truth, I press further, like a thumb on a bruise. 'I cannot believe he does not keep up with his little namesake?'

'Aye well, that he does. He calls, or we call at the house. I take it you have not seen him?'

I shake my head sadly. Of all the hurt I have endured, this is the greatest. My family have not called or written, and Matteo has cautioned I must take this as the sign it is, that – for now – things must lie. The dust must settle.

'How is he? My father?'

'You have not seen him so you will not . . .' Giuliana stops, gathers her thoughts, pulling the words together. 'He has not been well, has lost some weight, despite Tiberia's best efforts.' She sees the reaction on my face. 'But is still very much himself at heart, still as affectionate with the children . . . just a little . . . slower.'

I bite at my lip. The thought of my father being in any way diminished is almost impossible to imagine, this great colossus of my childhood.

'Do you think there is any possibility of my meeting with him?'

Giuliana's eyes flutter downward. 'I am so sorry. I have talked with him, told him of your need, your predicament. But he is adamant.'

'I do not believe for one moment it is he who is adamant, but Tiberia, judging. Always judging.'

'A *lot* has happened Costanza, it is a great matter for your parents to absorb. The affair ... affairs ... the statue which leaves little to doubt, Lorenzo nearly killing his brother, your attack. You have no idea how people have talked.'

'Oh, I have every idea of what people have ...'

'Nay. Not like Leonardo has heard it. About his own daughter. The words they have used. He has been near broken by it.'

A realisation runs cold through me, like a cloud covering the sun on a spring day. 'You mean I made him sick? Everything that has happened, it has made my father ill?'

'Nay. Well no one can say what makes someone ail – bad water, air miasmas – but Tiberia will not wear any more worry until your father mends. I will keep trying, I promise. He will be pleased to know you are ... recovering.'

When she leaves, Giuliana promises she will call again soon and kisses me on the good side of my face, and the touch of her lips is so tender it all but breaks my heart.

All that is left is to slowly find a new way to live. My wounds require daily care, which Livia tends to well and kindly. Matteo gives up the Fabbrica, a decision that surprises no one. Instead he takes over the main rooms on the ground floor, and commandeers the courtyard as his studio, shipping in marble and ancient statues he means to sell abroad.

Which is how I come to live among the broken statues, crowded with sorrow.

Chapter Forty-Three

'Tedium'

December 1638

Luigi Bernini sighs and feels a slight ache in the muscles that stretch between his ribs, a reminder of what has passed, of what that wench made his brother do.

He is sitting on a wooden bench in a large lecture hall packed with men, some wearing the black gowns of scholars, others in the garb of artists, draughtsmen or designers like him. At the front stands an eminent engineer, a doctor of mathematics, who is enthusiastically explaining the minutiae of a complex hydraulics system. Luigi Bernini looks out of the window onto the square, which is filled with more scholars hurrying at the pace of beetles, and sighs again. While the lecture itself is interesting, he finds the city of Bologna boring to the point of cruelty.

This was an inevitability. Stripped of his friendships, starved of his family, Luigi Bernini itches to find alternative entertainment of the kind he so casually indulged in at home in Rome. At first, he had hoped for a pretty daughter or maid who might service his needs. But his hopes were dashed as soon as he entered his lodgings.

It seems the lawyer had anticipated this and had taken great care to arrange a victualling house run by a woman so old she is well past her menses, with no daughters, no pretty housemaids, but who instead tends to a pack of weedy sons who are pious to the point of parody.

Despite the lecture room being full, it has ill-fitting windows and a piercing wind gusts its way through the wool jerkins of the men, biting at cold, white flesh, lifting the edges of carefully annotated papers, and turning the tips of fingers blue.

As the doctor of mathematics continues, Luigi blows on his hands to warm them. Then he takes up his quill, freshly cut this morning, and dips it into the inkwell before scratching a number of lines onto the paper. Head bent like a diligent schoolboy, Luigi Bernini works quickly, methodically, his mind whirring as the man talks, imagining a new system to move marble pieces around the Fabbrica with greater ease and safety. When he returns to his rooms he will add this paper to the pile of notations, sketches and structures he has devised to discuss with his brother.

It is a big supposition, that he will be allowed to return to Rome, that his banishment will not last a lifetime. Lorenzo did not come to visit Luigi after the attack, nor has he written. All because of Costanza Piccolomini. It is her fault this rift is so great. He is glad she is marked for what she did. It is only what she deserved for besmirching the Bernini name and causing so much trouble.

None of his family, not his brother, sisters nor mother accompanied the battered Luigi to Bologna, instead it was left to the lawyer, Ranallo, and his wife. The journey had been arduous, each bump of the wheel causing his broken body to jolt in pain. But far worse was the lecturing he endured the entire way.

'You must,' Ranallo cautioned, 'stay out of trouble. You cannot court any scandal. At all. Do you understand? There is much at stake.' Luigi had shifted in his seat, bristling with resentment but knowing last chances are hard to come by.

'This shameful incident,' Ranallo had continued, 'has reached the papal court. The Pontiff himself has intervened. The Bernini business is in very real danger of floundering. His Holiness can turn a blind eye once, but not twice. You must not take advantage of any virgins – chat to no married women – there can be no boys, no whoring, no tupping serving girls. You must not drink excessively or throw punches or fight in any way; must not carry a knife, dagger, sword or any other weapon. I have arranged for you to spend the next few months in sober study, a chance to use your fine brain for once; after all, are you not a Bernini? A family of known geniuses. Nay lad, now is the time to apply your mind, employ your thinking, commit your imagination to paper, impress your brother, be useful.'

But that was not the end. The lawyer had continued, droning on and on. 'And when you come back to Rome, you must return with ideas to elevate the reputation of the Bernini brothers even higher. Be an asset. And should you feel your temper or lust rising you must resist the urge, is this quite clear? Quit whatever situation you are in. Do not cause trouble.'

Luigi yawns again. It is a mind-numbingly tedious way to exist. Yet it is a necessity if his expulsion is not to last for ever. There is some small part of him, the little boy inside, who misses his mother, his sisters, even his magnetic older brother, and is afeared he will never be allowed to return.

And so Luigi Bernini broods. He writes reams of letters to the lawyer, and his sister Dorotea. *How much longer?* he asks. He tells them he counts the days until he can return. He complains this forced exile is most unfair. Demands they help. Wheedles and whines it is not he who has wronged, but instead he has been wronged. Pleads he was seduced by the Piccolomini woman. She is a temptress, a hazard to society, a risk to all Catholic women. What more can be done to make sure the Bernini name is secure? Is it not most unfair Costanza lives with her freedom while he is banished? Should she not pay a price too?

Chapter Forty-Four

'Prayers'

December 1638

L istening to the life outside my window is preferable to what lurks in my mind when I close my eyes. I have endured nearly four months of my dreams being polluted by Stefano's visit, or the remembrance of Lorenzo's last touch. Which is how I hear them coming: the clatter of their knives and the rumbling of their talk along the street.

The knock on the door is loud and long, with an insistent viciousness to it. Matteo springs up, bleary-eyed from sleep, the tension in his body manifest.

I lay my hand on his arm. 'Take care.' Our peace has been stolen once already.

He pats my hand. 'Whoever it is, I must attend to the racket and battering of stranger's boots upon our door, for they do not mean to leave.'

Dressed in only a nightshirt and barefoot, Matteo rummages

for a candle to light from the lantern outside our bedroom door. Then I hear the soft thud of his feet running down the stairs, his voice agitated.

'Cease! I am coming. I will be there in a moment. Can you not have some patience? For the love of God, stop banging, the whole neighbourhood will be awakened.'

In another time, I would have got up and found my own candle, before wrapping a shawl around my shoulders and padding after Matteo. But my courage has died. So, instead, I sit on the bed and listen to Matteo unlock the heavy bolts of the door, the voices beyond, irritated and hurried. There is an almighty din as the strangers enter the house, shouting in rough accents which speak in tones of violence.

Matteo is yelling too. 'What means all this? You cannot just walk in here ...'

One voice clearer than the rest. When he speaks, the hairs on my arm stand on end. 'We have come for Signora Costanza Piccolomini. We have a warrant for her arrest. She has been accused of fornication ...'

Matteo speaks again: 'You cannot arrive at a man's house and demand his wife. I will not allow ...'

But there is already the clatter of boots on the stairs. I do not wait for these strangers to arrive before jumping from the bed to find some slippers and a house-robe. I am just tying the belt when the first man enters the room, with a linkboy at his side. The child is as small and twitchy as the man is tall and still, and both are grinning. I feel my heart fluttering as if a hummingbird is taking flight in my chest.

'Costanza Piccolomini?'

I am unable to respond.

He repeats himself, irritated, but my name sounds strange spoken by him, and I look at him as if I cannot comprehend.

He takes a step forward. 'Don't play the dumb bitch with me. It won't help your cause.'

I move back to avoid his touch, as Matteo arrives breathless at the door.

'What means this? It is most unseemly to come to our bedchamber in the middle of the night in such a noxious manner. On what authority do . . .'

The man swings round. 'On the authority of the city of Rome, Signor Bonucelli.'

There is threat written all about his body, as he widens his shoulders and pulls back his neck, which is thick and sturdy.

'My name is Marcello Sagese. From the sbirri, the emissaries of papal justice.'

My stomach grinds and tightens, as reality punches me hard.

They are the street police: henchmen of the Governatore of Rome and known for their violence and corruption. Often more feared than the men they arrest. They come at night to be sure of bagging their prey and collecting their bounty.

'We are here to arrest your wife. This woman,' Sagese spits out the words as he points at me, 'has been accused of fornication and adultery. An official investigation has revealed that . . . in addition to your good self' – he bows mockingly at Matteo – 'she has committed carnal copulation with at least two other men: Lorenzo and Luigi Bernini. Brothers.' He leers. 'That she has spent hours in their company, allowed her breasts to be touched, and let herself be kissed and mounted, and other scandalous acts.'

I feel a sharp bile rise at the back of my throat. In addition to the man and the boy, two more henchmen have now entered our bedchamber. I can feel their eyes poking beyond my robe, nudging under my nightgown, salivating over my naked flesh. My skin flames with shame, and I wish I could leave this body, and all she is, and disappear. But I cannot. Instead, I must summon all my courage.

Matteo steps in front of me and starts to speak, but I say first, fast and flustered, 'Nay husband. I will go. There is no fight to be had here, for they will have me whether you say so or not.'

'A touching scene.' Sagese laughs grimly. 'Your wife may be a whore, but at least she has sense.'

I tremble as the militiamen move forward to pull at my arms. They bind my hands, pulling the rope taut against my wrists. I look at Matteo, who dips his head, then straightens it again and looks back at me, his face set dead straight, as if all life has been lost to it. I bite at my lip; I cannot allow the men of the sbirri the satisfaction of my tears.

Sagese grabs at my shoulders, and I feel a slipper fall from my foot. I stop to try and wiggle it back on, but I am propelled forward.

'Leave it,' another of the men says. 'You will not need it where you are going.'

Part IV

Chapter Forty-Five

'The Welcome Party'

December 1638

The men stop at the gate, as they are forbidden to set foot inside the walls of the convent.

Above, the moon is shrouded behind a thick veil of clouds, its light reduced to a murky glow. There are no stars. It is the kind of night in which constellations are lost and navigators flounder. I know once I step inside the high stone walls I will be swallowed from all view, absented from the world. Sagese thumps his fist against the wooden door, making me jump, and I make a silent plea: please, Lord, whatever lies on the other side, let it not kill me.

There is the sound of metal unlocking, and the door swings inward. From the shadows the face of a nun appears. She is young, round-faced, about my age.

'Is this her?'

'Aye.'

She looks at my face and frowns. 'Is she hurt?'

'Not by our hand.'

'You can take your leave now, we will handle matters from here.'

'You will tell the Abbess . . .'

'Yes, yes, I will tell her. You can unhand the woman now, we will see to her papers.'

It is a relief when Sagese lets go of my arm and I am released from his clammy hands. As least these men did not have me, and now I am given to the women of the convent. It is the first comfort I have felt since I was arrested.

Sagese roughly pushes me forward into the arms of the waiting nun. She pulls me through the door which she bangs shut against the men, and hurries me through a dim courtyard towards a square stone building set away from the street. I wonder, for the briefest of moments, about yelling, screaming for help, kicking the young woman escorting me, trying to get back to the door and somehow unlocking it. But I realise any attempt to escape would be futile; this is a place designed to keep its inhabitants firmly cloistered from the world.

The young nun walks quickly and I wonder at her ability to navigate her way in the darkness. She says no more to me, nor I to her, but she does not handle me as roughly as the men, and for this I'm grateful.

Inside the building, I am led to a room. It is enclosed on all sides, no windows, stale air: the kind of room where no good is done. Lanterns are set into the stone, their flames cast long, flickering shadows which lick across the unadorned walls and flagstone floor. Despite being sizeable, the room is bare of any furniture save for a stool set in the middle of the floor and a small table with a pail of water on it, by which is set a pile of rags.

There are two more sisters, who watch wordlessly as I enter. One is old, with small brown eyes which are nearly lost within the crevices of her skin. The second is taller than me, broader too, of middling age; her gaze is strong, impassive and the way her features are arranged, inquisitive eyes gathered in the centre of her face, reminds me of an owl.

It is this nun who addresses me, in a low, sonorous voice, well used to command.

'Sit down, Signora Costanza Piccolomini.' She motions to the singular stool set alone, like a lost boat on the high seas.

It is, I realise, all planned. I am expected. Slowly I walk to the stool and lower myself to sitting, so I am facing the three women. I panic, keeping my eyes lowered. I am not sure what to do, whether it is allowable to look directly at my jailors or whether I must remain submissive. This is the first time I have ever been in custody, and I realise I know none of the rules. From my downcast view I glance right, then left. I notice, with relief, that the door remains open.

The tall nun addresses me again. 'Welcome, I am the Abbess of the Casa Pia.' I see her hands gesture towards the aged nun. 'This is Sister Benedicta,' and then to the nun who met me at the door. 'And this is Sister Chiara.'

'You are here to pay penance for the dual sins of fornication and adultery,' the Abbess continues. 'The terms of your imprisonment are that you must work. You will wash clothes and linens in the convent's laundry. Your labour will be in service of the Church, and in return we will offer prayers for your soul.'

Questions hiss and spit within me, like fat from meat roasting on a fire. Who has raised such charges? When was I sentenced? And by whom? How long am I to be kept? What about Matteo? Does he know where I am? A washroom? I know nothing about—

These thoughts are broken by the sound of the Abbess, who is walking towards me with slow, deliberate steps. She silently circles the stool on which I am sitting, like a cat hunting a mouse, inspecting my body from every angle. When she returns to the front she puts her hand under my chin to gently raise my face to hers. Her fingers are strong and press into the flesh of my jaw. I feel her eyes running over the contours of my cheek, taking in my injuries, making a mental note of the livid, raised scars on my face, the blisters filled with pus, the swelling that still distorts my eye.

Our eyes meet for a moment. I am sure she can read my questions, understands my confusion, but refuses to meet them with any answer.

Instead, the Abbess breaks her gaze and stares at the collar of my nightgown, edged with fragile lace, eyes falling down my body to the single slipper, fine kid leather and embroidered with roses, and the other foot, bare, numb with cold and covered in the dirt of the city's streets just like a Caravaggio.

'First, your body will be prepared for your life with us,' explains the Abbess. 'Sister Benedicta will wash you and shave your hair. While you are at the Casa Pia you will wear a habit,' she continues with a note of disdain in her voice. 'Vanity is so often a woman's downfall. Here you will learn contentment and modesty.'

I nod in total compliance. Unexpectedly I hear a note being sung by a female voice – clear, sustained, a pure sound – followed swiftly by a chorus of women's voices, rising in unison from somewhere deep within the building and I am filled with deep sorrow. It is Matins. Two hours after midnight. The darkest hours.

Sister Chiara pulls me to standing and lifts off my nightdress; the sudden immodesty, even among this company, is shocking. Then Sister Benedicta brings the pail and sets it down next to the stool. She begins washing my body, squeezing a sponge of icy water under my armpits and between my legs. The water shocks my skin. She lets out a small groan as she slowly falls to her knees to wash my legs and feet. Her hands are swollen and misshapen with arthritis, and

I cannot help but think the ice water must feel more like torment to her than me. Yet my skin begins to pucker, my body shakes, for it is the end of the year and they do not dry me quickly.

Sister Chiara pushes me back down to sit naked on the stool. Sister Benedicta pulls at my hair, running her bony fingers across my scalp. Then she begins to brush it with long strokes down my back, just as Tiberia used to do. I feel her parting it in two, then she starts to weave each section into plaits, securing them at the bottom. She is behind me, so I do not know what is happening, but I feel metal on my neck, and hear the dull sawing of scissor blades.

My beautiful hair.

A memory flares: Lorenzo's fingers turning and twisting the tight tendrils at the nape of my neck, whispering, 'Venus, you are divine.' I close my eyes and try not to cry. The nuns have taken care with this task and I briefly wonder if it is destined for a wigmaker. Cristoforo, perhaps? I push the thought away.

Then Sister Benedicta takes a razor to my scalp. The blade jerks haphazardly across my skin, and gets caught time and time again, nicking and cutting my head. I feel a slow trickle of blood running own the back of my ear.

I try to shut out the rough scraping sound and focus instead on the voices soaring in grief, allowing every note to pass through me, permitting the music to hold me in its sweet embrace.

When it is done, Sister Benedicta steps back. I cannot help but raise my hand to rub my head, and despite knowing my hair has gone, am still surprised by the unexpected sharpness of the stubble on my scalp.

I am pulled to standing again. 'Signora, arms up,' whispers Sister Chiara and I follow her instructions obediently. I raise my hands and a shapeless habit is thrown over the curves of my body, erasing them entirely. The material is rough and itches everywhere it sits against my skin: across my shoulder blades and breasts, and under my arms. My feet are lifted one at a time and pushed into wooden clogs, which are heavy and tight.

The Abbess stands in front of me and inspects the work of her sisters. 'Good. Now Sister Chiara will take you to your quarters. It will do you well to comply while you are here, Signora Piccolomini. No more wildness. No more wilfulness.'

I am led by the young sister back out into the night. My arm rests on hers. The singing has ended and our wooden footsteps echo across the cloisters. The sound reminds me that we are mortal, anchored to this earth.

We arrive at a dormitory – another lightless room, other than the meagre spill from the lamps in the passage outside. I am shown to a pallet and thin straw mattress on the floor; a putrid-smelling bucket stands nearby. Above the bed hangs Christ on the cross, the sinews of his body straining against their shackles. Beside it is a small, roughly hewn table with a tallow candle set upon it. I sit in the pitch-black cold of early morning listening to the snores and scratching of a room full of women, and wonder how I have been reduced to this.

Chapter Forty-Six

'A Tableaux'

December 1638

B y my pallet there are marks on the wall.

Deep scratches of misery, made not by an animal but by the women who have lain here before me, dragging their fingers, again and again, until they left a permanent mark of their existence behind.

I trace the lines with my fingertips with the tenderness of a lover, imagining their nails ragged and worn. I think I understand the kind of relief the pain might have given them: a counterforce against despair.

Each day begins when the bells wake us for prayers. We rise like the fog on the marsh, spectres in the half light. The women have no modesty, but cavort and laugh in the most shameful manner. I do not join in but keep my distance; I have no need of friends like these.

Today they are particularly loud, being led in their ribaldry by

Rosa, a woman who is unpolished in every manner and makes vice-laden jokes in a voice just a touch too loud.

'Alive now, girls.' Rosa mimics the baritone voice of the Abbess. 'Time to use your God-given bodies to wash the stains of the rich, although it is a mystery how they appeared.' Rosa rocks her hips in an exaggerated fashion, mimicking a man pleasuring himself. The prisoners screech and holler.

'Utter disgrace,' mutters my neighbour, Carlotta. She is short, with agreeable looks, though not striking. Judging by her accent and demeanour, she was once a gentlewoman. She prays every night, hoarsely begging forgiveness from the Lord. I am told Carlotta's husband died, and she couldn't find a suitor before the money ran out, so she ended up selling first her possessions then her body. While the nocturnal sobbing is irritating, there is a gentleness to Carlotta which reminds me of Giuliana, and I cannot help but feel a little fondness for her.

Rosa is standing on her pallet now, cupping her hand behind her ear. 'What's that, signora?' she hollers. 'Disgrace, you say? Well, God gave us ponds, and men horns to use in them. So if anyone is disgraceful it's . . .'

Carlotta stands suddenly. 'Such naughty blasphemy!'

There is a roar of laugher as Rosa springs down onto the floor. 'I'm only trying to keep spirits up.'

Rosa walks towards the bed and, feline-quick, snatches Carlotta's grey woollen shawl from the mattress, throwing it over her head and fastening it under her chin, like a wimple. Then she pulls herself up to her full height and turns to face the women, eyes alighting on Serafina, a nervy, pale-faced girl.

Serafina joined the ranks of the city's working women at ten, when her parents died. One night a friend of her dead father took Serafina's maidenhead, leaving a coin or two to assuage his guilt.

Now she is fourteen with breasts and hair between her legs, and the premium she once charged has fallen away. Forced to take to the streets, Serafina was picked up by the sbirri.

Rosa puts her arm protectively around the girl, and Serafina basks in the reflected sunlight.

'Now, child.'

Serafina plays along. 'Yes Abbess?'

'Do you pray for the sinners?'

'Yes, Abbess. I pray for the sinners every night.'

'Good child. Kneel with me and we shall pray together.'

The women of the dormitory look on in glee at the tableaux.

'Dear Lord,' Rosa begins, wiggling a finger in a gap in the seams of the young girl's habit. 'Please send Serafina a new habit, for this one has more holes than a whore's stocking.' The women roar.

Rosa looks about the room. 'And Lisbetta. That poor daughter of vice. Send her only kerchiefs to wash, so that she may make light work today.'

The women cheer again. Lisbetta bangs her stick on the ground. She sits on a stool to work, because once, many years ago, a man threw her to the ground and kicked her half to death, rather than pay the pennies he owed her.

'Serafina?'

'Yes, Abbess?'

'Do not forget dear Silvia.'

'Which one is Silvia again?' asks Serafina.

'Oh, Silvia is the pretty one with the pert pomegranates.'

Rosa cups her breasts and hoiks them skyward while Serafina giggles. Silvia steps forward and reciprocates by shaking her ample bosoms under her thin nightgown. The women whoop. Silvia was attacked by a boy when she was fifteen, and thus spoiled. Being no longer marriageable, Silvia's parents could not afford a convent dowry, so she had only one option.

'We pray that on the day of Silvia's release,' Rosa continues, throwing her arms around Silvia, 'our girl meets a duke who loves large pomegranates so much that he sets her up for life in her own apartment, with servants and satins, so he can come and eat fruit whenever he wants.' It is a denouement which sends the women wild, while Silvia throws her head back and screams.

I do not want to look but find I cannot turn away. I have never seen these girls laughing as they are now, freely; their faces are almost childlike. It is the first moment of joy I have witnessed since I arrived at the Casa Pia.

'Enough!' shouts Carlotta. 'You will bring the Abbess down here in a wrath, and then we will all pay penance for your bawdiness. I will not have it.'

Then, unexpectedly, Carlotta begins to weep. 'It is too much,' she sobs. Raising her head defiantly she says with hushed fury to Rosa. 'You are too much. You are wicked and have no repentance. You allow your body to be used at will and are wanton beyond redemption.'

Rosa turns on her heel and faces Carlotta, furious. 'It is not I who will have to answer to God. It is not I who married. I took no vows of matrimony. I have not forcefully stolen the maidenhead of children – or beaten women until they are broken. I fear not my day of judgement, for I live fully in what I know to be right. And those who damn us? I say be damned!'

Carlotta makes a sound of disgust. Quick as a whippet, Rosa shoots a look at Serafina.

'Child,' she calls, still in the character of the Abbess. 'We forgot to pray for the Signora Carlotta.'

But Serafina does not respond; the moment has passed.

'What shall we pray for?' Rosa scratches the side of her head, as if thinking. 'Ah, I know. We shall pray that one day Carlotta wakes up and finds she isn't Such. A. Miserable. Old. Bitch.'

It is too much. Carlotta acts as I know Giuliana would, with horror and bewilderment, and I cannot stand it. Before Carlotta can say anything, I step forward and enter the fray.

'She said enough!'

Rosa turns to me and smiles. 'Listen sweetheart, this is not your fight.'

'You are vexing Carlotta, and I will not have it.'

The smile fades from Rosa's lips. 'Carlotta is vexing this whole place, with her airs and prayers. We're causing a little merriment, 'tis all. Lightening the day.'

'It is not kind. Carlotta is not of this world, as well you know.'

Rosa faces me straight on. 'If you lie on your back and make bedsport with anyone but your husband, then the Church orders you into this world. No exceptions. Not even for those who tup the Pope's favourite. We are all whores here.'

My old anger rises and I snatch Carlotta's shawl from Rosa's head. Holding it triumphantly aloft, I turn to the prisoners, but the women do not cheer.

Retaliation is swift.

Rosa lunges to grab the shawl back, and I instinctively pull it to my chest. She grips hard at the cloth and pulls, but the fabric in her hand is not the shawl, but my nightdress, a thin shift made from the cheapest of materials. There is a sharp rip as my gown tears from the yoke and falls to each side.

For a hushed moment Rosa doesn't say anything, then she steps forward. 'Sono desolata. Sweetheart, I'm sorry ...'

I put my hand up, palm out. Stop!' I growl. 'Don't take another step.'

I turn to the women, my gown still hanging open. Some avert their gaze, others stare, their eyes meeting mine. I see looks of pity and match them with disdain.

'My name is not Sweetheart. Or Venus. Or Whore. It is Costanza. And do not for a moment think this is any kind of humiliation. It is nothing.'

Rosa offers the shawl to hide my immodesty, but I push her hand away. Instead, I wrench the gown from my body and let it fall to the floor. Then I pick up the rough habit and shrug the itchy cloth over my head to cover my nakedness, determined not to cry.

* * *

After this, the women leave me alone.

I find solitude a strange place to reside. I am no longer a daughter, wife, mistress or friend, but someone entirely separate from the world. Without purpose. After the tumult of the last few months, it is a haven of sorts. A sanctuary in which I am not broken, bruised or betrayed.

Such solipsism means I succumb to the routine of the convent more easily, allowing my days to become endless.

Endless mornings, rising with women, the stale smell of night sweats upon their bodies. Endless dusks surrounded by the stench of dried urine. Endless hours sat squeezed next to my fellow fallen, in pews designed for the malnourished. Endless minutes praying for mercy, for the carnal lust I have indulged in.

I bend my knees to the unforgiving floor and fix my eyes upon Mary Magdalene, whose portrait hangs in the chapel. A woman who knew both sin and redemption. I pray, begging her to show me the right path, but she stares back, unmoved by my pleas.

Sometimes I allow my mind to wander. The question of who put me here and how long I shall serve, is one which constantly bedevils me. For as ill as Lorenzo thinks of me, it does not help him to have his mistress so publicly shamed. Who else? As mortified as my father was, it would be worse to have a daughter in the Casa Pia. Matteo cared for me throughout, and has never wavered in his affection for me, even if it was not the love of a true husband. The only person who would benefit from my being locked away is Luigi. By having me imprisoned, he could say I was the instigator, the perpetrator of all vile acts, the sinful woman who lured the brothers into vice.

I think about the men. Stefano, Luigi, Lorenzo. What is their penance? Where do they pray while I am incarcerated and genuflecting at the feet of my saviour, shorn hair itching under my cap, coarse wool rubbing at the nape of my neck? Do they go about as before? Free and walking the streets? Once such questions would have set a fire within me, licking and burning in fury, but all I feel now is exhausted by the way the world turns.

When I am not on my knees in prayer, I am elbow deep in piss, cleaning clothes in my new occupation as a washerwoman. It is an arrangement that must have been conceived by a wit: the stained women of Rome scrubbing the linens of the rich, until they are so white they shine with virtue and honour.

Chapter Forty-Seven

'The Secret Garden'

January 1639

'Come.' Lisbetta is holding out her hand shakily. 'Come with me.'

I turn over and sigh. 'Can you not leave me be?'

Every Sunday we are granted a few hours to ourselves. Most women spend it in the dormitory lying on their beds. Some sleep, others cluster together, sharing stories of brothels, pimps and punters. Sometimes they talk of the lives they left behind, but not often. There's more mirth in tales of turning tricks.

I never join in, but lie on my back under a meagre blanket, examining the ceiling, counting the cracks which splinter across the old plaster. These women have no solicitude for me, nor I for them. We are forced to be here, but should not be obligated to enter into false friendships.

This is the third week Lisbetta has offered her hand, the third I have turned her down.

I do not look at her but repeat my words. 'Lisbetta, please go. Leave me be.'

Usually the old woman shuffles off, but not today. Instead, she sits on my bed. It is an intimate gesture even in this crowded place, and the act of taking up my space irritates me. But she is infirm, and even in my worst moments, I am not lost of all compassion.

'Why? Why do you keep asking me to come with you?' It is the most I have ever spoken to her.

She speaks in an unhurried manner. 'Because I watch you. You speak to no one. Have no friends.'

God's blood. The bluntness of this answer irritates me even more. 'It is naught to do with you. I do not want or need companions in this godforsaken place.'

'Which is why, each Sunday, I ask you to come.'

'And I say nay. Leave me. So please respect my wishes.'

She does not move, but stares at me, as if divining leaves in the bottom of a cup. Behind us a group of women break into loud laughter, a raucous camaraderie which only serves to highlight the silence which surrounds me.

If Lisbetta will not move, I shall not speak. We sit for some time in silence, then she says quietly, 'I had hoped you would join me. Just once.'

Her words prick like a slender needle. Who dares hope in this place? It is just enough to make me want to move. I throw off the blanket in a petulant display of acquiescence.

'You win. Whatever it is, I will come this once. But do not ask me to speak. And when we are done, you must not make such a request again. Agreed?

Lisbetta stands unhurriedly. 'I am glad you are coming.'

My feet hit the icy floor. 'Christ, it is freezing.'

'Here.' Lisbetta reaches into her pocket and pulls out a pair of neat brown wool socks. I stare at them for a moment. They are so tidy that had I not known better I would have sworn they had been knitted by Tiberia's hand. The thought loosens like a skein of silk, unspooling back through the events of the last four months, pulling me to my stepmother's kitchen table, Giuliana, the sound of my father and Matteo laughing somewhere upstairs, and I feel such a wave of grief, I fear I shall sob. I breathe in and out slowly. That time has gone. Lisbetta is standing in front of me. I blink down the tears and wordlessly take the socks.

'Wrap the blanket around you, it will be needed,' she adds.

* * *

Lisbetta and I slip out of the dormitory and cross the courtyard unseen. Outside, winter's grasp is firm, and there is a chill in the air. The courtyard is stark under the silvery light of the pale sun and somewhere beyond the walls I hear the faint sounds of life: the clop of horses and shouts of children. She stops at a door set in the stone wall – one I have not noticed before.

Then Lisbetta produces a small iron key, which slips easily into the lock. I am astonished and despite my protestations to stay silent, cannot help but start to ask questions.

'You have a key? But how? Where did you get it?'

'From the sisters. I help with their garden.' She laughs. 'I am like an old dog, too lame to escape.'

The door swings open, and beyond is a large plot. I know little about husbandry, but can tell this one is well stocked and tended. There are canes, empty now, for beans to climb up. Clumps of bushes, lavender and rosemary I recognise. The soil is black, well-rotted and turned over. At one end there is a neat row of skeps for the bees; they are quiet, but it does not stop Lisbetta from limping her way down to them. She speaks in a low voice. I do not follow but can hear what she is saying.

'Do not be startled, I have bought a visitor today. Someone in need of the peace of your garden. A friend.' She turns and smiles. 'You must always tell the bees your business, or else they might take fright and leave.' She waves at the small wooden bench. 'Sit.'

I do as I am told. The seat is a little wet and chilly, and I am glad of the blanket I was instructed to bring, which I wrap around myself like a cocoon. Lisbetta says no more, but immediately sets about tending the garden. Picking leaves from the soil, pulling at dead twigs, tying up stems which have fallen, her feet shuffling patiently along the paved path. I am still a little mystified as to why I have been brought to this place, but am pleased for the solitude.

Lisbetta is different here. The hard decades of Rome's streets fall away, and she looks just like any other grandmother tending her kitchen garden. She continues on her rounds, lifting old rags and inspecting the plants that lie beneath; sometimes she is satisfied, other times dismayed, but does not stop in her ministrations. I notice each plant requires something new: the leaves must be turned over, ends pinched or else roots examined. I sit quite some time like this. Quiet, watching Lisbetta, listening to the life of the monastery and street blur.

A tiny brown bird, I know not its name, flies and perches on a branch near me. It hops in a quick jerking motion, inspecting me with black eyes as if it has an important message to tell me, but then turns as if it thinks better of the idea.

Lisbetta looks up. 'Hello friend, let me get you a little something.'

She hobbles to a metal coffer set on a stool and takes off the lid. Inside is grain, which Lisbetta carefully scoops and pours into a bird feeder hanging from one of the branches. She returns and sits next to me on the bench, clasping her now grimy hands in her lap. I have never been a lover of nature, but sitting here in this garden, it is the first calm I have felt in weeks.

'How did you learn ... what to do?' I gesture at the garden. 'All of that.'

'I grew up in the country. On a farm. My mother, grandmother, taught all us girls how to tend to plants, which ones to use for black or yellow bile, which will cause a headache to cease, which will bring on menses, which will cause excess bleeding. I learned what to watch for. And now I help the sisters in the infirmary.'

It is startling to think of Lisbetta as a small girl. I imagine her with dark plaits, eager to learn, a kind mother giving gentle instruction: 'Here you must turn the leaf like this, or see this flower head? When it is dried it can help calm a fever.' Lisbetta's clumsy little fingers learning the delicacy it takes to tend to living things.

I start with another question. 'Do you ever ask, "Why has this happened to me?"'

'Why not you?'

'No, I mean ... do you ever wish things could be different? That you could go back ...'

She stops me before I finish my words. 'This is the life I have lived. It could not be any other.'

'But what if there had been another way? If you had married, had a family? Stayed in the country?'

'I cannot know if my life would have been any better or worse. You can create the perfect life in your mind, but it is a fiction. I may have married a husband who beat me, or a man I loved dearly and lost too young. My children may not have lived. Or they might have grown into bullies, or selfish creatures who cared not for their mother. There are many ways to suffer.'

'I am here because a man decided to take something that wasn't his. I hate him more than I have words to say. I would do anything to go back. To say no.'

Lisbetta blinks slowly and contemplates the garden. A silence gathers and swirls between us. I had promised I would keep my business to myself, and yet here I am, spilling my thoughts at the first offer of kindness. Then she taps her stick on the floor, as if she were a judge calling a courtroom to order.

'It is no use hanging on to him like that,' she says eventually.

'Well, that is an easy thing to say.'

'I didn't say it was easy, I said it is no use. When you hold on to the hatred, the resentment, you allow him to live,' she taps at her skull, with her finger, the knuckles of which are painfully swollen. 'You give him space in your mind ... Paying no dues.'

I think of my dreams. Of falling from buildings and waking, immobile, to find Luigi standing over me, of being bitten by a thousand tiny insects, all with his leering face, of being attacked by a bear, my face clawed at repeatedly, and when I beg the bear-baiter to stop, it is Luigi, laughing at my plight.

'How do you do it? How do you evict them from your mind?'

'You must accept everything. Everything that has happened in my life has shaped me. Been thrown into the pot, blended to become the grey-haired woman who keeps asking the strange, lonely girl to come with her. I have used all the cruel things which have ever been done to me and determined my life by being the opposite.'

The little brown bird returns, circling the feeder before settling to peck at the grain. We watch it for a few moments. I sometimes wonder how a creature so small does not fall down in fright at the world. Everything is a danger, and its heart is so tiny, how can it stay alive in the face of the onslaught it must face daily?

'I do not think it is possible. To accept.' I pull the blanket closer around me.

'You see that tree?' Lisbetta waves with her dirt-stained fingers to a tree in the corner of the garden. It is large and old and gnarled. I nod.

'Look at the branches.'

I squint to look up at the branches stretching their skeletal fingers, straining to reach the white sky beyond.

'What do you see?'

'Nothing. The tree is bare.'

'Precisely.'

I shift. The old woman is talking in riddles now.

'Trees are honest, you see,' she continues. 'They know they must shed in order to renew. We are no different.'

I think about her words. How they sound wonderful but, like a fine gown, are of no practical help. The Berninis wormed their way into my flesh, into my bones, my marrow, and are now, even as we speak, eating me alive.

Chapter Forty-Eight

'The Washhouse'

January 1639

The washhouse is set off the high-walled quad, within easy access of the deep well set in the middle of the courtyard.

The task of cleaning the city's linen is not an easy one, and takes many hands, each woman assigned their own task. Outside the washhouse the soap is prepared by Lucia, a small, shrew-like-woman, who mixes lye soap with two bushels of hard-wood ashes to seven pans of water. The sinews of Lucia's arms flex and strain as she stirs the concoction in a great vat.

Lucia's lye is then taken in buckets by Frederica to Carmina, a mournful young woman, who pours it into great iron caldrons, setting it to boil. The fire for the lye is never allowed to die, and it makes the room so unbearably hot that some of the women – those in the midst of losing the curse of Eve – complain bitterly and take it in turns to stand in the icy breath of dawn.

Carmina's heated liquid is then ladled from the pot into smaller buckets to be poured into individual barrels, over which more women stand, immersing the clothes, pressing the sweat-, blood- and vomit-stained garments up and down in the murky water with great wooden sticks.

I am one of these women. I do not mind the heat and can tolerate standing in front of a large tub soaking linens in urine collected from the convent's chamber pots, because it is mindless work. I have even become accustomed to the terrible stench of pee, this being the most effective method to rid the cloth of the oils and stains of the body. Well, second most effective. It is said men's piss is better for the job – more pungent, I suppose – but that is in short supply in our community.

Today I'm thinking once again about Luigi Bernini as I plunge my wooden paddle in and out of the yellow liquid. About how he is free to go about his business however he pleases, and how I am in this place, elbow-deep in piss. I lift the stick again and again, violently drowning clothes in the urine, viciously pushing them under the surface of the grimy water until no more bubbles rise to the surface, before I release them, only to plunge the linen once more to the depths of the barrel.

Once my cloth is well soaked, I reach for the cenerandolo, a coarse linen cloth tightly stretched over a wooden frame, which I place over the top of the tub ready to strain the boiling lye. This is my least favourite part of the process – everything to do with washing is unpleasant – but I dislike this part because of the person tasked with walking round the washroom dispending the lye.

'Stand back!' Rosa shouts; her voice grates like a fishwife's. I am still positioning the cenerandolo when she begins to tip the bucket of ammonia-lye into my tub. It is typical of Rosa to be so haphazard. The fumes are the first to hit my eyes, stinging like bee venom. I close them in panic, and without thinking I rub at my lids with my pissy hands. This only makes matters worse, and when I open my eyes again tears have begun streaming involuntarily down my face.

I realise too late that I am standing overly close. Rosa, typically oblivious, carries on pouring the hot liquid which splashes from the pail onto my arm, falling like hot ash from a fire. The pain is instant, burning my skin, heat-seared scalds developing in seconds.

I stretch my arms out in front of me, in an unconscious attempt to relieve the pain. At first I believe it to be a mistake. 'Christ's sake, Rosa. Look what you've done. What are you playing at?'

But Rosa's tone tells me otherwise. 'Oh, do forgive me.' Her words may speak of contrition, but her tenor does not.

My blood bubbles like the boiling lye. 'You did this deliberately. You were too quick to pour, knowing I was in the way.'

'Don't be a clot.' Rosa is infuriatingly calm, to the point of condescending. 'Why would I deliberately hurt you? You think far too much of yourself, Costanza Piccolomini.'

Little blisters begin to form on my arm. '*I* think too much of *myself?*' I cannot help it; I am shouting now, incredulous. 'I think too much of myself? When it is *you* who swans about the place like the Queen of Sheba?'

The washroom stills, women stop at their work, those carrying buckets set them quietly to the floor, wooden sticks cease being plunged, tubs are not stirred, everyone is listening. There is a show to watch. Between the furnace of the constant fire and the monthly courses of the women, it is not unknown for debates to become heated, breaking the monotony for all.

Rosa puts down the pail slowly, deliberately and places her hands carefully on her hips. 'Come now, I can't possibly be the Queen of Sheba, can I?' She laughs, but it is a mocking snigger. 'Nay. I cannot be a Queen of anything, because *I* am a common puttana.'

The judgement of the word makes me wince. Rosa looks around

at the women, her audience, grinning at their enraptured faces glistening in the firelight. There is a complete quietness now, save for the bubbling of water and the crack of wet logs on the fire.

Rosa comes closer to me, so close I can smell the sour sweat under her arms and see the individual pores of her skin. She speaks slowly, purposefully, loudly into my face. 'Yet *I* am not the one marked for a whore.'

I don't need to look around to know the women are exchanging nervous glances now; this is getting dangerously close to a cat fight. The minute a skirmish begins the nuns will be in here, breaking up the aggression, hauling the offending women off to be punished harshly by the Abbess. A penalty which will be physical and severe.

The silence is broken by the dull thud of Lisbetta's stick hitting the floor and her hoarse breath as she struggles to stand. She means to intervene.

My own breath quickens and I clench my jaw. I would tear Rosa's eyes out, were I not so terrified of the sbirri taking me from this place to one far worse.

'Rosa . . .' Lisbetta's reedy voice attempts to command. 'Leave the girl alone . . .'

Rosa raises her hand. I am not sure whether it is a signal to stop Lisbetta from talking or whether she means to hit me. My mind quickens, like it did when I was seven and the neighbourhood bully was threatening Giuliana. Hit Rosa! Hit her first, land a blow, get in now, before she punches you, do not allow her to best you, to catch you unprepared. I am about to follow through on this command, but before I can strike in retaliation Rosa speaks.

'It does not help.'

What is the woman talking about? I look at her lost for words.

'The solitude and self-pity,' she continues. 'The thinking you are more than us. Loneliness will not save you from a broken heart,

Costanza. We all have our reasons for being here. You need to stick with us ... not fight us. Because we look after each other in this game. When the pimps and johns are long gone, it's your friends who will pick up the pieces.'

My heart pushes against my throat. I swallow, checking myself. Everything in me wants to scream. It was different. It was not a deal I made. I was in love.

But I do not. I have lived with these women long enough not to judge them. Instead, I lift my fingers to my face, wincing as the tips run delicately along the tender, raised scars across my cheek and nose, still swollen to the touch.

'He hurt me,' I whisper. It is the first time I have said it out loud.

Rosa's eyes narrow but her voice softens. 'Aye, Costanza. We know.'

It is an act of knowing, of quiet solidarity.

I look beyond her and notice for the first time that these women, who for weeks I have scorned and rejected, see me too. Even little Serafina. They may not know the details, but they know the nights with Luigi and the knife in Stefano's hand. They see the rejection by Matteo, then Lorenzo. They understand the hands of the sbirri on my breasts and hips. They see the humiliation and the shame.

They see me. And for the first time, I truly see them.

Chapter Forty-Nine

'A New Woman'

January 1639

The nuns serve us our meals as part of their devotion.

We stir and paddle, rinse and steam and scrub, and when we are done for the day, we make for the benches in the high-ceilinged dining hall set with long tables, rubbing our red-raw hands and stiff backs, waiting with rumbling bellies.

Sitting around the table is more company than I used to keep. Carlotta is joined by Rosa, Lisbetta and Serafina. They make light talk about the day and there are yet more jokes about men. Dirty, filthy, funny jokes that make the women squeal. Sometimes I think of Giuliana, her devout righteousness, or Caterina cossetted in her salon, and know they would not survive this.

We are tucking into our usual fare of watery stew and bread when a new woman walks in. Those who have just arrived at the Casa Pia attract a lot of interest. Oftentimes they are known by some of the women, Rome not being a big city. News can be gleaned from the outside world, updates on loved ones, precious rumour and gossip about friends or old foes, a connection with the world beyond. Women like Carlotta and me, arrested for events that happened behind closed doors, have less prospect for such a chance meeting, but we scrutinise fresh inmates nonetheless; it is part of the game.

As with many, this woman's eyes are downcast. Her head is freshly shaven and covered in red-crusted scratches where the blade has nicked her skin. I glance at her for a moment, the setting, the exposed scalp and the shift working together to obscure my memory from placing her, so different does everyone seem in this place. Then I see her face and have a fluttering recollection: a doorway, a young woman, smiling knowingly, dressed in only a chemise, an elaborate room, a startled gentleman pushing past me.

I stand abruptly and clamber over the bench to make my way to her, smiling, for I know exactly who she is, sure she will be glad of a friendly face.

'As I live and breathe! Bluma Bianchini, what are you doing here?'

Bluma's eyes widen in terror. 'You ... you must be mistaken, signora. I am Maria, Maria Campioni.' She holds out her hand. 'Pleased to meet you.'

'Oh,' I stammer. 'Oh, I am sorry. It's just you look like someone I used to know.'

Her eyes are barren, a wasteland of emotion. 'I have one of those faces ... aren't we are all just someone people used to know?'

I gesture to the bench where Lisbetta, Rosa and the other women are sitting. 'Why don't you come and join us ... Maria? It would do well to meet some people.'

She shakes her head. 'Nay ... but thank you. I would rather sit on my own.'

As she shuffles away to an empty bench, I notice her legs are marked with livid black bruises in the shape of boots, and there are spots of crimson seeping through her shift.

* * *

Later, when the meal is finished and we are walking back along the cold stone corridor to the dormitory, I manage to corner Bluma again.

'What happened?' I murmur, my lips hardly moving. 'How have you, a Jewess, ended up in a convent?'

'We fell on hard times,' she whispers back, her words short and biting. 'We needed money so I went out looking for business. Got picked up. Lied about my name.'

'God's blood. And Riva?'

Bluma shakes her head. 'I knew if they went to the house and found her . . . found out we are heathens, discovered how we lived . . . they would kill us both.'

'Surely—'

'Do not be so naive. The Church authorities would kill us, Costanza. We are an abomination. Riva would be tortured for her manly fashion. They would call her an insult to God. We Jews are not afforded the same protection as Catholic women.'

Bluma pulls away from my side, walking as quickly as her limping, battered body will allow. I feel foolish, and understand she would rather bear the pain such movement causes, than speak to me.

* * *

A few nights later I wake from another dream. I am at the Colosseum in a deep pit. I cannot escape, it is a dark, endless night, and the air freezes my breath. Somewhere in the distance I can hear growls. Menacing. A dark and ugly threat. I begin to claw at the earth to escape, desperately trying to find purchase. My soft nails rip and tear, and I can taste grit in my mouth, but still I continue to dig. Above me I hear the sound of the animals approaching, panting, snarling, straining at their restraints. Someone laughs. I know the laugh well. It is the same one I hear most nights. The same laugh I heard when I submitted, when I closed my eyes and wished I was elsewhere. Now I am half-awake I hear crying. Somewhere far in the distance. I stop my excavations and listen.

As consciousness returns, the sound becomes unmistakable: it is the stifled sobs of a woman. Normally I – we – the women in the Casa Pia – ignore such moans; grief is private, and there are many who experience it. I calculate the distance from my pallet, try to work out, counting along the beds, whose sobs they are. As I do the sums, it dawns on me who is weeping and I do not want to leave her without comfort.

I slip from my pallet tentatively, there is only scant light and I am careful not to knock the bucket or table, or stub my toe on another's bed. The dormitory is freezing, and I am glad for Lisbetta's woollen socks. A few more steps and I see the huddled figure lying curled and crying on the mattress.

I bend down and gently touch the woman's back. 'Blu . . . Maria. It's me, Costanza.' It seems madness to ask what is wrong, when the very fact of being in this place means everything is wrong.

'Go back to bed,' she hisses. 'I do not need you.'

I remember Lisbetta's gentle persistence, her continued offers of friendship.

'Maybe not,' I whisper. 'But I might be able to help. Just to listen?'

She sniffs but does not send me away.

I wait for a moment, then ask, 'Has something happened?' I am not well-practised at this. 'I mean . . . has something happened . . . beyond being here . . .'

A cold draught blows at my legs. My bed would be warmer than begging Bluma to talk, so I am relieved when she turns her face towards me.

Even in this light I can see her eyes are swollen, eyelashes gathered into small spikes. 'Please tell me. I have kept your secret … Maria. Riva once helped me and now I would like to help you.'

Bluma sits up, pulling her knees to her chest like a child. The air is chill. The other women shift and murmur in their sleep. One or two snore, some shout out, fighting imaginary foes in their dreams. I need to tread carefully.

'Can I sit down?'

She nods.

I perch on the end of Bluma's mattress, far enough to give her space, but near enough to give her comfort, and try again. 'Is it something … has something happened?' She nods once more. 'Something I could help with?' A shake of the head. 'How do you know? Can you not trust me? I have been a friend of Riva's a long time. Since we were girls. If she were here, do you not think she would urge you to rely on me?'

Another nod. A sniff. A breath in, then out.

'I will not survive. I will be uncovered … and then they will kill me.'

'I will help you learn the ways of Catholicism, so you can pass.'

She does not reply. I put my hand over hers and press down. As Lisbetta taught me during our time in the garden, I must give Bluma time. To think. To talk. She takes a great shuddering breath in.

'I am with child.'

It takes a moment for the information to register. Then my heart sinks. I could have helped Bluma with her catechisms, explained the Stations of the Cross. Many women in here gave up on the Church years ago, some are addled by drink, others are not always of sound mind, yet the sisters are happy as long as we are quietly reflecting on our sins. We could have got by. But a child? I press my lips together, grimace and curse inwardly. Bluma will be sent from the convent to somewhere far worse. She is right, she would not survive it.

'Are you quite sure?'

She nods. 'It is three months, maybe more, since I last bled.'

'Many things can stop you from . . .'

'Feel.' Her instruction is terse.

'I don't know what I'm . . .'

'Feel. It does not take a genius.'

I shuffle up the bed and Bluma lifts her nightgown to her waist. It is a profoundly intimate act, but instead of feeling lewd, it only serves to heighten her vulnerability. Despite the low light I can see the deep mottled bruises covering her legs and stomach, the shock of the dark triangle of hair at her crotch. She takes my wrist and guides my hand to her lower belly. Indeed, it does not take a genius to know what lies there. Under her skin I feel an unmistakable hardness, a warm little mound.

The words come before I have thought. 'I will help you.'

But I have no idea how, given we live under lock and key.

Bluma begins to cry again. 'It is impossible. I had hoped the beating, the kicking, would have . . . but it did not.'

'We will find a way,' I say firmly. She needs to hear these words, even if I am not convinced of the veracity myself.

'Here, move over. I shall stay with you tonight. You should not be on your own.'

'You should go back . . . people will talk . . .'

'Do you think we will be the first or last women to share a bed in this place? I can tell you we are well used to the sighs and moans, solo or with a bedfellow. Besides . . .' I look Bluma in the eyes, 'Riva is my friend, and so are you.'

She shuffles over, and I slip into bed next to her. We lie, her facing to the door, me curled into her back. It takes a while but eventually Bluma drifts off to sleep. I lay my arm across her, protecting her from the night air, from the scorn, the casting out, the uses men will have for her in the debtor's jail, and promise myself I will find a way.

Chapter Fifty

'Blind Eye'

February 1639

It is the delicate interlude between the harshness of winter and the awakening of spring, when the sun holds the city in her brittle grip.

I am kneeling in Lisbetta's garden (as I now call it), my knees resting on a piece of sackcloth, a trowel digging over the soil. If Giuliana could see me now she would laugh, for I have never shown the slightest inclination towards nature, or gardening or tending anything dainty or fragile.

To all who look at us, Lisbetta and I make the most unlikely of companions, yet spending time with her, in this plot, is one of the things that sustains me most. We talk of everything. She tells me of her childhood, feeding hens, milking cows, churning butter, turning cheese, of her brothers and sisters. She teaches me about plants, how to make holes in the ground and push bulbs deep into the black earth. Of the bushes that lie dormant only to come alive each spring, which plants will die after a season, explaining how nature invests all her glory in even the shortest of lives.

We talk of men, of mothers, of loss and lingering pain. She counsels me with words of understanding and comfort. I call her my wise woman and she smiles and tells me all the knowledge I need is held tight within me, like a seed which needs light and water; all I must do is listen and trust my own mind.

The earth in the garden is dark, full of well-rotted compost, alive with thick worms, which I hate but which Lisbetta says are vital to the health of the soil. 'It is a system.' She explains. 'We all exist for a purpose, even the worms.'

I am turning the ground over again and again, thinking absent-mindedly of Giuliana, my dirty nails, the whorls of my fingers stained with mud, imagining her mirth, when another conversation drifts into my mind.

A spring day. Giuliana and I walking along the river. An argument. Shock, hurt, shame. Herbs, apothecaries, remedies. Caterina's voice now: *There are ways.*

My hand stills, the trowel hangs in mid-air. Here, in this garden, there are herbs: for the nuns' dispensary and the kitchen. I look over at Lisbetta, who is pruning a tall shrub of some kind, gently pulling down the branches, carefully positioning her curved knife at the base of the twigs despite her trembling hands. I had promised Bluma I would not say a thing, but as I watch Lisbetta I wonder.

I stand and brush down my habit. 'Lisbetta?'

She stops and looks at me quizzically – I cannot have finished my task so soon. 'Aye?'

'Can I ask you something? It is very ... delicate.'

She stops, then hobbles over to the bench for a rest. 'You know you can ask me anything.'

'It is for a friend.'

'Go on.'

I join her and contemplate the bare branches of the tree. The sky is bluer today, washed with just a hint of colour.

'The herbs here, in this place. Would they ... could they be picked in such a combination as to bring on a woman's bleeding?'

She purses her lips. I wait while she counts numbers under her breath. 'Costanza ... are you?' She slowly points at my belly. 'Is there a child? In there?'

'Nay,' I say wearily. 'It is not me. A friend, I said.'

Lisbetta's eyes narrow. 'They all say it is for a friend.'

'But is it possible? To have the right combination?'

'With what is in the garden, and the storeroom, then yes, in theory it is possible to make a mixture to bring on bleeding. But it is not straightforward. There are risks. Once the quickening of the womb has commenced ...'

'It has not. I am certain. If there is no quickening, then you can help?' Despite the cold, I feel a warmth flood to my cheeks and a full feeling of satisfaction at my guile.

Lisbetta stares at me unapologetically. 'I can help. But did not say I would.'

'But it is for a friend, here at the Casa Pia, she is in dire need. They will send her to the debtor's prison ...' I hear the pleading in my voice, and do not mind; this is a desperate situation. 'I promised her I would help.'

'As I said, there are risks. I need to know who. Would have to attend ...'

'I gave her my word I would not tell.'

'You do not have to break your confidences. What if I guessed? If I guess then I can help, but I must insist on being there when your friend takes the draught ...'

'You will not guess.'

'Is it Maria?'

I turn, open mouthed. Lisbetta lets out a small chuckle. 'Close your mouth. You look like a carp. It was not hard to know. Few women have joined us recently, and you two are thick as thieves. I saw you creep from her mattress the other morning.'

'You must not breathe a word. Do you promise?'

'I promise.' Lisbetta runs her fingers across the front of her scalp, over the stubble showing from under her cap. 'You may not be able to see, but my head is full of grey hairs. There is something you need to know about grey-haired women. We have outlived our use ... we cannot bear children ... which means the world no longer needs us. This ...' She rubs at her head again, quivering fingers moving back and forth. 'This gives us great freedom and not a little courage. We use this freedom to help the young, to succour women, to mend the mistakes we ourselves have made.'

'Is this why you are my friend?'

'I am your friend because I like you, Costanza. Sometimes you just have to wait for some of your friends to be born.'

'I cannot imagine being old.'

'The young never can.'

* * *

I catch Bluma after evening prayers, pulling her into an alcove in the corridor just outside the dormitory.

'I have an answer.'

Bluma's face lights up, with what ... relief? And something else ... disbelief.

'You have? How?

'Lisbetta will help.'

Bluma takes a step back, the relief in her face clouding to anger.

'You told Lisbetta? You said you would not tell a soul. How can you trust that crazy old woman. How could you betray—'

'Listen. I told no one, Lisbetta guessed. And she is no more crazy than you or I. She is kind and tender and holds a knowledge of plants.'

'And where is Lisbetta going to get plants from in this place? Not even a weed is allowed to grow between the cracks of the flagstones in the courtyard.'

It is on the tip of my tongue to tell Bluma of the garden, of Lisbetta's great skill. But I am learning I am a keeper of secrets and a woman of my word.

'Lisbetta knows the sisters who work in the dispensary, helps out there sometimes. She can smuggle some plants to make a physick.' Now is the time to tackle the real objection. 'But she insists on being with you. Says it is risky.'

'Nay, nay, nay.' Bluma shakes her head vigorously. 'I will not have it. Have her. Just give me the potion and I will be done with it. On my own.'

'She will not. Lisbetta.' I hear the urgency in my voice as I whisper. 'She says she will not help unless she is there.'

'And you trust her? Some of these women, I swear, they are in league with the nuns, and you say Lisbetta helps in the dispensary? She will inform on me and then I am done.'

I touch Bluma's arm, a brush to reassure her. 'I promise. She is entirely trustworthy. And will help. Do you agree to it?'

'Aye.' Bluma shifts uncomfortably. 'If you say Lisbetta is to be trusted then I will agree. I hardly have any other choice, do I?'

'True.' I give Bluma a small hug, but her body remains resolutely impassive. 'Oh, just one more thing. There is no quickening is there? You have felt no movement?'

Bluma looks me dead in the eye. 'Nothing. I have felt nothing.'

* * *

Two nights later, after the women have climbed wearily into their beds, Lisbetta and I crouch at the end of Bluma's pallet.

We agreed Bluma would complain of stomach pains after the evening meal. That she would be in such discomfort, the attention of the sisters would be called to her state. Given the lateness of the hour, and being wholly trusted, Lisbetta would then offer to go to the dispensary for a physick. I was to accompany Lisbetta, on account of the darkness of the winter evening and her shakes being of particular peril.

We reached the dispensary quickly, an unassuming chamber filled with wooden shelves on which stood hundreds of jars and vases, each one holding meticulously dried herbs, flowers and roots, their colours dulled by time but still potent. In the middle stood a large wooden table, scarred from years of use and littered with texts, illuminated manuscripts and handwritten parchments.

Lisbetta had moved quickly, producing leaves hidden in the pockets of her tunic, instructing me to bring jars of herbs, hard blackened berries and the tiny heads of seeds. 'Hurry,' she had instructed. 'Do not let anyone see.' A pinch here. A scattering there. Lisbetta had pounded the pestle with surprising vigour, the powder releasing a musty, swampy scent. Once the grinding was done to her satisfaction, Lisbetta had mixed a little water, smeared the moss paste into a cup, then stirred it swiftly with some dark wine to disguise the smell, until it had dissolved completely. 'Here,' she said, pressing the cup firmly into my hands to take back to the dormitory. 'Carry it with care, there is no more where that came from.'

Now we are back in the dormitory, crouched by the light of a single candle, while Bluma drinks, taking great gulps at a time. The rest of the place is in darkness, and alive with the nocturnal mutterings of the women and the scratched footsteps of rodents.

'Take smaller sips,' Lisbetta whispers. 'Do not spill a drop of it.'

'But it tastes foul,' complains Bluma.

'It will do, but it must all be drunk. Every last part.'

A voice shouts out in the dark. 'God's blood. Can't you keep it down, you old bat? We've all had stomach gripes, cease with the fussing, can't you?'

I open my mouth to respond, but catch Lisbetta's eye warning me not to do anything that might bring about unwanted attention. Instead, I shout, 'Sorry ... we will try to be quieter. Poor girl suffers ... bad monthlies.'

Once Bluma has drunk the potion, I slip into her bed. I want to be near when it starts. Lisbetta leans over us and, mindful of the proximity of our neighbours and the bad blood we are already causing, whispers as quietly as she can. 'Come and get me. The minute the first pains start. Do you understand? As soon as they start.' Bluma and I stare up from under the cover like two children being admonished at bedtime.

'I will,' I tell Lisbetta. 'I promise.'

I close my eyes but can't sleep. Instead, I lie and listen to Bluma's breathing, feel the gentle beat of her heart under her nightdress, imagine the potion running through her veins, seeping into her belly. As some point I must drift off. It is the dead of night when I hear the first whimper, a small exhale followed by the slightest of groans. The sound fills me with a sudden, quiet dread. The early hours are a dangerous time.

I trust Lisbetta's physick, but women's bodies can be so temperamental; they cramp and bleed, cause strange pains, run hot then cold, and are not to be trusted. What if Bluma's body decides to do something strange, unpredictable, what if we cannot staunch the bleeding or she screams so loudly the sisters come and suspect a foul hand? What if I have caused Bluma's downfall rather than helping her? I find myself wishing this night to be over quickly.

Bluma moans again. I rub her back and murmur in her ear, 'Hold on. I will fetch Lisbetta.'

Bluma's body tenses with another cramp as I ease myself off the pallet, slipping one leg one leg at a time, then stand by pushing myself gradually from the wooden frame, avoiding quick movements which might attract attention, and tiptoe, like a night thief, to where Lisbetta lies, deep in slumber. She is slow to wake, but when she finally sees my face, she is alert, eyes blazing; she has done this many times before.

It does not take long. In less than an hour, Bluma is lying curled like a shell. She reminds me of Giuliana when she birthed Leonardo: skin grey and clammy, saying naught but quietly gripping her stomach. Bluma does not scream or shout, but instead endures it wordlessly, almost in total silence but for the odd, low-throttled moan.

'Is this usual?' I ask anxiously of Lisbetta.

'Quite normal. Loss can be a subdued affair.'

I stroke Bluma's hair, as Lisbetta keeps an eye on the bleeding.

'Still usual?' I ask again after five minutes.

'Yes.' She nods emphatically.

I run the words over and over again in my mind. Still usual. This is still usual. It is usual. But I cannot help but think it is not.

Lisbetta lifts the sheets again. 'It is done.'

She takes hold of Bluma's limp, white fingers, squeezing tight, and Bluma returns the gesture.

'You have done well,' Lisbetta says gently. 'We shall clean you up, then you shall sleep. Rest is imperative.' Then she looks up at me. 'Costanza, there is a bucket of water in the corner. It is cold but will do. You must sponge Maria clean and change the sheets.'

At the same moment, Carlotta appears, wrapped in her shawl. She is fizzing, a tumult of emotion running behind her eyes. 'I have been watching.' She almost stutters her words, so great is the effort to keep herself in check. 'I have been watching you. All three of you. This is no bellyache or monthlies.'

I glance at Lisbetta, panicked. We cannot have got this far to be undone.

Carlotta continues. 'This is a ruination. An abomination. What has occurred tonight is beyond wicked. It is a mortal sin. And under the roof of a house of God too. I cannot stand by and—'

'Cease.'

Carlotta stops talking and spins around. Another figure has joined us. Rosa. Immediately identifiable in the dark, her tall form casting an imposing shadow over the bed.

'Cease, Carlotta,' repeats Rosa quietly. Calmly.

'But Maria has—'

I glance at Lisbetta, whose weathered face is etched in panic at the thought of being uncovered.

'We have seen nothing,' Rosa says coolly, her voice low. 'Naught has occurred this night which is worthy of mention to a living soul.'

Carlotta bristles. 'You cannot say ... cannot tell me this is right ...'

'We have seen nothing.' Rosa states her words slowly, carefully. 'You may not know what happens when women are taken from here in disgrace. But I can tell you. Nothing good. Only awful things happen to girls taken by the sbirri. Things that make this existence, washing clothes in piss, seem like paradise. So, can we agree? Nothing happened here tonight?' Rosa's face is implacable, but her eyes blaze in the low light.

Carlotta pulls her lips tight. 'This,' she gestures at Bluma. 'Is still a mortal sin.' Her tone is more dejected than defiant.

'You are right,' Rosa concedes. 'It is. In the eyes of the Church, what has occurred here tonight is wrong. But what will happen to

Maria if she is taken to another place is also a sin. We must save one of our own. This is not a just world. But can we please agree; we have seen nothing?'

Carlotta looks down at the bed. Lisbetta is still holding Bluma's bloodless hand, I am crouched like a tiger at her back. There is a heartbeat, a moment of doubt, of reckoning, then reconciliation.

Then Carlotta says, 'What?' What are you staring at? I have not seen a thing.'

Chapter Fifty-One

'The Price of Bread'

February 1639

The year continues with a shudder, leaving the good people of Rome to use what little scudi they have on firewood and fat, to keep themselves warm.

While Bluma recovers quickly, Carlotta still cannot quite forgive us. The situation is recognised for what it is – an impasse – and an unspoken agreement is reached to sweep our quarrel into a corner, to stay with the dust mice and spiders. We live in too close proximity to allow real life, personal vocations or judgements to come between us.

Sister Apollonia, a cheery, ruddy nun of middling age, with a plump chin which spills from her wimple, makes her way between the benches of the supper table. As she passes by each woman, the sister dips a huge metal ladle into a pot which is pushed along on a squeaking cart by a hesitant kitchen girl. The spoon fills with a thin, greasy liquid with floating grey lumps of mutton gristle and some limp cabbage. Sister Apollonia lifts the spoon high, with not a little aplomb, before unceremoniously dumping it into our bowls.

All the women's bowls are filled except mine.

When it comes to filling my plate, Sister Apollonia sails on like a royal barge in full progress. I am puzzled. She must not have seen me, yet I am right here.

'Sister,' I shout good humouredly, 'I am sorry to halt proceedings but I am starving, and it appears you have forgot my portion?' I clasp my hands together as if in prayer, then hold out my bowl for a ladle of the not-so-appetising stew. 'I should be most thankful if my bowl can be filled.'

Sister Apollonia stops and turns slowly, giving me a frank stare. She doesn't utter a word, but simply shrugs her round shoulders, returns to her ladle duties, and resumes serving the next woman.

I try again. 'Sister Apollonia.' I hear a shrill tone to my words, spoken a little louder than I had intended. 'I have not had my food,' I explain. 'I have worked all day and am very hungry.'

This time, Sister Apollonia does not stop, does not look back, but ignores me, as if I have said no words at all, and gestures to the serving girl to carry on her duties.

I stand in one, clean action, back straight. This is confounding. I mean to catch the nun's attention, clamber over the benches and demand my food, even wresting the ladle from the reluctant sister's hand if needs be.

'Sit down.' Rosa's hiss is sharp with an edge of annoyance, and she pulls forcefully at my arm. 'Sister Apollonia has clearly taken a vow of silence . . . a penance for something or other. You will achieve naught by assaulting a nun with words.'

I bite my bottom lip and sit down reluctantly, staring at my empty bowl.

'What is the problem with Costanza's food?' asks Serafina,

which is exactly the same question I am asking. I perceive, rather than see, Lisbetta motioning the young girl to be quiet.

However, I do witness Rosa exchanging a knowing a look with Lisbetta, the kind of look mothers share when their children have stumbled into some secret known only to grown-ups. It cements a secret pact to cover up the truth, or at least explain the kindest version of it. Suddenly I feel as young and foolish as Serafina.

Neither Rosa nor Lisbetta answer, so I am forced to ask the question, which has begun to burn like an ember. 'What is wrong? Why does Sister Apollonia not feed me?'

It is Carlotta who answers. 'Because whoever was paying your keep is no longer offering up their scudi.'

My hungry belly turns. I had not thought about who might be paying for my food, my upkeep. I had just assumed ... assumed what? That the authorities covered my costs. But if this is not the case ... then who?

'Do you know who put you in here?' Carlotta continues. I cannot help feeling she is enjoying this. 'Was it your husband?' Carlotta has a long-held belief that no husband wants a ruined wife. 'Because if it was your husband, then he has given up on you. Stopped paying. Probably found himself a mistress, or is seeking an annulment for a new wife.'

I laugh loudly. 'I can assure you, Carlotta, my husband is not pursuing a woman.'

'How can you be so sure?' There is a smugness to her tone which is not kind.

'Nay. I can assure you, of all the things Matteo could be doing, pursuing a new wife is not one.'

'You are very sure of his love.'

'Among other things. It is not Matteo, I can just feel it.'

It is Rosa who intervenes. 'So if not your husband, who?'

I think through the list once more. 'It has to be a Bernini. I do not think Lorenzo would ... my coin is on Luigi Bernini. Somehow, he has contrived to have me locked up. And now he means to starve me.' I look at the women as the words I am speaking begin to sink in.

It is Serafina who grasps at the full meaning of the words first. She shoots an alarmed look at Rosa, then asks anxiously, 'Surely it cannot be that bad for Costanza?'

"Tis worse than bad,' Carlotta offers unhelpfully. 'Her lover has had her locked up and now refuses to pay. Her husband has abandoned her. She has no one.'

My stomach tightens and I feel a sharp bile rise and spit at the back of my throat.

'Here.' Rosa elbows me in the ribs and spoons half of her mutton-gristle onto my plate. 'We don't give up that easily.' As she talks, Rosa shoots a disdainful look at Carlotta. 'We are taught that when men whisper love it is everything. That we are possessions to be protected, like precious stones set in gold. But it is not true. We are our own agents.'

Suddenly I feel very weary. There are only so many times I can keep the Bernini brothers at bay – shoving and kicking them away – holding on to my mind. As if divining all of this, Rosa takes up her hunk of bread. She snaps it into two pieces and places one half firmly by my spoon. She gesticulates at the food, talking with her mouth open.

'Eat. It is in this way men justify their supremacy over us women.' Rosa continues waving the half chunk of bread in her hand up and down, like a judge banging his gavel, to emphasise her point. 'That we are frail and weak and must be controlled. And so, we submit. We make ourselves prisoners. These walls? This penance? This is not what binds us, Costanza. It is our submission to men that creates a prison of our own making.'

The words continue to leave Rosa's lips, but I am no longer able to listen. Instead I am distracted by a hurrying, running thumping at my breast, as if there is something I have forgotten, a notion I should have remembered.

It is Rosa again. 'The food is cooling. Eat!' She dips her bread heartily into the meagre stew and bites off another hunk. There is an aftertaste to Rosa's words. A tang, as if they leave a sour note, for I know them not to be true. Women can never be free. The only way to survive is to submit. Nevertheless, I eat the frugal portion carefully, savouring every bite. For it has been given in great friendship.

'A pox on all their poles,' I swear under my breath and the women laugh, for even though they are well-used to foul utterances, they are not accustomed to women who have been made into marble portraits using such profanity.

But Rosa merely pats my hand and says, 'Revelation is the price of bread nowadays. Now, wipe your face.'

* * *

In the Casa Pia there is ferment afoot.

The Abbess sits at her desk and sighs.

She has been told troubling tales of insurrection by the sisters, who recount stories of excitable mutterings at the table, at work, in the dormitory. In which the fallen women talk of men and the necessity of demanding freedoms, utter profanities, and encourage younger members of the community to take up against the natural order: that Eve must obey Adam.

The window is open and the cold air sharp on her skin. She understands. Of course she does. Was she not sent to a convent precisely because noble dowries had become so expensive? The youngest of five girls, four of whom had already been promised, her parents could not afford to pay for her marriage. The Abbess had not desired the life of the Bride of Christ, any more than these fallen women had sought their lives.

But over time she had accepted her lot, made peace with where she found herself, and she had prospered. A nunnery requires a natural diplomat and the Abbess is an exceedingly good one, playing the needs of the convent against the wants of the men of the Church. Greater piety means more money. She leads the novices and sisters in her care well.

Indeed, the convent is bigger than some noble estates, bringing in a good income with a well-stocked treasury, not to mention the laundry business. However, keeping the fallen women in check is as full-time an occupation as any might ask for. Mouthy, obstreperous, some broken in body or in spirit and well-used to fighting and clawing like cats on the street. What the Abbess has within these thick stone walls is more than she ever could have dreamed of from a life outside them.

But it will do the fallen women no good, tattling on about life with no men. For even here, in the convent, women cannot do without men. The sisters are married to Christ, give their confession to Father Pietro, and follow the instructions of the Bishop.

The Abbess pulls out the roll of the women paying penance. She has some alms she can use to take one or two in. Carnival will be upon them soon, a good chance to take in donations as the citizens of Rome try to assuage the guilt of their excesses by giving a generously to the convent.

She runs her finger down the names inscribed in neat block print. Costanza; now she would be a good candidate to become a nun at the Casa Pia. All of Rome heard that poor woman's scandal, and now half her face is ruined, a wimple would not be such a hardship. Besides, thinks the Abbess, she is a Piccolomini, a branch of the Cardinal's family. There are some who say he will make it to the Papal See one day. Costanza could be useful.

The Abbess tuts. She has allowed herself to be distracted. She will speak to the women of the need to work hard to earn their penance before they are released. That they must stop the ungodly badinage. For, if the Bishop were to hear ... The Abbess stands, smooths her skirts, and adjusts her wimple in the glass above the fireplace. In the grate the heart-flame crackles and wild shadows dance across her skin, which is pink and a little damp. She would have made a good wife.

But she has made an even more brilliant abbess.

Chapter Fifty-Two

'May the Saints Come and Meet You'

March 1639

'Rosa.' Carlotta's tone is brittle. 'The Abbess could not have been plainer at prayers last night ... you must cease all disruptive chatter ... keep your opinions to yourself ... or she will impose penance after penance upon us for being unruly.'

It is early in the day, the sun barely risen in the sky, but we have already said our prayers and are hard at work scrubbing. Rosa, weaving in and out of the tubs with her bucket of lye, continues with her task as she talks.

'I could not give two hoots what hawk-face says. It's all right for her, standing there in her fine wool habit, quarters full of tapestries and gold plate, assured of a warm hearth and full belly until she's cold in the ground.'

The din of the washroom swallows her words, so Rosa begins to raise her voice. 'We, us women who have nothing ... we must keep on. Keep our spirits alive. Penance,' – she spits the word – 'prayers and intercessions are useless; good friends, some coin and a sense of humour are what hold ordinary women together.' Rosa pauses for a moment, resting her pail precariously on the edge of a tub as she addresses the women like a preacher in a public square 'We must fight, or else what's the point? We may as well all give up now.'

Carlotta makes a violent shushing sound and whispers theatrically, 'The sisters will report you and then we'll have no supper.'

'You need to develop a stronger stomach, Carlotta.' Rosa picks up her pail and continues making her way among the women, warming to her theme of Carlotta's shortcomings; not just a lack of stomach, but a willingness to grovel to authority, and not forgetting a tendency to see a cup half empty, instead of half full.

Lisbetta joins the fray in strong voice, despite the evident tremors as she speaks. 'Leave Carlotta be, Rosa, she is right. The Abbess could not have been plainer. Foment will not be tolerated; and I could do without a penance of lying all night on a stone floor, prostrating at the feet of our Lord.'

Rosa stills, considering Lisbetta's words. 'So be it. I'll keep my mouth closed. But for your gammy leg, Lisbetta, all I say still stands.'

I listen to the discussion as I listlessly push shirts into the tub, watching them eddy in the yellow water. So lackadaisical is my technique that the noxious liquid splashes onto my shift and clog-shod feet, but I do not care. The supply of clothes is endless, and the room is cloyingly hot; my skin slicks with sweat as I feebly bang my stick against the wooden barrel. The work has been harder of late; my arms are weaker and I have not the stamina to thrash and dip the dirty linens with the vigour I used to.

I'm swaying my paddle without enthusiasm from side to side when my attention is caught by a commotion, the sound of women hurriedly dropping their sticks into their tubs, thump, thump. They are leaving their stations and congregating in the middle of the washroom, forming a knot, like birds descending on scattered seed.

'What happened?' I ask a passing woman.

She shrugs, 'Not sure. Accident? Or a fall? I think someone might have fallen? Or perhaps someone is ill?'

Bluma. A premonition ... a half-remembered fear ... as if I had been expecting this all along. Did we breathe a sigh of relief too soon? I imagine my friend on the floor, gripping her stomach, her white face contorted in pain. I drop my paddle too, wiping my hands on the front of my apron as I begin to anxiously push my way through.

Almost immediately a wash of relief runs over me. There is Bluma, standing on the other side of the group. But it is odd. Something is amiss. She has removed her cap and is running her hand roughly back and forth over her black-stubbled head. She looks up and catches my eye, her face alarmed, like an animal about to be caught. I know what fear is and want to reassure her. I begin weaving my way between the press of bodies when I hear something which stops me.

Sister Illuminata, who watches us work, has spotted the commotion and is coming over. 'Who?' she shouts stridently. 'Who is it? What ails them?'

A girl's voice answers, small and shaky. 'It is Lisbetta, Sister. Oh please do come quickly. She is ...'

'Lisbetta.' The name is repeated by half a dozen women with an audible gasp of shock.

'Lisbetta?' A wave of fear ripples through me.

'Move back, make room,' shouts the sister.

I too begin to elbow and push my way through the crowd. 'Nay,' I repeat under my breath. 'Nay, nay, nay.' I am praying nothing bad has happened. Naught which cannot be fixed or undone.

I reach my friend just as Sister Illuminata does. Her small, frail frame is being cradled by Serafina, who has tears running down her face. Lisbetta's stick lies redundant beside her. For a moment I am unable to register what I am seeing.

'Lisbetta.' My voice is pinched, constricted, like a too-tight collar. Something is off. The uncomfortable angle of Lisbetta's head, her eyes, which are open but appear not to see. The small trickle of blood falling from her nose; her mouth, which hangs open.

'Lisbetta,' I say again, more firmly, finally pushing through to kneel next to her, taking her limp hand. I am confused. She was talking only a minute ago, admonishing Rosa for being so strident. 'Lisbetta,' I call again, as if hearing her name will suddenly elicit a recognition of the outside world, reminding her we are here.

Sister Illuminata has joined me at Lisbetta's side. She looks up at the women from her crouched position, one hand on the old woman's rib cage, the other pinching her wrist. 'Someone fetch Sister Zita from the infirmary.'

'Is she . . . ?' Serafina can't bear to finish the sentence.

Sister Illuminata does not answer but folds her head into her neck and begins to pray gently; 'I commend you, my dear sister, to almighty God. Return to He who made you from the dust. May Our Lady, the angels and all the saints come to meet you as you go forth from this life.' Sobs break out among the women, a swell of tiny moans and cries. Bad things sometimes happen. But here, like this, on a commonplace Tuesday, when nothing was out of the ordinary?

One part of my mind refuses to acknowledge what is in front of me. 'Fetch a looking glass,' I order no one in particular and everyone in the room. 'Check her breath, mistakes have been known . . . Lisbetta . . .'

A hand weighs down on my shoulder. 'Costanza.' It is Rosa's voice. 'It is no mistake. Lisbetta cannot hear you.'

I want to say, 'I know that. I know she cannot. It is just I do not want it to be true.' But no words come, just a deep, low groan.

'Fetch someone ... from the sickroom,' I insist desperately. 'Someone who knows about such matters.'

At just this moment Sister Zita arrives, the infirmary nun who was so kind to Lisbetta. She is tall, thin and slightly out of breath, but ready to assume control. It is a huge consolation; here is someone who knows Lisbetta, who knows what to do. Sister Zita has tended to the sick of the convent for many years, has witnessed most all illnesses – but even she lets out a small cry of dismay when she sees Lisbetta lying on the floor.

Sister Zita kneels and completes the same checks Sister Illuminata has already performed. With two fingers, the nun tenderly closes Lisbetta's eyelids before standing and addressing the women.

'Tonight we will hold a mass for the soul of our dear departed sister, Lisbetta.'

Gone. Lisbetta is gone.

Instinctively I wrap my arms about myself to contain the swell of grief, but despite my best efforts, tears spill uncontrollably. The world blurs, the sounds of the women became muffled, and the once familiar surroundings of the washroom feel as if they are another realm.

* * *

Sister Zita and I wordlessly carry Lisbetta's body on a stretcher. Her body weighs so little, it is like carrying a bird which has flown into a window and stunned itself into death.

The crypt is a small, vaulted room, located deep in the bowels of the earth under the main building of the convent. There are great rectangle flagstones on the floor and the room is lined with shelves on which stand relics from earlier times; nuns whose bodies have been moved, their skulls and thigh bones preserved, each one meticulously arranged, so they may rise at the final coming.

This is not any place for the living.

The air is heavy, still, cold, but Lisbetta is untroubled. Together with Sister Zita I begin to prepare her body for burial. I didn't see her fall, didn't witness her last breath, and for this I feel mightily wretched. Everything I do now will be in Lisbetta's greatest honour, this woman who suffered greatly but still gave so much.

We move in an orchestrated dance around the stone table on which Lisbetta's body is laid. Sound is dulled in this place, and even when we whisper it is as if the walls absorb our words.

My friend has already lost the look of the living and her skin has a sunken, waxy sheen. She is dressed in the stiff, harsh shift of the convent, which we cut away to reveal a body shrunken by age and ravaged with scars, faded white, criss-crossing her body. They are in places and of shapes which mean they cannot have been inflicted by her own hand. Then whom? Her father, or a lover perhaps? Or they could be an accumulation of wounds amassed from a lifetime working on the streets. I touch at my own scar, the raw lesion which has made my face not my own, and feel hot tears springing at my eyes.

I dip a cloth into the bucket of water which has been left for us by unseen hands. It is warm and has been scented with lavender oil, which pools in slick puddles on the surface. I think of my first night, the freezing sponge bath, and smile at the perversity of providing warm water for the dead, but only cold for the frightened living.

Having wrung out the cloth thoroughly, I begin washing Lisbetta's body carefully, reverentially, softly wiping at each of her scars in turn, as if I could, in death, rub them away. Her fingers are curled in, like the feet of a sparrow, reminding me of the little brown bird resting on the branch. Under Lisbetta's nails there are still patches of dirt from the garden she loved so much.

Sister Zita brings two coins and rests them carefully on Lisbetta's thin eyelids. I wipe across my friend's brow and her hair, which is soft like a child's and sparse. Around Lisbetta's neck is hung a small cross on a chain. Sister Zita gently unclasps it, letting the chain fall into her hand. She considers it for a moment, then wraps it in a small cloth bag before carefully placing it in her pocket. 'I shall log this as Lisbetta's belongings,' she explains. 'I am not sure how she came to still have it. Our women can be very adept at hiding . . .'

Together, Sister Zita and I lift Lisbetta's frail frame onto the sheet we have laid out. I begin to breathe hard, great deep inhalations and exhalations, and will myself not to start sobbing, for if I begin, I fear I will never be able to stop. Sister Zita reaches across the table and lays her hand on mine. We stand like this for a few moments, surrounded by empty eyes with hollow gazes, my ragged breath filling the silence, until I can say 'we must continue'.

Sister Zita makes her way to Lisbetta's feet, slowly, carefully folding the sheet across the body to make a shroud. It is hard to believe I have never done this before; it has always been a task undertaken by the older women in our district. It makes me realise what grey-haired women do. Prepare the dead, fight for the living, patrol the dances and feast days, always in service, always watching out for others.

Slowly Lisbetta is swallowed by the white cloth. When Sister Zita respectfully tucks a posy of rosemary into Lisbetta's folded arms, sprigs from a plant my friend pruned and tended, I must turn away.

I am handed a needle and thread and together Sister Zita and I begin to sew. I remember every lesson my stepmother ever taught me, every admonishment, and begin meticulously passing the needle in and out of the cloth, careful not to hurt Lisbetta, making the neatest of stitches, of which both Tiberia and Lisbetta would be proud.

When we reach Lisbetta's face, Sister Zita pauses for me to say goodbye before closing the shroud. I lean forward and kiss my friend's forehead; her skin is cold under my lips. Tears fall from my eyes onto her face, great, fat drops, like the first storms of summer, flowing from my eyes to hers, so she looks like a statue of the Madonna weeping.

Lisbetta was my miracle.

Chapter Fifty-Three

'The Nursemaid'

March 1639

I am heartsore.

Grief descends upon me like a fine drizzle. Covering everything I am, seeping into my skin, my hair, my bones. It is like the weather. Some days my sorrow is calm, like the sun peeping from the clouds, with just enough warmth to nourish me. Other days it is a devastating tempest, a rage within, waking me from my sleep, buffeting against my mind, leaving me furious, exhausted and empty.

Sometimes I open my eyes and the melancholy is so overwhelming, I ask myself, how am I alive at all? How am I still breathing, when I am locked away from all those I love, and my friend is gone?

There is, I have realised, such a slim realm between the living and the dead. I had never imagined what it is to die. To no longer exist. Even after Luigi took my body, and Lorenzo so cruelly maimed me, it had never occurred to me that death was an option. Now Lisbetta has shown me how life must end for us all, and it is all I can think about, this constant, ephemeral line of impermanence tethering us to the earth.

Things matter less than they ever did. I cannot see the point of making my bed, of talking, laughing, making jokes. I pass through my days without traction, as if I am somewhere else entirely, yet my heart continues to beat so my body carries on the work it must do.

It is two weeks since we buried Lisbetta. I have just woken; sunlight the colour of pale butter falls in slices on the floor. The morning bells are ringing, loud, insistently. Wearily I swing my legs from the bed, but when I stand there is a strange sensation in my head, a spiralling, lights orbiting. I hear a whimper and feel a fluttering like a butterfly trapped in a glass, then blackness falls.

I awake on the pallet in the dormitory. It is dark now; I must have been asleep for hours. My eyes slowly adjust to the gloom and my brain feels as if it is expanding and contracting painfully against my skull. It takes me a moment to remember . . . I was standing and then . . .

My thoughts are interrupted by the scuffed sound of the door being pushed ajar and an elongated shadow falling across my body. It is Rosa. She carries a bowl, its contents filling the room with a strong smell of chicken and broth and sweet herbs, and I am instantly reminded of home, of Tiberia's kitchen, Papa sitting at my side.

'You gave us a fright.'

She kneels next to my mattress, carefully setting the bowl on the floor next to me.

'It was a fainting fit, 'tis all.'

I make to sit up, but feel as frail as a woman thrice my age.

'Here.' Rosa puts her arm around me and pulls me up gently, so my back is resting against the wall, my bones pressing against the spare stonework, which makes an inhospitable cushion.

'Nay, it was more.' Rosa purses her lips. 'I don't play nursemaid for many. Only true friends, and only when they are truly sick.'

I am startled. 'All I did was fall over.'

She stares at me. 'You fell over because you are hungry. As am I. But I share my food gladly, for I have a trunk full of dresses waiting for me when I leave.'

I doubt there are any dresses, let alone a trunk, but am grateful for her untruths; they are designed to make me feel better.

'But I have not suffered my face and heart to be sliced like you, Costanza. For while flesh can be sewn, a heart is not so easily mended.'

My veins pulse as I think of Lorenzo. The damage he inflicted on me and the sharp dread of ever seeing him again. 'I am reconciled with all that happened. It is better this way.'

'You are not reconciled here.' Rosa touches tenderly at my breast. 'You can decide to accept events as they have happened, but your heart can still ache. You have lost much.'

I think of Matteo, Papa, Giuliana, Lisbetta. Of my home. Of my face, how it is both me and not me when I catch a glimpse of my features in a window as I pass. Against my wishes, a tear spills in betrayal of my words, and falls down my cheek.

Rosa holds my hand, splaying my fingers wide, like a bat's wing. 'See? Your fingers are skin and bone.'

Then she brushes my cheek where the knife sliced, and I wince; it is so sore.

'Your face is alive with lesions. Your wound is festering in the dank heat of the laundry. It will infect and heat your blood.'

I touch at my cheek and calculate the months, like an almanac, in my head. August, September, and so on. It is seven months since

Stefano caused his wicked abrasion, and four since I was apprehended. My skin burns hot as I trace the pustules and bumps under my fingertips. I know it is infected, and badly so, and had hoped that my body would resolve the issue. Rosa is right. My comeliness has withered away, my breasts all but disappeared, and now I examine my fingers in the dull light of the candle, I can see my knuckles extending ungraciously from my skin. More tears fall.

'It is no good crying, Costanza. You have no reserves left for such self-pity. It is how we perish, and I have determined we shall not lose another of our sisters. You are going to live.'

'How? I have nothing left outside these cursed walls. I think I shall die in here.' My voice sounds more childlike than I would have wished.

'Nay, you will not. What you will do is eat this. I had to use every one of my considerable charms to get a bowl of nourishment; it was Sister Perseveranza serving tonight, and you know how difficult she is.'

Rosa lifts the bowl and spoons the liquid into my mouth. Her nursing skills are not well honed and it drips down my chin. She laughs and wipes it with her hand, which she then brushes on her shift. 'Once you have had a bellyful you must see the Abbess. Start fending for yourself. You need food, and if your husband will not pay then someone else must.'

Chapter Fifty-Four

'The Master's New Clothes'

March 1639

Spring unfurls all her frondescent fury.

The sunlight makes playful shadows on the floor of the sculptor's studio. Lorenzo Bernini has his arms outstretched while the tailor, Cristoforo, meticulously measures his arm span, his wrists, his neck – shouting out precise numbers to a boy dressed in a pale blue silk suit. Somewhere below the studio one of the Bernini sisters is at her music practice, her well-trained voice spiralling up through the floorboards, swelling and waning in perfect harmony with the chords being played on the harpsichord.

Lorenzo closes his eyes. He likes to hear his sister sing, but this is not the reason for his contemplation; in two months' time he will be married. The sculptor has made a good match, Catherine Tezio, a woman he can be proud to hold on his arm, from a good pedigree, well trained, assured to be compliant.

The last few months have been the most tumultuous of his life.

He still, even now, cannot fathom how things have come to pass in such a disastrous way. The excruciating meeting with Cardinal Barberini, nephew of the Pope. The pair sat in a sumptuous Vatican study, the Cardinal's long, thin, bejewelled fingers tipped into an arch, as he lay out the events of last summer, turning over each fact like a card shark with the winning hand.

'So, Signor Bernini,' the Cardinal had begun, his tone mild, his words anything but. 'It appears you have lost your mind over a woman.'

'Your Eminence, please, let me explain my madness. She was steeped in sin. I was completely fooled. Lost all capacity for reason.' He drops his voice, ever the showman. 'Believed myself to be in love.'

A terse response. 'She was married.'

The sculptor had looked sheepish at this. 'Aye. It was not one of my finer moments. She was . . . beguiling.'

'Then she had . . .' the Cardinal paused. It is a delicate matter for a man of the cloth to navigate. 'She had relations with your brother, Luigi. So you nearly killed him.'

'I was angry.'

The Cardinal leaned forward. 'In a church, Lorenzo. Your brother had taken sanctuary and you nearly beat him to death in a house of God.'

'Aye.' The sculptor looked at the priest with a frank, unrepentant gaze. 'I had lost all reason. My brother and the woman I loved. Together. Who would not do the same?'

The man in red shrugged. 'I am not an expert on affairs of the heart. But that was not the end. Then you sent a man to cut the woman's nose off.' He raised his eyebrows. 'Very Old Testament.'

'To cut her face, not her nose off,' the sculptor corrected.

'To maim her. Your mother wrote to me. Distraught. Saying you act as if you are master of all the world. That you respect no justice.

It is most unedifying, the chief architect of St Peter's Basilica acting
in such a manner. I might even go as far as to say embarrassing.'

'I was provoked.' There was, the sculptor recognised, something
defiant, peevish in his tone.

'You were exceedingly stupid. Now ... His Holiness, my uncle,
understands, "boys will be boys". Is prepared to overlook this' – the
Cardinal licked his lips – 'unfortunate ... incident. Is prepared to
let matters rest, on three conditions.'

'Oh?' The sculptor had smiled and tried not to look perplexed.

'First, you will be fined.'

Lorenzo shifted uncomfortably. 'Fined. Why should I be ...?'

The Cardinal leaned back into his chair. 'It cannot be let pass
you pay no penance at all. He has determined you will pay three
thousand scu—'

All pretence of a smile left Lorenzo's lips. 'Three thousand scudi?
It is a heavy penalty for such a ...'

'As I said, you will pay three thousand scudi. The sum is settled
and not open for discussion.'

Only then did it dawn on Lorenzo Bernini that this was not a
negotiation. 'And what are the other terms of this deal?'

'You must banish the man who did this.'

The sculptor's eyes flickered in momentary deliberation. 'Agreed.'
An easy decision. He would exile Stefano if it meant holding on to
his commission.

'And the third?'

'You must marry. A woman of good repute. Put this boyish
stupidity behind you. Set your mind to a sober union with a good
Catholic woman. Settle down. Have children. There can be no more
scandal. Do you understand?'

The sculptor squirmed. 'But what if I don't want to marry a ...'

'This is not up for debate, Lorenzo. The Pontiff has invested much in you. To keep working for the Vatican, you must marry. He orders it.'

'And if I don't?'

'It will be the end.' The Cardinal pressed his fingers together so hard, the tips began to turn white. He needed a resolution to this matter. 'It would be of much regret to His Holiness to suspend all commissions. He thinks you a rare and sublime genius, but you have to understand, Lorenzo. We simply cannot have you running around Rome nearly committing fratricide and chopping off women's noses.'

'Not chopped ...'

'It does not reflect ... well ... especially in these challenging times when we must assert the moral authority of the Catholic Church. His Holiness's will must be done.'

Despite his protestations to the contrary, the sculptor had known this was a good deal. He would keep his commissions and he had already been thinking about marriage. Calculated submission. Damage limitation. 'I agree.'

The Cardinal breathed out so quietly you would not know, unless you were stood next to his whiskered mouth, that he was relieved. His uncle would be happy. 'Good man, I knew you would see sense. I will see to it you have official absolution. We have much work to do to deliver the Glory of Rome and bring light to this century.'

The End. *The. End.* Those two words had reverberated around Lorenzo Bernini's head in the months since that meeting. He had not, at any time during his summer of madness (as he has now come to think of it) even considered that his actions could lead to the end of it all – his art, his career, his ambition.

He had returned from the papal palace and immediately called Ranallo, the lawyer, to his studio.

'I need a wife.'

If the request had come as a surprise, the primero-faced lawyer did not show it. Without missing a beat, he had asked, 'As you like, signore. And what are your requirements?'

'A woman of the like I could not fashion better even if I tried. I want a wife who is docile and pure, prudent, has no cunning side, beautiful but not vain, of an easy-going nature and such kindness – such capacity for hard work – she is called a gift sent from heaven.'

'A woman like this. It may take some time . . .'

Aware of his reputation, the sculptor had added, 'You must assure the father she will live an exquisite life, but only if she can put up with my nature – which is demanding – because I am no ordinary man. You have six months to secure the contract.'

* * *

'Signor Bernini, please, I implore you, straighten your back.' Cristoforo is now holding the tape along the length of the sculptor's spine. 'It is imperative we get the measurement precisely right.' Lorenzo's mind skips to Bologna, and his younger brother's labours in mathematics. The thought rubs at him like a boar-bristle brush. He has neither heard from, nor written to Luigi, but is kept fully informed by Dorotea. The boy will have to come home at some point, his mother and sisters will demand it, and besides, Luigi's design skills are missed.

'Signore,' Cristoforo pleads. Begrudgingly, Lorenzo Bernini stands a little taller for the tailor. The task of being fitted for his wedding clothes is most tedious, but he is determined to do things properly. Put on a show.

In the corner, the marble portrait of Costanza watches him. She is always observing; eyes blazing, lips parted, ready to admonish. Downstairs he has hung a full-length portrait of her in the salon.

Dorotea had been appalled. 'What will Catherine think? It is hardly fair to inflict a picture of your mistress on your new wife.'

'A woman's self-respect,' he had answered, trying not to be irritated by his sister, 'lies in her ability to tolerate her husband's imperfections. However great they may be. Catherine will not have an opinion. I am the master and I make the decisions in this house.'

The sculptor had been offered two Tezio daughters. He had chosen the younger, prettier one, who at twenty-two would be – he hoped – more compliant. 'This portrait,' he had continued, 'is my penance. A daily reminder of my actions. To reprimand myself. I am,' he had looked at his sister defiantly, 'a changed man.'

Indeed, he is. He rises before the sun to attend mass. Gives generously to the Church and religious orders. There is a small part of him, in a place so cavernous and deep he could never excavate it, that is frightened and ashamed. Frightened by his capacity to cause injury, by the way he lost control, by the excuses he is able to summon so easily, by the punishment he might face from an almighty God on the day of divine judgement, whatever the Pontiff says. And ashamed, simply for hurting the only woman he ever truly loved.

Still loves.

He is determined to remodel, remake his reputation, and so Lorenzo Bernini creates a new narrative from the wreckage of the old.

This marriage will change him.

God will save him.

'Hands down. Merci, signore. Now if I might ask you to stand with your legs a little further apart, I just need to measure ...'

Christ, this is wearisome.

'It is the talk of Rome that Lorenzo Bernini has finally agreed to be married. And such a fine match.' The tailor never pauses for breath.

'Well, I only exist to excite the gossips of Rome. I am pleased they approve.'

'Signore,' Cristoforo laughs nervously. 'I was merely saying . . .'

'How is Catherine's outfit coming on?'

'She will be the most splendid bride this city has ever seen.'

'Not her wedding dress, the clothes for her betrothal.'

Catherine's father, a lawyer for the Duke of Modena, had offered a most generous dowry, fifteen thousand scudi. Breaking with tradition, the sculptor had refused it. A game to be played. Instead, Lorenzo Bernini paid his future father-in-law two thousand scudi, simply because he could. Because it showed who was now the richer, more powerful man in Catherine's life.

'She will arrive at my house in the attire her father paid for,' the sculptor explains. 'The papers will be signed, then Catherine will divest herself of everything. Every last scrap of material, and she shall dress in garments I have paid for, so there is no doubt as to who is her master.'

'Signore. My apologies. I had misunderstood. It is all in hand.'

The sculptor makes a rare smile. He likes things being in hand. In control.

His sister breaks into song again, a haunting melody which sounds like weeping.

Chapter Fifty-Five

'The Magdalene'

March 1639

In the dormitory at the Casa Pia I grow weaker.

I do not think I can endure this torment, the grief that comes from such a prolonged separation from all those I love. The uncertainty as to whether they love me still. The knowledge that Luigi and Lorenzo Bernini did this to me, that they are predators who function in darkness; no light is cast on their actions, while I am bathed in well-lit scorn.

I am content to lie on my dirty pallet. The women come and go to their prayers and their laving, like tides turning on the sea, their footsteps providing a faint rhythm to my day. Rosa arrives with food, sips of soup and concoctions from Sister Zita, which make little difference. She tries not to say what we both think: these are merely sops, staving off the inevitable. I will not survive much longer.

Bluma sits nightly on my bed, telling me I must bear it all, to put the losses behind me, that Riva and Lisbetta would expect no less, both would be very cross with me – and her – if she were to allow me to perish.

Carlotta brings me a small handkerchief, which has gone unclaimed for long enough in the laundry no one will miss it. It is of the finest linen, edged with small, scalloped lace like the seashells of Riva's shirt a lifetime ago. It is the kind of trifle we both owned when we were ladies. My mind flutters to Caterina, the idle hours we spent on vanity, the scudi we wasted.

Inside the handkerchief Carlotta has tied dried lavender, to help my humours and stave off the bad air. She must, I tell her, reclaim it when I pass from this world, for it will fetch a ducat or two. Then Carlotta stands, busily rearranging her cap, and declaring she has never heard such nonsense in her life: good rest – 'tis all I need.

Serafina brings me a small painting of Mary Magdalene, which she does not stand on the table, but instead props on the floor, so that I might better see it from my pallet.

I do not know by whose hand it is, or indeed how Serafina came about it, but it is a fine rendition. In the portrait the Magdalene sits on a wooden chair, her head resting on her hand, alabaster skin shining. About her face there is such melancholy, it is as if she feels my pain. The Magdalene's eyes are closed, lids swollen from crying. Her other arm falls loosely, as does her chemise, partly exposing her breast. It puts me in mind of another portrait, another woman.

I spend so many hours contemplating the Magdalene that a space opens between us. I step in. I tell her again and again, about my life, how I brought this pain on myself. Of my blindness to what was there all along, and of the great distance I have travelled, each misstep taking me on a path further from my true self.

I close my eyes. The Magdalene talks to me, whispering in

myrtle-scented breath of repentance and forgiveness. The world quietens, and I listen. She tells me redemption is possible. That hope offers renewal, just as nature filling the bare branches with blossom and the moon waxes and wanes. I weep. She tells me I must fight instead of preparing to die.

Every day Rosa petitions the Abbess, who says she is too busy to come to my chamber. 'I beg you,' Rosa told me she pleads. 'You must see Costanza Piccolomini. She is too ill to move and needs an audience.'

'I will,' says the Abbess, and she never does.

'It is a game to her,' fumes Rosa. 'She will not come because I have asked. God save me from holy women.' Rosa paces the floor. 'There must be a better way.'

The next time Rosa saw the Abbess, she took a different tack. 'What if,' she postulated, 'Costanza were to die within these walls? A daughter of the Piccolomini house, notorious across Rome. But how is it she entered this place with but a cut on her face, and leaves in a wooden box?'

The Abbess had apparently looked up sharply. 'What is your meaning?'

'If Costanza were to die, it would be a tragic end to the Bernini scandal and there would no doubt be questions about her care. Even an inquiry, here at the monastery.'

Rosa told me the Abbess did not break her stare. 'Tell Costanza I will come after prayers, this evening.'

* * *

Rosa is at my side when the Abbess arrives at the allotted hour. With her comes Sister Lidwina, who keeps the record.

'I am saddened to see you,' says the Abbess, although her face speaks of alarm rather than sorrow.

Rosa stands. 'Costanza is as she is, for want of food and lack of medicine.'

I cannot lift my head, but know enough to say, 'Thank you for coming Holy Mother, I am honoured by your graciousness in attending to me.'

Rosa snorts.

'I must thank you Rosa, for bringing Costanza's plight to my attention. Perhaps Signora Piccolomini and I may have a few moments alone?'

Although it is dressed as a question, it is not.

Rosa stoops to kiss my head, and in a low voice breathes, 'Be resolute. You must have food. And money.'

I tip my head; I know what I must do.

After Rosa leaves, it is I who speaks first.

'I have no nourishment, only the mercy of Rosa. My husband has cast me off, but I beg you to write to him. Ask that he pays for my food. Tell Matteo that Luigi Bernini has contrived to have me locked up and now he – or more likely his brother – have stopped paying for my keep.'

The Abbess gestures for Sister Lidwina to hand over the document she is carrying.

'It might be more tangled than you would believe, signora.'

She inspects the parchment, reading the words writ upon it carefully.

'It seems it was not Luigi Bernini, nor his brother, who instigated your arrest. But your incarceration is the result of an inquiry, made after a barber surgeon reported your injuries.'

My heart crunches into a ball. 'Francesco Neve? I had thought him to be an honourable man.'

The Abbess looks up from the paper. 'And you can continue to think the same, for Signor Neve was required by law . . . as all barber surgeons are . . . to report treatment of the cleaving of a face or limb. It is a grievous crime.'

She carries on reading. 'The inquiry took evidence from two main witnesses: the Widow Vanna, and a Caterina Panzetti. Both gave testimony of your unlawful adultery and fornication with two men, Lorenzo Bernini and Luigi Bernini. I believe they are brothers. Caterina swore you had confessed to carnally knowing both men. Given this evidence, and the scandal of your conduct, the Governatore of Rome approved your arrest.'

I blink. 'Caterina?' I repeat the name. My heart sinks like a lead weight.

It was Caterina who gave evidence? Her words had me bound to this place? All those confidences. Whispered secrets. The hours we spent in each other's company. The shared confessions. She herself was not without sin. To what end? My mind floods with questions. It does not make sense. Why? It must be some strange mistake. A clerical error. Caterina was my friend, everyone knows this.

My face must betray my confusion, because the Abbess stops.

'Yes. That is correct. A Caterina Panzetti. Do you know her?'

'She was . . .' What is the word? I cannot think. Nay, not a friend. That is not the right word. Not anymore. A quell rises in me, like the waves of a rough sea. All those details, all those intimate moments with Lorenzo that were shared with Caterina, only for them to be used in such a way.

I repeat the news again. 'It was Caterina . . . Caterina Panzetti was responsible for having me bound to this place?'

The revelation has the same effect as throwing a lit taper into a pitch-black cave.

Inside, I detect the flickering of an old and familiar feeling. A rising wrath. I want to open my mouth and scream until I am hoarse, until the angels in heaven above can no longer bear my rage and cover their ears, until Caterina Panzetti in her cossetted salon hears my fury at her betrayal, and understands she will be punished. If not in this life, then the next. I smile, as if saying hello to a long-lost friend, and put my hand on my heart, feeling its reassuring thump.

The Abbess seems taken aback. Perhaps this is not how she expected the interview to go. 'It is what is writ here,' she offers by way of explanation.

'What of Luigi Bernini?' I demand. 'And Lorenzo Bernini, who instructed his man Stefano to inflict this cruel injury upon my face? What did the Governatore rule for them?'

The Abbess inspects the parchment again, and consults Sister Lidwina, who jabs at something written at the very bottom of the page.

'Luigi has left Rome. There is no record of a Stefano. Lorenzo Bernini received his penance and absolution direct from His Holiness, our Papal Father. He must pay a large penalty ... And marry.'

'Lorenzo's punishment for my disfigurement is that he must marry?' I ask incredulously.

The Abbess responds sharply. 'His Holiness cannot be questioned.'

It is fruitless to persist. 'I pity the poor girl, whoever she is.' I drop my voice. It is not Lorenzo Bernini I care about. 'And what of my husband? Do you know if he is ... well?'

A beat of silence. A little brown bird hops onto the window sill.

'Your husband has written to the convent more than once,' says the Abbess kindly. 'To reiterate his willingness to ... to take you back into his care.'

The bird stops stock still for a moment, cocks its head to one side and examines me intently. 'This,' it seems to say. 'This is what I came to hear,' before disappearing as quickly as it had appeared. Matteo. This man. This good-hearted man is waiting. He will open the door, grasp my hand, call me wife and take me back into our home. There is a future if only I can persist. 'I am still left with naught to eat.'

The Abbess looks upon me without passion. 'It is wretched,' she says flatly.

'What can I do?' My voice cracks.

Sister Lidwina reaches to whisper in the Abbess's ear and she nods in response.

'Each year we set aside money for a few church dowries. To pay for fallen women to take their vows and commit their life to Christ in penance, and we think you ...'

'Nay!' I interject.

Only minutes before, I would have gladly accepted such an offer. But now I think of the men, of Luigi, Lorenzo and Stefano, the spring sun on their faces, going about their day in a state of freedom. Lorenzo, preparing to marry. Matteo in his steadfastness.

I feel the serpent rising, coiling inside. Instead of lamenting this sensation, I rejoice at its reappearance, at my blood coursing through my veins, a righteous indignation that it is not I who should cower from the world, but they.

'Nay,' I say again, more quietly. 'It is a good offer. One I am grateful for, but I have a husband and friends, and a life beyond these walls. A place I wish to return to. Therefore, I need the authorities to pay my keep, if it is they who have imposed this sentence on me.'

The Abbess's eyes narrow. 'Very well. Sister Lidwina will help you to compose a letter to the Governatore, pleading your case and explaining your husband is not obligated to pay for you. That you are abandoned by everyone, and gravely ill, only being kept in life and limb by the discretion of the other women.' At this, she pauses. 'You understand we cannot pay for you. If we did for one woman, the Governatore would insist we pay for all women. Then where would we be?'

A letter is my only hope?

'I thank you for your kind guidance, Holy Mother, but I shall write it in my own hand, for only my own words can adequately and persuasively tell of my anguish and need.'

'Very well. Sister Lidwina will provide you with a quill and parchment. I shall offer some advice if I may? I see a great many women pass through these gates. All have suffered calamity, known sin. Repentance is one thing, forgiveness quite another. It is forgiveness which allows the soul to thrive, where calm resides.'

She looks at the painting on the floor.

'The Magdalene knew this; she repented and was forgiven by our Lord. Your repentance will be similarly welcomed.'

The Abbess turns to leave.

'May I offer some advice in return?'

She turns to look at me, unaccustomed to not having the last word.

'Serafina. She is a child, and too good for the life which awaits her beyond these walls. She should have my dowry; she would make a much better nun than I.'

The Abbess smiles. 'I think you may be right, Signora Piccolomini. On both counts.'

Chapter Fifty-Six

'Fare Thee Well'

April 1639

I write the letter to the Governatore. It is sent, and I wait. A pastime I still detest.

I tell Rosa of the revelations: of Caterina's great betrayal.

We are seated on my small pallet, and it is a comfort, her body next to mine, reminding me of the hours Giuliana and I spent as girls.

Despite the Abbess's warnings she cannot pay for my keep, she seems keen to stave off the potential scandal of my taking my last breath in her care, so sends meagre meals to my bed, broth with eggs and white meat. My face is starting to heal thanks to the tinctures and dressings of Sister Zita, who has been tasked with redoubling her care for my wounds. I am grateful for the small jars she sends, which smell of healing eucalyptus, reminding me of Lisbetta.

Time is beginning to steady me. I no longer feel on the precipice of death.

'I trusted her words and always believed she gave me wise counsel.' My stomach knots, remembering all the ways I confided in Caterina.

'It is a sore thing, to be used so,' Rosa commiserates. 'But I am not surprised.' She bites at the side of her nail, muddling her speech with fingers and teeth. 'I know something of Caterina,' she says idly.

I sit up at this news, unmoored by the magnitude of what it means.

'How so? Why did you not say?' I try to take in Rosa's full aspect, but it is hard to do so in the gloominess of the flickering light.

'There are many things I choose to keep hidden in a place like this.'

This feels like a betrayal anew. That Rosa could know the true nature of Caterina, and not have said a word.

'I only met Caterina Panzetti once or twice. I was on the arm of a man everyone knew was paying me. I had no idea she would have given you away in such a manner. Even though . . .'

'Even though?'

'It was a party. Lavish. Lorenzo Bernini was there, and Caterina.'

'You have met them all? Why did you not say?'

'It would have served no purpose, Costanza. Your story is yours alone. If they remembered me at all, they would only know me as a harlot . . . I am not important enough to be named.'

'But you knew them. You knew that life?'

'Aye . . . I did. But in a place like this, being from that world does not make you friends.' She inspects her hands, which are sore all about. 'I remember them all. It is my trade, to watch men and know secrets. Caterina is in love with Lorenzo Bernini. It was clear that night and even clearer now. She watched him all evening; it is what the lovesick do.'

A shiver casts itself over my body. Such stupidity. Of course Caterina loves Lorenzo. Why else would she make herself available to me in such a way, if not to steer the course of our friendship to her own ends. To place herself at the centre of our affair, making herself of use to both artist and muse?

I laugh. It begins as an abrupt outburst, which extends into a full-throttle belly-howl.

'I am such a fool. You should have said something.'

Rosa is quiet and looks at me. 'I am to be released this evening.'

I stop laughing. I should say something, tell Rosa how unexpected and awful this news is, that she will leave a huge gap in our lives, but can only manage a meagre, 'Oh.'

'I shall share something, because it does no good for folks to be about your business, but you are my friend and I do not have many. In my work, girls come and go. Most do not use their real names.'

Rosa is well known for plain-speaking, so I am stumped that she has kept this many secrets well hid.

'Is Rosa your given name?'

She shakes her head. 'Nay. I first came to this profession half a lifetime ago. When I was thirteen, I was picked up by an old woman who procured beautiful young girls who had nothing more in the world than desperate parents and poverty. This bawd would take such young women and sell their maidenhead to the highest bidder.'

I think of Rosa-who-isn't-Rosa at the tender age of thirteen and imagine a spirited and clever girl.

'At that age, my looks were almost perfection,' she says, her typical immodesty making me smile. 'A pretty face, long lustrous hair which shone red-gold in the sun, small hips and high breasts. Such was my beauty, I commanded a high price from a noble bidder, a young duke, wanting his first taste of pleasure in the secure knowledge the girl in question was not tainted by disease.'

She looks at the ceiling in recollection. 'He was nervous, and I had no idea what was to happen. There was much fumbling and not a little pain . . . when he was done and the sheets stained, he sighed and turned over to face me, and told me he loved me. The bawd, sensing a great fortune could be made from this infatuation, had her more experienced girls to instruct me in all the ways a woman can pleasure a man. The duke kept me for many years, even after he married.'

'And now?'

She shrugs. 'He is dead.'

'And you were arrested?'

Rosa smooths down her shift. 'I was always coveted. Cast my net wider. Other dignitaries, not a few cardinals. Men can be so jealous.'

'I'm so sorry.'

'Don't be!' Rosa's eyes flash. 'I am good at my profession, well versed and practised in making men happy. I am known and liked enough by wealthy patrons to have been missed. I shall live finely. And, I promise you this, even if I must sleep with a thousand cardinals, I will make sure you are provided for, Costanza.'

I look at Rosa for a moment and see her anew. For all her lewd speak, she has a refinement and understands the politics of power far better than I do.

Rosa leans forward and whispers. 'And if you ever need me, ask among the working girls for Margherita. Like the daisy. It is my real name. They will know you are to be trusted, and will tell you where I am.'

Truth shimmers in the breath between us. 'You are a good friend, Rosa.' Then selfishly, I think entirely of myself and begin to cry at the next grief I must endure.

Rosa leans forward, straightens my cap, and then holds my head in her strong hands, her fingers wrapping around my face as she kisses me fiercely upon the lips.

'You will survive this. You will live your life in colour, Costanza.

Glorious colour. For you are a phoenix, and you will rise from these shady ashes of calumny and shame, and you will shine. You must live. Blaze! You must wear fine clothes and decorate your walls in crimson. Your fire will be felt long from now, I promise.'

Then she kisses me again.

'I must go.' She stands and sweeps from the room without a backwards glance, and I am at once heartbroken and lifted to the skies. For who does not want to follow in a meteor's footsteps?

Chapter Fifty-Seven

'A Case of Tender Politics'

April 1639

The Governatore sits at his desk. The trees outside his study quiver in the spring breeze, their trembling shadows falling on the expensive Turkish rug. As head of justice for the city, he is busy. Too busy to attend to the likes of the two letters he has before him.

He reads his correspondence with a glazed eye. The first is a letter from the Abbess of the Casa Pia:

> *To my venerable Father from your humble handmaid of Christ, with all subjection and devotion I seek your solicitous care and wise counsel for a poor, fallen woman who finds herself in our care, Costanza Piccolomini . . .*

He furrows his brow and rubs at his temples, which pulse with annoyance. Women's affairs are rarely simple. There is a small twitch of recognition. Piccolomini. Like the old Popes. He knows the name – the woman Lorenzo Bernini lost his mind over? A case of tender politics if ever there was. This will attract the personal attention of the Pontiff, who intervened on Bernini's behalf. Good artists are hard to come by, pretty women are not.

He skims the Abbess's letter:

> *Grief tortures the woman. I ask you, with pious prayers, that*
> *this tribulation may come to an end soon before she is altogether*
> *wasted away. If the lady were to end her on time on earth within*
> *our walls, it could call into question all our care, and it would*
> *change the aspect of the harm to slaughter. No allowance has*
> *been made for this woman's keep. Therefore, I seek your sage*
> *counsel. Within is a letter from Signora Piccolomini. Are you are*
> *satisfied with her penance? I pray that you send me wise words.*

He is chary now. The Abbess is an arch demarche, virtually Machiavellian in her diplomatic manoeuvres. It is typical of her to lay this decision at his feet.

He picks up the letter folded within the Abbess's. It is written in tightly lettered script, neat, if not polished. He reads through the words:

> *Most Illustrious Sir,*
> *I am Costanza, wife of Matteo Bonucelli, and have for the*
> *past few months been so sick I am indisposed to live. I have been*
> *incarcerated, abandoned by everyone, so I must call on your*
> *mercy and beg you send me with some food, that might cure me*
> *of my most grave and deadly illness. If you will not send money,*
> *then I ask that you consider giving approval for my release, so*
> *that I might be reconsigned to my husband.*

I implore you, please help. I place all my hope in the prudence of Your Most Illustrious Lordship. Before I finish, may I remind you that without food a woman cannot live. I lay myself humbly at your feet and pray to God for your happiness.

It is no decision at all. The Governatore is not going to be responsible for this woman's death, and risk reignition of a scandal surrounding the Pontiff's favourite.

And he is not going to pay coin from his own coffers to keep her.

The Governatore picks up a quill from the row of newly sharpened points and dips it into the midnight ink before scratching across the bottom of Signora Piccolomini's letter in capital letters:

I DETERMINE THAT YOU CAN RESTORE HER TO HER HUSBAND, 7 APRIL 1639

* * *

'Signora Piccolomini.'

I open my eyes. It is Sister Chiara, whispering to me agitatedly. She is pulling at my sleeve. 'Wake up signora, you must dress.'

Rousing myself is not easy. It is still dark outside, and the light from her small candle is frugal.

'What is it? What is the rush?'

'The Abbess wishes to speak with you. Now. Hurry.'

I raise myself slowly. For all Sister Chiara's extortions to be quick, I am still not strong enough for fleetness but must amble like an old lady, steadying myself as I stand, and cautiously passing my tunic over my head, lest I should fall. My breath is laboured as I pull the rope about my waist and fix my cap against my hair, which scratches in its growth against my scalp.

Sister Chiara waits until I am done.

'Good.' She nods, then leads the way from my small quarters.

As we pass through the convent all is quiet. The sisters are sleeping, as are my friends. Only the moon is our company, her soft silvery light falling upon our faces as we creep along the corridor, our clogs lightly scratching the surface of the stone.

We mount the stairs to the Abbess's quarters. It occurs to me that if the Abbess is awake at this hour, tending to the business of the monastery, then when does she sleep? I am filled with a nervous surge of hope. I have been waiting for a response to my letter, and I can only hope that this early morning call is to bring me good news at last.

Sister Chiara knocks gently on the door, and the Abbess tells us to enter. I am curious to see her living quarters, and they do not disappoint. The walls are hung with rich tapestries in bright colours, and there is a large desk, ornately carved, behind which she is seated. The Abbess does not rise as I enter but bids me to sit on a chair in front of her.

Her eyes are resolutely fixed upon me and betray no emotion at all. Even here, at this ungodly hour, she is tidy and pressed.

If it had been glad tidings, I would have expected half a smile at least, but her countenance is so grave my heart now hammers in fear. I immediately chastise myself for having allowed hope to bloom. I surely should have learned by now that it is fateful to wish for the best.

'We have had a response from the Governatore.'

I wait for her to continue but she does not.

'What does he say?'

I cannot believe she is making me ask this. But I shall play her game.

'He has recommended you are released to the care of your husband.'

I raise my eyes to the vaulted ceiling as I feel myself crumple in blessed relief. I should be angry at the Abbess for playing with me like a cat with a half-dead mouse, but I cannot be. I will be freed from this place, but to return to Matteo? The possibility feels suddenly, unexpectedly stillborn. That was the life of another Costanza.

'Thank you, Abbess,' I murmur.

'Do not thank me. It is the decision of the gracious Governatore. In the decisions of God's men we trust.'

She stands and pulls a small key from her pocket.

'Before you go, I have something for you.'

I cast my mind back to the fateful night I stepped inside the monastery, and for one awful moment think she is to return my ripped nightgown and single slipper.

Instead, the Abbess slips the ornate key into the lock of the chest, and turns it until there is a click. Perhaps it is the papers for my release? She lifts the lid and pulls out a neat coin purse.

'This was left for you.' For one moment I wonder if it is from Lorenzo. 'By Rosa. Or, at least, the woman who goes by the name of Rosa, although I think if we checked the parish records we might find such a woman never existed. No matter. This is for you.'

The Abbess turns and places the purse in my lap. It is new, and smells of recently tanned leather, strong and feral. The weight of the coins presses against my thighs, speaking clearly of their number and value.

'I do not understand.'

'She came back.'

I look at the Abbess, still not comprehending her meaning. 'Rosa came back and asked me to hold this purse in safekeeping, until your release.'

I wonder how much is contained within the smooth leather wallet, and it is as if the Abbess has read my mind. She smiles for the first time in all the time I have known her. 'You have a good friend. I believe there is more than eighty scudi within.'

Enough to leave Rome.

'It is a miracle!' I utter as my eyes flicker to the small, stained window, issuing a thousand thanks to Rosa, who is somewhere beyond the convent's walls.

The Abbess draws herself to her full height. 'I can assure you it is not a miracle, for such things are gifted by the grace of Our Lord. And there is nothing miraculous about men paying women for their bodies.'

Then the Abbess lowers her voice and comes to stand so near, I can smell the scent of her body, warm bread and incense.

'You were badly used, Costanza. I have seen many women come through my gates, and most have suffered, been forced to lie with men, lied to *by* men, their bodies hurt, used as sport by men. Nay, my women are not wicked. The truth is that most are not fallen, but instead have been pushed by circumstance. Your face will heal, and in time your heart will too. I will carry you in my prayers that God will keep you safe.'

Then she bends and smiles again, 'Well, God . . . and Rosa.'

I am taken to the gate by Sister Chiara, the same nun who met me all those months before.

'I shall pray for you, Signora Piccolomini.'

Once I would have mocked the idea of a nun offering her prayers for me. What did I need of such things? Now I know that the world is a ferocious place to exist, and the prayers of the sisters are offered in love and not judgement.

'I should like that. Thank you, Sister. And when I look to the canopy of stars above, I shall feel your words falling like a blessing on my shoulders.'

Sister Chiara hesitates for a moment, then thrusts her hand into her pocket, drawing out a clenched fist which she slowly opens. Nestled in her palm is a small cloth bag I recognise.

'Here,' she whispers, pressing the pouch into my hand. 'Lisbetta talked many times about you. Sister Zita said you should have it.'

I bite at my lip, eyes burning wet, and open the drawstrings. Inside is the little gold cross on a chain.

'Thank you,' I whisper to Sister Chiara.

In that moment we are not jailer and prisoner, holy woman and whore, but women and equals. I am reminded that I can be seen beyond my scar.

I pause in silence in front of the great wooden doors which stand between this moment and the rest of my life.

Then I turn to Sister Chiara and hug her hard. It is a most unseemly act, to hug a nun, and she is taken by surprise. Slowly I feel her embrace return, her thin fingers pressing into my back, and she murmurs in my ear; 'Godspeed, signora. Do not forget us.'

'That I could never do.'

I had half-expected the Abbess to come and see me from the door, if nothing more than to ensure my most sensitive person has been properly discharged to the world – to see the back of the threat of scandal. But she does not.

I turn and step over the threshold into the street, once more a free woman.

Chapter Fifty-Eight

'To the Future'

April 1639

The night bleeds into day, and overhead the soft sky is streaked with fine filaments of tender light. As the heavy door closes behind me with a clunk, I take a breath. Although I have dreamed of this moment, I am suddenly afraid.

The morning breeze whispers her breath against my skin. The world is awakening and the street is already busy with sellers and muleteers. Behind me, in the convent, the women will be amassing for morning prayers before starting their day. I feel the comfort of that steady routine behind me, and for a moment it pulls me back. But I am not built for a life of silent devotion. I have come too far and learned too much to spend my days in contemplation. I walk along the road, listening to the dull clod of my clogs as they hit the ground, hoping that they will divine the route I should take.

But it is a false hope and soon I am at the end of the street.

Straight ahead is Matteo, and the home we share. It is as easy and difficult as that. To go back to my old life is tempting. I realise now that Matteo had meant all along to care for me. And in my months of confinement I missed him, our home, our life filled with beauty and light and art. But in his world there will be Lorenzo Bernini, and I worry I lack the courage for it.

Left, towards Giuliana, my old life and the people who loved me most. I think for a moment of Mother Gavia's big bed, and the hours we spent as girls prostrate upon it, pining for a world beyond. Giuliana was there at the start, she has known me before and during, and will forgive it all. I could rent a small place on the road of my childhood.

If I turn right, I will pass the new buildings, where cardinals and dukes conduct their affairs. Somewhere there is Rosa, although I doubt that is the name she is using still. With a few scudi in my pocket to pay the right ears, I am sure I could track her down. We could be companions. Perhaps I could persuade her to cease her trade, and start a new business, collecting and selling ancient and modern art, for she knows enough men with the coin to want fine things.

Or if I turn around, and pass the convent, I will eventually come to the Tiber, that great benefactor of Rome. And from here arrange passage to – to where? Florence, or Naples? Or perhaps Spain, France or England. Somewhere my name would not be known, and my face could be explained away as an accident with a sword or scythe. Somewhere I could leave the ghost of Costanza, Bernini's beloved, behind.

I stand for a moment and feel the warmth of the sun on my face.

Then I begin to walk.

Epilogue

'Seek Your Own Story'

Some Years Later

My life can be divided neatly.

Before the Bernini brothers. And after.

Before I met Lorenzo and Luigi, I had lived in a state of blissful ignorance. After coming into their orbit everything became unfixed, untethered. The velocity of such alteration took time to settle.

For a long while I did not feel like myself. My body was not my own, my face did not belong to me, my smile was different, the life I returned to was not mine. Only now am I discovering my point of centre again, and find myself able to stand on firm ground.

Matteo waited patiently for me to return. Taught me I could be safe. I still see my half-sister Cecilia, who is married to a good man and has babies of her own; we talk of Tiberia, and the other siblings, Michele and Cleria, who remain distant.

Not long after I was released, I was forced to face more seismic grief. Papa had fallen ill while I was in the Casa Pia, I saw him just once before he died. Giuliana had also fallen pregnant and did not survive her third birth, another boy. Marco, now a widowed father of three, quickly remarried – another young girl from our district. I mourn Papa, Giuliana and Lisbetta greatly and deeply, but never again have I considered giving up.

Although I have not seen Rosa again, the women of the convent changed me. Even when I saw no future, they held me, sustained me, picked me up, dusted me down; they had bet on me when I had lost the ability to bet on myself. I learned through their strength never to let anyone diminish me again.

Now I know better. Life is short, can end abruptly, before you have a chance to do the things that matter. Before you have a chance to say goodbye.

I returned to the paintings I visited with Lorenzo. Studied them with more intent. Accompanied Matteo on trips to studios, talked to art dealers. We opened our home to visiting painters and sculptors from the great European courts. I read, attended mass, learned to negotiate with suppliers and cultivate patrons; I helped my husband to build his business.

As for the Bernini brothers, Luigi eventually came back to Rome, tail between his legs, and now helps Lorenzo manage his engineering projects, designing fantastical gardens, magnificent fountains, a new frontage for the Basilica.

Lorenzo married. His wife is expecting another child; they have several already. I feel genuine sorrow for Catherine Tezio Bernini. From what I hear, my likeness hangs from the wall. I see Lorenzo from time to time, at parties or exhibitions. He looks changed – perhaps not as much as I, but haunted somehow. I imagine it a great burden to know the depths of your own wickedness.

I have only seen Caterina once. In those first few months after I left the Casa Pia I worked hard to regain my strength, walking every day and feeding my body with good food. There was a route I took, avoiding my old district, which led me down to the river. It had been an autumn morning: a gentle crispness about the air and leaves fallen underfoot to create a tapestry of fiery reds, gold, ochre and burnt oranges – nature's farewell. At first I wasn't sure it was her. Caterina had appeared thinner, reduced somehow, wearing an outfit I had observed before – a dress that had seen better days.

My first instinct had been to turn, walk the other way, cast myself into the shadows of a nearby building. At the same moment, Lisbetta's chain shifted on my neck and as I ran my fingers along the fine gold necklace I had a change of heart. Instead of slipping away, I walked purposefully towards Caterina, my step quickening alongside my thoughts, almost giddy with the anticipation of contriving a confrontation I had dreamed about for so long.

She did not see me until it was too late. At first she was confused at a stranger stepping directly into her path, then a horror descended, as Caterina realised who I was, and what was about to occur.

'Signora Panzetti. I would like to say it is a great pleasure but . . . that would be a lie.'

Caterina gave a little cry. Her eyes widened as she took in more closely the destruction Lorenzo's instructions and Stefano's blade had caused. She had no rouge on her cheeks, no staining upon her lips; her skin was pale and more aged than I remembered.

'Costanza . . . I . . . I,' she stuttered, scrambling for words. 'I heard you had been . . . you were back at home.'

For a fleeting moment I imagined raising my hand, slapping her across the cheek so hard it would leave a red welt for days, instead I chose my words to wound.

Caterina shifted nervously from one foot to another.

'Have you seen Lorenzo?' I asked. 'I hear he is most happily married. A changed man, so they say. Another child on the way.'

'Nay ... I ... we ... Paolo has been busy ... we do not ...'

Cruelly, I let her words flounder, like a fish pulled from the pond, not even extending Caterina the kindness of saving her from what we both know.

'Ah yes.' I smiled. 'I had heard you had both been cast out into the cold.' I tipped my head to one side. 'Seems the Bernini brothers can be ruthless. Extending loyalty only to their own.'

It was nasty, I know. Matteo had recounted the public snubbing of the Panzettis, the social disgrace they had suffered, the financial problems Paolo was facing, having borrowed greatly on his relationship with the Berninis, which had now fallen away. News I had received with not a little glee.

I expected to see a flare in Caterina's eyes, like sunlight bouncing off water. But there was nothing. Just emptiness. She too had been hollowed out by the Bernini brothers, left with only Paolo to sustain her. At that moment I felt a sensation I had not expected: pity. I suddenly wished for the conversation to be done.

'It is a cruelty, to be caught in their wake.'

'It is.' Small words, uttered in a small voice.

I thought of the perplexing emotions we hoard, of how strong feelings are unexpectedly and inexplicably sparked by small acts, catalysts that remind us of our common battles.

Each life is intricate. Each of us are woven from love and loss; experiences that bind us together more than set us apart. For who among us does not have their own struggles, does not carry their own heavy load?

I have learned a great many things, but above all, never to be confined by the tales other people tell of you.

Always seek out your own story.

This is mine.

Afterword

The real Costanza Piccolomini, and what happened next

Costanza returned to Matteo and to their house at the foot of the Quirinal Hill on Vicolo Scanderbeg. Here, they lived together for another fifteen years until Matteo's death in 1654. While it's impossible to know if any marriage is truly happy, in his will Matteo described Costanza as his 'dilettissima moglie' – his most beloved wife – and left her everything he owned, including the house and his flourishing business.

In the intervening years, Matteo had become a well-established sculptor and entrepreneur. He set up a foundry in the garden of their home and, after a brief but no doubt necessary interregnum, began working again for Gianlorenzo Bernini, alongside other private patrons. In 1650, Matteo was commissioned by Velázquez to produce twelve bronze lions for King Philip IV of Spain, which can still be seen in Madrid today. But it wasn't just the production of new art that kept Matteo busy; records show he also restored antiquities, employing several men from Lucca, and was involved in the trade of ancient sculptures.

After Matteo's death, Costanza took on the running of the art dealership and was addressed as 'Costanza Scultora' (sculptress).

Surviving correspondence shows a woman who knew her art and was no pushover when it came to negotiating. Costanza developed a strong network of rarefied patrons: men close to the court of the reigning pope, Alexander VII. She also built up an enviable private collection of the leading artists of the day, including Poussin's Plague at Ashdod, which today hangs in the Louvre in Paris.

We will never know what long-term impact Costanza's brutal attack and subsequent incarceration had on her. Nor do we know if she ever saw Gianlorenzo or Luigi Bernini again. What we do know is that alongside Matteo, Costanza used her undoubted tenacity, resilience, knowledge of art and keen intellect to build an impressive life for a seventeenth-century woman, especially one who had been born into relative poverty and publicly scorned.

Perhaps we see this most clearly in the physical environment Costanza chose to create for herself. She added considerably to the value of the house on Vicolo Scanderbeg, ornamenting the front door with luxurious travertine blocks (not unlike the kind Caterina boasts in the novel). Costanza's stairs had peperino treads and her bed was bedecked in expensive embroidered silks. Her sala was a room with windows, facing the street. This would be where she received her visitors and business associates. Costanza decorated the sala in unashamed luxury, lining the walls with three hundred panels of costly red leather embossed with gold, and two red chairs resplendent with green fringe. Given the trauma she suffered, there is something defiant and unexpectedly pleasing in the unapologetic flamboyance of Costanza's personal style.

The art she chose to display in this room tells us even more. For although her house was filled with many pictures and sculptures, Costanza selected just four paintings to hang in this, her most precious of sanctuaries. The first was a portrait of Venus, the ancient goddess of beauty and desire; the second was Susanna from the Old Testament, a woman under the surveillance of older men; the third was Mary Magdalene, the penitent; and finally, the fourth picture was a half-length portrait of Costanza herself.

Author's Note

On Saturday 13 March 2021 I attended a vigil for Sarah Everard, whose murder had been confirmed the day before.

It was lockdown, so my wonderful friend Anya invited the women in our local WhatsApp group to join her and her sister in a moment of reflection in the little park at the end of our road, in an 'unofficial, socially distanced, mask-wearing way'.

A group of us gathered to mourn a young woman we had never met. The UK was still in the depths of lockdown, isolated and frightened, and it seemed there was some kind of compulsion at play, for women to stand together in grief and silence, two metres apart.

A serving police officer would later be jailed for abducting Sarah and killing her. I recognise here that many women, especially Black women and women of colour, have never felt safe or protected by the police, but I've thought a lot about what prompted us to leave our homes that evening. The conclusion I have come to is that we all had our own stories and understood how fragile the space is – between what happened to Sarah and us returning safely to our own families. How frequently harassment, threats and acts of violence happen to women, and how rarely they are taken seriously.

One by one we lit candles, watching the meagre flames flicker in the failing light, and left them burning in tribute in little glass jars along the banks of our local river, an ancient Thames tributary.

When I returned home, I felt overwhelmed by desolation and fury.

Desolation at Sarah's death at the hands of a man who decided her fate for her. Globally, 81,000 women and girls were killed in 2020. How can we live in an age where that number of women *and girls* are so unsafe? And of these around 47,000 of them (58 per cent) died at the hands of an intimate partner or a family member, the equivalent to a woman or girl being killed every eleven minutes *in their home*. What's more, where trends can be calculated, they show that the magnitude of such gender-related killings remains largely unchanged over the last decade.

My fury stemmed from the knowledge that we have not begun to address this endemic violence against women. The data has only existed for decades. The reality has lasted centuries. I felt, and still feel, furious at women's everyday lives; the way we constantly scan for danger, limit our activities to daytime hours, the assessment we make of the footsteps of a stranger, the keys gripped in knuckles, hair tucked in hoodies, the inconvenience of taking the longer but well-lit route, the Saturday night mantra of never leaving a mate behind, the weekend A & E departments crammed full of girls paralysed by date-rape drugs, the safety calls on first dates to reduce the very real threat of violence we face for just meeting an unknown man.

Sarah's death also coincided with the burgeoning independence of my own daughters. I was suddenly having to navigate the very nuanced path of teaching my girls how to assess their own risk, without explicitly stating what those risks were. It was stomach-churning to realise how little has changed since I was a teenager, and now I was preparing my girls for a lifetime of low-humming fear in order to stay safe.

Something snapped.

Why, I asked myself, am I doomed to repeat this depressing cycle? Why do we prioritise male narratives (Sarah's killer was known as 'the rapist' to his colleagues) over female safety?

Costanza's story began hammering at my door. I first heard about Bernini slashing the face of his mistress on a BBC programme about Rome, her disfigurement mentioned in passing by two male presenters. She was not even named. Then back to the brilliance of Bernini.

It was the casualness of the reference. A lifetime of a woman's pain brushed over in a few words. The prioritising of Bernini's narrative – of his genius as an artist – over this misogynistic attack on a much younger, vulnerable woman.

I started to research Costanza, finding Sarah McPhee's remarkable non-fiction book *Bernini's Beloved*, to which this novel owes a great debt. I read Bernini biographies. In the depths of the pandemic, from my tiny office, I walked the streets of Rome online, visiting churches, Caravaggios, piazzas. The dialectic of the undoubted brilliance of Bernini and his capacity for incredible violence converged.

In Control, another superb non-fiction book written by Jane Monckton Smith, a former police officer, helped me to recognise Gianlorenzo Bernini's behaviour in its pages – throughout his life we see elements of the eight stages of coercive control at play.

Monckton Smith challenges the idea of a 'crime of passion'. Instead, she argues these attacks are not spontaneous, unpredictable or beyond forensic understanding. In fact, intimate partner killing is one of the most predictable forms of homicide.

I read up on acid attacks and the psychology of modern female disfigurement. The #YesAllWomen and #MeToo movements influenced my writing, as did the filmmaking of Céline Sciamma, who shot *Portrait of a Lady on Fire*, the story of a woman artist and her female lover, through an unswerving female gaze. Around this time, I was made redundant. So many of the midlife women in my department were let go that we formed an informal club as a bit of a joke, but it was a timely reminder of the patriarchy at play.

It was overwhelming, trying to untangle my thoughts about being a woman and a mother in this moment. I needed to look at things with a different slant, to find the roots of contemporary violence against women in a four-hundred-year-old story. For centuries, Costanza's pristine marble likeness has been mute. Now the reality of her haunted me. My only response as a writer was to begin telling the story of this hunted, hounded, disfigured woman, as well as her incredible defiance and phoenix-like rise to wealth and success.

So Costanza became, in some ways, my attempt to unravel my very complex feelings around the murder of Sarah Everard, of dangerous men hiding in plain sight, of misogyny and patriarchy, and the ongoing need to surface this behaviour, to talk openly about its impact on women.

To break the cycle.

Why? Because we can no longer afford to ignore inconvenient truths.

We must confront the past and prioritise women's narratives over those of more powerful men.

Historical Note

Costanza is a work of fiction. As with most women throughout history, unless they were royal, or lived notable lives, we know little of Costanza's life. What little we do know is thanks to the painstaking academic research of Sarah McPhee.

Wherever possible, I tried hard to remain truthful to the time, and any inaccuracies are mine and mine alone. Every author has to make decisions in the best interests of their novel and *Costanza* is no exception.

To start at the beginning. We do not know where Costanza was born, only that it was around 1614. Her mother's name is uncertain, and it is speculation that Tiberia was her stepmother, but I liked the idea of this relationship and ran with it.

Parish records show that by the time Costanza was married in 1632, she had three younger siblings: Michele (8), Cecilia (6) and Cleria (3). A 'blood sister', Anna Maria, is mentioned in Costanza's will. In the story I made her brother and sisters slightly older as I wanted to explore the impact of Cecilia's burgeoning womanhood, and all that it implies as another facet of Costanza's story.

Jane Monckton Smith's *In Control* – and her definition of the eight stages of coercive control – informed many of my decisions on plot.

Stage one is described as a history of control or stalking; we know Bernini described his dominant element as fire and displayed recurrent patterns of control, even trying to undermine his wife's final wishes with his own will, seven years after her death.

Stage two, early in the relationship, is the commitment whirlwind. Bernini's own son Domenico describes his father's affair with Costanza as 'fieramente inamorato', or *wildly* in love.

The third stage is a relationship dominated by control. The scene in the novel in which Lorenzo dresses Costanza is taken from a real chapter in his life. On the day of his betrothal, Bernini indulged in a practice called 'stripping of the bride' – famously recounted in Boccaccio's fourteenth-century *Decameron* story 'The Patient Griselda' – a parable about the virtues of a woman's obedience to her husband.

Lorenzo took his future wife to his house. There he made his bride strip off her own clothing, then dress in garments supplied by him. The old clothes were sent back to her father, thus signifying that Bernini was now master over his wife. Indulging in a little anachronism for a moment, what might once have been called an old-fashioned custom looks very much like coercive control to modern eyes.

Stage four is the trigger, an event to challenge control. In Costanza's story this is undoubtedly Lorenzo Bernini learning that his brother, Luigi, slept with his mistress.

Stage five is the escalation of control, such as the advent of stalking. We know from records that Lorenzo Bernini put Costanza's house under surveillance, lying to his family to do so.

Stage six signifies a change in thinking. I truncated the scene where Lorenzo beats Luigi. In reality, Lorenzo Bernini went berserk, chasing his brother through St Peter's, beating him with an iron rod, breaking two ribs, then when his brother took refuge in

San Maria Maggiore, Lorenzo kicked at the doors and marched down the aisles and chapels, sword in hand, ready to kill his brother. Having beaten his brother, Lorenzo's fury then turned on Costanza.

Stage seven is the planning of a homicide. Bernini not only instructed a servant to slash Costanza's face, but the man came armed with two flagons of wine, much like the Greeks and their horse in Troy, to gain entry from an unsuspecting Costanza. This was a systematically planned and cruelly premeditated attack.

Stage eight is homicide and/or suicide, or – in the case of this novel – Costanza's face being irreparably damaged, to save Bernini's own.

If we know nothing of Costanza, we know even less of Matteo, save his letters and his art. We don't know if he had an affair or if he slept with men, but I was keen to explore the wider dynamics of sexuality at play in Catholic Rome in this period. We also have no knowledge of whether Matteo willingly 'leased' his wife to a more powerful superior, a practice not uncommon in this period. Given their long and successful union after Costanza's release, I like to think he was not a willing participant in her downfall.

Nor do we know if Costanza's relationship with either Lorenzo or Luigi Bernini was fully consensual. The Bernini brothers were born to a mother, Angelica, who was just twelve when she married her husband, Pietro, who was twenty-five at the time. Unusually, the marriage bans were read a week apart, perhaps suggesting Angelica was already pregnant when the pair wed. Despite the misconception that marriage at such an early age for girls was common in this period, this is not the case. The age gap between Angelica and Pietro hints at an unpleasant broader family dynamic in which Pietro was highly dominant and expected the women in his life to be submissive in all areas of life, including – one presumes – sexually.

If a 'rockstar' artist approaching his forties having an affair with a woman in her twenties of lower social and economic status raises questions, then the relationship with Luigi raises profound concerns.

The next description is distressing, and involves a minor.

We have already witnessed the recorded violence between the brothers, but Luigi Bernini was also a known sexual predator. Records tell us that when Luigi was sixty, he violently raped 'un putto' – a boy – somewhere near his brother's statue of Constantine in St Peter's Church, the holiest place in Catholic worship.

We know this because a case was brought to bear. As now, it was rare for rape cases to be brought forward in the seventeenth century, and even rarer for these to include the charge of sodomy. But the boy Luigi attacked was the godson of a cardinal, who was not going to let the matter lie.

The events described tell us a number of things. First that Luigi was a rapist, capable of acts of unspeakable violence against minors (the boy suffered sixteen fractures during the assault). He was disinhibited, unable to control himself and unafraid of the consequences. It is highly unlikely this pattern of sexual attack would have developed suddenly in a man in his sixties, and it was probably prevalent throughout his adult life. All of which must lead to questions as to whether Costanza's 'affairs' – a women sleeping with two brothers – were as titillating as some 'nudge-nudge-wink-wink' historians have suggested.

Caterina is wholly fictional. The inspiration for her came from *Bernini's Beloved* in which Sarah McPhee explains that women were often the subject of community surveillance and that even the appearance of immodesty could lead to investigation. In other words, family, neighbours, friends, would give evidence on your conduct to the courts. The idea of a former friend turned informer intrigued me. We have no idea how Costanza came to be incarcerated, but it's not inconceivable that a neighbour or acquaintance, a Caterina or a Widow Vanna, named her a 'donna dishonesta'.

Similarly, the Abbess of the Casa Pia is also a figment of my imagination. The prelate of the monastery was Monsignor Bovio. However, I wanted to pay my respects to the hundreds of young noble women who were sent to convents, sometimes unwillingly, as their parents could not afford more than one or two dowries. Many of these women were exemplary leaders and managed complex finances and estates. There was no laundry room either, although this was a feature of convent business, but the idea of fallen women washing the dirty laundry of Rome's rich was an extended metaphor too delicious to ignore. As for Costanza's letter to the Governatore, while – astonishingly – we have the original, I have rewritten for the purposes of clarity and brevity in the novel.

Finally, I want to touch on names.

Costanza was born a Piccolomini, the name she used throughout her life, and I have used in this novel.

The record of Costanza's marriage to Matteo still exists. It reads that Matteo, son of Giovanni Bonuccelli of Lucca from the parish of Sant'Andrea delle Fratte, and Costanza, daughter of Leonardo Piccolomini, maiden of Viterbo from the parish of S. Lorenzo in Lucina in Vico San Silvestro, 'contraxerunt matrimonium per verba de praesenti'.

Such is the fluidity of seventeenth-century names, Matteo has been known by many names, Bonarelli being the one art historians have adopted from payment documents. I have chosen to use the spelling Matteo used in his will – Bonucelli – in the novel.

Pietro Bernini's son was born following five daughters. He bestowed upon this much coveted boy the names of both his grandfather (Giovanni) and his father (Lorenzo). In surviving documents,

Bernini's first name, Giovanni, is usually abbreviated to Gio or Giovan, which eventually morphed into Gianlorenzo, the name he is most popularly known by today. However, as an adult, Bernini considered his name to be simply Lorenzo, and so it is styled in the novel.

Lorenzo's wife was called Caterina Tezio Bernini, but by the time I decided to include her in the novel my original Caterina was so firmly lodged in my mind, I decided to anglicise Caterina Tezio's name to Catherine.

There are many other instances in this novel where I have forsaken true accuracy over accessibility, language being the most obvious. I have however, researched extensively and faithfully, and every decision I made was in the interests of telling a compelling story, one which is more than the sum of its parts.

Rachel Blackmore
October 2023

Acknowledgements

First, to Juliet Pickering, my agent, a tireless mentor and supporter of women, thank you for believing in me, and in Costanza's story. It's a privilege and joy to work with you. And thank you to everyone at Blake Friedmann for your hard work behind the scenes, debuting with you has been a dream.

To Christina Demosthenous, my dazzling editor, who made this book so much more. When there is a lack of narratives, readers are served monochromatic stories. Thank you for shifting the dialogue, seeking out the renegades and bringing colour to this world.

To the Dialogue Team, Emily Moran and Millie Seaward, who shared my excitement in telling Costanza's story from the get-go. Thank you for your sparkling creativity, immense skill and the great care you have taken in launching Costanza, we could not have been in safer hands. Thank you also to David Bamford, Eleanor Gaffney and Karyn Burnham.

For all the readers, booksellers and bloggers, who took Costanza into their hearts. Your passion, dedication and love for stories is important, thank you.

For my Mum, Stella Blackmore, who taught me how to be a warrior woman and whose unstinting support led to me following my dream. And my sister Kate Blackmore, who is wiser than anyone else I know and has taught me more than I can ever say. Thank you for being my biggest cheerleaders, for reading all my early words – even the crap ones – and still believing. I am forever grateful to be a Blackmore Woman. This is for you.

In memory of Harriet Becher, who was a first reader of Costanza. Harriet's fierce intellect and keen inquisitiveness drove many key decisions in my early days of writing: her voice is woven into these pages and her friendship made me a better woman. Like Hakim, Naima, Raif, Dorothy and Will, I miss her every day.

A novel isn't written without the help of a village, and I am lucky to have the most luminous of writing friends. Much of the first draft was created in the company of Alice Speirs, thank you for a friendship like no other. And Sam Kilgour, the wisest of women, who dropped everything and read the first completed draft in a day. Look, I found the chicken!

For the writers of London Writers' Salon (LWS) and the mother-writers of Calliope. Thank you to my historical fiction LWS co-host Kat Trigarszky, whose patience, humour and friendship is the best of all things. To Parul, Matt, Lindsey, Niamh, Abbey, Sallyann, Tracy, Lisa, George and Lucy who accompanied me from new writer to author, and reminded me to enjoy the process and have fun. To all my fellow writers, it is a privilege to share in your company and creativity.

A special thank you to the community of writers who leaned in and helped with the research of this book. The inestimable Nicolas Laborie for introducing me to the sculptor, Emma Elliott, who generously shared her studio for an afternoon so I could experience for myself the sensation of working with Carrera marble. To Marian Edmunds and her partner John Pitt, a stone carver, who so beautifully and eloquently described the visceral and emotional process of taking chisel to rock. To Lara Lightfoot for sharing her experiences of being an artist's model, which helped me understand Costanza so much better.

Beyond thanks to the Irish Writers Centre Team, Betty, Cassia, the judges and my fellow winners. Without your faith in Costanza and the Novel Fair, this book would be gathering dust in a top drawer. Thank you also to the Historical Writers' Association and *Harper's Bazaar*, whose short story competitions gave me faith to carry on.

To Anne Moore, my GCSE history teacher, whose lessons I still remember and ignited a profound love of the past. Teachers are superheroes.

Special thanks to the writers who have generously shared their knowledge and helped me understand my voice and craft during mentoring sessions and courses: Nikesh Shukla, Holly Dawson, Marti Leimbach, Imogen Hermes Gowar and AK Blakemore.

To Kate Hinchy and Emma Castillo for being brilliant, smart, funny women and for giving me such great love and support. Thank you Emma for sharing this funny old thing called motherhood, from NCT to teenagers. Thank you Raj for the endless cups of tea, and Sam and Ethan for sharing such great holidays and chips on the beach.

To Anya Delap for holding me up – literally and metaphorically – in my most fragile moments. And Simon, Finn, Rafe, Harley for your friendship. Also, to my St Johns community, the school Mums and Dads, my dear friends and lovely neighbours, thank you for looking after us and each other.

To Sarah Domeyer, for being part of our family, and everything that comes with our loud, busy, messy lives.

To Shane Matthews for everything you have done and continue to do.

To my Dad, John Blackmore, who I miss more than anything

and who would have been so proud to see my name in print. I once complained I had no time to write. Dad told me to be patient, that the right story would come then I would feel compelled to create. You were right Dad, the right story came.

And finally, to my guys, Louis Patrick, Bea, Frances and Corin, for your endless curiosity and zest for life. I love you beyond words and am so proud of you all.

Costanza Book Club Questions

If your book group has read Rachel Blackmore's *Costanza* and you're looking for some inspiration to kick off your discussion, we've got just what you need.

1. Costanza and Lorenzo begin the story at very different points in their lives. How do their circumstances and personalities shape the events of the novel?

2. *Costanza* is based on a true story. How effectively does the author blend historical facts with fictional narrative to create a compelling story?

3. Seventeenth-century Rome is a contradictory place; both pious and licentious. How does the setting influence the novel, and how effectively does the author immerse readers in the atmosphere of Baroque Rome?

4. Costanza finds herself caught between Bernini and his jealous younger brother, Luigi, with life-changing consequences. How does the novel portray male rage and its impact on women?

5. Desire, betrayal and resilience are central themes in the novel. How do these themes drive the plot forward, and what do they reveal about the characters?

6. Bernini's desire to create Costanza's likeness in marble – and her reaction to the sharing of their intimacy without consent – is a turning point in the story. Discuss how this moment mirrors the use of digital imagery in modern society.

7. Despite her arrest, Costanza ultimately refuses to be defined by her downfall. What role does female friendship play in Costanza reclaiming agency over her life? Which friendship left the deepest impression on you?

8. Tiberia, Giuliana, Caterina and Rosa represent alternative paths Costanza might have taken. How do their characters help our understanding of choice vs fate in the novel?

9. Reflect on the conclusion of the novel. Are you satisfied with how the story concludes for Costanza and Bernini? What lingering questions or thoughts do you have after finishing the book?

10. In her Note to Readers, the author explains how she came to write *Costanza*. How does this information deepen the reader's understanding of the themes explored in the novel?

Bringing a book from manuscript to what you are reading is a team effort.

Renegade Books would like to thank everyone who helped to publish *Costanza* in the UK.

Editorial
Christina Demosthenous
Eleanor Gaffney

Contracts
Megan Phillips
Bryony Hall
Amy Patrick
Sasha Duszynska Lewis
Anne Goddard

Sales
Caitriona Row
Dominic Smith
Frances Doyle
Hannah Methuen
Lucy Hine
Toluwalope Ayo-Ajala

Design
Hannah Wood

Production
Narges Nojoumi

Publicity
Millie Seaward

Marketing
Emily Moran

Operations
Kellie Barnfield
Millie Gibson
Sameera Patel
Sanjeev Braich

Finance
Andrew Smith
Ellie Barry

Copy-Editor
David Bamford

Proofreader
Karyn Burnham